Dying to Heal

Dying to Heal

Dr. Alan Fluger, DC and Richard Warren Field

PISIFORM PUBLISHING

ISBN 978-0-9829024-0-0

Pisiform Publishing

Yorba Linda MPO
P.O. Box 2021
Yorba Linda, CA 92885

Dying to Heal is a work of fiction. All characters and events are imaginary. Nothing in *Dying to Heal* should be construed as medical advice or care.

Book design and production by Joel Friedlander
www.TheBookDesigner.com

First Printing, March, 2011

Dying to Heal is dedicated to chiropractors of the past who perfected their healing methods while confronted by a hostile medical establishment determined to destroy their profession. The ultimate justice for those determined healing pioneers will be a collaboration between conventional and alternative approaches to healing. The "winners" of this collaboration will be the patients who will benefit from the best of both approaches.

Acknowledgements

For Dr. Alan Fluger:

With deep appreciation to my mother and father who loved me first.

With overwhelming gratitude to my beloved wife Marian, who was there from the beginning.

To my family, Laini, Lance, Kent and Aaron to whom I am so proud of.

To Adrienne, Cara, Erin and Happi; thank you for all your help.

To my partner, Rick, who made all this possible for me to achieve my dream; I thank you.

For Richard Warren Field:

My thanks to Linda Black for her review and comments on the *Dying to Heal* manuscript.

My thanks to my family: my wife, Carrie, and my children, Michelle and Ryan, for their support, and for their input as they experienced first hand the benefits of "alternative" health care.

My special thanks to Dr. Alan Fluger for introducing me and my family to the concepts of chiropractic, and to the benefits of his care.

Chapter 1

"I hope I haven't found you too late," Eldon Stafford said as his daughter Brianna greeted him at the door of her small one bedroom apartment in Brea, California, part of Southern California's Orange County. Fifty-eight year old Eldon Stafford, Chief of Staff at Orange County Memorial Hospital, successfully projected a distinguished, often imposing presence. He stood six feet four inches tall, with a broad frame, and with his excess weight well-hidden by a perfectly tailored dark gray suit. He had a full head of hair, mostly gray, but with black streaks still sprinkled in. "We'll have to discuss why you have been hiding." Stafford wiped a few beads of sweat off his forehead and paused, catching his breath. "But there's still time if we get you to the hospital immediately. I have the best people standing by and-"

"Dad."

She was trying to interrupt, but Stafford was determined to get his words out. "Denial is a normal reaction to a serious illness. That's okay. There is still time-"

"Dad, just listen for-"

"We can talk on the way."

"Dad. Check me."

Stafford looked at his daughter closely for the first time since he'd arrived. She was a thin girl, but not gaunt. She had not been healthy in recent years, but today, her serious brown eyes sparkled with vitality. Her flowing brown hair shined. She wore jeans and a white t shirt. He knew men found his little girl, now almost twenty-eight, attractive. But he rarely considered her in that context. She had been sick. He was a medical doctor with almost ten years of higher education. He needed to help her, whether she resisted or not. And he had expected resistance. But he had not expected her to ask for an exam. "My bag's in the car."

"I'll wait."

Stafford hesitated. Would she wait?

"I'm not going anywhere. I wasn't hiding. Not from you." She smirked.

"I'll be right back." He turned and walked briskly toward his car, parked on the street in front of the apartment complex, about a hundred feet along a bush-lined walkway. So, she hadn't been hiding from him. But her statement implied she had been hiding from someone. His office staff and hospital colleagues had told him she'd been deliberately evasive.

Yes, his brilliant daughter, possibly possessing more raw intelligence than he had, sometimes liked to be contrary. He and his wife had focused on raising her the right way. They'd been in college when the full force of the 1960s had collided with the culture. Stafford had never been a front-line protester. But he sympathized with his generation's dedication to changing the world. He and his wife had taught Brianna: "Question authority." He never dreamed his brilliant daughter would go off to college at the liberal University of California at Berkeley and follow their "question authority" instructions to the letter by becoming a conservative foreign relations student, modeling her ambitions after the career of Condoleezza Rice.

Her studies had taken her to an internship with a conservative Orange County Congressman. Her PHD thesis was about the Bush Administration's initial reaction to the attack against the country on September 11, 2001. As part of that thesis, she got an interview with Condoleezza Rice, and her positive treatment of the Bush Administration's performance earned her many battles with her professors, which she seemed to enjoy the most when they were the most intense. So was his daughter being contrary now?

Stafford stopped. He looked back.

Brianna Stafford stood just past the open door of her apartment, arms folded, wearing a confident grin as she watched him.

Stafford turned back toward his car and picked up the pace of his walk. No, she didn't look like she was going to bolt. But he'd better hurry anyway. She could change her mind.

He reached his car, a top-of-the-line silver Lincoln Towncar. He pressed a button on his keys; the locks popped open. He opened the door and grabbed his black leather bag from where it was sitting on the front seat of his car. He took in a deep breath and paused to gather himself. More perspiration ringed his forehead. He gritted his teeth. He'd been continents away, half a planet away, when he'd gotten the call. "Your daughter had a full-blown asthma attack. She's in the hospital." That wasn't what had scared him. His best, most competent colleagues were attending her. He could monitor her progress by staying in contact with them. At that point, he hadn't needed to cut short his trip. But the next report sent him into a frenzied series of calls and a rushed flight back from the physician/pharmaceutical convention in Copenhagen, Denmark. His daughter had left the hospital, possibly under the spell of some creepy, self-appointed "healer." How could his staff have allowed her to escape the benevolent control of the most advanced, state-of-the-art care modern medicine had to offer?

He arrived back with his daughter. He fought to catch his breath.

Brianna smiled at him as he entered the living room and set down his bag. "Maybe someone should check you," she joked. "You seem a little out of shape."

Stafford wiped his forehead. "I don't get enough exercise."

Brianna's smile remained as she raised her eyebrows. "You don't have to hurry. I'll wait as long as we need for you to see how well I'm doing."

Stafford scowled. He would be the judge of how well she was doing. He faced his daughter, pulled out his stethoscope and put it to his ears. He put the round end of the stethoscope over his daughter's heart area. A nice strong beat sounded—a calm beat, probably not nearly as elevated as his own heartbeat right now. But, it wasn't her heart that was the problem. He placed the round end of the stethoscope over her lung area. "Take a deep breath and let it out."

Brianna seemed to shrug as she complied.

"Again." Doctor Stafford frowned as he moved the round disk over her lung area. Was there something wrong with the stethoscope? He pulled the disk away. He tapped on it. It picked up the sound loud and clear. He put it back over his daughter's chest. "Deep breath again. Really deep. Then out."

Brianna complied again.

"One more time."

Brianna breathed in and out again, grinning confidently, without a trace of impatience.

Doctor Stafford raised his head slowly. He pulled the stethoscope out of his ears and let it dangle loosely around his neck. There was only the slightest hint of wheezing. He heard nothing like a full-blown asthma attack. That rumbly, mucousy sound, that ever-present confirmation of breathing passages obstructed—it was there, but barely detectable, vastly reduced from what he had expected to observe. "They told me you had an acute asthma attack," he finally said to her.

"I did."

"They told me-" Doctor Stafford looked into her eyes. No jaundice. The frenzied hospital call had indicated jaundice, which should have been evident to the naked eye. He reached into his bag for his opthalmoscope. He would check more closely to make sure. He switched on the device's light. "Hold still." He looked in her right eye. It was clear. "They said you had... you were suffering from an acute jaundice condition." He looked in her left eye. "Your eyes were almost pink, they said, looked like they were going to sink right through the back of your head."

"It's true."

Doctor Stafford switched off the light on his opthalmoscope. He shook his head. "This has to be verified at the hospital." He snapped open his cell phone. "Larry. It's Eldon Stafford. I need a chest x-ray, blood work and a full body scan set up for my daughter. Have it ready to go the minute I get there. We'll be there in-"

"Dad. You don't need to test me. I'm healthy."

Doctor Stafford looked at his phone. "Have it ready—we'll be there," he said into it before he snapped it shut. "We need to be sure."

Brianna Stafford shrugged.

"It's… a miracle." Stafford nodded slowly. "We've come a long way with medical science. But occasionally? Something like this happens. A miracle."

"It's no miracle." The voice came from Galen Reed, a brown-haired man of about forty, just under six feet tall, dressed in a blue shirt and white slacks. But the intensity in his eyes and facial expression seemed to contradict his unassuming appearance. He walked from the kitchen adjoining her living room.

Eldon Stafford tensed. "Who are you? Are you the one who…"

"I've been helping your daughter become healthy."

Brianna Stafford spoke up. "I told him I thought you might come home from your convention. He called me this afternoon and told me he sensed I would need him here today. I have learned not to-"

"So, you're a quack and a psychic," Stafford said to Reed.

"Sometimes I have a fore-sense of events to come. I don't try to explain this to anyone—I don't even try to understand it myself. Often, it's just a rough feeling—sometimes the event comes to me very precise and vivid. I think if a person is acutely aware of his or her surroundings, the mind can process all that awareness and offer an insight into what will-"

"Spare me. Who knows how much harm you caused to my daughter when you convinced her to-"

"When I convinced her to leave the hospital that was killing her?"

Stafford tensed. The audacity of this so-called healer! How could the man so casually bash the hospital, a place that had extended so many lives, a place that represented the triumph of modern medical science over disease? He considered bombarding the man with a few choice words to counter his impudence. But he stopped himself. Until he could explain his daughter's dramatically improved condition, he would keep his temper in check. He was a trained medical professional, able to contain his emotions, superior to other people in intelligence, in education and in demeanor. Stafford set his jaw and glared Galen Reed down. "You're going to try to convince me that you helped her, and the hospital didn't?"

"I'm not going to try to convince you of anything. I welcome your exams. I want your daughter to have those tests as soon as possible. I'll let reality do the convincing."

Stafford turned to his daughter, deliberately directing his remarks to her only. "They're waiting. Let's get going on those tests."

"As long as Doctor Reed comes along," Brianna said.

Stafford grunted and grimaced at the title her daughter was giving to this man. "Brianna, there are restrictions-"

"Dad, either he comes, or I don't."

"Brianna, now is not the time to be stubborn and contrary."

"Oh. So Dad, does that mean there is a good time?"

Galen Reed spoke. "Doctor Stafford, I will not create any trouble. I assure you, I want these tests as much as you do."

Eldon Stafford looked at his daughter. He recognized that smug expression she wore when she had the upper hand. He looked at Galen Reed. "No trouble is right. You better keep a low profile or I'll toss you right out of there."

"Low profile." Reed nodded. "Sure."

Stafford looked Reed up and down. He did not want this man along. But his daughter's health was more important than any battle with this so-called healer. He would have to put off dealing with this fool until sometime in the future. "Let's go," he said.

Chapter 2

"Looks negative," Stafford said, peering over his glasses, reviewing his daughter's chest x-ray with a meticulous stare. "But we'll get the radiologist's report." Stafford stood next to his daughter who lay on a bed in a small examining room next to the emergency room area of Orange County Memorial Hospital. Brianna lay on her back, wearing a light blue hospital gown.

"I'd like to have a look," Reed asked Stafford, taking care to project a polite, undemanding tone.

Stafford frowned and made no move to hand the x-ray to Reed.

Brianna tilted her head and directed a disapproving look at her father.

Stafford handed the x-ray over to Reed. He looked like a man who wanted to make some sort of objection, but held it back.

Reed looked at the x-ray. He nodded. "A nice healthy set of lungs." Reed decided now was not the time to extol the virtues of standing x-rays.

"I told you; we'll wait for the radiologist."

Reed grinned and shrugged. "Sure."

"Besides, the scan will tell us more."

"You mean pump her full of rads for what could be a bunch of false positives," Reed quipped.

"We'll know how to read it here. This is not some fly-by-night clinic. This is Orange County Memorial Hospital."

"So you do realize those things are not always reliable."

"For people who don't know what they're doing. But we know what we're doing here. I can do without the snide comments."

Reed nodded with an amused grin. So Eldon Stafford didn't seem to like scans either, though he wasn't going to admit it. But he had apparently decided to use every tool available to check his daughter's condition.

"Eldon." A man of about forty-five, almost bald, wearing a thin white coat over a white shirt and tie, breezed into the room. He had a band with a mirror around his forehead and a stethoscope around his neck. A badge with the name "Lawrence Middleton, M.D." hung slightly tilted on his front shirt pocket. He blinked quickly three times then rubbed his eyes. Doctor Middleton looked at Brianna. "Good. You got her back here."

"Yeah," Stafford said, tight-lipped. "Is the scan ready?"

"Got one ahead of her, but it's almost done. The next one can wait; it'll just be a little behind."

"Thanks."

"Young lady, you gave us quite a scare," Middleton said to Brianna.

"Sorry," Brianna Stafford said. She didn't seem sorry.

"But it looks like you're back on your medication, getting your condition under control."

Brianna smirked toward Reed.

Middleton then looked at Reed. He gave the impression that he wondered who Reed was, but was not willing to ask.

"What about the blood-work?" Stafford asked Middleton.

Middleton looked back at Stafford. "I put a rush on it."

"Good."

"Do we have the records of the blood-work from before she left the hospital?" Reed asked Stafford.

Stafford frowned. "I'll get it."

Reed smiled and nodded a silent thank you. Good. Stafford might not like his involvement, but he was not going to resist obviously appropriate clues in the search for the truth.

Middleton looked at Reed again.

Stafford picked up a phone on the wall of the room and punched in an extension. "This is Doctor Stafford. Bring my daughter's records to examining room seven." He hung up.

Middleton asked Reed "You are…?"

"A friend of my daughter's," Stafford volunteered quickly.

Middleton frowned, but did not follow-up. He looked back at Brianna. "So, when did you restart the medications? I thought you just got here."

"We're going to hold off on that for now," Stafford said.

Middleton looked puzzled.

"Yes, Dr. Middleton," Brianna said. "It seems I may not need the medications anymore."

"You might just find the blood-work shows that the medications were causing her more trouble than the asthma," Reed stated, trying to be gentle, but realizing after he said it that the remark itself was too provocative to be delivered gently.

"Who are you?" Middleton's face tensed. "A friend? You sound like a lawyer. A lawyer friend maybe? Slinking around here for a payday?" He looked at Stafford. "We're letting lawyers wander around here?"

"No." Stafford drew in a deep breath. "My daughter thinks this man has somehow cured her."

Middleton's eyes widened and his nostrils flared. "This is the guy, isn't it—the guy who talked her into leaving the hospital! He's some chiropractor! He almost killed your daughter! What is he doing here?"

"It was the hospital and the so-called care she got that-"

Stafford interrupted Reed. "My daughter insisted he come along. My preliminary exam showed her symptom-free. She would only come back here if he came too."

Reed did not follow up after the interruption. He realized Stafford had been wise to cut him off. Yes, Reed was annoyed to be accused of "almost killing" Brianna Stafford. Yes, Reed enjoyed suggesting the truth to these men, that the hospital had come closer to killing her than anything else, including her underlying asthmatic condition.

But shoving it in the face of these proud professionals was unlikely to accomplish anything constructive. Reed's older colleagues had told him of the condescending, often malicious treatment they had been subjected to by the mainstream medical profession, and the bitterness created by that treatment often pervaded relationships between the practitioners of the different approaches to health. Reed wanted to see a different tone evolve. So he needed to project conciliation and collaboration even in the face of antagonism and hostility. It was good Stafford had cut him off. Reed was not on his turf. This was a time to tread lightly—tread lightly and look for opportunities.

"Your daughter? She's why he's here?" Middleton asked Stafford.

"Yes."

"Um, I'm not sure. It's not hospital policy."

"Probably not."

Middleton shrugged. "Nearly symptom free." He glared again at Reed.

Reed shrugged, but stifled a smirk.

"I'll check on the scan." Middleton left.

"Low profile," Stafford said through gritted teeth.

"I remember," Reed acknowledged.

"You can't start up with that 'hospital-killing-her' crap."

"I'm glad you cut me off."

Brianna looked at Reed, puzzled by his comment.

"The point is still valid," Reed clarified. "But it was the wrong time and place to make it. Your father is right about that."

A young woman walked in holding a hospital file. "Doctor Stafford?"

"Yes."

"Your daughter's file?" She handed it to him.

"Thanks."

The young woman left.

Stafford looked through the file.

An orderly walked in, pushing a gurney. "They're ready for the scan."

Brianna got down off the bed. "I can get there without the wheels."
The orderly swallowed. "Um…"

"It's hospital policy," Eldon Stafford told his daughter.

"Okay," Brianna agreed, again wearing a confident smirk. "Be nice to my, my 'friend,' while I'm gone."

Stafford nodded. He looked back at the file as the orderly wheeled Brianna from the room. Stafford said nothing. The only sound in the room was the crinkle of papers as Stafford paged through Brianna's hospital records.

Reed wondered if he would be banished to the emergency room waiting area. When Brianna first arrived at the hospital, Stafford had directed Reed to the waiting area where he had spent his time watching "I Love Lucy" reruns while Brianna got her x-rays and blood-work.

It had been many years since Reed had been in a hospital, back to the days when he went to the hospital every day as an employee. If anything, the emergency room at Orange County Memorial seemed even drearier than he recalled it. The place still had a dull gleam of worn stainless steel punctuated by fading and cracked white tiles. He recalled the bright white paint, reflecting the light in the area in a harsh, nearly violent way, almost calculated to subliminally agitate people already in discomfort from whatever ailment they had present-ed with. People crowded into the hard plastic chairs—babies coughed and cried, grumpy, frazzled people slumped uncomfortably, some sleeping, apparently settled in for long waits. And the place smelled like alcohol and cleaning potions combining in an unsuccessful at-tempt to obscure odors of blood, urine and body odor.

Reed suspected some of the conditions of these patients could have been addressed at the preventative stage, conditions that could have been completely avoided. But he knew some patients neglected their health until the point of crisis, then filed into the emergency room as a last resort, encouraged to come there knowing that no matter what condition they presented with, the hospital had to take them in. The system encouraged the overcrowded emergency room, so Reed found himself understanding the tired, sometimes flip attitudes of the nurses dealing with the seemingly endless flow of incoming patients. But though he knew they were overworked, with doctors often working brutally long shifts, he also knew the patients needed alert evaluations not tainted by weariness. No matter what the defects of the system were, the patients needed to come first.

Patient Brianna Stafford certainly came first. She had breezed right past this human bottleneck, escorted into the hospital by her father. Galen Reed wondered if Brianna Stafford knew how lucky she had been to avoid the scene in the emergency room waiting area.

Reed thought about the hospital's need for a renovation. Someone with some financial authority would decide that enough wear and tear had accumulated, and that appearances needed to be addressed. But would they take the opportunity to upgrade the emergency room into a truly patient-friendly place, or would they just replace old steel and white tiles with new steel and white tiles? The atmosphere could be so much more comforting, so much more conducive to healing and health. But Reed knew, from his brief time as a hospital employee, what the answer to his question probably would be. They would squeeze out the funds for the renovation, spending as efficiently as possible to upgrade an area that served so many patients who would never pay the hospital the full cost of their services.

So was Eldon Stafford going to send Reed back out into the emergency room waiting area, now that Brianna was off for another test?

Stafford turned another page. He frowned.

Reed wanted to see the records. But now was not the time to insist.

Stafford closed the file. He picked up the phone and punched in a number. "Eldon Stafford here. Is my daughter's blood and urine work ready?... How long?" He sneered. "Alright. Have someone bring up the results immediately when they're ready." He hung up the phone.

Reed felt the presence of an acutely uncomfortable silence. But he resisted the temptation to fill it with some forced remark. It was Stafford's move. And he didn't want to irritate the man into banishing him back out into the waiting area.

Stafford picked up the file and held it in front of him. "We'll want to see what it looks like now." He handed the file to Reed. "They did blood and urine when she was first admitted, and again, just before she left."

Reed took the file as he nodded. "Thank you."

"I'm not conceding anything until I see the results of that scan."

Reed nodded again.

"The scan was negative for an acute asthmatic condition," Middleton told Stafford as he entered the examining room. Brianna Stafford lay on the examining table. Galen Reed stood with her. He looked at Brianna and nodded with a confident grin, satisfied his assessment of Brianna's case had been confirmed with an objective test.

Stafford raised his eyebrows.

"You're one lucky young lady," Middleton said, but he sounded like he was scolding her. "Sometimes miracles happen. Sometimes… patients get away with noncompliance with doctor's orders. I wouldn't press your luck. Count your lucky stars and get back on your medications starting right-"

"I'm sorry," Reed interrupted. "But it wasn't luck."

Middleton eyed Reed.

Stafford looked weary and drained as he took a deep breath.

"And I can't let you put her back on those drugs you had her taking." Reed looked at Stafford. "You saw the lab results."

"Elevated liver enzymes. Elevated white blood count." Stafford paused. "Up from the initial blood work at time of admission." Stafford frowned. "I'll grant you—patients have adverse reactions to medication."

Middleton looked at Stafford with disbelief.

"But stopping the medications didn't clear up her asthma," Stafford added.

"No, it didn't," Reed agreed.

"So she was lucky," Stafford said.

"Very lucky," Middleton added sternly.

Reed shook his head. He stepped over to Brianna Stafford. "Lay on your stomach." Reed looked at Stafford. "Doctor?" he summoned. Reed began feeling along Brianna's spine. This was a moment of opportunity. Maybe Middleton was in a defensive mood, but Stafford seemed genuinely open to an explanation. How often did someone with Reed's healing skills get a chance to demonstrate them to a prominent member of the medical establishment?

Stafford joined Reed.

"She still has some alignment problems at her thoracic spine, specifically at T3, and a little less pronounced at T2. That's the controlling area of the spine for the lungs and respiratory system." Reed raised his hands from Brianna Stafford's back. He motioned with his fingers to Eldon Stafford. "You'll feel it."

Stafford gave him a look of disbelief.

Reed took Stafford's hand and raised it to Brianna Stafford's back, almost before he could react. "Right here." Reed guided Stafford's hands to the place he was referring to. "You can feel the right side is not matched up with the left side, a sure sign of a vertebra out of alignment. You'll also feel some spasming in the surrounding muscle areas."

Stafford pulled his hands away. "I'm not sure. I kind of see what you mean, I guess. I just don't know if it really has the relevance you attribute to it."

"I'll adjust the vertebrae, and you will feel the difference." Reed reached down to feel for the spot again before making the adjustment. "These adjustments, in combination with homeopathic remedies and nutrition and diet programs alleviated your daughter's-"

"Eldon. This guy has no legitimate credentials for a hospital. This stuff isn't allowed here."

Reed held off actually completing the adjustment.

Middleton continued: "No back-cracking, or neck-cracking, or whatever other silliness he's going to try to con you with."

"He's not doing any of the procedures. He's just showing them to me."

"He's got his hands on her. Your daughter!"

"It's a good thing he did get his hands on me," Brianna said, eyes boring into Middleton.

"Eldon," Middleton said, shaking his head. "This is a medical hospital, one of the most prestigious facilities in the country." He stepped to the door and looked out into the hall, as if worried who might be aware of what they were doing. "You've got to stop the guy."

"It's okay," Reed said raising his hands, palms out, as if to show he held no weapons and harbored no hostile intent. He looked at Stafford. "I wanted you to see your daughter's health was not just a happy accident."

Middleton shook his head again as he walked out the door.

Eldon Stafford breathed in and out. He found a small stool on rollers and sat down. He looked up into the air, seeming to focus on nothing in particular.

Galen Reed started to say something about the results, but remained silent. He fought the instinct to fill the silence with some sort of conversation, an instinct as naturally human as eating or sleeping. Sometimes people had to get to a destination without a guide, to be sure they'd arrived at the right place, at the desired destination. Galen Reed sensed what his next move should be. Don't hard-sell the answer; let Stafford sell it to himself.

Stafford looked at Reed. "You're an interesting man," he finally said. "And a sincere man." He paused a moment. "You believe in what you do." He looked up. "And I believe in my years of training and experience."

"I've seen these ideas work time and again, and I've associated with colleagues who have had the same experiences. It's not just 'belief.'"

Stafford smiled. "Okay." He paused again, as if fighting himself, struggling to decide which words to speak, or whether he should say anything more at all. "I think… I guess I should… I'm going to say— thank you."

Reed felt a rush of warmth course through his body. Successful healings always made him feel euphoric. But this one—this one he sensed could have far-reaching positive consequences. "I appreciate

your willingness to express your gratitude. A man in your position…
well, I know it doesn't come easily. It speaks to your character and
integrity, and I-"

"Yeah. Okay. Just…" He turned to Brianna. "You have to promise
you'll call me if you run into problems. This is all nice. But if you-
" He paused. "Don't shut out your doctors just because of this one
situation."

"I won't. I'll keep an open mind—about everything."

Stafford nodded.

"Doctor." Reed looked at Stafford, trying to lock eyes, to read
him closely. "It has been my pleasure to help your daughter. And sir,
I would like to help you, too."

"What?"

"I'd like to help you resolve your own medical problems."

Stafford's head moved forward and his eyes widened with disbelief. "My medical problems? What could you possibly know about my
medical problems?"

"A lot. I know quite a lot."

Stafford squinted, apparently annoyed with what he probably per-
ceived as pushy behavior.

"I see things, doctor. And I honestly want to help you." Reed
paused. "If you're interested, come see me at my office. Your colleague is right. This is not the appropriate place to go into details. But
trust me—I can help you too."

Chapter 3

"Blood pressure?" Natalie Corey's eyes narrowed with skepticism. "You came to my office for blood pressure? You didn't tell me Brianna Stafford had high blood pressure." She sat at her desk. Galen Reed stood next to her. Natalie Corey had a pleasant face with a few aging lines just beginning to form. Her frizzy black hair was neatly styled in waves. She wore a pastel-orange blouse and gray pleated slacks. Her office presented a deliberate, intriguing contrast. She displayed so many live plants, hanging from the ceiling, lining shelves at various different heights, that the room gave off the pleasant natural scent of an outdoor garden. But she also had a sleek, flat computer screen somehow connected with an unseen CPU. Few papers cluttered her desk; few books stacked up on her shelves. Reed had seen her access most of what she needed on line.

"Brianna Stafford is not my only patient," Galen Reed reminded her.

"No. But she is your project patient."

Reed frowned. "You understand what this could mean."

She smiled. "I understand what you think it could mean."

Reed held back his annoyance with her attitude.

Natalie Corey typed on her computer keyboard and clicked a few times with her mouse. She turned the monitor toward him. "Here's the latest in natural remedies for high blood pressure."

Reed looked at the list. Hawthorn. Calcium and magnesium.

Garlic. Fish oil. Argentum Nitricum. Belladona. Glonoinum. Lachesis. Natrum Muriaticum. Nux Vomica. "Nothing new."

"No. And really, you know as well as I do: healthy diet—eat your oatmeal, your bran, your fiber; exercise; reduce stress"—she grinned—"in your office, Chironosis™—combining chiropractic and hypnosis to reduce stress."

Reed smiled slyly. "That kind of attitude can't be good for business."

"We don't do things here the way they do at the drug companies—you should know that."

"I know."

"Besides, business is great. I just hope people aren't replacing their chemical 'miracle cures' with new potions of 'natural' miracle cures."

Galen Reed nodded. "Believe me, I keep an eye on that."

"So how is the Brianna Stafford project going?"

"Project. I wish you wouldn't call it that. It's an opportunity."

"They haven't connected it up at all, have they…"

Galen Reed shrugged. "No reason for any kind of 'connecting.'"

Natalie Corey frowned. "These are not stupid people. They're not people who can't put together two-plus-two."

"I don't think it's that important that-"

"Not important? Are you serious?"

He grunted. "More important to me than it is to them."

"It might not be good if they connect this up before you tell them."

"I will. When the time is right." He paused. "It wouldn't be such a bad thing, you know. I'm not doing anything wrong."

Her expression cooled. "No. I guess not. Not anything you haven't done before, anyway." She looked down at her hands and the computer keyboard. "Well, it's great to have you stop by, whatever the reason."

"This place is amazing."

Natalie Corey smiled. "Some of these plants are the fresh herbs we actually sell."

"Fantastic." He took in a deep breath, absorbing the fragrant herbal odor. "The boys are with you this weekend?"

"Yeah."

"Sunday night?"

"I'd appreciate it. It's always a hard time for me."

"I'll be over. Call me after your ex picks them up."

"Okay." She looked away toward one of her hanging plants, then back at Galen Reed. "Do you ever wonder what would have happened if I hadn't been stupid enough to marry Sy, the real estate tycoon?"

Galen Reed shook his head. "No. The timing wasn't right for us."

"Maybe I should have waited."

"I might have made you wait forever. And where would your two sons be?"

She smiled. "You reduce it to the logical point…"

"And you never would have gone from that cute vitamin store clerk I fell in love with to a key executive for this natural remedy company if you hadn't been forced to find a career to support your sons. Everything flows together for a reason. It doesn't always flow smoothly. But you and I? Our best days are ahead of us."

"You always say that."

"I know it's true. And I know you make light of what you call my 'project.' But you, and this place right here, could end up being a part of it."

"Why am I such a sucker for dreamers?"

"Because no matter how hard you try to fight it, and throw in a little fashionable dark cynicism, you are one of us."

"Heaven forbid," she said, but with a smile, she contradicted her words.

"That was quite an afternoon," Brianna Stafford said to her father. They sat down in their booth of the Imperial Highway Grill restaurant and began looking at their menus. It was still early evening, so the restaurant was close to empty. A television showing a football game flickered soundlessly, mounted from the ceiling, four tables away. It added a little light to the dimly lit establishment. "I hope it wasn't too upsetting." She raised her eyebrows and grinned.

"It was an excellent afternoon," Eldon Stafford said. "I found out my daughter is healthy."

"And it doesn't matter how I got that way…"

Eldon Stafford looked down at his menu.

"Or whether you understand how I got that way…"

Eldon Stafford looked up from his menu. "I suppose you think I should go see him."

"I never said that."

He narrowed his eyes suspiciously.

"I wouldn't ever suggest that."

"Good." He looked down at his menu again. "Because you know, I can't."

"Can't."

"That's right."

"I understand 'don't-want-to.' I respect that. But Dad—can't? That doesn't seem right."

"A man in my position…"

"A man in your position can afford to look past the straight-and-narrow."

Eldon Stafford's eyes drifted up, as if taking him out of the conversation for a moment.

A young waiter with short brown hair stepped to the table. "Do you need a few more moments?"

"I'm ready," Brianna Stafford said.

"Um, yeah," Eldon Stafford said. But he didn't look ready. "Um, let me look."

"Can I bring you something to drink while you're deciding?"

"Cranberry juice," Brianna Stafford said.

Eldon Stafford looked at his daughter as if she'd chartered a submarine to go to Mars.

"Good for asthma," she explained.

"Hmmm." He looked at the waiter. "Scotch, with some ice."

"I'll be right back," the waiter said just before he walked away.

Brianna Stafford looked at her father. "I remember when I was eleven. That bus tipped over and they filled the hospital with kids, banged up, with all sorts of injuries."

Eldon Stafford's eyes snapped to attention as he looked at his daughter.

"You were on t-v, telling the world about how the children were doing. Mommy took me in—she wanted to show you off, to show me what my daddy did."

He swallowed as his eyes glistened, apparently trying to hold back tears.

"You walked around, giving orders to doctors and nurses, doing everything you could to save those kids. I was so proud—my dad, the healer of hurt kids, the saver of lives."

Eldon Stafford rubbed his eyes. "But not able to heal his own daughter."

Brianna Stafford's eyes widened. So this was her father's mood. She'd finally brought it to the surface. And this mood of her father's was familiar to her. "Dad. No matter how great a healer you are, you can't know everything."

He closed his eyes. "I know." He opened his eyes and looked up, away, as if speaking to more than just his daughter. "I helped those kids. We... we were flawless. But my own wife—and now my own daughter..."

"Oh Daddy. I didn't mean to—"

"It's okay. I shouldn't be this way." He looked back at her and smiled. "I mean, I saw the tests. Wow. My brilliant daughter. You took this on—yourself."

"Not by myself..."

"I know. You utilized that chiropractor fellow. But I mean, you found him."

"Yeah. Sort of."

"What do you mean 'sort of?'"

"Shauna talked me into going to this health food expo."

Eldon Stafford laughed. "Health food. Isn't that a little left-wing radical for you?"

"I don't think healthy food or good health habits have any particular political affiliations. In fact, the personal responsibility of good health habits fits right into a good right-wing platform."

"All-right. Truce." Eldon Stafford held his hands up as if surrendering, at least temporarily. "What happened at this health food expo?"

"There was a guy there talking about how food can be medicine."

"And that was this Reed fellow?"

"Dr. Reed? No. But the guy said he works with Dr. Reed. I told him that for my asthma, I had to take real medicine. He said, sure, I was probably taking steroids. I said no way—those are for bulked up football players and baseball hitters. He told me to look at the bottle. I laughed it off."

"The steroids are in small doses-"

The waiter returned.

"The chicken salad," Brianna Stafford told him. "With the vinaigrette dressing."

"Corn beef on rye with fries," Eldon Stafford requested.

The waiter nodded and left.

"Dad, steroids?"

He shrugged. "That's how we've kept you breathing for over ten years."

"Well, the steroids thing wigged me out a little and made me curious. Here I am, almost four-point-oh in grad school, hobnobbing with cabinet officials and very powerful political types, members of Congress and their staffs, and I seem to be completely ignorant about the medications I was shoving into my body. So when the guy called me about a free evaluation from Dr. Reed, I decided to do it."

"Maybe Dr. Reed made you sick."

Brianna Stafford shook her head. "I didn't really take him seriously at first. I told him I was the daughter of a doctor-head-of-a-hospital. He could try his voodoo-witchdoctor back-cracking on me, for entertainment. I giggled when he felt my back and acted goofy when he did the adjustments. I'm not sure why he kept treating me."

"You weren't paying him?"

"I think I paid for the second visit. Only that one."

Eldon Stafford's face showed puzzlement.

"I stopped taking the steroids, but I didn't get to him regularly. Then I had a bad attack. He came to see me in the hospital."

"Yeah. I think I know the rest."

"After he talked me into leaving the hospital, he treated me every day, explaining it all as he went."

Eldon Stafford raised his eyebrows. "Like he explained it to me."

"Yeah. A little more detail, but yeah."

"So... this isn't some sort of rebellion against me, like sticking it to your hippie parents?"

"No." Brianna shook her head. "I wouldn't be stupid with gestures like that. And Dad, from everything you tell me, you weren't really a 'hippie.' More like a hippie sympathizer maybe. But even that was just you as a kid. The truth?" Her eyes watered as she looked at him. "I'm proud of you."

"Even when I couldn't—when the doctors couldn't save your mother?"

She shook her head again. "Sometimes things just happen."

"They just happen. Someone like Galen Reed just happens to cross paths with us."

Brianna Stafford nodded.

"I haven't been feeling well. He's right about that."

She stiffened and eyed him intently.

"I'm taking all the God Damn drugs they're giving me—according to the God Damn instructions, the same sort of instructions I give to patients every day. And I feel—lousy." He drew in a deep breath and let it out. "It's just this, this getting old, is so annoying."

The waiter placed a chicken salad in front of Brianna Stafford and a corned beef sandwich with French fries in front of Eldon Stafford.

"The great healer who raised me would have done anything, tried anything, anything logical, to help a family member who wasn't feeling well."

Eldon Stafford looked up, then down at his food.

"So do it for yourself. You're a family member. It's just us now. Do it for me."

"I told you—a man in my position can't."

Brianna Stafford shook her head. "Not 'can't.' 'Won't.'"

"I don't think you understand."

"I do. I just don't agree."

"I shouldn't have even let him in the hospital."

"You did it for me."

"True."

"So, go see Doctor Reed. For me."

A grin seemed to sneak on to Eldon Stafford's face for an instant. "You really are a lot like your mother. Whenever I miss her, I don't have to look far."

Brianna Stafford smiled as she sniffed back a tear.

Chapter 4

"I don't know a Doctor Middlebury," Wyatt Greevey said into his intercom. His nostrils flared as he sneered. Greevey maintained a perfectly coiffed head of thinning silver hair. He sat at his desk in front of a state-of-the-art flat-screen computer monitor, clicking his mouse through some emails. "Why did you give him an appointment without talking to me?"

"He doesn't have an appointment," his secretary's voice told him through the intercom.

"We met briefly at a banquet in Zurich. We sat together," Lawrence Middleton said through the intercom. "I'm sorry to come without an appointment, but-"

"I don't really handle the day-to-day with doctors," Greevey told him. "See the appropriate pharmaceutical rep."

"It's not a product question."

Greevey frowned. "Alright, Doctor. Lucky I'm not scheduled."

Lawrence Middleton walked into Wyatt Greevey's office.

Greevey stood up without smiling. "Doctor Middlebury."

Middleton seemed to force a smile. "Middleton, Mr. Greevey. Lawrence Middleton. Orange County Hospital."

Greevey motioned Middleton to a chair across from the desk. He had heard the name correctly. Deliberately mangling the name would help let the doctor know his place. "What needs my personal attention?"

t"I guess... you don't remember me."

Greevey raised his eyebrows and shrugged.

"We were at the Zurich convention in 2007. You told us all about the wonder of the drug technology, how we will partner together—doctors and progressive pharmaceutical companies—to help people live to unprecedented ages."

Greevey shrugged again. He'd made this speech hundreds of times. Sometimes he'd even embellished it to describe his own vision, how he had seen as a young man starting out in business in the 1960s, that investing in this collaboration would create value for society by producing longer, healthier lives, and make investors who saw this potential very rich. His holdings in three major pharmaceutical companies, and in hospitals and even a few insurance companies, had him thoroughly involved in the system. He couldn't remember Middleton, so couldn't remember how much of this he had shared with him. "So, sure. I'm sure I said those things. What brings you here today?"

"You talked about your vision. Your vision as a young man."

Greevey nodded. He must have given the whole presentation at that table. Would this man ever get to the point?

"And we talked about modern-day Luddites."

"Oh yeah." Greevey recalled this discussion. "Luddites" did not come up very often. "Orange County Hospital? Stafford. Doctor Stafford."

"He's the one who made the comment."

"Yes. He called them touch-feely charlatans."

"Right. And I said they would have tried to resist the light bulb by bottling daylight."

Greevey frowned. "You're the one who said that?" Greevey didn't mention he thought it had been a dumb, non sequitur comment, injected just to say something—anything. Why was this man here?

"I did. I said that after the Luddite comment."

"Stafford's a good man. How's he doing?"

"He allowed one of those Luddite charlatans into the hospital." Middleton looked at Greevey with the eyes of a man bringing a grave threat.

Greevey wasn't sure how to respond to this. "That's what you're here about?" he finally asked.

"You said at that banquet, that people will be led astray by phonies who will try to convince the people that the expense of technology is not only unnecessary, but that it may be harmful—like the original Luddites who told the world that automated looms would-"

"Dr. Middleburg, if you-"

"Dr. Middleton."

"Alright, Dr. Middleton, if you're concerned about a matter of hospital policy, why are you here? Peggy Squire is perfectly capable of handling your concerns. Why don't you set a meeting with-"

"I'm not a cardiologist or a cancer specialist."

Greevey frowned. So this Dr. Middle-whatever was not one of the big stars of the hospital.

"She's a million-dollar-a-year hospital executive. I'm just a struggling doctor, just a modest six figure income before overhead, before the insurance companies, landlords and employees and their benefits get done with me."

Greevey shrugged. Was the man trying to cry poor?

"But I do write a lot of prescriptions." Middleton nodded, tight-lipped. "A lot. I believe in the mastery of modern medicine."

"Well, good," Greevey said. This man wasn't going to be passed off to a hospital exec. Greevey decided courtesy, quickly executed, time-efficient courtesy, was called for. "Doctor, I wouldn't worry about Eldon Stafford. He's also committed to modern medicine. He's one of my biggest allies in southern California. If he had some… person you found objectionable… in the hospital, I'm sure he had his reasons."

"I really am sorry to take up your time," Middleton said, "but I'm not sure you understand. His daughter was very sick. She thinks she was healed by some chiropractor. Doctor Stafford had the man in the hospital-"

Greevey shook his head. "Eldon Stafford is not going to let some chiroquacktor run wild in the Orange County Memorial Hospital."

"The guy was doing adjustments—hands on—right in the examining room!"

"I'm sure you didn't see what you thought you saw."

"I'm telling you, I-"

"And even if you did, Dr. Stafford certainly didn't sanction it. Maybe he just wanted to see what the guy did to his daughter."

"It didn't look like that."

Greevey scowled with disbelief.

"It looked more like he was getting a demonstration, taking instruction. When I asked him about it, he didn't say anything like 'I was checking to see what he did.'"

"What did he say?"

"Not much. But later, he told me we should be open to new ideas."

"New ideas. Sure. That's what we're about. New cures. That's made us rich. You know, we work with some chiropractors. Manipulations under anesthesia. Perfect collaboration between modern medicine and chiropractors. A responsible way for the good guys to bring modern medical science to the back-cracking fad."

"Manipulations under anesthesia?"

"Yes. I'm surprised you haven't heard of it. I'm sure Dr. Stafford has."

Middleton seemed flustered. Greevey assumed this would finally get him to leave. But Middleton spoke again. "This wasn't under anesthesia. He was demonstrating. Showing technique. Instructing. Dr. Stafford had the clear appearance of an observer, a pupil."

Greevey smiled. "And you find this disturbing…"

"I thought you would want to know. You're on the Board of Directors. You have influence there."

"And you figure you have influence with me because you write a lot of prescriptions…"

"Look, I just thought you would want to know of such irregularities sanctioned, maybe even encouraged by a doctor with a lot of authority at the hospital. He's got that title, Chief Consulting Physician—they gave that to him when his wife died."

"And you don't think he should have the title or the authority. Maybe you have someone else in mind?" Greevey flashed a sly smile.

Middleton's face tensed. "I'm not trying to take his position."

"So, if the hospital made a change, you wouldn't be interested…"

"I didn't say that. I'm capable. I wouldn't turn away from a position I could handle if it came my way. I'm ready for it."

Greevey nodded. "Thanks for coming by."

Middleton stood. "I just don't want to see a good man duped into collaborating with ignorant charlatans. And if he falls under the spell of this man, just because his daughter had some kind of lucky result, he has a lot of influence. This is California. Southern California. A lot of trends start—right here." Middleton started toward the door.

"I'm sure everything will be fine. Stafford's one of the best."

"Yeah." Middleton nodded as he continued to the door.

"But I'll check into it."

"You don't have to patronize me. I'm sorry I wasted your time." Middleton left.

Greevey smiled and shrugged. He looked at his computer monitor and clicked on an email. He shook his head as he thought about Dr. Middleton's visit, a visit that seemed to him an attempt by an ambitious man to improve his position. Not the first time such a ploy had been attempted. Greevey pressed the intercom. "What do we have on that guy?" Greevey asked.

"You don't remember him?" the secretary's voice asked through the speaker. "He was offered the Chief of Staff position down at San Diego County Medical Center about five years ago. He turned it down—said he wasn't ready."

Greevey's smile disappeared. "Hmmm. So I wonder if I misread this."

"Sir?"

"Um, schedule McTavish in here—first thing tomorrow."

"Now you're bugging your dad?" Clyde Minden flashed an

incredulous smile at Brianna Stafford. They stood in line to get tickets to a movie. "This Reed guy has you acting like an idiot."

"Do you understand?" Brianna Stafford asked, irritated with his attitude. "I don't take Singular anymore. I carry my inhalers but hardly use them. Yes, my dad might understand that and be impressed. You, on the other hand…"

"I'm too thick. Just a dumb football player."

"You're acting thick, about this."

"Brianna, I'm not some pampered housewife who lifted a twelve-pack of soda and tweaked her back. I've got the real thing, from playing offensive tackle in Division One college ball. Some guy chanting herbs and touchy-feely won't make me feel better."

"Chanting herbs?"

"Whatever he does."

"You have no idea. He would make sure your vertebrae are aligned and-"

"I don't want to know what he does, Brianna. I need the real stuff. I can stand next to you right now only because I am on drugs to stop the pain. I've got three discs popped out. Your dad has me seeing the best back-cutter in Orange County. I wouldn't embarrass him by going to your Galen Reed character."

They reached the ticket window.

"Two for 'Ambush Dawn,'" Clyde Minden told the ticket clerk.

"Twenty-two please."

Clyde Minden handed him the money. The tickets popped out of the dispenser. The clerk handed the tickets to him.

Clyde and Brianna entered the theater.

"Popcorn?" he asked.

"Nothing," she said. "None of this stuff."

Clyde smiled. "Oh yeah. That's right. We need to go to the health food movie theater. A place where the movies always have the turnips living happily-ever-after."

"They might be smart to sell healthy snacks at the theaters. I'll bet they'd sell more."

"For the two or three twerps who would buy them?" He got in line for his popcorn.

"Trust me—it would be more than two or three."

Clyde shrugged.

"Doctor Reed could help you. You should give him a try before they start cutting you open."

Clyde tightened his lips. "I don't know why you don't get it. I have a serious back condition. I know other guys who've had the same thing. Back surgery is the only way. Sure, I'll have to deal with some problems in the future. But it's the price I pay for football—number five in the country, playing on national television in the Sugar Bowl three years ago. You tell me how many guys can say that."

"I'm not the only one who doesn't get it."

"Yeah, it's me. Two MRIs showing my discs popping out. You're right, I don't get it. Let me tell you, what I really don't get is why you're trying to get everybody in the world to see Dr. Reed. Why don't you ask everyone in this line to go?" Minden turned. "Hey? Anybody for a back crack?"

Brianna did not look back. She didn't want to see if there was someone behind them who might just be paying attention. "Not everyone. But those closest to me, of course. I know what he can do."

"For a little backache, or maybe one of your stuffy nose or lung things."

"He can do a lot more."

"You have a crush on him."

"What?"

They reached the snack counter. "One medium popcorn and a large coke." He turned to Brianna. "You want anything?"

"They have bottled water." She pointed to the shelf next to the Milk Duds. "I'll take one."

Clyde smirked. "Don't get wild on me."

"That's eight dollars, seventy-five cents."

Clyde handed over a ten dollar bill and took his change. They walked away with their snacks, toward theater twelve, with "Ambush

Dawn" in light blue light just above the entrance.

"I do not have a crush on Galen Reed."

"You better not." He hugged her with one arm as they walked. "Maybe he has one on you."

Brianna Stafford frowned. "That's ridiculous."

"You say he doesn't bill you."

She didn't say anything.

"You are a gorgeous girl."

She smiled and hugged him back. "There's nothing like that. He's my doctor."

"Doctor." Clyde frowned. "Like your dad."

"Not exactly. Different. But effective in his own way."

"Well, if I were you, I'd want to know a little more about why he's so involved with a non-paying patient."

"He's a great healer. Money is not his main priority."

Clyde let out a chuckle. "Believe me, I see it at my desk all day long. All of these doctors, of all types and philosophies—back-cracking, needles, chants and fire-dances—they all have one thing in common. They want the money. They come whining to the insurance company trying to squeeze the system for every dollar."

"And you squeeze them right back." Brianna showed him a mischievous grin.

Minden shrugged. "It's my job."

They walked into the theater. The lights were out, and a preview was running.

"So you're a charity case? Or for some reason, he thinks you are?"

"I'm a starving student."

"With big connections in Washington. An up-and-comer."

"Oh yeah. I'm sure that's it. He figures I'll get all the world leaders and diplomatic corps to come out and see him in Orange County for chiropractic care."

"I could see you trying."

"Hmm. Maybe I should."

"He's hot for you. I bet he'd bill me."

They worked their way down a row toward some seats. The theater was only about one fourth filled.

"Make an appointment. Find out."

Clyde snorted. "Nice try." He lowered himself into his seat, grunting as he adjusted his positioning.

Brianna Stafford watched him and scowled.

Chapter 5

"I said to drive me to the hospital," Eldon Stafford insisted to his daughter as she pulled into a parking place in front of Galen Reed's chiropractic office. It was a nearly moonless night. The parking lot to the enclave of one-story office buildings was empty.

"Just let him look at you—hear what he has to say." Brianna flipped open her phone and pressed a number for a speed dial. "No one ever has to know."

"Drive me to the hospital or I'll call 9-1-1 and get my own ride there."

Brianna saw her call connect.

"I'm two blocks away," Galen Reed's voice said through the phone. "Does he know you're bringing him to me?"

"He just found out now. And… he's not real happy about it."

"Brianna! I told you! I cannot indulge in this New Age claptrap!"

"Then indulge me." Brianna snapped her phone shut.

Eldon Stafford sneered but offered no further protests.

Galen Reed pulled through the parking lot in his blue Impala. He drove right up to where Brianna Stafford was parked, and did not take the time to angle his car between the lines of a parking place. He burst out of his car.

Eldon Stafford did not move from the passenger seat. He rolled down his window.

Reed took a few quick steps to him.

"Would you please tell my daughter to get me to the hospital?" Stafford asked, more commanding than questioning.

"You already told her. She brought you to me."

Eldon Stafford's eyes turned steely and stern. "I need to get to the hospital. We'll run some tests and find out why I feel so bad. I am having acute discomfort—my condition is serious—we can't be fooling around here, playing games so my daughter can prove a point. Or more likely disprove a point."

"The hospital will pump you full of more drugs. They will make you sicker."

Stafford seemed to absorb the information, but tensed and clenched his teeth.

"You're on blood pressure medication, at least five years. Statins for cholesterol, longer than that. What else?"

Eldon Stafford aimed a scolding glare at his daughter.

"I didn't tell him. You didn't even tell me about the prescriptions you've been taking until we were on our way here."

"Hmmph."

"Abdominal pains? In the liver area? Any fever?"

Eldon Stafford breathed out. "I don't know about the temperature. The pains. Yeah. On and off. But real bad tonight, which is why I have to get out of here and get to the God Damn hospital!"

"Any change in your health?"

"Yeah, well, nothing really. A sore back. I took a few anti-inflammatories. Now I think the sore back might be related to something else. So I need to get to some real doctors, in a real hospital, and-"

"Like the ones who killed your wife?"

Eldon's face flashed red. "Brianna, drive me away from here—now!"

Brianna Stafford's eyes widened. "Not cool, Doctor Reed! Not cool at all!" She had never seen Reed seem so competitive, so blunt and decisive—so undiplomatic.

"I'm sorry." Reed seemed to know he had gone too far. "That was a cheap shot, even though-"

"Brianna..." Eldon Stafford looked like he was about to seize control of the car himself.

"Bottom line, Doctor," Reed stated. "Throw away your drugs and come into my office."

"Throw away…" Eldon Stafford appeared to gather himself. "You would have me ignore high blood pressure and high cholesterol?"

"Absolutely not. We will approach them differently."

"Like he did for my asthma," Brianna said gently. "Like he did for me."

"Give me an hour. If you still feel you need the hospital, then your daughter takes you."

"I don't negotiate with terrorists."

Galen Reed nodded. "Okay. That one makes us even for the comment I made about your wife. I shouldn't have said anything about that—wrong time, wrong place. But Dr. Stafford, I know I can help you."

Eldon Stafford looked at his daughter. "You're not taking me to the hospital until I deal with this fool."

"Give him a chance," Brianna told him. "Give yourself a different choice." She paused. "And if you're worried about a 'man in your position,' no one will know but the three of us."

"We have doctor-patient privilege too."

"Doctor-patient," Eldon Stafford muttered disgustedly as he got out of the car. "Coerced guinea pig is more like it."

"I wish you didn't feel that way." Reed moved toward the front door of his office and pulled his keys out of his pocket. "But I will take this opportunity to help you any way I can get it."

"Those blotches on the skin on the backs of your hands," Reed said to Eldon Stafford. "Your blood pressure medicine is thinning your veins and arteries. You are probably more susceptible to a stroke now than before you started taking it."

Eldon Stafford laid face down on the high-low examination table. He tried to remain focused on his impatience. But the inquisitive, curious part of him couldn't help but assess Galen Reed's process.

He took in a deep breath. He would try to relax as much as possible through this mostly irritating diversion.

Galen Reed moved his fingers down Eldon Stafford's spinal column.

"That's nonsense," Stafford finally said, responding to Galen Reed's comment about the blood pressure medicine.

"The blood thinning chemicals in the drug you're taking have thinned out your blood vessels to the point that some of them have become fragile and broken. Blood is leaking into your tissues."

Stafford shook his head without replying. He would endure these ramblings to pacify his daughter, and get on his way to the hospital. He had suffered through Reed's exhaustive, intrusive questions about his medical history. Reed had insisted the questions were essential, so though Stafford answered the questions as minimally as he could, he did answer to avoid his daughter's disapproval. Now he regretted he had been so forthcoming about the medications he was taking. He also grunted through the orthopedic tests Reed administered, tests Stafford remembered from medical school, but only used in his own practice in a cursory way to set up referrals to orthopedists. Did Reed fancy himself an orthopedist? Stafford grimaced with impatience. Orthopedics had nothing to do with his current symptoms—Reed was wasting their time. Good thing the tests could be administered quickly. He'd gotten through all of that, and figured Reed was nearly through with his tinkering. His promise to Brianna would be kept, and he could get to the real professionals.

"And the statins. They must have you on a high dose. Your liver is taking a pounding."

"You can't know any of that without tests."

"Iridology, Doctor. Accepted in many cultures, including some medical establishments in Europe. The eyes are more than just the window to the soul. Take a look in a mirror, at the lower left quadrant of your right iris. You'll see a grouping of little back dots. This is an indicator of liver weakness or even liver damage. And it doesn't take iridology to evaluate the yellowing in your eyes. I'm sure you've noticed that."

"Old age."

"Old age with heavy drugs. Not the stuff law enforcement goes after. The legal stuff the drug companies push. Old age can be done without them."

"Oh, I see. Go back to the days of no drugs, when people lived to ripe old ages of forty and fifty."

"Not at all." Galen Reed felt down Eldon Stafford's back. "Just apply the knowledge differently."

Eldon Stafford rolled his neck and shoulders, resituating himself.

"I found part of your back problem." Reed pressed on Stafford's lower back. "L4-5 and L5-S1 are out of alignment. You also have short leg syndrome—your right leg is a little shorter than your left because of a femoral rotation related to the sacro-iliac dysfunction. I'd like to confirm it with x-rays, from a standing position. I've got a machine here. It'll take just a few minutes."

"X-rays"

"Right this way."

Reed led him out to the room with the x-ray machine.

"No fractures. No bone pathology," Reed said as he held the x-ray they had just taken. He handed it toward Stafford.

"I saw it," Stafford said. "Let's get on with this."

"This confirms my initial impression, that-"

"I know," Stafford said. "Typical chiroquackery bullshit." Stafford lay back down on the table.

Reed came around to the head of the examining table and made eye contact with Stafford. "Why is this so hard to accept? Why does it have to be so inconsistent and incompatible? It's simple, really. The spine is the center of the entire body. Everything branches out from the spine. The spine evolved first—it's an older structure biologically than most of the rest of our bodies. The central nervous system, right? So wouldn't it stand to reason that if the spine is not positioned at its optimum, the body loses some of its function, its efficiency, its ability to heal? Your lower back is out of alignment." Reed stepped back to the side of Stafford. "Anti-inflammatories attack the symptoms of the damage to your back, the muscles that have been thrown off by the misalignment. Those drugs attack your stomach and liver as well. What I do will address the actual problem. Relax." Reed applied a quick burst of pressure to Stafford's lower back.

A cracking sound resulted.

"Hey!" Stafford reacted to the sudden action, but realized the sudden pressure wasn't painful. If anything, if he allowed himself to admit what he really felt, he would have to admit he had a sensation of the bones in his back locking back into their correct positions.

"That, sir, was an adjustment."

"Are you trying to break my back?"

"Quite the opposite. I'm putting your back into a better position to help you heal."

Stafford looked ahead without speaking.

"There are a few other places where the vertebrae are out. I'm going to adjust them, to give your body the maximum ability to heal your liver."

Stafford started to object, but felt another burst of pressure further up his back, then another just above it.

"Wait here. I need to get some ice."

"Ice. To reduce the swelling from all the damage you just did?"

Reed put ice packs on Stafford's back. "Even putting things back in place causes a disruption. So the ice—it's good for the body's recovery."

"And you do this to people all day."

"With very positive results—yes."

Stafford shook his head. "The body will heal itself."

Reed put towels over the ice packs. He smiled. "Exactly. And isn't a lot of mainstream western medicine based on this? Set a broken bone. Let the body knit the two pieces back together. Catch a cold? Rest, while the body's immune system kicks out the virus. What I do is to make sure the bones encasing the central nervous system are in place, unlocking your body's maximum capability to heal itself. Naturally.

Without drugs that create new damage—you call it 'side effects'—new damage that then also has to be healed." He shook his head. "Chiropractic is not some quirky idea, swirling around mainstream medicine like an extraneous eccentricity. It is a perfect partner with all modern medical technology if utilized properly."

Eldon Stafford didn't like being lectured. He wanted to tell Reed to keep his flaky propaganda to himself. Who did this man think he was, lecturing an educated, respected medical doctor? But he held back the obligatory indignation. Because despite what his years of training and experience were telling him he should say, he had to admit an undeniable fact—he felt better.

"So, should I tell Brianna to get the car started to rush you to the hospital?"

"No," Stafford answered quietly.

"Good."

"But I can't just throw away the drugs."

"You can. Maybe in stages. We can work on that. But eventually your body, with an optimally aligned vertebral column, will let you know you've done the right thing."

Stafford shook his head. "Cholesterol clogs arteries. I've got too much of it in my blood. Something has to be done."

"Doctor, those studies refer to a correlation between cholesterol and heart disease. But it may be a correlation without a cause and effect. There's no real proof that high cholesterol leads to arterial sclerosis."

"Hmmph. I don't know about that. But, okay. All right. You've helped my daughter. You've explained how you can help me. And I'm a wild-eyed fanatic fool if I try to deny that I do actually feel a little better, and that some of what you said made some sense. I'll give it a shot. So what do we do?"

"I want to adjust you three times a week for a month and then reevaluate. And I want to wean you off the drugs. Meet me on the sly. At night."

Stafford eyed him.

"I want only one thing in return. If I help you—if my methods benefit your health—I want you to admit it. To me, to Brianna, and anyone else you feel could benefit from the information."

"I'm not sure about that. You'll want me to take out an ad in the national press?"

"No." Reed shook his head. "No. You choose who else to tell. Brianna and I are the only ones I am saying you have to tell."

Eldon Stafford moved his shoulders and rolled his head. "I gotta tell you—I do feel better."

"Good. But one session isn't enough."

"Tomorrow night?"

"Sure."

"One other thing. Do you really think the hospital killed my wife?"

Reed swallowed. "I'm sorry. I never should have pounced on you with that."

"Apology accepted. Rude delivery noted and now disregarded. Do you believe it's true?"

"Yes."

Stafford stretched, tensing, then relaxing.

"Do you have the records?" Reed asked. "We can take a look at the situation, maybe find out, one way or the other..."

"I can get them."

"So, are we going to the hospital?" Brianna Stafford asked her father as she strapped in her lap and shoulder belt.

Eldon Stafford strapped in his lap and shoulder belt. "I still don't feel all that great."

Brianna started her car.

"But I do feel better."

Brianna nodded. "No drugs. Just chiropractic care." She put her car in gear, pulled out of the parking place and started the car toward the parking lot exit.

"I still need some tests."

"So—the hospital?"

Eldon Stafford took a deep breath. "Not tonight. I'll get the tests at the hospital during a slow period."

Brianna grinned.

"I'm not certain about anything right now. I mean, the visit forced me to relax. Just lying down for the adjustments probably had some therapeutic value."

"You found adjustments, for the first time, to be relaxing?"

"Well, no. Not in the moment. But the process of lying down—taking the frenzy out of the situation…"

"I'm glad you feel better."

"Me too."

"Sorry. Yeah, I should have called back." Eldon Stafford carried his cell phone toward the bathroom of his luxury Costa Mesa condominium. Stafford was shirtless, wearing pajama pants.

"We're glad you're okay," Lawrence Middleton's voice said, speaking through Stafford's cell phone.

Stafford walked back into his bathroom. "I will want those tests. I'll stop in tomorrow."

"Afternoon? I'll supervise myself."

"I'll stop by around three."

"Good."

"Thanks Larry."

"No problem. Get some rest."

"Right."

The call ended.

Stafford put down the phone. He stood at the counter and looked in the mirror. He frowned at his flabby upper body, with sagging chest muscles and protruding belly. If this torso had presented to his examining room, he would have lectured its owner on exercise and diet. He moved toward the mirror and inspected his eyes. He pulled down the lower eyelid of his right eye. A little pink—it had been a long day. But Stafford could not see anything in his eye to indicate he had a damaged liver. Dots in the eyes—voodoo medicine!

Stafford looked at the purple blotches on the back of his left hand. He looked at another under his right armpit. It was hard to dismiss that finding. Yes, those blotches could be explained by the medication. Yes, the medication could thin and break the blood vessels, causing blue, deoxygenated blood to leak into the tissues.

Stafford scrunched his shoulders up and down. He rotated his head on his neck, and flexed his spine by throwing his spine forward. His back did feel better. He didn't have chronic back pain, but his neck and lower back occasionally tightened. These areas felt looser, more flexible—more healthy.

Stafford wanted to dismiss what had happened at Galen Reed's office. He wanted to dismiss the perspective Reed had presented. But he couldn't get himself to reject the ideas. Over thirty years of training and practice—he had to admit Reed's ideas could have merit. He thought back to his undergraduate days at Cal Berkeley in the mid 1960s. Even at that time, he'd been committed to becoming a doctor. His father, a successful insurance agent with plenty of money, had committed to finance his entire education. So Eldon Stafford answered his father's commitment with a commitment of his own, to excel at his studies and complete his medical training.

But he had not been oblivious to the activities of his fellow students. Question authority. Don't trust anyone over thirty. Make over an unjust world with a burst of youthful idealism and energy. Don't let the "Establishment" insist on mindless conformity to old ways when new ways could be better. Now he looked in the mirror and saw a middle-aged man who by every objective definition was the "Establishment." Was he a fool back then when he had accepted the "question authority" ethic? And could he trust himself, a man almost double the age of thirty? No, he didn't have to go that far. But mindless conformity was never good. Open-mindedness could never be a mistake. So what was there to lose by reevaluating his approach to health, even his own health?

Stafford looked to the right of the bathroom sink. He saw the bottles of pills. He picked up the one labeled "Benicar." He needed to take one tonight, for his blood pressure. He opened the bottle and looked at the pills. He pushed his lips forward and exhaled a burst of air through his nose. Fine—he'd test blood pressure tomorrow too. One night wouldn't kill him—would it? He looked off to his left, at a small waste basket next to the toilet. Throw them away? He wasn't going that far. He slammed the bottle back down. He looked at the bottles of Lipitor and Motron, also sitting on the counter. Throw them away? Not tonight. He would gather more information.

He looked back into his eyes. He stared in closer. He saw a little black dot in the lower left quadrant of his right eye. Could that dot really mean something significant? It was just a dot. Stafford knew better than that. His training had taught him—there were few if any meaningless anomalies on the human body. Everything meant something—just a simple matter of decoding the meaning.

Stafford reached for his toothbrush, but stopped. It wasn't time to retire for the night yet. No, there was another occurrence from this evening that gnawed at him. It had festered in the background while his own healthcare was an immediate issue. Now, it was front-and-center.

Stafford grabbed his cell phone and hit his speed dial.

"Eldon. You still okay?"

"Yeah Larry. I'm fine, thanks. I just called to ask a favor."

"Name it."

"Could you have the folks dig up my wife's hospital records, and have them waiting for me when I see you tomorrow afternoon?"

"Um, I can try. That's before the computer records. It might take some archive searching."

"Okay. Put the records people on it."

"Sure. Your wife?"

"Yeah. Just some… well, her case came up recently. I'm curious about a couple of issues."

"Her case came up?"

"Yeah. See you tomorrow."

"Sure."

"Thanks for your help."

"No problem."

The call ended.

Eldon Stafford walked into his bedroom. He took a bottle of Scotch from on top of the headboard and took a swallow. Some ailments required a less sophisticated, more ancient form of medication.

Chapter 6

"Your back is better," Galen Reed told Brianna Stafford who was lying face down on the high-low table. "Alignments are improved. We're still working hard on T2 and T3 for the lung area. I worked that one again today. How's your breathing been?"

"Good. Better."

Reed's hands moved to her neck and shoulder area. He kneaded both sides at the base of her neck. "You do seem tense."

"Tense?"

"More than I can remember except for maybe your first visits."

She didn't answer.

"And quiet. More quiet than ever."

"I have a lot on my mind."

"Most people do. And the stress from all that 'lot on your mind' reduces the body's ability to heal."

Brianna again did not say anything.

"Well, try to relax. It will help your progress-"

"Why did you bring up my mother like that?" Brianna asked, the question bursting out of her as if she had held it back and could no longer restrain it.

Reed now understood the stress. "I regretted it the minute I said it," he admitted. "But to hear him going on and on about how much in a hurry he was to get away from me to go to the place where-" Reed let out a deep breath. "Well, I remembered what you told me about your mother, and it just came out of me."

"It was mean. It was a cheap shot. He felt terrible about what happened to my mom for many years. He considered it a major failure of his life, and considered me the biggest victim of that failure."

"I understand. I am sorry."

Brianna rotated her neck.

Reed kneaded her neck muscles again. "If it helps, I think your father is past the outburst. It may have opened things up to find out what happened."

"She died—that's what happened. I told you about it so you would know me, and know my father, and understand us, not so you could use it against him."

"I'm not using it against anyone."

"You shouldn't have brought it up."

"Shouldn't have brought it up? It's an integral part of what is developing here."

Brianna turned over to face Reed. "And just what is developing here, Doctor?"

Reed shrugged. Wasn't this obvious to her? "Brianna, this is an enormously important connection. One of the most prominent, respected MDs from this area is experiencing effective chiropractic care—first, administered to a loved one, and now as a patient. The possibilities, the potential." He shook his head. "You can see it, can't you?"

Brianna eyed Reed. "My father asked me how you came to treat me. I told him it was a coincidence. I told him I was a lousy patient, that I giggled through your treatments, that I wondered why you even kept treating me."

"Coincidence." Reed paused a moment. "I hardly ever believe in it. I've told you, I have moments where I sense the future. I had a feeling Sal, the nutritionist who referred you, was going to meet someone important that Saturday. I saw your name—your last name—on his list, and saw how-"

Brianna backed up and brought her arms over her chest. "This sounds creepy, Doctor Reed."

"Have you been helped?"

"Yes."

"Has your father been helped?"

"I think so." But she still sounded apprehensive.

"I know that hospital. First hand. As an employee, and as a patient. I am certain I am destined to make a difference in some way related to that hospital, or the people there, probably both. And the difference I make there will resound and reverberate well beyond Orange County, or California, maybe even beyond the country. So when I saw the name Stafford, and realized who you were, I decided this was the moment it would start. And I am ready. The time is right. Not back then. Not back when…" His voice trailed off as he paused. "The time is now. The door will open from my association with you and your father."

"And that's what it was about."

"It was about getting you well."

Brianna lay back down and relaxed. "Okay. How can I argue with that?"

"And why should you?"

There was a knock on the door. "Dr. Reed? The next patient is ready," a female voice said from just outside the door.

"I'll be right there." He turned to Brianna. "Let's get you on the rollers."

Brianna Stafford nodded and moved to the intersegmental traction table.

"Feeling good?" Galen Reed asked as he reentered the examining room where Brianna was relaxing.

"Sure. But… I'm still unclear about a few things."

"What do you need to know?"

"What do you mean—'employee?'"

"Of the hospital?"

"Yes."

"I worked there many years ago, in collections. I saw first hand—it was no place to get sick."

"Collections?"

"You sound like you're asking for my life story."

"It seems like a long way from collections at a hospital to healer."

He smiled. "It has been a long journey, but I know I have arrived at the right destination." He paused. "I've always been a little restless—three different schools to get my Bachelor's degree. But I always had a sense I would work in something where I helped people. I was going to be a teacher. But when I came out of school, the job market was tight. I worked at a collections agency, then took the job at the hospital verifying insurance and doing collections because the hours allowed me the flexibility to work on a Masters degree. But what I saw at the hospital…" He shook his head. "I thought there must be a better way to heal people, a better approach to health itself. So, I enrolled in the Modern School of Health. It opened my eyes to the shortcomings of the established MD-type approach. I am so grateful now that I couldn't find a decent teaching position, though it was frustrating at the time. But this is where I will make my mark. This is how I will help the most people in the most profound ways."

"Why didn't you just go to medical school?"

"You know by now, I am a creature of intuition. Conventional medicine was not my calling. I saw who was going into pre-med. They were mostly people who were very smart, doing pre-med because that's what smart people did to get into a line of work that would make them a tremendous amount of money. I heard few if any talk about an inner voice calling them to heal the sick. I couldn't see myself in that world, surrounded by those people. And my inner voice hadn't been specific yet."

"But the hospital…"

"Yes, the hospital." He gritted his teeth through a grin. "I was also a patient here, a long time ago. I was playing basketball and got knocked down pretty hard. I went in for x-rays. The grim-faced doctor approached me, with the longest expression I had ever seen. He told me the gunshot to my thigh would render me unable to walk normally ever again. Gunshot? I told him he had the wrong x-ray, the wrong patient. He insisted. The x-ray tech insisted. All procedures had been followed—they couldn't be wrong. They were Orange County Memorial Hospital. You know what it was? A quarter in the pocket of my shorts. Somebody saw a quarter and called it a gunshot wound. Some poor emergency room resident with next-to-no sleep for over two days. No, I was not going to be part of that system."

"So you knew from your days in the hospital who my father was."

"And that he had a daughter named Brianna. Yes."

"Well I'm sorry Doctor, but I feel used. You treated me to get to my father! You had this agenda, and I was just someone to use."

Reed nodded. "I understand that at a superficial level, your concern seems reasonable. But let me ask you—have I cheated you in any way?"

"No. If anything you've been generous."

"If I help you, and you tell your friends and family, have I used you?"

"No. Of course not. That's not-"

"If I decide to help someone who I know could offer a lot of good to a lot of people as a result of our association, have I done anything wrong?"

Brianna took a deep breath. "No, when you put it that way, I guess not. It just has a kind of... stalker feel to it."

Reed shook his head. "Trust me, this association between your father and me is meant to happen. Lots of good will come from it—I've seen it in my mind, how it will work. I've seen that I just need to be patient enough to let him get there with me."

Brianna looked skeptical.

"He's healthier already. You know it's true. And he's getting your mother's records. There's been a delay, but they're supposed to be available this week, and he's agreed to review them with me. If I was a negative influence in your lives, a 'stalker,' would things be heading in such a positive direction?"

"No, they wouldn't." Brianna paused a moment. "He's going to have you go over the records with him?"

"Yes."

Brianna raised her eyebrows. "Wow." She nodded. "Just remember, it's a sensitive subject, Doctor. Don't hard-charge into it."

"Sounds like good advice."

Chapter 7

"What happened to my regular rep from your company?" Lawrence Middleton asked as he motioned Seymour McTavish to a chair in the functionally furnished private office of his private practice suite a few blocks from Orange County Memorial Hospital. "Is he okay?"

"Absolutely." McTavish sat down. Seymour McTavish was about forty, with a stocky build, a weathered face, and brown hair cut as short as it could be without displaying a completely shaved scalp. "He'll continue to be your personal rep from Havitol Pharmaceutical. I handle... I work on special projects for Mr. Greevey."

Middleton twitched his nose and eyes as he wondered about the phrase "special projects." "Listen, tell Mr. Greevey I'm sorry about coming to his office. I'm embarrassed I bothered him. And I'm really not trying to move in on Dr. Stafford's position. I guess I just found some of his behavior peculiar, and I needed to tell someone about it." He smiled. "I probably should have told my minister, or consulted a counselor."

McTavish's serious eyes homed in on Middleton for a short, awkward moment. "Actually, Mr. Greevey is glad you came to him."

Middleton frowned. "He didn't seem glad."

McTavish chuckled. "Well, you know, that's his way. He's a busy man and he gets cranky. I often kid him about being a grump. Wyatt the Grump, I always say." He chuckled again.

"Well, I got the feeling I was bothering him, that I had made an extremely unfavorable impression on a man who barely knew who I was, and didn't want to know."

McTavish raised his eyebrows in what seemed like a choreographed, contemplated movement. "He is very favorably impressed, and grateful. Impressed with your insight, grateful you shared it."

"Oh, well, thank you. But, like I said, I'm not sure this is really an issue."

Again there was a silent moment while McTavish appeared to organize his thoughts, and his approach. So Greevey had changed his mind about Middleton's visit and had sent his "special projects" person to communicate it. There was something more behind this than a PR visit, something that might just benefit Lawrence Middleton.

Middleton considered that he had probably taken McTavish by surprise by minimizing the issue. Greevey apparently wanted more information. Fine, Middleton would help him along. "Is there something else I can do for you?"

"Yes, there is," McTavish said. "We have been examining the situation, and have other sources of information and measures in place. But I wanted to know from you—have you noticed anything peculiar about Dr. Stafford?"

Middleton frowned in thought. So now Eldon Stafford was a "situation." And he, Lawrence Middleton, had detected it. Yes, there was definite potential for benefit here. "Peculiar." Middleton hadn't expected this type of request, and had to ponder. But he became uncomfortable with the awkward silence while he thought, and blurted out the first thing that came to his mind. "Actually, he looks a lot better lately."

This seemed to surprise McTavish.

"He came in not long ago for some follow-up tests. He must be on some new meds. A few weeks ago he came in for some tests—the day after he almost admitted himself to the emergency room. His liver enzymes were off the charts. He complained of abdominal pain. He seemed like a mess, but also seemed guarded about how he was going to deal with it. The follow-up tests showed liver enzymes within normal ranges. His blood pressure was just over borderline, and his

cholesterol was up slightly from the earlier readings. But he just...
seemed to feel better."

"New meds? Did he mention new meds?"

"No." Middleton looked down, then up. "No, he made some cryptic comment. Something like 'I discovered a fountain somewhere—I'll let everyone know if it works out.' I took that to mean he didn't have time to go into it, or didn't want to say what he was doing."

"Has that chiropractor guy been hanging around?"

"No. Haven't seen him at all."

"Interesting." McTavish seemed to deliberate over what to say next. "Because, his prescriptions for our cholesterol medication, and our blood pressure medication—filled prescriptions—have dropped 62% over the last month."

"You guys track that?"

"We can, sure. We usually use the data to track the use of our new medications. It helps us to come after, um, contact the doctors who maybe didn't get the word on one of our new products that could really help their patients."

"Ah, yes. I mean, we are incredibly busy. So if some of us are behind on the literature, you can find those doctors and advise them."

"Exactly. It's how the system works to bring modern medicine to a busy, more-and-more complex world."

"Well, maybe Dr. Stafford just didn't write many prescriptions last month."

"It's the lowest for both of those medications in the last five years. That includes vacation periods."

"Hmmm. What do you think it means?"

"I don't know. That's part of my, my assignment. To find out."

Middleton shrugged. "If he's on new meds, they seem to be working."

McTavish nodded. "I'll pull our competitors' data."

"Really..."

"I've got connections with my counterparts. They'll help."

Middleton shrugged again. "Okay."

McTavish stood to leave.

"Oh, there was one other thing," Middleton couldn't believe he'd almost forgotten to mention this, under the heading of "peculiarities." "He asked to see his wife's hospital records."

"His wife. I didn't know he was married."

"She passed away. From some kind of flukey illness."

"When was that?"

"About seven, eight years ago."

"And he asked for the records—when?"

"When he came in a few weeks ago for the first tests. They're in a storage facility out in Riverside. I put in a request. They're still not here."

"How did she die?"

"She went into the hospital with a swollen foot. It turned out she was a lot sicker than that. Things just kept getting worse. Everything the doctors tried—no help. She just got worse and worse. Until she died."

"Call me when they come in. I'd like to see them before he does."

Middleton gave McTavish a wary look. "I'm not sure that would be proper."

"You're worried about confidentiality? She's long dead—she has no right to confidentiality. We're both worried about Dr. Stafford's strange behavior recently. You're the one with the smarts to flag this for us. I know you'll keep helping."

Middleton nodded. What could sharing records for a long deceased patient harm? And helping these powerful men could help him—in the present. "I'll contact you when they come in."

"So you decided to come," Natalie Corey said to Galen Reed as she greeted him at the front door to her home.

"I just ran late. I told you that when I called." He walked in.

Natalie Corey's house décor exhibited the same contrasts as her office. Sleek, stark modern objects, like a prominently displayed flat screen high definition television and the angled shapes of designer furniture contrasted with a scheme of hanging and potted plants. "Ran late? I waited in that restaurant for almost an hour."

"I did call. My session with Eldon Stafford took-"

"Calling to say you'll be a few minutes late is one thing. Calling to tell me to wait indefinitely is quite another."

"I am sorry. It's just that he is progressing so well, and he is more receptive each time. I don't want to-"

"It's just like ten years ago." Natalie shook her head. "This is what broke us up. This obsessive, my-world-first behavior."

Galen sat on her white leather couch.

Natalie remained standing as she eyed him.

Galen got the sense that she wasn't sure she wanted him to stay. "Ten years ago. A long time ago."

"I'm not talking about ten years ago. I'm talking about right now."

"But you related it to ten years ago."

"It's even the same family."

Galen nodded. "I think we should talk a little about ten years ago. Actually about seven or eight years ago."

"It's stuff like this that broke us up." She finally sat down, not next to him on the leather couch, but in a leather chair diagonally to his right.

"I know. You would wait somewhere for me. I would never show up and forget to call. I was immersed in-"

"You think it was about not calling? That you can fix this by calling to tell me you'll be putting me second to whatever comes along?"

Galen slumped into the couch. "I'm sorry. It's just that, it's that I have the chance to make sense of everything, to turn one of the darkest times of my life into something positive. I am sorry, but this-"

"Galen. 'I'm-sorry-but' means you're not sorry at all."

Galen grimaced. She had a point. She had a way of cutting right to the heart of this sort of issue. She was right—he wasn't really sorry. He was just trying to justify himself, and get her to agree.

She shook her head. "This isn't going to end well. It didn't before. And it won't this time."

He felt himself grin just slightly. "That's your real fear. That I'm repeating what happened before."

She shot him a dubious look.

"That's why you keep saying it—'ten years ago,' 'back then.' You say it's not about that, but it is." He moved to the edge of the couch and reached for her arm. "It will be different. I'm different. You're different. They're different. The whole dynamic is changed. I can't undo the past, but I will build something positive from it."

Natalie moved her arm away from his touch. "I'm not big on mindless affirmations. Saying something over and over again will not make it happen."

"No. I've never been big on that either. I'm not doing affirmations. I'm just trying to tell you, this is not ten years ago. We were so much younger and less experienced with the world then, less confident, less assured. I was just getting started. Look at you. You were a clerk in a vitamin store who took my antics without a peep. Now you're an executive with a great company, and you aren't going to let me slide by with any crap. If we'd stayed together, you never would have evolved to this point."

"No. I would have been spared a lot of grief with the real estate tycoon, fighting for custody, fighting off bankruptcy…"

"And you wouldn't have two wonderful sons."

"You know, you can only play that card so many times."

Galen smiled. "But I haven't used them up yet."

A little grin slipped onto her face. "Almost."

"All I'm saying is that we have arrived at this time, the best possible reality. We didn't get here smoothly. You went through the failed marriage. I went through a sequence of new-age airheads. But here we are, you and I, in position for an amazing collaboration."

"I saw Brianna Stafford the other day. She was in one of our stores. Boy did that bring back memories."

"The next generation."

Natalie raised her eyebrows. "'Next-generation' looks good on her."

"What?"

"Young adulthood looks good on her."

"Um, yeah."

"So I don't need to worry about her?"

Galen's eyes scrunched together with disbelief. "She's a patient. Real young."

"So was I."

"That's different. You were a friend first, then a patient."

"She was a young girl back then."

"Who lost her mother…"

Natalie Corey took in a deep breath. "I wish you could convince me this won't come to grief."

"I promise—it won't."

"What happens when they find out this isn't all coincidence?"

"The name on Sal's list was a coincidence. My reaction? An opportunity to fix something that has haunted me for a long time, a chance to exorcise some demons."

"Life doesn't work that way."

"Not always. But I know it—as certain as I can be about anything—I know life will work that way this time. I can see it, vividly, inevitably… Out of the demons will come something truly amazing."

Natalie took a deep breath and shook her head. "I hope you prove me wrong."

"You're part of it. You'll keep me from, from doing too much 'obsessive behavior.'"

"Great. That's my favorite thing to do."

Galen Reed shrugged sheepishly.

"All right. Truce."

"A truce. Good." Galen looked around. "Where are the boys?"

Natalie Corey moved next to him on the couch. "They're with their father this weekend."

Galen Reed grinned and nodded as they cuddled with each other.

"My back does feel a lot better." Eldon Stafford stood up. He drew a deep breath. The room was filled with a lavender scent.

Galen Reed smiled. "I didn't think you'd keep coming back if you weren't getting decent results."

Stafford took another deep breath. "I have to say—at first I thought it was the forced relaxation of coming here a few nights a week. I thought that, by itself, was making me feel better."

"That's part of it, certainly. Taking that stress down a few notches."

"Of course. But the back alignment thing—I have to admit. I really do see the effect."

"Good. That's important to me."

"Now, before you get too puffed up about it, we need to acknowledge it hasn't been the only thing that's helped."

Reed smirked. Stafford was more and more talkative after each session. Reed sensed Stafford had been holding back his reactions to the treatment, keeping them to himself. At first, Reed's only validation of the effectiveness of his treatments had been Stafford's return visits. But visit by visit, Stafford had warmed to the effects of Reed's treatment more and more. "What else has helped?" Reed finally asked.

"Quite simple," Stafford told him. "You made me pay attention to things I've been telling my patients for years. Fix the diet to bring down cholesterol and fat—that has taken down my weight, which, of course, makes me feel better. My cholesterol numbers are up slightly, but nowhere near where they were when I started taking the medicine. And cutting salt and sugar, along with getting back to regular cardio-vascular exercise, has taken down my blood pressure. Even this thing about pickle juice—you remember telling me that?"

"Of course. I tell all my patients about it."

"I can't imagine an MD giving that sort of information to a patient. We really are trained in more high-tech remedies. But last week, I thought I was getting a cold. I had the sore throat, the whole set of symptoms that comes on. I couldn't believe I was doing it, but I gargled the stuff, just like you said to do."

Reed smiled.

"The cold never came."

Reed nodded. "That juice keeps those pickles from going bad. If you take a pickle out of the jar and leave it, it spoils rather quickly. So common sense tells us there is something special about the juice. Just ask the lady from New Albany, Mississippi who lived to 115. She says her secret was vinegar and pickles. Not blood pressure medicine and statins."

"I remember you telling me about her, the second visit."

"Good."

"So I don't think the back-cracking stuff is essential. Having someone else push me to do the things I knew I should do—that may be the most important part of this."

"I'm not trying to claim you need only vertebral alignment for health. I don't minimize it—a healthy spine is a key component. But my profession is not just about the spine. It's about a different approach to health. And you've experienced it—first hand."

"I don't know if it's that different."

Reed smiled as he raised his chin. "It's a subtle but profound difference, Doctor. You see, you're talking about adjustments, about my work realigning your spine, as if this is a way for a healer to impose a cure on an illness. You almost sound like you think I offer my care as a substitute for the drugs. But really, everything I've done has positioned your own healing processes to work more effectively. You know, even something you might consider our most intrusive method, our chironosis™, which uses hypnosis, simply acts to focus the mind and body. Spine alignment helps, of course. But the information about diet, exercise, reducing stress, even the hypnosis—these are just ways to get your body to do what it can do better than any drug, any healer. I've simply given your body the tools to maintain health. My focus is not on curing illness, though I can certainly facilitate that. But my focus is on maintaining, even increasing, health, wellness."

Stafford appeared to consider the remarks. "We do that too," he finally said. "But probably not enough," he quickly added.

"No argument there either," Reed said smiling.

"I'll bet not." Stafford sat down on a chair in the examining room.

"Do you have a minute to talk?"

Reed's smile broadened. "Sure. Let's go into my office."

"How about the Imperial Highway Grill?"

"It's pretty late for a meal."

"We'll have a snack. A healthy snack."

Reed smiled again.

"Um, I have my wife's hospital records."

Reed nodded as he took in a deep breath.

Chapter 8

"I referred two patients to you," Stafford told Reed as he ate his fresh fruit cup, accompanied by some whole wheat toast that Stafford dipped in a small plate of garlic-flavored olive oil. They sat at a table not far from where Brianna and Eldon Stafford had eaten a few weeks before. Dinner rush was winding down, but most of the tables were still occupied.

"Thank you. That may be the biggest compliment of all."

"I know you could help these people. They really do need a focus away from cures, toward maintaining their health. I know that's what you'll do for them."

"Count on it." Reed took a bite of his chicken breast salad. "You do realize, Doctor Stafford, that we could do a lot more good than just help a few patients."

Stafford shrugged. "I'm not sure about that…"

"If the established medical profession dropped this focus on sickness, and focused instead on health, we could transform the entire healthcare system. We could overturn-"

"Wait a minute. Now, I've seen the good you've done for me. And you can help people who need to focus more on healthier behaviors. But curing disease, healing sick people—that's what we do. And this system of ours is the greatest ever, the most advanced ever. Dedicated people, researching new drugs, pioneering new surgical and other medical techniques, have extended lives that would have been lost just a few generations ago. Heart attacks used to be disabling at best, often fatal. Cancer used to be a death sentence. At a lower level, torn knee ligaments used to need major reconstructive surgery, with a loss of some function almost certain. Now we can do a scope on some of these injuries and have the patient walking at full function in a matter of weeks. If you're talking about replacing-"

"Not replacing. Forming an alliance. What if we could prevent some of these conditions you are so proud of your ability to treat? What if we could prevent most of them?"

Stafford shook his head. "I don't see it. Not as part of some broad change."

"It's because of your training. You're trained to detect illness, then throw a drug, or a surgical technique, or some other form of treatment course at the illness. If you can go beyond-"

"But that is what we do," Stafford insisted. "Sure, prevention is not a bad thing. But doctors cure sick people. What else are we for?"

"We could be so much more."

"We'll have to agree to disagree."

Reed sighed. Stafford seemed to be closing out the discussion, far short of what Reed had wanted to accomplish.

"Let's take a look at the records."

Reed raised his eyebrows. "Yeah."

Stafford reached into his briefcase and pulled out two stacks of about two hundred pages of medical records, fastened together with metal strips at the top. "It was a sad trip down memory lane for me. But I didn't see anything there confirming your suspicion that the hospital killed her."

Reed nodded.

Stafford handed the stacks over to him.

Reed thumbed through the stacks. In the dry detail of medical narrative writing, full of oversized, passionless words—full of numbers: measuring tests, measuring time, measuring deterioration, full of scrawled nearly illegible notes—the story of Susan Stafford's death could be reconstructed. She had entered the hospital with a swollen foot, leading to an initial diagnosis of cellulitis. For some reason the emergency room doctor had put heat on the foot, making it worse. With Susan Stafford getting more uncomfortable, experiencing more pain, her blood pressure went up. The recorded symptoms seemed to multiply—collapsed lungs, failed kidneys. He had a good idea what had happened. He put down the first packet and picked up the second packet, expecting to confirm his suspicions. The records weren't tabbed, so he figured the section he was looking for would be grouped, without any clear label, in the second packet. But it wasn't there. Reed grabbed for the first packet again. He tensed as he stopped breathing a moment. "It's not all here."

"What are you looking for?"

"The drugs. What did they give her? There's one page, from when she first got there. Where's the rest of it?" Reed let out a long breath.

"I saw that. It looks like a few pages of the drug records are missing."

"Do you remember?"

"I remember they pulled out all the stops."

Reed suspected "all the stops" had been exactly the problem. But he was smart enough not to mention it, not without something concrete to point to.

"These records are almost eight years old. I don't know if we can expect-"

"Doctor, you've been through these records. Does it strike you that they left anything else out?"

"No."

"Every little bureaucratic cover-thy-ass memo, log-sheet, chicken-scratch on hourly reviews—it's all there except for the complete pharmacology rundown. Doesn't that seem odd?"

"So, in your mind, what does it mean?"

"I'm not sure. Where did you get the records?"

"Dr. Middeton saw to it."

"Well I'm sure he didn't get them himself..."

"No, um, they came from an offsite storage location. Not even in the county. Maintained by an independent contractor, not even a hospital employee. That's why it took so long."

Reed looked at the records. "These are copies."

"They look like it." Stafford's face flashed with an insight. "Sure. You have some ten-dollar-an-hour clerk making copies of hundreds of pages. A mistake was made."

Reed was amazed at how charitable Stafford remained even when faced with circumstances that at least merited some suspicion.

"We'll just request the originals."

Reed leaned back. "Not a good idea. We need to hope those pages became, um, lost, after the copy stage. We don't want to give anybody the idea, or the opportunity, to get rid of the originals."

"You're getting paranoid."

"Paranoid." Reed paused a moment. "I'm young, a relative newcomer to chiropractic healing. My older colleagues have told me stories about the efforts taken to destroy the chiropractic profession. I'd like to think it can be different. Some of my older colleagues carry so much bitterness they insist it will never be different. They believe the established powers, the wealth, the people who owe their privileged positions to this system, will never allow it. They could be at work here."

Stafford sneered. "We're talking about an error by an overworked clerk. Anything else is… silly."

Reed felt a surge of anger. "Look, do you want to know what happened to your wife or not? If you don't, fine. But don't kid yourself—with what we have right now, you might as well not have gotten any records at all." Reed picked up one of the packets. "You still don't know. I think somebody's messing with this. I don't know who or how, or even why for sure. But if you want to know, there is a way for us to find out." He tossed the records down on the table.

Stafford scowled as he cleared his throat. "Of course I want to know." He paused a moment, scratching his chin. "And it does bother me that those drug records are missing."

Reed kept his eyes on Stafford.

"I'll have my secretary order the originals, and have them sent directly to the office-"

Reed shook his head. "Have her find out where they are. Or find out yourself. Whatever you think would draw the least attention. Then we go get them. Ourselves."

Stafford looked down at his food.

"You know how it works. Fundamental diagnostic technique. We need to rule out the unhealthy condition, if we think it is not there. You want to rule out my paranoia? That's how. We need to get the complete records."

Stafford nodded. "I'll call you when I have the location."

"Good."

"This is the first time they've gone out afterwards," McTavish said into his cell phone as he watched Reed and Stafford leave the Imperial Highway Grill. "They just finished eating."

"What did they talk about?" Wyatt Greevey's voice asked through the cell phone.

"I couldn't get close enough."

"Did they look happy, or annoyed? Were they connecting—or not connecting?"

"It looked intense. At one point they were looking at records."

"The wife's."

"Probably."

"You fixed them."

"Yeah. Absolutely."

"Any ideas?"

"This is just one doctor. One guy getting friendly with a chiropractor. Is it really worth all this effort?"

"He's a damn influential doctor, with a ton of talent and ability. Yeah, it is—worth the effort."

"Well, okay. I'll get the other thing started."

"Good."

"It'll take some untraceable cash."

"I'll have it for you."

"I'll be in touch."

"You come to the Throne on the Range and order grilled salmon?" Stu Javolly said to Eldon Stafford as they sat together in a booth at the elegant, high-priced Costa Mesa restaurant. "These people offer the best center-cut steak in the area." Stu Javolly was in his early forties. He dressed in an expensive, dark blue suit, and wore a blue and red tie.

"A bit heavy for lunch," Stafford said, "and I had a hamburger earlier this week. I like to take my red meat in moderation."

Jovally tilted his head and lifted his eyebrows in an exaggerated gesture of disbelief. "Doctor, you and I both know—we are no longer confined by the strictures of diet. We have pills that allow us to indulge." His eyes flashed with an exaggerated smile.

"That we do," Stafford answered.

"It's amazing isn't it—this country expanded on beef, cattle, big ranges, cattle drives. America eats better than the rest of the world, and eats more meat, protein to grow big strong kids and big strong adults. But admittedly, we developed the heart attacks to go with it."

Stafford nodded.

"But in true American fashion, we found a way to have our beef and eat healthy too! A little pill that pulls the fat out of the bloodstream. Some would say a miracle—I say a triumph of modern science and U S of A can-do innovation!"

Stafford nodded again. "You have your center cut, and your little pill that pulls the fat out. I'll take the salmon."

"Your choice," Javolly nodded with a smug grin. "And isn't that America too? The land of choices!"

Stafford let out a long breath. "So, Stu, what's on your mind? You asked for this lunch."

"You're right, I did. I did, it's true. And you're a get-to-the-point man, a busy man. I respect that." Jovally reached for a sip of his double martini. "So I will—get to the point, that is. We noticed your prescriptions for our products, particularly for cholesterol control, have dropped way off."

Stafford held a cold but otherwise neutral expression. "I don't do quotas."

"Oh, please, Doctor, don't misunderstand." Jovally gushed, leaning forward, seeming desperate to connect. "This isn't something we see as your failure. This is our failure. Our failure to maintain our connection with-"

"Why does it have to be anyone's 'failure?' Why can't it be that I just—that my patients just didn't need the medication?"

"Oh, well, sure. Sure. That could be true."

"Could be?"

"Well, of course, it is, if you say it is."

"I do."

"Well, then it's true."

Stafford leaned back, maintaining his neutral expression, trying to disguise his growing regret that he had agreed to this meeting, and his growing trepidations about its true purpose.

"Dr. Stafford, is there anything Havitol Pharmaceutical can do to meet your needs, and the needs of your patients?"

Stafford fought laughing out loud. What a canned sales-rep question this was, apparently the default question in the event of trouble! Should he ask the man if Havitol Pharmaceutical was tampering with his wife's records? Of course not. This clown wouldn't know anyway. "I'm fine. Leave me your card. I'll call you if I need something."

"Oh. Yes. Of course." Jovally reached into his inside coat pocket and pulled out a business cardholder. He pulled out a card and handed it to Stafford.

Stafford took it without comment.

"I also brought some asthma medication—for your daughter, um, Brianna."

"That's alright. She doesn't take it anymore."

"Oh. Well, that's good, I'm sure. Well, I also brought some of your cholesterol and blood pressure medication."

"I don't take it anymore."

Jovally forced a smile, but seemed supremely flustered. He chuckled nervously. He looked down at his satchel of samples. "That's... I'm sure that's, well, quite good!" He chuckled again.

"It is."

"One would almost think you have no need of our products anymore."

"My patients will. And when they do, I will write them prescriptions."

"Of course, well, good."

The waiter brought a salad with vinaigrette dressing to Stafford. Jovally had not ordered a salad. Stafford picked up his fork and started eating.

"I need to lay my cards face up," Jovally said with exaggerated earnestness. "We talked about you. Management and I. When we saw your numbers drop, we talked about you. And we came to the conclusion that we at Havitol Pharmaceutical have neglected you. Yes, it's true. I know you'll say it's not true—that's the kind of polite, classy man you are. But it is true. And we're sorry. I'm sorry. And it's my butt on the line because of it. You're an important man, and we should not have neglected you."

Stafford swallowed a bite of his salad. "I appreciate the meal, and the concern." Stafford almost followed with his insistence that he had not been neglected, but decided this would not successfully restrain the sales patter of Stuart Javolly. He took another bite of salad.

"Other men of your importance have been hired by us as consultants."

Stafford looked at the man. Where was this going?

"Your influence, your knowledge, your experience—it's valuable and you deserve to be compensated for it."

This was a sales pitch of some sort, Stafford surmised. He waited for Jovally to finish it.

"Some of our doctors take their consulting fees in cash..."

Stafford looked at him with unguarded disbelief. Was the man offering him a cash bribe?

"Which would be completely improper without a 1099 report filed with the IRS," Jovally quickly added.

Stafford frowned. The man had hinted at some sort of bribe, and had correctly read Stafford's disbelief. "I have plenty of work," he finally replied. "I don't need any consultant work for cash or otherwise."

Stafford continued the meeting without saying much. He thought about excusing himself to use the restroom, calling his secretary and having her page him with some sort of "emergency." But he decided to remain for the duration of the lunch. The grilled salmon promised to be tasty. He nodded politely and offered the appropriate hmm-hmms throughout the representative's recitation about the company's latest breakthroughs and their applications. He had read about most of these products—he prided himself on keeping up with the literature.

Stafford believed one thing Javolly had said. They had been talking about him. But what had they really been saying? His peers at Berkeley would have told him to beware of corporate greed. He had largely dismissed what he had come to consider was a youthfully simplistic view of the world. But maybe it was time to consider how corporate greed had potentially infiltrated this situation. His secretary had obtained the records location. It was time for a road trip with his new friend, Galen Reed. It was time to find out if Reed was even partially right about those records.

Chapter 9

"I'm not sure I understand." Wyatt Greevey frowned impatiently. "You tell me he said he'd write the prescriptions his patients need." He sat behind his desk, his eyes boring in on Stu Javolly.

Javolly squirmed in his chair, adjusting as if trying without success to get comfortable. "It's not just what he said. It was the way he said it."

Greevey flared his nostrils. "When I hear that, I know I'm listening to speculation not necessarily supported by anything solid. Facts. People I admire—and reward—come to me with facts."

Javolly nodded. "I understand. Fact: he didn't take the free medication I brought for himself or his daughter. Fact: his prescriptions are down for some of our best sellers, and he gave no assurances he would pick it up, or even any explanations on why they were down."

"But he said he'd write what he needs to write—his patients will get what they need. He's not ruling out prescriptions."

Javolly paused. "Sir, everything indicates he's going to cut them back."

Greevey took an exaggerated breath and released it. "Okay. I see that." He looked down at nothing in particular and tapped his desk. "Maybe we need to sign him up as a consultant." He looked back at Javolly. "Did you talk to him about that?"

"I did." Javolly tilted his head, then looked back at Greevey. "It didn't go well. I pulled it back."

"What do you mean?"

"If you could have seen the look he gave me…"

"All the doctors need money these days. What do you mean 'the look' he gave you?"

"It was a look of"—Javolly seemed to search for just the right word—"of indignation."

"Does he understand that a number of select doctors are working with us this way?"

"I didn't really get into that."

"Hmm. If you presented it in some sleazy way…"

"I don't think I did."

"But it went over that way."

Javolly gulped. "I guess."

"Alright, well, thank you for your report."

Javolly stood. "Sure." He left quickly.

Greevey leaned back in his chair. He scrunched his lips as he reflected. Was this Eldon Stafford development worth his time? The man was one doctor. But, he was an influential one. Still, the man was not writing an article condemning prescription drugs, or in any way publicizing his apparent change in attitude. The system, erected by men like Greevey, was not vulnerable to one doctor's change of attitude, was it? Greevey raised his eyebrows. This was a question in his mind. Since it was a question, Greevey was still looking for complete information. Otherwise, he would not be asking a question, he would be formulating an answer. He had built his success by making the right decisions based on meticulous analyses of comprehensive information.

Greevey nodded silently, then pressed the intercom. "Is McTavish still in the building?"

"I'll check," his female assistant/secretary replied.

"If he is, ask him to come up."

"Yes sir."

"I think Jovally screwed up with Eldon Stafford." Greevey leaned back in his chair.

"He's one of your best guys." McTavish settled back into his chair, across from Greevey, the same chair Javolly had just occupied.

"Doesn't mean he can't screw up."

"I guess anyone can."

"I prefer no screw-ups."

"Of course. But Javolly—he's a true believer. He sees his role as doing good in the world, bringing medicine to the sick, convincing doctors to make maximum use of our company's great technological breakthroughs."

Greevey smiled. "And you don't, you don't share his sense of mission."

McTavish shrugged. "Sure."

"Well, I think his 'true-believer' nature got him fouled up and put Stafford off. A guy who believes he's on a worthy mission is probably not the best guy to propose what will be in essence, a bribe. I can't tell if I have a problem or not. I can't tell if Stafford could cause us trouble, or if he just didn't take kindly to Javolly."

"So Stafford didn't like the consultant idea."

"No. Apparently not."

"Maybe I can pose it to him. The system squeezes doctors so they need money. It makes them more needy, more flexible when we need something."

"You're a cynic, McTavish. Thank goodness you're my cynic."

"Come on. So are you."

Greevey drew in a deep breath. "No. I am closer to a true believer. I was one of the architects of this system, a system that brings us longer and longer lives for more and more people. I know it's not a perfect system, but it's the best system available. And as an architect, as a guy with a lot of power and responsibility to keep the system running, I've learned that you can't always count on the better side of human nature." He smiled. "Controls keep the system functioning the way it should. Controls, McTavish. Controls to keep the power. Controls to keep people in line with the system. Controls that work best when people barely know or understand how they're being controlled, or even that they're being controlled at all. And if a lonely voice in the cogs of the system gets wind of it, good controls will have a dense complexity that keep that lonely voice from doing anything but grumbling speculation, speculation that falls on the deaf ears of the machinery of the controls."

McTavish wore a blank expression.

Greevey smiled. McTavish was not a man who appreciated the more esoteric aspects of Greevey's exercise of power. These subjects should be saved for someone with more appreciation for the ideas, ideas Greevey had converted into reality, and now proudly watched their effective function every day from his perch in the hierarchy.

"You think Stafford could be one of those lonely voices."

"I don't know. And I don't know if it matters. But 'I-don't-know' is the problem. Plan B is ready?"

"All set."

"Put it in motion."

"It'll be done."

"Um, there's a, a note on the chart." The young clerk's eyes narrowed as his forehead tensed. "I think I need some sort of permission or something." He stood at a long plain counter in the front office of the Riverside Document Preservation Specialists warehouse, located on Market Street just south of the 60 Freeway in Riverside, California, about forty miles east of Galen Reed's office. Behind the counter was a door that appeared to lead into the huge, hangar-like building. Eldon Stafford and Galen Reed stood at the counter.

Stafford motioned to the business card he had slapped down on the counter. "You see the name and title on that card, don't you?" He pulled out his driver's license. "It is me, no question."

The clerk swallowed and nodded.

"You see the name on the chart?" Reed asked. "This is his wife's file."

"Well, um, I don't know why the note. Maybe the wife, um, is insisting on her patient confidential rights."

Stafford's face tensed with emotion. His nose twitched.

"His wife died. This is the chart that, that relates to her death."

The clerk shook his head. "But the note. I'm not supposed to let this go without-"

"I'm responsible for the note," Stafford insisted. "I am counter-manding it."

"Okay, um, if you could wait for my boss-"

"We've driven an hour to get here. We're not waiting," Stafford told him.

"You know, I really don't get it," the clerk said. "Don't you have the file?"

"Why would I be here if we had it?"

"Well, I copied it myself. Every page. I sent it to your hospital, the hospital on your card."

"You sent everything," Reed repeated. "Everything?"

"Yeah. Everything."

"All the drug records?" Reed asked.

"Everything in the file."

Reed looked at Stafford. "We're just going to have to call for authorization."

"I will not," Stafford said. "I've identified myself. There is no reason to make a call."

"But I have the number right here. We could have this cleared up in thirty seconds."

"Are we implying I need permission to get copies of my wife's records? These people work for the hospital, for me."

"The guy's just a low level clerk. Give him a break and let him cover his hind-side."

Stafford smiled. "Hind-side?"

"We are medical professionals. Should I have said gluteus maximus? Otherwise, we'll be sitting on our gluteus maximuses waiting for this young man's boss."

"Sir, if I could just make the call. I'm sure it'll be fine."

Stafford scoffed. "Fine. Call someone else for permission. Sure.

Stop the next homeless guy who walks by here too. Get permission from everyone."

"The number is 714-555-8011," Reed told the clerk.

The clerk punched the number into his phone. "Hello, um, this is Brent Twill at the storage in Riverside? I have a Doctor Stafford here?... He wants to see a chart, for Susan Stafford. But there's a note on it... Um, well, yeah, his card says he's-... I'm just making sure. It says to get approval from an administrator.... He is? Oh. It still seems, well, like I should wait for my boss... But I, I'm, maybe I could talk to an administrator... I do?... Okay... Bye." The clerk looked at them. "I'd be more comfortable if we waited for my boss."

"Young man, I could pull this entire account," Stafford said. "Your boss won't be thrilled with that. You spoke to Records. You're an intelligent human being. We want a complete copy of that file."

"Copy?" The clerk seemed to freeze with indecision.

"Wait." Reed frowned in thought. "Just let us look at it. We're just looking for—we wanted to look at one section in particular. You could do that much for us."

"Just look at it?" Stafford asked Reed.

"Yeah. Make it easy for this guy."

Stafford shook his head, scowling.

They both looked at the clerk.

"I guess that'd be okay." The clerk handed over the file.

Stafford opened the file right to the green tab labeled "Pharm." Reed looked at Stafford. They exchanged looks of recognition. All the drug records were there, about ten pages more than had been in the file Reed and Stafford had previously reviewed.

Reed reached into his front pants pocket, below the view of the clerk. He clasped his cell phone and pushed a button.

Stafford's cell phone rang. He pulled it off his belt and looked at it. "My office. I'll take it outside." Stafford stepped out of the front counter area.

Reed smiled at the clerk. He took the file and turned to the pharmacy section. Yes, there were many more records. From a quick glance, Reed could see they depicted a messy situation. He wondered how Stafford would react when he saw them.

The phone rang in the front counter area. The receiver was mounted on the wall over next to the door into the back area of the facility. The clerk moved to answer the phone, turning sideways to face it.

As the clerk moved away, Reed brought his briefcase up on the counter. He opened it so the lid was blocking the clerk's view of the file. He pulled some papers out of the briefcase and wrote some notes with a pen on a pad on top of a stack of the papers.

Reed glanced at the clerk. The young man seemed absorbed with the phone call, his attention not focused on Reed. Reed quickly separated the drug records from the hospital file and placed them under the pad and papers he had taken out of his briefcase. He continued reviewing the rest of the file pretending to make notes.

The clerk hung up the phone. He returned to Reed. Reed did not look at him immediately, but maintained the appearance of someone intently studying and making notes.

A few moments later, Stafford walked back in. "My office. I better get back."

"The records seem in order," Reed said.

Stafford nodded. "Well, while I was on the line, I had my office check." He grinned sheepishly at the clerk. "It turns out we do have that copy you made. Got buried with the incoming mail, I guess. Sorry to trouble you."

"Oh, well, that's okay."

Reed collected his stack of papers and put it on his briefcase, the stack that now included the pilfered complete drug records from the Susan Stafford hospital file.

The two men smiled politely at the clerk as they left.

Stafford let out a huge sigh of relief as they walked toward his car. "We needed the whole plan. I thought you were a little nuts."

"I didn't think they'd give up that file."

"You got them to call Brianna at her number."

Reed nodded, feeling relieved as well. "That's why we had to time this so the boss was at lunch. She would have looked up the number."

"Did you have any trouble getting the records out?"

"You got my signal. No trouble at all. He must not have recognized your voice when you called in."

"Yeah. The start and finish of my acting career."

Reed smiled.

They arrived at Stafford's car. Stafford pressed his key ring to unlock the car. He got in the driver's side; Reed got in the passenger side.

"Did you look at them?" Stafford asked Reed, his face pale and anxious.

"A quick glance." He reached in his briefcase, pulled out the records and handed them to Stafford.

Stafford swallowed. He acted like someone about to wade into a pool, knowing that in order to swim, he needed to endure that first uncomfortable contact with the water. He thumbed through the records. "Okay. She comes in with a swollen foot. Cellulitis." He turned a few more pages. "They get her on Indocin. It's an anti-inflammatory. Looks like they were thinking antibiotic, but didn't go with it right away."

"Look in the first part of the file. They put heat on an inflamed foot."

"Probably not good. But not the end of the world."

"Well, it increased her pain, which increased her blood pressure. All the stops, right? So they were watching that blood pressure."

"Okay." Stafford looked back at the drug records. "Yeah, I see it here. They medicated the blood pressure. Lasix. It's the brand name for furosemide."

"Furosemide."

"Right." He shrugged. "Pretty strong stuff. It's a diuretic. Got to have regular blood tests if you're on the stuff. It's not my favorite for b-p, but it's a perfectly good medication, and an appropriate one under the circumstances, with my wife under hospital supervision."

"Did your wife have any drug allergies?"

Stafford frowned in thought. "She was hardly ever sick. I'm not sure." He snorted with a grin. "I'm not even aware if she knew."

"See what happened after they gave it to her?"

Stafford looked back at the file. "Well, I know her lungs collapsed, her kidneys went berserk, from some kind of fast-moving infection, some flukey thing."

"It was a classic sulfa drug reaction."

"Sulfa drug." Stafford paused, apparently going over the facts in his mind. "Lasix is definitely a sulfa drug."

"So was she allergic to sulfa drugs?"

An expression of nausea came onto Stafford's face. "Oh my God." He paused again. "I do think I remember—she might have been-" He plowed back into the file. "But the timing. That infection just raged through her." Stafford frantically pawed through the file. "The dose of Lasix was started at-" He thumbed back through the file. "It wasn't an infection, was it?"

"Doesn't look like it."

"I think she told me, years ago, about a childhood allergy…"

"Did she tell them?"

Stafford thumbed to the form with the intake information. "Looks like she said no allergies. People don't always know. And when they're in distress, they may not remember." He looked up with a grim expression. "But we should have been alert to it, once she started falling apart."

Reed didn't say anything.

Stafford seemed to choke back powerful emotions. "She comes in with a sore foot. We throw heat at it, cranking up the pain, cranking up the blood pressure. Then the drug we give her for a condition we caused ends up torturing her to death! My God. You're right. The hospital killed my Susan."

Reed still did not say anything.

"We pumped her full of more crap, but none of it for a drug reaction."

"'Pulled out all the stops.' Isn't that what you said?"

Stafford's lips tensed, his nostrils opened, and tears rolled down his cheeks. "So. You're right."

"I'm sorry."

"I mean, you're right, aren't you? The hospital killed her. Right? This is victory. You should be happy. You told me so."

"Victory." Reed tensed. "No. Nothing about this makes me happy. Believe me."

"I don't know how we didn't see this. There they were, attacking each symptom as it popped up." The tears flowed. "How could we have lost our way on this?"

"By thinking about illness and symptoms instead of getting her to wellness."

"What?"

Reed shrugged. Stafford's "what" question, indicating he didn't understand Reed's statement, pointed to the exact problem.

"I suppose if you were there, it would have been different."

Reed felt the air flow out of him. He drew some shallow breaths. "No. Believe me, I'm not saying that. I am not saying that at all." Stafford was making too many assumptions. Reed would correct one of them at some time in the future, but now was not the time.

"Sounds to me like you are."

"I'm sorry. If I gave you that impression, then I take it back. Me being there, or not... That isn't the issue..."

"I don't know how I'm going to live with this." Stafford shook his head. "I don't know."

"The way all of us live with, with things like this. We move forward. We try to make the future better, because there is no option I know of that allows us to fix the past."

Stafford started his car. "We have a long drive ahead of us. Suddenly, I find I am so tired. So overwhelmingly tired." He looked at Reed. "Could you drive us back?"

"Sure."

Chapter 10

"Why didn't we destroy the whole damn file?" Greevey asked McTavish. McTavish sat up on the edge of the chair, looking across Greevey's desk. "Or at least get rid of the records that could embarrass us?"

"Well, um, we had no idea they would go all the way to Riverside and run a scam to steal them." McTavish squirmed in his chair.

"A scam?"

"The way I understand it, they came in while the supervisor was at lunch, and somehow the file now no longer has all the drug records. This sounds like a calculated, deliberate scheme to me, a scheme to take those records and stay undetected."

"Okay. So what does it mean?"

McTavish pushed some air out of his nose. "It means they know—they know we're holding the information back."

"Why didn't we at least destroy the drug records in that file?"

"We destroyed most of them in the copy."

Greevey shook his head. "Yeah. I know. Didn't expect them to go to Riverside." Greevey twitched his nose. "So I'm asking again, what does this all mean? What is he going to do next? And in the final analysis, do I need to worry?"

McTavish brought a file up from his lap. "Our friend Dr. Middleton told me the records show very aggressive prescription medication to try to deal with Stafford's wife. He said something like 'the bad results are easily explained by the uncertainties of medicine.'"

Greevey smiled. "Bad result." He shook his head. "I'd say."

"But the point is, you really can't blame the drugs."

Greevey lifted his eyebrows. "You mean you can't, and I can't. A jury, or the newspapers? They can blame anybody they want, including the hospital, and the drug companies—both."

McTavish's head tilted. His face became serious, as if pondering. "Well no jury's ever going to see this—the statute of limitations is long gone. The newpapers? It's a page-23 story."

"Page-23? Not with a key doctor at that hospital involved." Greevey frowned. "So what is our dear Dr. Stafford doing with all this?"

"I'm not sure."

"Well that's what I need to know, Seymour. That's what you need to bring to me."

"I've been working on it. But his car hasn't left his home. He must be in there, because there's phone calls."

"We're tapping his phone?"

"No-no-no. But I spread some cash around, and found out who he's been talking to. By the way, I'll need a sign-off from you. Those penny-counters down in the accounting department-"

"Run it through me. I'll kick it down for approval. What did you find out?"

"There were calls to his office. Nothing unusual there. Calls to three banks, and an accountant and an attorney."

"Attorney?"

"Yeah."

"What kind of attorney?"

McTavish reached into his file. "I don't know. I have his name and address."

Greevey turned to the keyboard of his computer. "I think we better find out, don't you?" He clicked on "Google" in the "Favorite" category of his internet browser.

"Yes. Also, there is an interesting omission from his calls."

"Yeah?"

"No calls to his daughter, or that Reed fellow."

"Hmmm." Google emerged on his screen. "What's the attorney's name?"

"Sheldon DeCastro."

"Got a city?"

"Anaheim."

Greevey typed "Sheldon DeCastro," "attorney," and "Anaheim" into the box for the search parameters. "Why do you suppose he hasn't called his daughter? Or Reed, for that matter, his partner in file-stealing?"

"Not only that, but he's not picking up his daughter's calls to his cell."

Greevey watched as the results of the Google search appeared. He smiled. At the top of the list of matches was a link to a website for The Law Offices of Sheldon DeCastro, estate planning and tax expertise. "Hmm."

"Got a match?"

Greevey raised his eyebrows. "Yeah. Maybe we've been looking at this thing all wrong. Eldon Stafford is one of those upstanding, stalwart types. He's not a blame-everybody-else guy." He nodded. "He must have been involved in some of those decisions about his wife. Not his name on the charts—doctors don't treat their family members. But he had to be involved. So the records, maybe he sees them as his failure."

McTavish flashed a smile of realization. "And he's wondering if he can live with the guilt."

"Keep an eye on him," Greevey said. "But maybe this whole thing is going to work out just fine."

"Brianna. I didn't think you had an appointment today." Galen Reed's eyes narrowed with puzzlement as he walked from one treatment room to another. "Um, have them show you to a-"

"What's going on with my father?" she demanded.

"I don't know." He gestured her into his office. They stepped inside, but Galen Reed did not sit. They stood at the door that Galen Reed gently closed. "He cancelled his appointments for this week."

"He called you? When?"

"No, his office called."

"Have you spoken to him since your little adventure together?"

"Little adventure." Galen Reed scowled. "No. But I assume he's had a lot to-"

"He hasn't spoken to anyone," Brianna stated caustically. "Except his secretary. Long enough to tell her to cancel everything."

Galen Reed shrugged. "So he needs some time. I don't think that's-"

"Didn't you consider, in your little mission to dredge up my mother's death, that you might just cause a lot of harm?"

"No, I didn't. And I don't think-"

"You've called into question his whole life. He never was the same after she died. There's no way you would know this, but my father was once the star of the hospital."

"He still is pretty important over there."

"He is. But before my mother died, he took on all the tough cases, especially cancer. He did some amazing things. After my mother died..." She shook her head. "Something in him wilted. He kept working—he was still the same brilliant man. But those high-profile, high-risk cases, those cases with death hanging in the balance—he couldn't face them anymore. They gave him a title. He still contributes—don't doubt that for an instant. But after my mother died..." She took a deep breath. "He learned to live with it, with time passing. And now, for some reason I just don't understand, you had to throw this back up into his face, to open this old wound that had nearly healed—what, so you could lord it over him somehow?"

"No. Not at all. Facing how his wife died, and why, will help him, help me, and maybe help a lot of other people."

"You just don't get it. When my mother died, it shook him, pushed him down, pushed him toward the bottom. I think he carried on for me. I was a young, adolescent girl. He couldn't let it affect him because he cared about me. Now, you brought it back, at a time when I don't know what he'll do!"

"Let me tell you, being 'pushed toward the bottom,' as you say, is sometimes exactly what we need to make real progress toward accomplishing something great. You've got to take down the old building to put up the new one."

"Oh that's so clever. So visionary. So chic revolutionary. So Chè Guevara. Have you stopped to consider it just might destroy him?"

"Destroy him?"

"Yes! He's flesh and blood! He might not behave according to your New Age model of progress from destruction."

"He's not going to hurt himself."

"How do you know?"

"I've seen this. I've seen how this will all work." Galen Reed paused. "It's not just his wound."

"I know. It's mine too. It's ours together."

"That's not what I was referring to. There were other people involved on the periphery who-"

"I'm not really interested in a long examination of this. I need to know what's going on with my father now."

"This will work out, Brianna. We've just got to let your father get there, at his pace."

"Oh. The psychic Galen Reed."

"Call it whatever you want. He is not going to hurt himself."

Brianna drew a deep breath. "I need you to come with me. We are going to his home to make sure he's okay."

"He is. I know he is."

Brianna's cell phone rang. "Hello?"

"It's Doctor Middleton. You called?"

"Yes. Have you heard from my father?"

"No. Just some weird instructions from an attorney, about routing his salary to a trust of some sort."

"A trust?"

"Yeah. He faxed it to personnel. They'll look it over and give it to payroll. I don't get involved in that."

"Thanks for the quick call back."

"How come he hasn't been in? Has he been sick?"

"Uh, no, um, I'm not sure. We'll call you back."

"Let me know if I can help."

"Thanks. Bye." Brianna Stafford ended the call. "Are you coming with me or not?"

"We need to give him time. He'll let us know how he's going to absorb this, in his time, at his pace."

"Well you can afford to take the risk that he'll 'absorb this' in a good way. I can't. I won't." Her faced tensed. "I will never forgive you if my father, if he, if something happens." She slapped her phone shut and stormed out of Reed's office.

Galen Reed stepped over to his desk and sat. He knew he had a patient waiting. He also felt confident that he was right, that Eldon Stafford's reaction to the hospital records pertaining to his wife's death would not lead to self-destructiveness. But should he entertain just a little doubt?

Reed picked up the phone and punched in a number.

The line connected. "This is Eldon Stafford's cell phone. I am unavailable right now. Leave your name and number and I'll call you back when I can. If you have a medical emergency, call 9-1-1 or get to the closest emergency room as soon as possible." The line beeped.

"Eldon? Dr. Stafford? It's Galen Reed. Just checking in with you. Call me if you need to talk." He hung up.

The cell phone had picked up the call immediately. Maybe it was off. Reed punched in another number.

The line connected. "This is the home of Eldon Stafford. Please leave your number and I'll call back when I can. If this is a medical matter, please call my office. If this is a medical emergency, call 9-1-1 or get to the closest emergency room as soon as possible." The line beeped.

"It's Galen Reed. I just tried your cell. Just checking to see if you're alright. Call me, um, if you need to." He hung up.

Galen Reed reached into his bottom desk drawer. He picked up a file off the top of the items in the drawer. The file was labeled "Susan Stafford." It was a little yellowed, and in an old file format, with a lot more handwritten information on it than his newer files, which had a sleeker look with more computer-generated forms and labels. He opened it. On top was a clipped newspaper article: "Noted Physician's Wife Dies." Highlighted in yellow was "The cause of death is listed as 'complications from an infected foot.'" He swallowed hard as his eyes watered.

The intercom sounded: "Mary Schuler is ready in four."

He pressed down his speaker button. "Thanks."

Reed's cell phone sounded. He looked at his phone, then pressed the button to receive the call. "Eldon. Dr. Stafford."

"Hello. I guess I have been a little reclusive. Mysterious."

"Well, yeah."

"I have to tell you, I'm a little mysterious to myself right now."

"Are you okay?"

"Probably depends on your point-of-view."

"You're taking this mysterious thing all the way..."

Stafford chuckled. "I suppose. It affected me, Galen. A lot. I've been trying to puzzle through it. Went a little insane, I think. Even got in touch with an old friend, God Almighty Himself, who I'd kind of left out of my rolodex since my wife died."

"Any answers there?'

"Yeah. The usual one. God helps those who help themselves."

Reed nodded. "That's the one I've always gotten."

"Listen, be patient with me. I have my response. To the hospital. To the medical profession. To you. Yes, you're involved. It's a good response. It'll answer all concerns. Just-"

"Let you get there in your own time."

"Exactly."

"I understand. But I don't know if your daughter's going to be so patient."

"I know, she's been calling me. I should probably call her back."

"You could do that. But you may not have to. She's on her way there now."

"To my house."

"Yup."

There was a brief pause. "But I'm not ready. And the house…"

"I'm just telling you, she's coming."

"Okay, thanks for telling me."

Chapter 11

"Dad!" Brianna Stafford called out. She banged on the front door of his Costa Mesa townhouse. "Daddy!" She pounded again.

No response came.

"Daddy!" She pounded again.

Again, no response came.

Tears welled up in her eyes. She pulled out her keys and fumbled urgently through them. She found the right key and inserted it into the lock, turned it, and shoved the door in.

The odor of Scotch permeated the air. "Daddy!"

She looked inside toward the living room. On the hardwood floor, next to the coffee table, about five feet from the flat-screen television on the entertainment center hutch, was a broken whiskey bottle. Dirty dishes, an empty pizza carton, and three empty dirty glasses sat on tables around the living room. The brown liquid from the broken bottle formed in round splotches on the floor. When Brianna looked closer, she saw smaller round drops of red, fresher than the brown liquid.

"Where are you? Daddy!"

She heard water running. The drops of red trailed out of the living room toward the back hall of the townhouse.

Brianna followed the red-dotted trail through a sparsely decorated hall toward the back of the townhouse. She reached the bathroom. A larger pool of fresh red liquid had collected at the door.

She burst into the bathroom.

Eldon Stafford stood at the sink, his hand under the tap with the water running. He wore a t shirt and boxer shorts. His face looked haggard, with dark smudges among unshaven whiskers.

"Daddy!"

He looked up, apparently startled. "Brianna. I forgot you had a key."

"Well I do! What are you doing?"

Eldon Stafford's eyes darted, and he grinned with embarrassment. "I was trying to clean up. I cut myself."

"On the bottle?"

"Yeah." He looked down at the sink. "Damn finger bleeds like a geyser." He looked up at her. "I don't think it needs stitches."

"Daddy, why didn't you answer the door? Why didn't you call me back?"

He turned off the tap. "I, I'm sorry." He reached in the medicine chest for a band-aid. "I've been going through it. I didn't want to-"" He paused and let out a stream of air. "I didn't want you to see me this way."

"You shouldn't have had to go through anything." Brianna Stafford scowled. "Galen Reed has been a big help to me. I'm not sure he's been very good for you."

Eldon Stafford wrapped his finger with a large band-aid. He pressed down on the cut. "Galen Reed woke me up. He got me healthier, and woke me up. I owe him a lot."

Brianna looked at him. "He didn't need to bring this stuff up about Mom."

"He didn't need to. But he did. And I'm glad he did."

Brianna assessed her father, and his words. He seemed so human, so vulnerable.

"I'm not sure how much a daughter wants to hear about her father, and his struggles…"

"Struggles?"

"I've been sleepwalking since your mother died. Deep down I

knew something wasn't right about what happened to her. It took Reed to get to the bottom of it. It took Reed to challenge a lifetime of assumptions and education."

"I'm sorry I brought him into our lives."

"I don't think you're hearing me. I'm glad you did."

Brianna shook her head. "I don't understand."

"I know what I need to do," he said. "Let me get cleaned up. I'd like to clean up my home a little. Call Galen Reed. Tell him to be here in about two hours."

"Reed?"

"Yeah. He is a big part of this."

"But-" Brianna Stafford shook her head.

"I know what needs to be done. I've taken steps. Everything will be explained. I just want Reed here." He walked out of the bathroom and into his bedroom.

Brianna Stafford followed him.

"Let me take a shower. Then we'll get the living room cleaned up. After that, I'll lay it all out." He took a pair of slacks and a polo shirt out of his closet, and grabbed a pair of fresh boxers from his dresser.

"I don't-" She paused. "Dad, whiskey?"

"A little at night, to numb things, I guess. I'm done with the whiskey, done with the numbing. That ends now." He walked out toward the bathroom.

Brianna followed him. "Daddy. Numbing from what?"

"From everything. From what's happened to me. From what happened to your mother. From what my long years of education and training, and then experience and success, were powerless to prevent." He opened the bathroom door and walked through. "It'll all be clear soon." He smiled. "I love you Brianna." He closed the bathroom door.

"Daddy. Daddy?"

She heard the sound of the shower water starting. She stood at the door for a few moments. Was he stable? If she waited, would she open that bathroom door and regret she had not intervened? He sounded so committed to some course of action. He sounded vulnerable and defeated, but somehow determined all at the same time. Her father wouldn't hurt himself and leave her with Galen Reed to pick up the pieces. That would not be a final moment he would possibly bequeath to her. But the father she had grown up with would never consider "numbing" anything with whiskey. She reached for the doorknob. But what was she going to do? Burst in on her father while he was taking a shower? She brought her hand down.

She heard the door to the shower stall shut.

Brianna Stafford took her cell phone out of her purse. She punched number five on her speed-dial options.

Galen Reed answered. "Hi Brianna. I'm-"

"I need you to come over here right away."

"Is there an emergency?"

"Emergency. I don't know. My father says he's going to explain everything, his reaction to all this, and he wants you here."

"Good. I have three patients left. Tell him I'll come over right after."

"He's in the shower."

"So tell him when he comes out."

"What if he doesn't come out?"

"What? That's silly."

"He's acting weird. There's a broken whiskey bottle." She paused. "I'm scared."

"It's going to be okay. I'll be there as soon as I can."

"Okay." The call ended.

"Javolly!" called a voice from across the underground parking structure.

Stu Javolly looked across the structure in the direction of the voice. He spotted Seymour McTavish walking toward him. Javolly looked around. The dimly lit structure was empty except for the two of them. Javolly took a nervous breath. He did not relish meeting Seymour McTavish alone anywhere, much less under these circumstances.

"Hey, it's okay, I don't bite," McTavish said with a smug grin as he approached.

"You've been waiting for me?" Javolly asked.

"Sort of. You sure do work late." McTavish reached Javolly.

"Sometimes."

McTavish eyed him, still grinning. "I make you nervous?"

"No. Of course not." Javolly's eyes darted away.

"I'm not here for the old man."

"Mm-kay." Javolly stood at the driver's door of his metallic blue BMW 530i with a personalized license plate of "PHARMREP." He held his keys. He wanted to open the door and get in, but decided he should wait to see just why Greevey's corporate fix-it man had sought him out.

"I want to talk to you," McTavish said. "I think the old man's pissed at both of us." McTavish still seemed to be smirking.

Javolly looked at him. "I don't think he's upset with me—not that I know of."

McTavish scratched his left eyebrow. "You think the old man was happy with your handling of Eldon Stafford?"

"Dr. Stafford is just one doctor. I don't see what the big deal is."

"Tell me you're smarter than that."

Javolly frowned. He wanted this conversation to be over. He certainly had given his recent encounter with Eldon Stafford a lot of thought, but wasn't inclined to share his reflections with this man. "I've-"" He shrugged. "I've got to get home." He looked down at his car door and pushed his electronic remote key. The car locks popped open.

"The old man is no fool, and neither are you. I've seen your sales records. You're one of the best. But the patents are running out and there's nothing new coming down the pipeline from R and D. This is not a time we need less enthusiasm from key doctors for our products."

Javolly frowned again. "People will still need the drugs. They'll still get sick. They'll still need our products to get well." He opened his car door.

McTavish shook his head. "You're on salary? On profit sharing? You have company stock?"

Javolly got into his car. He threw his briefcase behind him into the back seat. "Commission. What's the point?"

McTavish raised his eyebrows. "Commission." He chuckled. "Generics for the big patents'll cut your commission, well, from a BMW 530i to a white Hyundai compact. That's what the old man's looking at."

Javolly put the keys in the ignition. McTavish leaned toward the open car door. "He doesn't need an Eldon Stafford cutting back on his 'scripts."

"So that's why you think Mr. Greevey is upset with me."

"You were supposed to keep the guy from cutting back."

"Yeah, well, he wasn't open to any of my suggestions."

"I believe it," McTavish said. "I let Stafford get those damn records about his wife. That's why the old man's pissed at me."

"Okay. Suppose this is true." Javolly shrugged. "What're we supposed to do?"

"Work together. You're the rep for Stafford and Middleton. Talk Middleton up. I think he's an ambitious guy who can keep us posted on various, well, whatever details come along. He's a guy with lots of soft spots. Second marriage. Second family. And he isn't done paying for the first one."

Javolly's lips scrunched forward. "That little piece of information part of Havitol's R and D work?"

"Sure. We like to have an idea who we're doing business with. This guy Middleton is a plodder. An overachiever, not as smart as most guys doing what he does, and he can't help but be aware of it. Didn't connect too well with the wife in his first marriage, and seems to be away from home working a lot for a happy husband, so the second one may not be going much better. He knows I'm not a sales rep, and he treats me with some distance. I also need to keep a low profile. I'm working this from some other angles—you don't need to know. So you can work the guy's soft spots from your direction."

Javolly looked away as he shook his head. "I don't see the need for all this. I sell life-enhancing, life-preserving, life-saving products. The market for what we offer isn't shrinking, it's expanding. We don't need 'various details,' or 'low profiles.'"

"Ah. Yes. A believer. We save the world so the world will save us. So why do we need someone like me?"

"I didn't say that."

"Yeah. Well, the old man has been around a long time. He knows the world doesn't work that way. We may have great products. But we still have to protect our turf. That's why the old man needs someone like me. Be glad I'm on your side."

"You said 'may have great products'—do you believe we do?"

McTavish blasted a burst of air from his nose as he smirked. "Does it matter?"

Javolly looked away. "To me it does."

"And to me, maybe it doesn't. Can you work with me?"

Javolly fingered his keys. He looked at the BMW logo on his steering wheel. "I'll keep telling Dr. Stafford and Dr. Middleton about how our products can help their patients." He looked back at McTavish. "And I'll keep you posted."

"Good. Trust the old man's instincts on this."

"Hm. I guess he's picked up a thing or two over the years."

"Count on it. If he's got alarm bells, we should too."

"I'll grant you that."

"You took long enough getting here!" Brianna Stafford opened the door to Eldon Stafford's townhouse.

Galen Reed walked in. "Traffic. Brea to Costa Mesa at this hour—you know what it's like."

"He was in the bathroom. A long, long shower. Then he went into the bedroom." Brianna Stafford's face tensed. Her eyes darted toward the hall leading to the bedroom.

Reed shrugged. "From the looks of this place, he's been through some tough reflection. He probably wanted to get cleaned up."

"He keeps saying you have to be here. He'll explain everything when you get here."

"Well, good." Reed glanced around. He saw what looked like a living room to his left. "Let him know I'm here."

"You let him know." Brianna Stafford grabbed his arm and yanked him toward her father's bedroom.

They arrived at the closed door to the bedroom.

"Daddy! Galen Reed is here."

"I'll be right out," Eldon Stafford's voice said from inside.

"Daddy! Please come out now!"

"When I'm ready, sweetheart. Wait for me in the living room."

"How long?"

"Not long. I won't make you wait much longer."

"Daddy…"

"Living room."

Brianna Stafford's nostrils flared and her lips tensed. "Be out soon." She walked away, toward the living room.

Galen Reed followed her. He could sense Brianna Stafford's concern. "You need to relax."

"Relax! My father is acting very strange. I'm worried about him. You don't care—you made whatever point you wanted to make. Bravo. Score one for Dr. Reed." She sat on a chair, but on the edge, as if ready to move at the first indication she should.

"That's not the way I look at it."

"Why not? Victory of some sort over established medical practice. That's what you're about, isn't it?"

"Actually, this could help-"

"Oh, cut the b-s, Doctor!" She bolted up. "I'm not waiting. Help me if you want!" She moved quickly back toward the bedroom.

Galen Reed let out a long breath as he stood up. He wasn't going to sit by himself in the living room. He walked to catch up to Brianna Stafford.

Chapter 12

"Daddy?" Brianna's voice sounded from outside the bedroom.

Eldon Stafford sat on his unmade bed wearing a polo shirt, but still in boxer shorts. Papers were spread out in scattered piles. His brief-case lay open. The door to his bedroom was closed. "Brianna. Please wait in the living room."

He picked up a letter with a report from his attorney. He had made all the arrangements. But this was such a radical action. Would it be truly worthy of the memory of his wife? Or was this an eccentric impulse that would end up mocking their life together? Did it contradict what they were, an esteemed doctor and his wife?

"Daddy, please open this door." Brianna seemed to be whimpering. Why couldn't she be more patient?

"I will, sweety."

He picked up a few stacks of papers and put then in his briefcase. Maybe he should call it off. It was so extreme. Life didn't have to be so turned upside down by an event that had occurred years ago and had retreated into the past for everyone else. He shook his head. Everyone but him. And on this, his vote was all that counted. He raised his jaw, then gripped his briefcase and snapped it shut. It was time to go forward.

"Daddy, whatever you're thinking, you still have people who care about you." She sounded like she was sobbing.

Stafford suddenly realized how his daughter had interpreted his actions. He'd been so absorbed in his own inner turmoil that he hadn't considered how his behavior would appear to others. "I'll be right out," he called out. He found a pair of slacks and a belt and put them on. He looked around for shoes. A pair of slippers would do. He started for the door, but remembered his briefcase. He reached back, grabbed it, and bolted to the door.

Eldon Stafford pulled the door open to see his daughter, teary-eyed, with Galen Reed standing behind her. "Brianna. Shame on you for thinking-" He wasn't sure how to complete the thought. "Let's go to the living room." He quick-walked ahead of them, in effect now leading them to the living room.

As he caught up to and passed Galen Reed, he muttered "you could have tried to calm her down."

"I did."

"Then you could have done a better job of it." He went into the living room and took a chair next to the coffee table.

Galen Reed sat on the couch.

Brianna Stafford took a chair across from her father.

Eldon Stafford looked at both of them. He opened his briefcase. "You had an effect," he said to Galen Reed. "What you forced me to see. You had a serious effect."

Reed nodded.

"I've been through a lot." His eyes glistened. He smiled. "You can see from the mess around here."

"It's too bad, Daddy, that you had to go through all this." She scowled at Reed.

"It's like taking medicine," Eldon Stafford said to his daughter. "Sometimes it tastes bad, but the healing can start."

Reed's head jerked back. His eyes widened as a look of concern came on his face.

"Or like an adjustment," Eldon Stafford quickly added.

Reed grinned slightly.

"What do you mean, 'healing?'" Brianna Stafford asked.

"Sorry. Bad metaphors."

Reed smiled.

"Like I said, I've been through it. I almost said hell, but it was more like purgatory. I exiled myself from the spiritual side of me." He swallowed as he dabbed his left eye, then his right, with his index finger. "I couldn't understand. All that church I went to. All the good things I'd done. And God took her, in some flukey way. No meaning. I decided there was nothing really. No meaning." He let out a deep breath. "It's meaning that I have reconnected with."

Galen Reed smiled as his eyes also glistened. "I think I'm there with you."

"You will be, if I have this right. Because I stopped flailing out, cursing that there was no meaning. I started asking—what is the meaning? What good could come from something so terrible? Find the good, some good, any good."

Brianna Stafford's eyes lowered. "What if there is none?"

"That can happen, if you ask the wrong questions." Eldon Stafford looked at Galen Reed. "The meaning, the way to find some good, is for you and I to join forces."

Galen Reed's smile broadened and two tears rolled down either side of his face. "We can do wonders, Doctor."

"I know we can—Doctor."

Galen Reed relaxed back onto the couch.

"I'm not just talking about a daydream, a chit-chat of feel-good, of what might be. I've been on the line with my attorneys, and my bankers. We're going to open up an office, a clinic. I'm bankrolling it. We'll start out at a day a week, seeing patients—together. We'll put both of our healing heads together and map out a course of action for each patient, with a bias toward non-invasive, non-drug solutions to medical problems."

"Problems." Reed's eyes became attentive; his expression became serious. "You mean illnesses?"

"Exactly."

Reed frowned.

"We'll fill the examining rooms, don't worry," Eldon Stafford said.

Galen Reed's expression didn't change.

"We'll get the chronic conditions in, like asthma, allergies—and of course, chronic back pain!" Eldon Stafford nodded emphatically as he flashed a big smile.

Galen Reed nodded and smiled back, but it looked forced.

"We'll get anyone in who needs a focus on wellness, or has expressed an interest in that kind of approach."

Galen Reed nodded and smiled again.

"I also know some high-profile athletes and celebrities who will eat up this kind of exotic approach to healthcare. The word will get around."

"Once a week."

"To start, yes. That won't be a problem will it?"

"Um, no. I'll make room in my schedule."

"Oh, and I'll be publicizing this at the hospital. The clinic'll have my name on it. That will feed patients to us."

Galen Reed sat up. "You're going to put this out at the hospital?"

"Absolutely. The place where Susan-" His words caught in his throat. "The place where we failed her. It's fitting."

"It's a huge step. And it won't come without some, some friction."

"I know. But I've got the credibility and good will to make it work."

Galen Reed scratched his head. "Well, I'm in, of course." He smiled, but the smile quickly drew back. "We'll see how it all works out."

"You seem concerned. Too extreme, maybe? Too sudden?"

"No. Long overdue. And maybe not extreme enough."

Eldon Stafford eyed Galen Reed, puzzled by the remark. He had hoped for more enthusiasm from Dr. Reed, but had to consider that while he had gone into seclusion, and had focused all his energy immersing in the idea, Galen Reed had only just been exposed to it.

"It's like anything," Galen Reed said. "We'll get it started and see how it works out. We'll make whatever modifications are needed as we go. But I'm proud and privileged that you've thought to include me in this."

Eldon Stafford smiled. "Good."

"I'm sorry I'm not able to see you," Lawrence Middleton said as he moved briskly through the hall of his private practice office toward an examining room. The examining room door was shut. A file sat in a slot-like shelf just outside the door. "But I'm behind and I need to see all these patients before I get back to the hospital this afternoon."

"I understand," Stu Javolly said to Middleton as he trailed behind him. "But I had a couple of things to talk to you about-"

"It'll have to wait. You can push your literature on your company's latest breakthrough later, after my office hours. See my appointment girl."

"I did. I couldn't book anything with you for three days."

"I'll call you."

"It's not just about our latest breakthrough. It's also about Eldon Stafford."

Middleton looked at Javolly. "You're Greevey's right-hand man at Havitol..."

"For sales, yeah."

"For sales." Middleton picked up the chart in the slot. He twitched his nose as he looked at the notes taken by his nurse. "Wait for me in my office."

"I'll be there." Javolly walked toward the end of the hall toward the back of Middleton's private practice suite. He turned left around a corner and saw Middleton's private office. He walked in and took a chair. He set his sample case down and looked around. Bachelor of Science from Penn State, Doctor of Medicine from University of California Irvine School of Medicine, Residency completed at Orange County Memorial Hospital—Dr. Middleton's educational credentials hung conspicuously on the walls of the office.

Javolly pulled out his cell phone. "McTavish," he said into the phone. The line rang.

"Yeah," McTavish answered.

"I'm at Dr. Middleton's office. Anything new?"

"No, not really. Same thing we had before. Stafford and Reed have joined together somehow, whatever that means."

"I'll try to help. I'm waiting for him right now."

"Try to get a read on whether he's sympathetic to us or not."

"Of course."

"Call me."

"Yeah. Bye." The call ended.

Javolly looked down at his sample case. He opened it up. There was a new drug he was pushing, a drug to clear up severe cases of psoriasis. The drug was the result of extensive, costly research and development, including genetic engineering. According to the literature, the technology would help patients dramatically. The market was limited, so it was important for Javolly to inform as many doctors as possible about the new drug so it could be prescribed to as many appropriate patients as possible. He took out a sample, matched it to some literature, and put it on Middleton's desk.

Middleton walked in just as Javolly's hand left the objects he had placed on Middleton's desk.

"No time for the sample," Middleton said. "I've got four patients waiting, but for mostly routine stuff. So I'm squeezing in a quick discussion."

"It's just a new treatment for severe cases of psoriasis-"

"Those go to dermatologists."

"You might have use for-"

"I'll take a look later. You said you wanted to talk about Eldon Stafford."

"Yes."

"What do you want to know?"

"He stole records about his wife, went into a snit, and came out joining with some chiropractor to set up a clinic."

Middleton's eyebrows raised. "Well, he is back at the hospital. But he seems different. Like New Age aliens kidnapped the real Eldon Stafford and put some strange substitute in his place."

"Strange how?"

"Well, you said it. This clinic. He put up a notice, encouraging patients to come for what he calls 'alternative healing approaches.' He has fliers and brochures in all the waiting areas. No one's said much, um, except some of the support staff—the janitors and orderlies, people at that level, even a couple of nurses—have said they're going to sign up."

"What about administrators? What're their attitudes?"

"Administrators." Middleton shot a look of disbelief at Javolly. "Dr. Stafford is the administrator who would be in a position to say something about this. The other people in administration, the penny counters, the billing people—they leave these sorts of judgements to people like Eldon. They'll let him call the shots on all things medical, until it costs the hospital money. A few notices out doesn't."

Javolly scratched his cheek. "If you were in charge, what would you do about a doctor putting out notices like this?"

Middleton shrugged. "I'd put a stop to it. For one thing, it's advertising, pure and simple. For another, I'd need to know what 'alternate' approaches he's talking about. I wouldn't want the hospital connected with some off-the-wall mumbo-jumbo."

Javolly shook his head. "Too bad about his wife's death. Looks like it's shaken him up, maybe even ruined a fine medical doctor. I'll talk to Mr. Greevey about this. He'll want to go over this with the hospital board of directors."

"I'll help in any way I can. Make sure Mr. Greevey knows I'm on board."

"I will."

"I mean, when I talked to Mr. Greevey recently, he didn't want to hear from me."

"That's changed. Look, there's no doubt, he's a busy guy. Besides Havitol, he's on the board of directors at the hospital, and owns a big chunk of Health Solutions Insurance. But he's got a special interest in this."

"Good. I like Dr. Stafford. But he's clearly caught up in something. While he's working through it, we need to make sure he doesn't cause damage to any patients, or the hospital."

"Absolutely. Glad we see this the same way." Javolly stood.

"But listen, I don't really have a lot of time for this."

There was a momentary silence. Middleton wasn't standing. Javolly got the idea Middleton expected him to say something.

"You can't keep coming to my office like this, unscheduled."

"Just for quick visits for information?"

"While we've talked, I could have seen three patients. I could have written five prescriptions. Your Mr. Greevey's insurance company buddies squeeze me from every direction. I have to work twice as hard to make half the living my predecessors made thirty years ago. I've got an ex-wife who still grinds me for money. Those kids are all grown up, but they keep coming back to the well—me. My current wife can't understand why she isn't living as well as my ex-wife did. I only have one kid with her, but more expenses and less income. Not a good formula. So my time is valuable; I've got lots of obligations." Middleton squinted; Javolly sensed irritation. It was time to work those "soft spots" McTavish had referred to.

Javolly looked at him. "Um, we don't expect your time for free. We have special doctors on our payroll as consultants. I'll get the arrangements started."

Middleton grinned. "It's nice to see you understand. I'll take a long look at the psoriasis drug. Sometimes the insurance companies are slow to process the referrals. I'm sure my psoriasis patients will appreciate having something to take while they wait to get into a dermatologist's office."

Javolly nodded. "Right."

Middleton stood. "I do need to get back to those patients." He breezed out of the office.

Javolly looked up at the degrees on the wall again. He was busy too—he had a long list of doctors to call on, and calls to make to McTavish and Greevey.

Chapter 13

"The x-rays are negative," Eldon Stafford said as he walked into the examination room of his private practice suite. "You just have some neck and back strain." He grinned, enjoying his contacts with patients on his first day back.

A frumpy woman in her mid forties looked at him. "Oh." She lay face-up on the examination table.

"You're two days post-accident. Normally I would prescribe pain medication, an anti-inflammatory, and ask you to see me in two weeks about physical therapy if the symptoms persisted. But, well, I have a new clinic, a new approach to healthcare. I wonder if you'd be interested."

"What is it?"

"You would be seen again by me, and also by a gifted healer, trained in chiropractic. He and I together will collaborate in reviewing your condition, and come up with a treatment plan that will combine the best of both healing approaches."

She grimaced as she adjusted her position. "Some friends have said I should go to a chiropractor."

"Well at this clinic, you get both."

"My HMO, though. I don't think my HMO covers it."

"You let us worry about that."

"You mean…"

"I mean we'll figure out how to get compensated. We are excited about the potential for this type of collaboration. We'll get the insurance paperwork to go through."

"Okay. Sure."

Eldon Stafford handed her a business card. "Give us a call to set an appointment. This Friday is wide open."

"Okay, thanks. What about the prescriptions?"

"If you can manage to the end of the week, let's see what we can do without the drugs."

The woman grimaced. "I'll try."

"Good. I'll see you Friday." Eldon Stafford left the room.

He walked to the next examination room. He smiled and his eyes widened as he looked at the name on the chart. He didn't even open it. He just took it and walked into the room.

"Good morning," Eldon Stafford said, still beaming the same excited smile he had been wearing since his office had opened. "How are you feeling?"

The thin woman in her late twenties looked up at him with a weary expression. "Better now. I had a horrible episode yesterday. Couldn't move. I had to call in sick. My husband had to take care of the kids."

Stafford glanced at the notes at the top of the chart. "I see. Three episodes in the last ten days."

"It's been terrible. I need something stronger."

"Did it help?"

"No. The other stuff didn't help at all. I need something stronger."

Eldon Stafford paused to formulate his approach to this patient. "Migraine headaches is one of those conditions that seems to defy consistent successful treatment. I'll write you another prescription. But I have another suggestion for you."

She looked at him hopefully.

"I've started a clinic in partnership with a gifted healer, a chiropractic healer. We'll see you together and-"

The woman's expression changed to a sheepish grin, as if she was holding on to an embarassing secret.

The change of expression took Stafford by surprise. "You, uh, have something to say about chiropractors?"

"I've been seeing one."

Stafford frowned. "Has it helped?"

"Sometimes. I don't really, uh, do it consistently. My health plan cut me off after ten visits, and it seems weird to be seeing him and seeing you."

"Come in and see Dr. Reed and I. We'll put our two approaches together and see if we can't get these things under control."

"How soon?"

"Friday."

"Okay."

Stafford handed her a card. "Call us."

"I will."

Stafford left the examination room and walked to the front area of the suite. "Delores?" he called out as he approached three women at the front reception area.

All three women turned to look at him, but Stafford's attention focused on Delores Hart, his office manager for twenty-five years. She had neatly coiffed black and silver hair, with a healthy energetic face. She wore a tailored suit.

"How many more?"

"Four. They're all in rooms."

"Good."

"Doctor?" She got up from her seat and walked over to him. "I noticed you referred a number of today's patients, even some of your long-term patients—to some clinic?"

"Yes." Stafford raised his eyebrows and grinned slightly. "I'm setting up an experimental clinic with a chiropractor. I'm referring people there who I think we can help."

"Really..."

"It probably sounds strange."

Delores Hart grinned back. "Not really. A lot of people see chiropractors. I know some of my friends do, and say they get a lot out of it."

Eldon Stafford smiled as he shook his head. "Do you know, almost half of the patients I mentioned this to have seen chiropractors, some even concurrently with my care."

"I believe it."

"It's quite an eye-opener. It seems that people are embarrassed to tell their doctor—I wonder how widespread this is."

"This is a great idea you have, Dr. Stafford."

"Thanks. We'll start it at one day a week to see how it goes, but then hopefully build it up to something a lot bigger."

"Who's staffing it?"

"Just Galen Reed and I right now."

"No, I mean who is running the front?"

"Oh." Stafford realized he should have understood this question more quickly. "We've got two temps lined up. Galen's, uh, Dr. Reed's staff is taking the appointment calls. I'm planning to do the billing through this office."

"Dr. Stafford, this sounds great to me. I would like to be involved."

Stafford looked at her, considering the idea. Delores Hart had been with Eldon Stafford for over twenty years, almost since the beginning. She'd been the young wife in a failing marriage, with recent training at a technical school and a few years experience as an assistant in a medical office. She had joined the office staff at the bottom, and had simply stayed until staff attrition had placed her at the top. He would always remember how attentive and helpful she had been when his wife had died suddenly. He wasn't sure he really wanted her for this venture, but he wouldn't refuse her. She had earned the privilege of choosing this assignment, and seemed to have enthusiasm for it. And he knew she would make sure his office functioned smoothly while she worked the new clinic.

"They'll do without me here for one day."

Stafford smiled. "Okay. You're a part of it." He paused. "It'll be interesting."

"I'm looking forward to it."

"I've got an appointment for injections Thursday," Clyde Minden told Brianna Stafford. They sat in the stands of a high school basketball game. "That's it. I'm not seeing Reed."

"You're not listening," she told him impatiently. "It's not just Dr. Reed. It's my dad, too."

He smirked. "You're calling him 'Dr. Reed' now? How does your dad like that?"

"My dad calls him 'Doctor' all the time."

The crowd cheered as a player from the team with the light blue uniforms swished a three-point shot.

"Damn." Clyde Minden grimaced. "Play some defense! Get a hand up on that guy!"

"Is Drew-"

"It's not my cousin's fault. He's down low at power forward."

"So no one'll blame him if-"

"He's already got a full ride to Oregon State. I'd just like to see the team get to the state finals."

"Clyde, about your back…"

"Brianna, I've got one thing to say about this, and it's an old expression that has never been more appropriate—get off my back."

"You respect my dad."

"Of course."

"You even admit Dr. Reed has helped me a lot."

"Yeah…"

"Shouldn't you see them at their new clinic before they start with the needles, maybe even the knife?"

"We've been over this. I've got serious back problems. Blown out discs."

The crowd cheered again.

"Alright Drew!" Clyde Minden yelled out.

Brianna looked down on the court and saw Drew Minden trotting back on defense, accepting a few quick slap-handed congratulations from his teammates.

"Power. Just sticking with it and going back up with power." Clyde

Minden shook his head smiling, then pumped his fist.

"Did you play?" Brianna asked him.

"In high school. I came off the bench. Not in college."

"Does your cousin play football?"

He grinned slyly. "He's not tough enough."

"Tough enough." Brianna turned her head and looked at him. She looked back at the game. "Is it part of being tough to get your back carved up by a surgeon? Sort of like a purple heart of football?"

He sneered. "Brianna, give it a rest."

"Would you 'give it a rest' if you thought I was doing something foolish?"

"You? Do something foolish? Miss summa cum loudly about anything and everything?" He chuckled. "Nag a guy to death? Maybe."

She eyed him.

"I'm not being foolish. I'm going with the trained professionals."

"My dad is starting a new clinic that could offer you an alternative to getting your back cut into. You won't even consider it. I'd call that foolish."

"You really think your dad would have me go to a chiropractor for a disc problem? I see the claims files in my office. Blown out discs need surgeries."

The teams huddled on the sideline during a timeout.

"My dad referred almost twenty patients to the new clinic. I know he would want you to come in."

"Right." He snickered.

"He would."

"Okay. Let's call him." Clyde pulled out his cell phone. "Give me the number."

"Now?"

"Right now."

Brianna took the phone from him. "Fine," she said as she punched in her father's cell number. She brought the phone to her ear. "It's ringing." She handed it to him.

The game resumed. But though the crowd continued reacting to the plays being made, Clyde Minden and Brianna Stafford focused on the phone conversation.

"Dr. Stafford… It's Clyde… I'm okay. Hey, uh, Brianna seems to think I should come see you about my back at some new clinic you have… That's what I told her… Make sure?… I don't want that guy-… That's what I've been telling her. Guys I know who have what I have always get the surgery. I at least need the injections… I guess that's true—no real downside of getting another opinion…" He let out a deep breath. "Okay. I'll call in for an appointment… Friday… Okay. I wasn't looking forward to those needles. I'll put that off just a bit longer… Yeah. Thanks. Bye." The call ended.

Brianna Stafford smiled but waited for Clyde Minden to confirm what was apparent from his end of the conversation.

"Well, he agrees my back is much worse than some guy caught in a fender-bender, and that the injections are probably my last hope to avoid surgery. But he said to come in so they could have a look."

"Good."

"Well, I think he's getting me in to humor you." He snickered. "Daddy's girl."

She gave him a dirty look.

"He did tell me to bring in all my films. When they get a look at how messed up my back is, this foolishness will be over and I'll get on with the real treatment. But it's okay. I'll humor you, and your dad."

"I really believe you won't regret it."

"I hope not."

Their attention turned back to the game.

Chapter 14

"Eldon Stafford." Natalie Corey smirked as she shook her head. "You're going into business with Eldon Stafford." She looked away for a moment, then back at Galen Reed. "Maybe my company should partner up with Havitol Pharmaceutical. Start a line of herbal Prozac." She jabbed a fork into her salad. They sat across from each other in a booth at Coco's Restaurant, down the block from the Brea office of Natural Healing Remedies (NHR).

Reed's jaw jutted forward. "It's once a week. One day. It starts Friday." He paused. "I'm not really sure how it's going to work out."

"You're not sure?" Natalie laughed derisively.

"No, I'm not. He seems enthused, but I'm not sure he really grasps what needs to be done, that he's really on board all the way."

"Galen, this has got 'mess' written all over it."

He took a deep breath. "It could be huge, I'm telling you. I know you don't see it. But it could be the first step to something extraordinary."

"Well then, wonderful. But you may have to find another supplier. We don't carry Lipitor or Viagra."

"Very funny." Galen looked down at his turkey sandwich. He took a bite, though he barely had an appetite. "I tell my patients—avoid stress. Look at me. I can barely eat."

"So why do it?" Natalie asked. "Why put yourself through it?" She took another bite of her salad, then looked back at him for a response.

"I know what's stressing me. And I'm still not sure—do I tread lightly, go along with what he set up, kind of dip my toes in the water? Or do I get aggressive, tell him what we really need to do to dive all the way in?"

Natalie looked away, seeming to pause in thought. "I'm always in favor of full communications."

"Even if 'full communications' could end the opportunity..."

"Opportunity." She took a sip of water.

He looked down at his sandwich and thought about taking another bite.

"All this involvement with the Stafford family—you can't count on it to drive away your demons."

He looked at her. "Demons." He narrowed his eyes. "What you call 'demons' is just, it's just unfinished business."

"I see new business, with nothing getting finished, just new frustrations and stresses for the future. Demons in training."

"You're not going to help me with this, are you..."

"I'm trying to help you."

"Oh. I see. Trying to discourage me is trying to help me."

"Yes. That's exactly what it is."

He eyed her. "Well, you can't discourage me."

Natalie shrugged. "I guess not." She swallowed. Her eyes moistened, but no tears came. She tightened her lips and her expression became stern. "And if we end up the way we did the last time-"

"Natalie." He shook his head. "I'm not the same guy. It's not even close to being the same situation. We'll be fine."

"Doesn't matter. We're not married. There are no promises here."

Reed reached across the table and put his hand on hers. "I promise you, it'll be fine. It could be great." He smiled a soft, affectionate smile. "It would be easier for me if you would just root for me, even if you think I'm crazy, flat-out wrong."

Natalie put her other hand on top of his. "You know I'll always want the best for you. I did then. I do now. And if you're really committed to doing this thing, of course, I hope with all my heart to be wrong about it, and that it succeeds. I just wish you would leave that M-D world and do what you do, what you do magnificently. The Staffords—they'll bring you grief again."

"I'm not denying the possible down side. There's risk in every-thing in life—the bigger the ambition, the higher the risk. But we're all a part of the same world. And we have so much to gain if we can bring both worlds together. It's worth the risk."

She smiled. "Okay."

"Get ready for a lot of orders."

"We don't carry Vicodin."

"Very funny." But this wisecrack of Natalie's seemed more playful, not as caustic as her earlier ones. He brought his hands back to his side of the table, picked up his turkey sandwich and took a big bite."

"Are you stalking me?" Eldon Stafford called out irritably as he turned the key to lock the front door of his townhouse. He looked at his watch. It read 6:53. He took in a deep breath of crisp morning air.

"I'm sorry about this, Doctor." Stu Javolly walked briskly toward him. "But I wasn't sure you'd been getting my messages."

"I got them." He put his keys in his pocket and deliberately avoid-ed offering any apologies or explanations for not calling back.

"Well, then, um"—Javolly seemed taken off guard with Stafford's blunt demeanor—"I thought it was important we talk."

"Call my office. Make an appointment."

"You'll call back?"

"If I have time…" Stafford walked past Javolly toward his car, parked around the corner from his townhouse.

Javolly followed. "I really think we should talk."

"I've gotten the latest bulletins from the corporate seers at Havitol. I know about your company's newest miracle cures. Your company sells miracle lotions and potions. I'll call you if I need any." Stafford kept walking.

Javolly kept following. "That's not what I wanted to talk to you about."

Stafford stopped. "What is it?"

"I've heard some rumors about some new office, some new clinic you're working on?"

Stafford scrunched his lips and squinted. "So?"

"With a chiropractor?"

Stafford shrugged.

"I don't know what you're trying to do, but you could be courting real trouble."

"What're you talking about?"

"Chiropractors hate us. They'll turn you against us. And you'll open yourself up for huge trouble."

Stafford turned to walk away. "This sounds like a threat."

"No. I'm sorry. I don't mean it that way at all. We consider you a friend, and we want you to be aware of the trouble we have seen with this sort of arrangement."

"A big corporation is my friend. How interesting. And wants to warn me about trouble? I have no idea what you're talking about. And I think you have it backwards. The chiropractors can't prescribe your products, so it's you who doesn't like them." Stafford started walking.

Javolly again walked with him. "They try to cut us out with a bunch of voodoo herbal concoctions and old-wives' potions. They con their patients away from real medicines."

Stafford stopped again. "So what does that have to do with me? I'm not a chiropractor. Get to the point."

"The point is he'll drag you into disaster. No one expects a D-C to offer any real medicine. But they damn well do expect their M-Ds to. And when someone comes into your little operation with the back-cracker and has a real problem, and you don't give him what an M-D should have, and the result goes into the toilet, that patient'll come looking for you. He'll say the M-D should have known better. I know you're set pretty well. But one bad result, and some PI attorney will take it all."

"You've got a great imagination. Now I gotta go." He resumed walking.

"I'm just trying to help you, Doctor."

Stafford was through talking to the man. The attempts to attack the new clinic with destructive pessimism struck Stafford as weak and grasping. Why would this pharmacy rep spend his time chasing Stafford to make such an effort?

Stafford popped the locks open on his car with the remote on his key-ring. The pharmacy rep's behavior seemed peculiar. The man seemed overly preoccupied with the project. But Stafford was too busy to give the encounter much more thought.

"Do we need to do complete physicals on all these people?" Eldon Stafford asked. They stood at the front desk of the new clinic. Furnishings were sparse. It had the look of a new place where not everything had been moved in yet. The waiting room included only a bare minimum of chairs, tables and reading materials. A few fliers sat in a mostly empty rack at the front desk. Empty file shelves stood along the wall behind the front desk. One generic painting of three brightly colored triangles hung on the wall.

"I need to do a complete initial exam and history, like I did the night I started treating you," Reed told him. "X-rays before any adjustments, especially with complaints of back pain or back trauma."

"No matter what the patient complaint is?"

"Absolutely. I need to get a sense of the whole patient, regardless of the complaint. And I cannot do any adjustments on the spine until I am sure fractures and other bone pathologies are ruled out."

Stafford nodded. "Okay. Let's have you see them first, then me."

"Sounds practical."

Stafford frowned. "How should we work the actual consultations?"

Reed took a deep breath. "We need to discuss each patient?"

"Well, yes. How else can we collaborate?"

Reed raised his eyebrows. "The problem is that we'll both be trying to see patients, then squeeze in conversations about them. We could end up keeping patients waiting for a long time."

"Hmmm." Stafford looked at Reed. "Sometimes they wait in my office."

"A key to my approach to health is to teach patients to lower their exposure to stress. We can't advise low stress, then keep people waiting in our office for extended periods of time."

"True enough."

"Since we are going to discuss every patient..."

"We'll call them with our diagnosis and treatment."

Reed thought a moment. How much should he say? In an optimum collaboration, Reed would see the patients and start the initial care. Stafford could get involved if more intrusive measures were needed. But Stafford clearly wanted direct involvement with every patient from the beginning, at least at the outset of the clinic's operation. Though cumbersome, it wasn't an unreasonable request for the man putting his resources and reputation on the line. Reed would go along for now, anticipating they could work out a more efficient patient examination process later. "Okay. So I see them, you see them, we sit down at the end of the session and go over the cases, decide on a course of care, then call the patients for follow-up."

"Wow. Yeah, that seems like quite a process."

"Health care by committee..."

Stafford paused in thought. "Well, that's why I had them book the last patient at three o'clock. We'll have plenty of time."

Reed nodded. "I could screen them..."

"That's not really a collaboration," Stafford said. "No, we both need to see them. We'll have the time."

Reed wanted to argue that a "collaboration" could involve any examination sequence they wanted to agree on. It didn't need to mean equal time with every patient. But he held back the thought.

"We'll start off with this process. We can fine-tune it later."

"Sure."

Stafford looked at his watch. "First one's here in fifteen minutes." He smiled.

Reed returned the smile. "This is going to be a sensational day."

Stafford smiled.

Chapter 15

"A bunch of these are easy," Eldon Stafford said. He sat back in a chair behind a desk in the office he and Reed were sharing. They'd put in the hard work of seeing all the patients. Now came the moment Stafford had been anticipating, when two approaches to health care would combine to elevate the quality of care for these patients. Reed sat in a chair on the opposite side of the desk. "The three strained backs are all yours. No drugs. A steady schedule of adjustments is in order. You set the frequency."

"I agree on two of them," Reed said. "But Jimmy Puccinelli, the car accident. I'm a little concerned about him."

"Seems pretty standard," Stafford said. "Neck pain. Lower back pain. No radiating pain. No priors. You got the x-rays. So you think there's something more wrong?"

"No, no. That's not the problem. Thirty-one year old male, well-nourished, healthy height and weight. My exam revealed no spasms, no subluxations consistent with his complaints, inappropriate responses to tests... I'll tell you, I don't even want to write this up as an injury due to an accident. If he really has a sore back, we can try to alleviate his discomfort. An adjusted, healthy spine will be good for him under any circumstances. He states subjective symptoms, and I'm reluctant to call him a liar. But I'm afraid he is trying to build up a claim with an insurance company. Someone digging around in this file and looking at test results might very well call him a liar."

"What do you do with this type of thing?" Stafford asked. "I'm sure this happens all the time."

"Not that often. I don't seek out this stuff. When I get a case like this, I treat it honestly. Anyone can benefit from chiropractic care because every visit gets the patient some progress toward a healthy spine. But I'm not going to be a co-conspirator with this guy in milking the system. That's not what we set this up for."

"Should we cut him loose?"

"I can help him. I'll just keep all the documentation on the level. I told him his symptoms were mild, and entirely subjective. I told him my treatment would amount to well-care, but that we could provide it."

"And he said…"

"He said okay. I think he understood."

"Sounds good." Eldon Stafford pulled out the next file. "Clyde Minden. I'm really interested in what you have to say about him."

"I need him in here five days a week. Inversion therapy, possibly chiropractic traction. It'll take some-"

"I think you're reaching on this one," Eldon Stafford said.

"Reaching…"

"I know I'm the one who told him to come in here. But my God, did you see the film?"

"Yes, of course."

"He's got ruptured discs at L4-5 and L5-S1." Stafford shook his head. "This isn't some muscle strain and a few misaligned vertebrae. You do the adjustment process on him and you'll make him worse."

"It won't make him worse, and we have a good chance of improving his condition without drugs or surgery. This is the whole idea of the collaboration. With the inversion therapy, we use gravity to get those bulging discs, which are a lot like jelly, to retract back into their spaces. It can take time and patience, and a little scar tissue'll form. But after getting the retractions completed, regular visits can maintain the health of the spine. It's a lot better than cutting out pieces of his discs and fusing the vertebrae, which only sets up the inevitable follow-up surgeries."

Stafford shook his head. "Ruptured discs. They need to be repaired."

Reed nodded. "Uh, we need to recognize that discs are looked at differently by our professions. If a disc is really ruptured, then the annulus fibrosis is torn, and the nuclear pulposus is leaking out. There can be a bulge without a rupture. It is important to differentiate. I have heard MDs use the terms 'bulging disc,' 'ruptured disc,' and 'herniated disc' interchangeably. But these conditions can differ. I know you're aware that bulges can be present without any symptoms. As I say with just about everything, we should start with the least intrusive care. I've seen inversion therapy work well with these conditions. We need to give it a try."

Stafford looked at him. "Hmmm."

"Least invasive first, right?"

"If it has a chance of success."

Stafford looked at a stack of files between them. He picked them up, looking for Galen Reed's notes on each one. He scowled, with his eyes creating a more intense facial expression as he went through each subsequent file.

Reed waited without saying anything.

"You've recommended chiropractic care for every single one of these cases."

"Yes I have."

Stafford eyed Reed. "Look, the neck and back stuff is easy. And I understand some of these others. The forty-three year old with asthma. I wouldn't have believed it before, but I saw what you did with my daughter. Work him off the drugs—I'm all for it."

Reed nodded.

"The kid with the hamstring. Basically, he needs rest, then probably p-t. That's a huge muscle in his leg, Galen. His spine alignment isn't going to be an issue."

"The old R.I.S.E. I know you guys have it too. Rest-ice-support-elevate. Ultrasound treatments will help the tissues heal. But please don't dismiss proper spine alignment for optimum health. And we'll adjust the knees and ankles, to put the joints in optimal positions. I can do all of that to assist the body's healing processes."

"What about a little pain medication?"

Reed shook his head. "I wouldn't suggest it. Pain will let him know he hasn't healed yet. It will encourage him to follow the home-treatment regimes I'll give him. And this boy is bursting at the seams to get back on the baseball field. If the pain is masked, he might be tempted to start up sprinting before his body is healed."

Stafford nodded. This seemed logical. "Alright. I understand." He picked up another file. "But this carpal tunnel—this needs an orthopedic consultation. It looked real severe to me. It's going to need some injections, maybe surgery. She should be on an anti-inflammatory—I think she's got tendonitis to go with it."

"Well, again, you're talking about going to the big guns before we've tried some gentle persuasion. We can adjust the wrist, give her some ultrasound treatments, and give her a support for the wrist. There are aroma therapies, herbal remedies, homeopathic remedies—they can be tried on the inflammation before we declare chemical warfare. We also need to address the habits that created the condition and change them." He paused. "Non-invasive first, right?"

"On everything? You're reaching, like a politician trying to get every vote, or a kid trying to get all the cookies because he doesn't want to share."

"These cases can all be handled at the chiropractic level."

Stafford picked up another chart. "Here's an elderly lady. Eighty-four. Twenty pounds overweight, with high blood pressure and pre-diabetic. Her hip is worn out, and she's got three herniated discs butting up against the cord. She needs a total hip and some spinal injections. She's too old for two surgeries, especially not two in quick succession. So I'd give her the total hip, and the injections. I wouldn't be yanking her around on an adjustment table."

"No, you'd poke her full of drugs, cut her open and subject her to whatever overheated staph infections are floating around the hospital."

"That's a bit extreme."

"It's a bit extreme to say I'd be 'yanking her around over an adjustment table.' Give me some credit. I take my patients as they come. The very old and the very young merit a careful approach."

Stafford shook his head. "You're rooting for chiropractic like it's the good guy, like it's the home team. I thought we were trying to strike a balance."

"An ideal combination. It may not be balanced."

Stafford drew his head back with a look of irritation as he took a deep breath. "Well here's a good one. Do you really think the lady with the migraines is going to leave here without a prescription?"

"Yeah, she's an interesting one. First of all, that medication covers the symptoms. We need to get to the root causes and-"

"She's had CAT scans, x-rays and a brain MRI. We saw them. They're all negative."

"The CAT scan and the MRI results basically rule out a tumor or other brain abnormality that could really be devastating to her. Those were good news. The neck x-rays." Reed shook his head. "They were taken lying down. I need to see x-rays with her standing up."

"Standing." Stafford frowned. "What does that get us?"

"The x-rays in a supine position are fine for looking for fractures. But we need to see how the spine curves. When the patient is standing up, we can see if there is an abnormality with the overall position of the spine, not just whether one of the vertebra has a crack in it."

"So, we find someone who will do a standing x-ray-"

"We can do them right here. Your x-ray tech has probably had some exposure to them somewhere. If not, the training is minimal."

"Fine. Until then, what does she do for the pain?"

"If she can lay off the pain medication, she should. I wouldn't encourage her to take it. When I took her full history and did my complete exam, I noticed she is complaining of pain in the abdomen. Could be stomach, could be liver, could be both. The pain medication is destroying her stomach, maybe her liver as well."

Stafford looked through the chart. Yes, the abdominal complaints were indicated in Reed's notes on her general medical history and condition.

"That's why it's part of my process to look at the whole patient."

Stafford felt a surge of irritation with what sounded like a chastisement.

"I did find a couple of cervical vertebrae out of alignment. I can adjust them and see if that helps. If she's gorging on pain medication, we won't know if the adjustments are working."

"And you're going to flip Brianna's boyfriend upside down."

"I've seen it work."

"Look, I'm going to tell you, I'm disappointed. I thought we would be working together on this. I feel like a singer in a duet who's being drowned out by his partner."

"Non-invasive first. That's what-"

"You keep saying that. But I'm the one out on a limb here. I had in mind we would be working together, not with you handling all the treatment."

"I'm out on the limb with you," Reed said. "We're both-"

"I put up the resources. I made all these referrals. And if someone gets a bad result, that patient is coming after the M-D with the deep pockets, not the D-C. You haven't thought of that-" Stafford cut himself off. That seed planted by Stu Javolly had taken root. It had seemed a ridiculous concern at the time. But if Reed was going to overreach to the point of absurdity, maybe Javolly had a point.

"We can get a policy that-"

"And I'm telling you, the insurance companies are going to balk at paying anything reasonable for your care of some of these more serious conditions."

"I thought we weren't worrying about that. I thought we would start the revolution and let our billing staffs figure out how to collect."

"Yeah? Well maybe I didn't think this thing through enough. Maybe we should have gotten down and dirty with the details before I jumped in. Because as far as I'm concerned, because of your attitude, this is not working!"

Reed paused and allowed a little silence before responding. "This isn't working because we still have a fundamentally different way of looking at our patients. You see parts of sick people who need chemical potions and clinical procedures to make them better. I see whole people, less healthy people, who I want to bring to optimum health with as little chemical and procedural intrusion as I can."

Stafford thought about Reed's statement. Were they dealing with a conceptual mismatch? Should Stafford consider reassessing his concepts with an eye toward harmonizing the two approaches?

"And you didn't really bring me anything tough."

"Ruptured discs? Migraines? Carpal tunnel? Those are easy? I see M-S patients, and cancer patients. Are you going to adjust those 'whole people' to health?"

"I've had success with both."

Stafford felt himself flush with a surge of warmth. His stomach churned. "Now you've got to be kidding me. You're not going to tell me you can cure M-S and cancer with chiropractic care! You're starting to sound a little nuts." Stafford felt the blood drain from his head. "I can't believe I may have partnered with a whacko."

"Wait a minute," Reed said, now showing some annoyance. "Cure? I didn't say cure. Are you telling me you have a cure for M-S?"

Stafford didn't answer.

Reed continued. "And I know there are effective treatment courses for cancer. By maintaining optimum vertebral alignment, we-"

"Put the body in a position to heal itself. I know. You've said it a hundred times."

"It's true a hundred times."

"So chemo is just-"

"I've adjusted patients to help them deal with their chemo. It can't hurt, and many have told me it helped."

Stafford shook his head. "Placebo effect."

"I don't think so. I've had many positive results, with really obvious, easily observed improvement, to have it all explained by the 'placebo effect.' But even if that's true in some cases, do you really object to any method of relief for a cancer patient undergoing chemo, even if it might occasionally be a 'placebo effect' situation?"

"It's bull-crap. Like saying you can treat M-S."

Reed lowered his head and let out a long sigh. "M-S is a terrible scourge. As much as we chiropractors value a smooth-functioning nervous system, M-S is about as close as it gets to a body's worse-case scenario." He shook his head. "Are you up on your M-S?"

Stafford usually referred M-S patients right out to specialists. But he had some knowledge of it. "The Myelin Sheaths cease to function properly—not something you're going to fix by lining up vertebrae."

"The sheath tears. Since this is the insulation around the nerves, the nerves can't carry electoral impulses properly. It compromises the entire nervous system."

"Okay…"

"The usual standard treatment is anti-inflammatories. This suppresses the immune system, the body's ability to heal itself! This just makes the situation worse. First thing I do is get the M-S patient off the drugs as quickly as I can. We do everything we can for the whole body of the patient. We formulate the best possible nutrition, exercise, rest—we reduce stress as much as possible. And yes, we get the spine as close as possible to perfect alignment. I can't cure it, Eldon. I'm not claiming that. But I can put the body in a position to heal it. Send me your M-S patient."

"You'll have me taking M-S patients off of anti-inflammatories? I'll be sued into oblivion." Stafford shook his head. "I need to rethink this whole thing." He tossed the file he was holding onto the desk, bolted up and walked out, toward the front desk.

Delores Hart was the only staff person still left.

"Cancel next week's appointments," Stafford told her. "Galen and I-" He caught himself. "Dr. Reed and I still have some issues to work out." Stafford now wondered if he should have accepted the "doctor" title for this man so quickly.

Reed approached.

"What do I tell the ones who were here today?" Delores Hart asked.

Stafford looked at Reed. "Tell them we will call them within the next week with our, our conclusions."

"Your problem is that you're not willing to go far enough down this path," Reed told him.

"That's my problem?" Stafford tilted his head and reflected that he was drawing the opposite conclusion—he had gone too far.

"It is. For this to work, we-"

"I've had enough for one day. I'm a bit, a bit overloaded, I'd say. Too much stress, Dr. Reed. Too much of my life is going out of alignment."

Reed rolled his eyes.

"Excuse me?" The voice came from the waiting room.

Stafford looked into the waiting room. It had been over an hour since they had seen the last patient. It hadn't occurred to him that anyone was still in the waiting room. He spotted Jimmy Puccinelli. Puccinelli was a dark-haired, clean-shaven man in his thirties with a wiry build. He looked like he was in great shape, at first glance, the epitome of a well-conditioned athlete.

"Did I hear you say you'll call next week?" Puccinelli asked.

Stafford looked at Reed.

"'Cause I need to get my treatment started. Right away. I got a lot of symptoms, and I need treatments. I need to be off work, too."

Stafford looked at Puccinelli. "Dr. Reed will treat you."

Reed stepped up. He pulled his business card holder out of his pocket, pulled a card out and handed it to him. "Call the office. We'll get you started next week."

"I need a note for work."

"What do you do for a living?"

"I take in freight at the loading dock for Discount Warehouse."

"Set an appointment for Monday. I will reevaluate your symptoms and consider your work situation. I may recommend light duties."

Puccinelli gestured a flip of a wave with his right hand. "You know what? It's okay. I shouldn't miss more time. I'll get through. I can get them to put me on the forklift."

Reed nodded.

Puccinelli looked down at the card. "Is this place going to be open? 'Cause here is a lot closer to me than this other place."

"We'll let you know," Eldon Stafford told him.

"Okay. Then, I'll see you." Puccinelli left.

Reed turned to Stafford. "It's been a long day. Let's both chew on this thing and talk next week."

"Yeah."

Reed headed back to their shared office to get his belongings. Stafford did not follow.

Chapter 16

"It's been a month," Brianna Stafford said as she got up from the intersegmental traction table, a table with rollers through the middle to massage the vertebrae as the patient lay face up. Her late afternoon session had ended. "The last time I took any prescription drug, or inhaler, was a month ago."

Galen Reed nodded. "That's wonderful. Your body will thank you."

She smiled. "I think it already is. I feel great. I've joined a health club. I do laps in the pool. I never had the endurance before to do more than over and back. I don't feel tired after the workouts—I feel more energized!"

Galen Reed returned the smile. "That's what I'm here for." He escorted her toward the reception area. "Sorry we ran late today."

"It's okay," she said. "I schedule toward the end of my day, so I'm fine with however long it takes. You have such a relaxing place."

"Part of the program."

She turned to face him. "Doctor Reed, what happened with my dad?"

He paused, pondering her sudden change of mood and subject. How candid should he be?

"With all the good you've done for me, and for him, with all the enthusiasm he had for working with you, I thought you two might be on your way to a really remarkable collaboration."

Galen Reed still wasn't sure how much he should say, how involved Brianna should be with this issue. "I think we plunged before we worked out all the details," he finally said. "It's probably my fault. I didn't say enough about how I thought it should work. I loved his enthusiasm for the concept, and let him take the lead without much input from me. We'll need to fix that."

"He's not talking about it that way."

Reed felt a twinge in his stomach. This was the sort of conversation—Brianna Stafford in the middle between him and her father—that he wanted to avoid. But, he wanted the information. He took a deep breath and wiped his forehead, even though it was dry. "What is he saying?"

"It's not so much what he's saying. It's what he's asking."

"Asking..."

"Again, how I met you, how you started taking care of me, if you made any wild claims about what you could do for me."

Galen Reed's eyebrows lifted.

"He seems to be having second thoughts about the whole idea. He's asking questions like he thinks you're some kind of faith-healer or con man."

Galen Reed bristled. "He ought to know himself what I'm able to do, and that I'm not a flake."

"I'm not disagreeing with you. I told him somewhat the same thing."

"What'd he say?"

"He said he thinks you have an exaggerated sense of what you can do, and that you could be dangerous."

Galen Reed scowled. "Dangerous?"

"He couldn't have meant it."

Her statement did not diminish his scowl.

"This comes at a really bad time, Dr. Reed." Her eyes moistened. "Clyde had injections yesterday. He says if they don't work, he's going for the surgery. He knows my dad seems to have changed his mind about you, and he says he's not coming back to see you."

Galen Reed took in another deep breath. "He's got to come in. He needs to at least give me a chance to help him before he takes the extreme, and mainly irreversible step of surgery."

"I don't think he'll do it."

"Do you want me to talk to him?"

"I don't think it would do any good. It's my dad's opinion that's influencing him."

"If I could just show him—I'd use his film to explain how I can help him, and what surgery will do to him."

"I'll try." But her tone suggested that she was not convinced any effort would be successful.

"It's a big step he's-"

"Hello!" Natalie Corey's voice sounded from the waiting area, and her tone resounded with impatient annoyance. "Galen! Are you coming out of there at some point? I'd like to have dinner some time before we're limited to the 24-hour drive-thru at Jack-in-the-Box."

Galen Reed stepped up to the front desk.

Brianna Stafford followed.

"Sorry," he said to Natalie Corey, who was standing next to a table in the waiting area. "I ran late."

Natalie Corey stepped up to the counter that looked out into the waiting area. "That's what your staff told me as they left—about fifteen minutes ago."

"I'm sorry," Brianna Stafford said as she moved next to Galen Reed. "I've been keeping him."

Natalie Corey lifted her head in apparent surprise. "I didn't know you still had a patient," she said to Galen Reed.

"We're done," he said. "I lost track of time." He hesitated a moment. "Um, we were talking about her father, uh, Dr. Stafford."

Natalie Corey nodded with a blank expression.

"I'm Brianna Stafford," she said with a perky smile. "You must be-"

"The girlfriend, for lack of a better term," Natalie Corey said.

"Well, he's an extraordinary man, your Dr. Reed."

"Yes," Natalie Corey agreed, again without any apparent emotion.

Brianna Stafford frowned. She seemed to assess Natalie Corey, and then narrowed her eyes in thought. "I'm sorry—I just get the feeling... have we met before?"

Natalie Corey looked at Galen Reed.

"Maybe you've seen Natalie in here before when you've had an appointment."

Natalie Corey smirked. "That's not likely. I don't come in here that often." She looked at Galen Reed again. "I started coming in here when we have a dinner date because otherwise he keeps me waiting, until I starve, or get bored." She scolded him with a chastising expression.

"It's true," he admitted. "I get wrapped up."

"Well, I won't keep you any longer." She looked at Natalie Corey again. "You really do look familiar."

Natalie shrugged.

"The vitamin lady," Brianna Stafford said with a triumphant smile.

Galen Reed looked at Natalie Corey. "The vitamin lady."

"I do remember you! You worked at the vitamin store, where my mother-" She cut herself short, but continued after the brief verbal hitch. "My mother and I, when I was a girl, when she was alive, came into your store to buy things."

"I did work at a vitamin store."

"Not anymore?"

"No, actually, I moved up with the company. Now I make the decisions that supply that store, and a number of stores like it."

"I haven't been there in a long time—to that store. There's a place closer to me..."

"Well, good. As long as you get your health products somewhere," Natalie Corey said politely.

"I remember you as a very nice lady."

"Thank you. I was younger, back then."

An awkward silence intruded into the conversation.

Galen figured Natalie was not sure if she should admit she knew exactly who Brianna Stafford was. And Brianna was waiting to see if Natalie would acknowledge recognizing her. He attempted to rescue the moment. "I'm sure Natalie saw a lot of customers."

"Yeah, of course. And, my mother and I haven't been there in a long time. I definitely look different now, and-" She again cut herself short, then resumed. "And my mother died. A long time ago. At the hospital."

"I'm sorry," Natalie Corey said.

"It's okay. It was, like I said, a long time ago."

"But you will always miss her. I know that's true with my father."

"Well. It's good to see you, vitamin lady," Brianna said smiling. "Those are happy memories for me."

"I'm glad," Natalie Corey said.

"I'll see you." Brianna walked through the door into the waiting area and waved a smiling farewell as she left the office.

Galen Reed walked into the waiting area and gave Natalie Corey a quick kiss and a hug.

"So you're still okay with the daughter," she said.

"Of course."

"I don't know why it's 'of-course.'" She chuckled.

"Brianna knows what I've been able to do for her."

"Put that feistiness into her, huh?"

"That's her personality. When she's healthy, she can express it."

"I'll say."

"Not so feisty about her boyfriend, though."

"The guy with the back?"

"Yeah. He's already gone for the injections. He's probably going for the surgery."

"And?"

"And I need to stop him."

Natalie Corey's face registered disgust as she snorted out a blast of air. "He's a grown-up, right? He gets to make his own choices."

"That's not the point. He's going to make a bad choice."

"So you're going to take him on too?" She shook her head. "This is what I knew would happen if you got involved with the Stafford family again. You want to save them from the mistakes of their world. It's not going to work that way, Galen."

"It's different. I'm older. I'm smarter. I'm stronger."

"I'm-I'm-I'm! But they're the same! What're you going to do? Kidnap him and brainwash him into deciding to reject the MD drug-'em-and-cut-'em standard care?"

"I'll talk to Stafford. I'll get another shot at Clyde and convince him."

"And if you can't. That's what worries me. How is it going to affect you if you can't?"

"I'll be fine, as long as I know I gave it my best. That's the key."

"I'm not going through this again." She shook her head. Her face tensed as she appeared to fight tears. "I'm so sick of dreamers. I'm so sick of having to pick up the pieces when the dreams fail."

"I'm not your ex-husband."

"I always attract dreamers. Before him. Before you. I don't know why. I don't want to. I just do."

"Admit it. You really do love-"

"Don't tell me what I love." Natalie Corey sneered with anger, an anger that seemed to fight off any tears that were coming. "I saw this with my parents. Dreamers. They were going to change the world." She smirked. "I grew up in a commune, up near the Oregon border, until I was ten."

"You never told me-"

"Because it was stupid. My father finally took a job with Nestles down in Glendale." She laughed, but with a caustic tone. "He and my mother said they were joining the corporate world in a good way, a way that would bring pleasure to people. Did they think I was stupid? I know a rationalization when I hear one. It was time for them to put dreams aside, to pick up their toys and put them in the toy box—time to grow up! We went from living in dirt with a bunch of weirdos to living in a real home. And my life could join the world."

"This is not an idle fantasy," Reed told her. "And I know it is going to work out. I have seen it."

Natalie Corey shook her head. "See! I cannot escape the dreamers of the world!" Her breathing quickened. "Not again." She turned toward the door. "I lost my appetite." She started to leave.

"Just hang on," Galen Reed said. "I've got to lock up."

"Take your time. I'm going home. Call me. Call me when this Stafford thing has run its course. Or, don't call me." She left.

Reed bobbed his head with frustration. "Damn." He turned to lock up his office.

"Just thought I'd poke my head in for a second," Seymour McTavish said as he entered Wyatt Greevey's office.

Wyatt Greevey looked at his computer terminal. It read "8:16 pm." "'Poking your head in?' At this hour?" Greevey flicked his pen onto his desk and rubbed his eyes.

"I got a call. Thought you'd want an update on the Stafford thing."

"Sure. Got any good news for me?"

"Actually, I do. The whole thing seems to be falling apart."

Greevey's eyes widened. "Really."

"Yeah. It looks like they can't get together on how it should work."

"How good is your information?"

"I have an amazing source, right in the middle of things."

"Who is it?"

"Um, you may not want to know. Not for anything I've done, but for what I have the capability to do if it's needed."

Greevey frowned. "But this is certain."

"The information is, absolutely. As far as the operation totally falling apart, that isn't certain yet. But it's heading there."

"Good. This little problem might just fix itself."

"Yup. I've got a great Plan B standing by. But we may never need it."

"Plan B."

"This is where you don't want the details. Keep deniability in place."

Greevey's eyebrows raised as he leaned back in his chair. "Yeah. All right. So you'll let me know what I need to know."

"Right."

"Well, keep up the good work."

"You bet." McTavish left the office.

Greevey picked up his pen. Deniability. Did McTavish think he was in the CIA? What kind of mess would he get Greevey tangled in with "Plan B?"

He put his pen down. Did he have McTavish's cell phone number? He thought about bringing him right back in to get the details of "Plan B." He reached in his pocket and grabbed his cell phone. He flicked it open, but did not see McTavish's number in the speed dial menu. So he'd never entered the number. Just as well.

He looked back at his computer terminal. Earnings were still flat, with no hint of improvement. In two weeks he would have to report this disappointing news to the shareholders. He frowned. On second thought, this Stafford problem was not really important enough to warrant more time. If "Plan B" was needed, he would press McTavish for more information at that time.

"It's not a matter of who loves who," Natalie Corey said to Galen Reed. Reed listened to her voice coming through his phone as he sat on the couch in his home. "I know you love me. It doesn't mean you won't hurt me again."

"I'm trying to tell you that it's not-"

"Galen, I'm tired. I'm tired after a long day. I'm tired of thinking about this. I'm tired of arguing about it. If you're really different, then you're calling the wrong person."

"The wrong person... You think I should call-"

"You know. You make that call, and you spell it all out, warts and all, past and all. Good night. Do not call me again until you have acted on it." The line clicked.

Reed grunted. He put down the phone. Things were different. Why couldn't she see it? Why was she being so difficult at a time when he needed her support the most?

He looked at his phone. He understood what she was saying. Call Stafford. Confront him. Spell out all the baggage. What was he waiting for? He'd proven his effectiveness. He didn't have to defer to the M-D world. But would a call like she was asking him to make do any good? Was Natalie baiting him into a course of action that would wreck the collaboration?

Time to stop cogitating. Natalie was unsupportive and annoying, but she was right. Why should he wait for the great Eldon Stafford to contact him? They needed to talk. Reed would make the call.

Reed picked up the phone. He punched in Stafford's number.

"Eldon Stafford."

"Eldon. It's Galen Reed. We need to talk."

There was a short pause. "Yes. We do."

"You're right. We did jump into this too quickly. You and I need to hash out the details. What's your schedule over the next few days? Let's get together-"

"Look, I think the whole thing was a mistake."

Reed wasn't sure what to say. He did not expect such a blunt repudiation of their collaboration, a collaboration Eldon Stafford had seemed so enthused about not long before.

"You there?" Stafford asked.

"Uh, yeah."

"So, anyway, I'll continue to refer some patients. But this idea of putting us together… not workable. I got caught up, in the stuff about my wife's death, and Brianna—I lost my objectivity."

"We didn't set it up right."

"Because it can't be done."

"Let's talk about it."

"Sorry. I'm done. I'm dismantling the clinic."

"Eldon. Dr. Stafford. Promise me you won't do anything definitive until we have a chance to talk, in detail, about how this could work."

"I'm not making any promises."

"Let's meet tomorrow."

"No time. I've been avoiding the hospital. I need to face the place squarely for the first time since, since our visit to Riverside. All I've done since then is stop in and drop off a few fliers and kind of brush by everything. It's time for me to get back to work."

"Okay, so we can't meet right away. At least tell Clyde to hold off. Have him wait until you and-"

"I can't do that. He needs the surgery."

"Eldon, please. I've seen patients start down this back surgery path. One leads to another, to another and another. Pain pills. Injections. Rehab after rehab with painful p-t. He's too young to start down that road."

"I'm not going to argue with you about Clyde. It's his choice."

"Just get him to talk to me before he makes it."

"I'll let him know you want to speak to him. No guarantees."

"He'll listen to you. Just get him to call me."

"If he wants to. I've got to go."

"Well, good luck at the hospital tomorrow. I know it won't be easy."

"No."

Reed paused. Maybe this was the wrong time to push. "I'll call you tomorrow night. Let's set up a meeting then."

"Fine. Bye." The line clicked.

Reed closed his phone. He still had Clyde's file in the office. He would try the young man himself, first thing tomorrow.

Chapter 17

"It's not gonna work." Clyde Minden lay in his bed, face tense with pain, as he looked up at Brianna Stafford. Brianna Stafford held a tray with two hands. On it was a glass of orange juice, some soup, and whole wheat crackers.

"Can you sit up?"

"Yeah." He grimaced as he squirmed his way up to a position with his head slightly elevated.

Brianna Stafford extended the legs on the bottom of the tray and set it down in front of him.

"Thanks."

"You were doing better than this before the injections."

"Don't start up with this again." He took a gulp of orange juice, then picked up a cracker. "And tell your buddy Reed to stop calling me."

"What did he say?"

"I don't know. I haven't picked up, and I'm not calling back. And I'm not listening to any long-winded voicemail messages either."

"Clyde. At least call him back."

Clyde crunched a cracker, then scooped out a bite of soup.

"Clyde?"

He swallowed, then looked at his tray. He grimaced, then shook his head. "I know you mean the best for me. But I can't keep fooling around with this. I put in for some time off. I'm scheduled for the surgery next week."

"Clyde—no!"

"It's set. It's decided, a done deal."

Brianna Stafford stiffened. "You can't take it back, once you do it. You could try Dr. Reed's methods first, and then-"

"Brianna, please. This was a hard decision. I don't really want your opinion. I want—I need your support."

Brianna Stafford paused. "You and I may have different ideas about what support really is."

"To me right now? It means no more arguing about it."

"And to me? It means not allowing someone I care about to make a terrible mistake."

He shook his head. "I'm tired of explaining this."

"I'll be here for you, Clyde. But don't expect me to agree with this."

"Okay. Fair enough." He grimaced as he adjusted his position. "You'll see."

"I hope so. I have never wanted to be wrong about something more than this." She looked away and sniffled. "Nothing would make me happier."

He smiled. "Thanks."

Brianna did not return the smile. She wanted to be wrong, but was certain she was right. And she could not smile, thinking of the consequences for Clyde if she was right.

"Eldon." Lawrence Middleton stood to greet Eldon Stafford. He had been sitting at a desk in the examination area of the emergency room at Orange County Memorial Hospital. He looked up from a CAT scan result on a patient with complaints of intense abdominal pain. The scan was negative. The x rays had been too. "It's good to see you." He extended his hand.

"Yeah." Stafford extended his hand and they shook. "Time to get back to business."

"How's the clinic going?" Middleton asked.

"I don't know." Stafford's clipped tone told Middleton that Stafford did not want to discuss the subject. Middleton figured the clinic was not going well.

"What do you think of this one?" Middleton asked, picking up the chart that went with the CAT scan results. "She's in with severe abdominal pain, nausea. No fever. We're waiting for the blood and urine work."

Stafford took the chart and thumbed through it.

"We're thinking some kind of stomach virus."

Stafford nodded. "I'll look in on her."

"We're keeping an eye on her. I'm not sure if we'll actually admit her. But she seems real weak and in a lot of pain. I'm hesitant to send her home yet. She may be at the beginning of a nasty virus."

"Well, still, maybe something she can take on at home."

"True."

"What else have we got?"

"In the emergency room?"

"Not just here. In the hospital."

"The usual stuff, I guess." Middleton rotated the computer terminal at the desk toward Stafford. "Take a look." Middleton hit a few keystrokes, then gave up his chair to Stafford.

Stafford sat down. He took hold of the mouse. "Lot's of new moms," he commented as he scrolled through screens showing the patients admitted to the hospital and their admission diagnoses.

"Aren't there always?"

Stafford smiled. "I suppose." He frowned. "Is it my imagination, or do we see a lot more liver problems these day?"

"People live longer, and we're doing a better job of taking care of their hearts. Something's gotta give."

Stafford nodded. "Someone'll do a study and let us know why."

"Sure."

"Room 5-0-6."

Middleton looked at Stafford, puzzled by the reference. He looked at the screen. "Car accident. Compound fracture of the right leg. The airbag might have saved her from a lot worse. A nasty head-on with a drunk driver."

"That's the room Susan was in."

"Susan." Middleton didn't place the name immediately. "Your wife." He had now figured out the reference, but had no idea what to say.

Middleton paused a moment. "A long time ago."

"Yeah."

Stafford scrolled through some more screens. "A bunch of elective surgeries."

"Sure. We don't need to get much involved in those. The surgeons have them under control."

"Of course. And they expect us to have things under control."

Middleton looked at him. This seemed a strange remark.

"You know—the crazy staph infections we've been seeing, the right drugs on hand, the right nurses in place…"

"Sure."

"And we do have it under control. Most of the time."

"Pretty much all the time."

Stafford looked at him, eyes squinting, but with a smug grin, as if he knew something Middleton didn't know. "The modern hospital. The best facility modern technology can offer."

Middleton again wasn't sure what to say. Was Stafford being sarcastic, or asking a question of some sort, or making a straight comment?

"I'm going to reacquaint myself with the place," Stafford said. "I've been away awhile."

"Not that long. You've taken longer vacations than-"

"Some separations are not measured in time or space."

"I think I understand." But Middleton made the comment because he didn't like the awkward conversation.

"I barely understand myself." Stafford grinned. "I need to get re-oriented, get back into this. I'm going to take a walk around."

"Need company?"

"No. I'll let you get back to whatever you were doing."

"Okay."

Stafford walked away toward the emergency room beds.

Room Five-Oh-Six. Code blue. Stat. Code blue. In his memory, Eldon Stafford heard the final emergency summons to his wife as if it had happened just a few days before. He wished it would leave his mind, but it kept echoing from his memory into his present-day thoughts. Present-day activities would drive this recollection away, wouldn't they?

He reached the woman with the severe abdominal pain. "Still having pain?" he asked her. She lay in an emergency room bed with an i-v hooked up to her right arm. Doctor Stafford grasped an aluminum clipboard that held the woman's chart.

"Doctor?"

"Yes, I'm Dr. Stafford. I'm Chief Consulting Physician here, helping out, offering an extra opinion." Room Five-Oh-Six. Code blue. Stat. Code blue. The memory echoed in Stafford's mind again. Keep working—dissipate it.

"I still feel, just terrible—my stomach."

"Your stomach." Stafford knew people often referred to their stomachs when they could mean anywhere in the abdomen. He looked through the chart. She had come in, doubled-over with abdominal pain. The initial diagnosis was "gastroenteritis." She said she had no appetite, and was noted as looking pale. He thumbed through every page of a thin chart and grinned briefly as he realized he missed the detailed "whole-patient" notes Galen Reed gathered on their new patients during their brief collaboration. He looked at her. A few droplets ringed her still pale forehead just below her hairline. "Any vomiting?" he asked her.

"No," she answered. "But I feel like I might."

"So nausea."

"Yeah. I guess."

"Fever?"

"I don't think so."

Stafford looked at her chart. Her temperature readings had been about a degree and a half below normal. Stafford put his hand on her forehead. She was damp, and cool. "Hmmm." He looked at the medications. "I know they think you have a virus of some sort."

"Something's been going around."

"Something's always going around." He thought a moment. She probably belonged at home, but he didn't want to send her away in so much pain. Acetaminophen wasn't easing her discomfort. "I'm going to have them switch up the meds a bit—we'll try some Motrin. I'll check back."

"Thank you."

Stafford nodded, put the chart back next to the bed, and walked away. He spotted a nurse. "Switch the meds for bed seven. I put it on the chart."

"Yes, doctor."

Stafford smiled and nodded.

Room 5-0-6. He hadn't been back there since he and Galen Reed had gone through his wife's hospital records. Room 5-0-6. Room Five-Oh-Six. Code blue. Stat. Why was this still plaguing him? Susan had faced her battles in that room years ago. The hospital and doctors had failed her in that room—years ago. Stafford was sure many patients of Room 5-0-6 had been successfully treated since then. He needed to face down this demon haunting him. Room Five-Oh-Six. Code blue. He needed to go there, now. If he could see it again as just a place, a small place, situated in a much larger place capable of producing great good, he could stop fixating on Room 5-0-6.

He had dabbled with this Galen Reed project, a flirtation with extremism, with potential medical heresy. It had been an escape. Room 5-0-6 confronted him as one of the demons spawned by his wife's tragedy. He would face down that demon. Now.

As he walked to the elevator that would take him up to Room 5-0-6, his mind flooded with a soundtrack, and back-of-the-brain images from days past. "The origins of the modern hospital can be traced to the golden age of medieval Islam." Textbook illustrations, drawings of medieval Muslims tending to patients, flooded his mind with the soundtrack. Hospitals. A great institutional achievement. That's what he'd learned. Modern western medicine had taken this institution from these initial beginnings and had brought humanity unprecedented health. That's what he'd been taught.

He was vaguely aware of his progress up the elevator. He responded with an automatic nod and grin to someone who had said hello to him. But images from outside his immediate surroundings flooded him as he closed in on Room 5-0-6. Groans and screams of pain entered his private soundtrack. Where was this soundtrack coming from? Susan had never screamed. She had grimaced, even forced smiles through her discomfort as she waited for the trusted doctors to heal her. But she had never screamed.

Room Five-Oh-Six. Code blue. Stat. That memory continued, but had been forced to the background. An explicit memory came to him, from a movie he had first seen in the mid 1960s, "Zulu." The company surgeon was standing over a wounded soldier with a saw. Rows and rows of bloody men lay on the floor of a chapel. The soldier's eyes tensed with a disbelieving agony. The young solider quivered. His face was covered with sweat. "Bite down on this, lad," said the calm voice of the white-haired surgeon as he handed the young man a stick to put in his mouth. The boy's mangled left arm dangled from his shoulder. The surgeon wore a torn red uniform, with blood all over his arms. He placed the saw above the wound. Groaning voices multiplied in Stafford's mental soundtrack, male and female—they no longer corresponded to the movie clip, which had mercifully faded from his memory. And what did that image have to do with the modern hospital? A battlefield hospital from the late 1800s depicted in a movie had no relevance to Room 5-0-6, did it? But he felt a sinking feeling as he knew why his subconscious had chosen this image. There was a terrible connection. It was the kind, confident face of the surgeon, the soft assurances of the venerable medical master, about to saw off a young man's arm without anesthesia.

The soundtrack of male and female shrieks kept reverberating through his private soundtrack. Another image came to mind, an image of a painting. He rubbed his eyes, but this wasn't an image in his line of sight. He realized he could not clear his mind by clearing his sight. The image was stuck in his mind. In the painting, a surgeon, dressed in a suit that looked like it was from the 1890s, or maybe the early 1900s, beamed triumphantly as he stood holding a bloody body part. He stood over a patient on an operating table. The man had apparently used his medical training, the flower of science and modern medicine, to cure some afflicted person. The painting was an obscure memory. He couldn't bring it all into focus. He couldn't remember when and where he had seen this painting. But he smiled. The flashback to this painting was a gift, reminding him that modern medicine was a gift to humanity, and he was one of its lead practitioners.

He exited the elevator. Room 520. He was almost there. The soundtrack and extraneous images faded. The demons were about to be put in their place.

"Please help." This wasn't coming from Stafford's soundtrack. The voice was coming from Room 517.

Stafford walked in.

An elderly woman lay face up on her bed under the covers except for her head. Her face tensed with pain. Tears rolled down her cheeks. "Please help," she said again.

Stafford picked up her chart. Cancer. Breast cancer that had spread into her internal organs and her spine. No hope, just a lot of pain. And lots of medication prescribed for the pain. "What can we do for you?" he asked.

"The pain. Stop the pain."

Stafford looked again at the chart. "I'll check with the staff to make sure we have your medication at the maximum possible to keep you comfortable."

"Doctor?"

"Yes."

"Is my son here? My sister?"

"I'll check."

Stafford walked out of the room and walked to the closest nurse's station.

"Dr. Stafford," greeted one of the nurses behind the desk.

"Hi. Hey, uh, Estelle Gustafson, 517. She seems in a lot of distress."

She nodded. "I'll check it myself. She's in the last stages."

"I know. Where's her family?"

"They were here just last night. They'll be back."

"She's calling for them."

"Okay."

"Thanks." Stafford walked away from the nurse. She had been polite. But Stafford got a sense of "business-as-usual" from her. Would Estelle Gustafson have been much better off at home, with her family, with plenty of pain medication available? How did that medieval Islamic innovation help Estelle Gustafson today?

Room Five-Oh-Six. Code blue. Stat. Code blue. Stafford's attention shifted to Room 515. There were big, bold signs mandating that no one could go into the room without complete protective garments, mask, gloves, head-covering and light-blue disposable garb to cover all exposed areas. This was a "quarantine" area.

Stafford looked for the nurse. She was looking at a chart outside Room 512. "The burn ward full?" he asked her.

"That's not a burn. Staph infection."

Doctor Stafford took a deep breath. "Did the patient get it here?"

"Probably."

Doctor Stafford put on the light blue garb consisting of material that felt like a cross between a stiff paper towel and an overstarched pajama. He put the gloves on, and put the mask over his face.

The nurse shrugged, but made no effort to join him.

Stafford stepped into the room.

The patient was an elderly man, lying on his back, asleep. He was under a tent. An IV ran into his right arm. Stafford stepped over to see what medicine they were administering.

A small bag read "Vancomycin."

Stafford raised his eyebrows. He stepped out of the room.

"They've got the heavy artillery on this one," he commented to the nurse, who was still standing outside Room 512. Stafford removed the garb and placed it in a hazardous waste collection bin.

"Nothing's killing it," the nurse said. "The patient's immune system is his only hope, and-" She didn't complete the thought by stating the obvious.

Stafford put his mask in the same hazardous waste collection bin. He stepped immediately to a sink behind the nurse's station. "These staph superbugs may curse us for years," he said as he squirted some pink disinfectant soap out of a bottle and onto his hands as he washed them.

"Too much medicine," the nurse said. "Too much antibiotic running around. The price we pay for winning the war on bacteria."

"Winning?" Stafford tilted his head toward the quarantine room. "Not for him, huh."

"No."

Stafford's mind flashed to a memory. He was sneering and dismissing a report on television news. The negative know-it-alls, with a policy of bad-mouthing to get ratings, were peddling another doom-and-gloom version of reality without really understanding the facts they were reporting. Stafford recalled waving dismissively at the obnoxious comment: "Preventable hospital error is the eighth leading cause of death in the United States, higher than vehicle accidents, breast cancer, and significantly higher than AIDS." He recalled thinking that the raw numbers showed a lack of understanding. "Preventable error," he thought, was a subjective term. Stafford breathed out as he thought of the man in the quarantine ward with the staph infection, that he probably picked up while in the hospital for something else. It looked like he'd be in that eighth leading cause group, and soon. Stafford wondered what he had come in for. He shook his head. He didn't want to look. And he suspected that if the man could speak, he would tell Doctor Stafford that it was he who did not understand the numbers, not the news reporters. Staph infections. A hospital innovation for the 21st Century.

Room Five-Oh-Six. Code blue. Stat. Code blue. Time to get on with the visit to Room 5-0-6. Medieval medical innovation. The ideas combined and started to take his mind out of the moment again. The doctor from the movie "Zulu" morphed into the triumphant doctor from the painting of the surgeon. He wanted to get his mind off these images. Room 5-0-6 was just ahead.

But Room 512 got his attention. A man lay in an oxygen tent, sleeping peacefully. Stafford walked in and picked up the chart. Pneumonia. A raging bacterial infection confirmed with a culture. Expertly treated with an antibiotic known to be effective against this particular bug. The modern hospital at its best. He put down the chart. He smiled as he drew in a deep breath. This was exactly what he needed, on the way to Room 5-0-6.

He felt a crescendo of emotion as he reached the room. He remembered looking in and seeing his wife hooked up to an i-v, hooked to vital signs monitors, flashing and beeping. He remembered how she had looked up at him, pleading, and smiling with the confidence of someone who, though in distress, believed the people helping her would pull her through. Though too weak to speak, her eyes were saying "I'm in trouble, but I know you will save me." He remembered later seeing her covered with a sheet.

Room 5-0-6. The image of the confident white-haired surgeon with the blood-soaked arms flooded his mind again. He looked in, almost expecting to see Susan.

Chapter 18

Room 5-0-6. He saw a young woman. Her right leg was casted and elevated. She had on a light blue hospital gown, and flipped channels with her television remote control. She looked at Stafford. "Another doctor?"

"I'm Dr. Stafford, Chief Consulting Physician here."

"Oh. Hi."

"How are you feeling?"

"A lot better than a couple of days ago."

"Good."

"Something else I can tell you, Doctor."

"Yes?"

"I hate drunk drivers."

Stafford smiled. "So do I." He looked around the room. "5-0-6." His head floated, like he wasn't sure of his surroundings.

She looked at him with a puzzled expression.

"It'll be a good room for you." It was something to say in the moment.

She continued to look puzzled. "Sure."

"I mean, it's been a good room for a lot of people. A lot of people have recovered in this room."

"I would hope so."

Stafford found himself back in the moment, and realized that what he had been saying probably didn't make sense to the young patient.

"You can be sure of it." His jaw set firmly. "We will take good care of you."

"Thank you."

"I'll check in on you again."

"Chief Consulting Physician?"

"Yes."

"I really appreciate you taking the time."

Stafford nodded and walked out. Room 506 wasn't so bad. It had been the location of some sad mistakes many years before. But this was a place of healing, of broken bones mending. And Room 506 could do the job as well as any other.

How about 507 across the hall? He stepped across and saw a man, who appeared to be in his late 50s or early 60s, lying in bed. He nodded to the man, who was awake, but had a look of discomfort on his face. Stafford picked up the man's chart.

"I heard what you said to that girl," the man said to Stafford with a weak, scratchy voice.

Stafford was surprised to see the man's age was forty-eight.

"She's lucky," the man said.

Stafford grinned. "Head-on collision. I'll bet she doesn't feel lucky, but I've seen some awful consequences of head-on collisions."

"I'll bet," the patient said.

"Back surgery?" Stafford asked.

"Yeah. My fifth."

Stafford felt a chill creep through him. "Five?"

"Four before this one." He smiled. "I hope Room 507 will be good for me, like you said 506'll be good for her."

"I hope so."

"Gee Doc, you sounded a lot more confident with her."

"I'm sorry. I'm sure it'll be good for you too." Stafford hoped the man didn't sense that Stafford had made the only obligatory comment possible.

"I don't know," the man said. "The first surgery was supposed to fix my back. About five years later, I needed a second one. Three years after that, I got a third, and I swore it would be my last. But here I am, on number five. I don't know—I seem to have no choice. I just ask, I ask over and over again, why did the Good Lord give me such a horrible back?"

Stafford picked up the chart. He fought to maintain a neutral expression to avoid alarming the patient. As he flipped through the reports and notes, he got an idea of what this patient had been through. The first surgery over ten years before, was a fusion of the last lumbar vertebra, L5, with the first sacral vertebra, S1. When the remaining lumbar vertebral and sacro-iliac joints, and the hips and knees, overstrained to compensate for the effects of the fusion, a second fusion was performed, of lumbar vertebrae L3 and L4, L4 and L5. This led to another back surgery at L5 and S1 to correct problems left over from the first surgery. The resulting problems caused by the distortion of the lower body function created the need for a hip replacement. Now, surgery number five, was to place a titanium rod in the patient's back from L1 thru L5. Notes in the chart chronicled the results of these trips to the operating room: weight gain from inactivity due to chronic pain, constipation and other digestive problems, impotence, and finally morphine addiction and long periods in a wheelchair, with the hope that this fifth surgery would bring him back from his nearly hopeless physical state. There was a note about depression and an expression of serious thoughts of suicide.

Stafford wasn't sure what to say. He couldn't say what he was thinking, that he was wondering if this man offered a glimpse of Clyde Minden's future, and that maybe if he had seen someone like Galen Reed twenty years before, he could have lived a totally different life. But he had to say something. "I'll check in with you after the surgery. I'm sure you have a top surgeon working with you. I don't want to step on his toes. But I will check back with you. We will try to make this room a good one for you, the last room you'll ever be in for pre-op for back surgery."

"Thanks, Doctor."

Stafford almost grinned—he attempted a confident grin—but

realized he probably still wore a tense expression on his face. He didn't want to stay in the room any longer. He was afraid he would give himself away.

Stafford stepped out of the room and looked across the hall. Room Five-Oh-Six. Code blue. Stat. Code blue. Room 5-0-6 was still there. Room 5-0-6 had spread to Room 5-0-7 for the man with the back surgeries. And 5-0-8 for some other malady.

The triumphant surgeon from the painting—where was he right now? The image popped back into Eldon Stafford's mind. The memory shifted from fuzziness to more clarity, as if the edges of the painting now filled in, and a full context became available to his recollection. Yes, the surgeon in the painting was triumphant. His assisting colleagues were dutiful and unemotional. An audience observed the procedure from behind a glass partition in front of a balcony above the room. The faces of the people, watching the surgeon's efforts—what were those expressions? The memory crystallized as if choosing this moment to clarify. Focus formed to jagged edges. The expressions—they were expressions of horror, of incredulous revulsion. The surgeon had performed a clumsy amputation on a young, brown-haired boy. This wasn't a painting celebrating modern medicine. The painter clearly created images to condemn this surgeon.

Now that Dr. Stafford had recalled the entire painting, he remembered where he'd seen it. Protesters at one of the pharmaceutical/physician conventions he had been to—he recalled it being the most recent convention in Denmark—had distributed a flier outside the convention, protesting what they described as "the carnage, maiming and devastation" of the "unholy alliance between the butchers of modern medicine and the international pharmaceutical cartels." He'd been disgusted by the image when he'd seen it, and had been disgusted by the creepy, ignorant people who were inflicting their warped ideas on people in and around the convention. He was annoyed that this extreme image had pummeled its way into his consciousness. And as he thought about it, he still felt the image was over the top. But his mind also drifted toward that young soldier biting down on a stick, waiting for a confident saw-wielding surgeon. So just how far from reality was that painting of the surgeon? Five back surgeries, and counting?

The walk up to Room 5-0-6 had not served its purpose, of bringing Eldon Stafford back into the hospital routine. Susan was gone. It had happened in Room 5-0-6, through the over-indulgences of "modern western medicine." Eldon Stafford would never slip back into the hospital routine again, not the way he had lived it before—he understood that now.

As he walked back out away from Room 5-0-6, back up toward the higher numbers—Room 5-1-7, Room 5-2-0—another image flooded into his mind. This one was from a movie about Henry VIIII. He couldn't remember what movie this was, and the actual memory was hazy, but he recalled a fat, yellowish Henry VIII asking to be bled. Some creature who fancied himself a leading medical authority of the day was going to cut into this man and draw blood, with the idea that such a process would make the man healthier. Henry VIII was yelling for the man. The man came into a room with a canopied bed. Henry VIII frowned with impatience. The "healer" brought a satchel full of sharp objects and a container for the blood. He was slightly built, balding, with mostly gray hair. He took one of the sharp objects and cut into Henry VIII's thigh. Henry VIII grunted, and gritted his teeth, but maintained the resignation of a patient swallowing foul-tasting medicine. Then Stafford's mind re-costumed the man into the suit worn by the triumphant surgeon form the turn-of-century painting. This shifted to another costume change, to the light green surgical garb, and pictured him cutting into Room 5-0-7's back, to cut out pieces of his vertebral discs.

Stafford got on the elevator. Room Five-Oh-Six. Code blue. Islamic medieval innovation. An improvement on the medical technologies of the day. Didn't those people think they were using state-of-the-art medical technologies? The man cutting into Henry VIII? Sure, he was bringing the best modern medical know-how of the 1500s to his important patient. Everyone thinks they live in the modern age. What would they say about the current state of western medicine, and the evolution of the great medieval Islamic innovation a few generations from now? Stafford could picture it. Some dignified commentator would say: "They had so much drug and surgical technology, but used it as if taking a sledge hammer to a thumb tack on a bulletin board on the wall, and then wondering why the walls were smashed in everywhere. They engaged in the classic folly of saving the patients by killing them, of failing to see when the cure was worse than the disease, forgetting Hippocrates' elemental, vital advice—physician, first do no harm!" True success would come to those who could open their minds beyond the conventions of the day, achieve a vision of what could be, and lead others on a clear path toward that vision.

Stafford found himself trudging toward the woman in the emergency room with the debilitating abdominal pain. She wore the same expression of ongoing pain he had left her with.

The entire atmosphere of the hospital now seemed different to Eldon Stafford. Every edge of counters, tabletops, chairs, gurneys, desks, of weirdly-shapen machines—the edges seemed to be jarring and artificial. The colors seemed cold and inhuman—faded white, scratched silver—the place didn't seem to offer any sort of warmth, compassion or comfort to humans suffering. Indifferent and inhuman. The surroundings radiated indifference and inhumanity. If caregivers seemed distant and uninvolved, they were simply taking the cues from their surroundings.

"Feeling any better?" he asked. The answer looked obvious, but he wanted to get her talking, to try to find out more information.

"No. I still feel awful."

"Think this is something you could ride out at home?"

"I don't know. I wish I knew what was wrong."

"Stomach virus?"

"Feels awful."

Stafford picked up her chart. The blood and urine test results were now available. Everything looked within normal ranges, including the white count, except for the liver enzyme readings, which were about ten times normal. "Your blood work's back."

"Anything there?"

"I'm not sure."

She shook her head. "I tell you doctor, they say these things come in threes. I don't want to know what the third one is."

Stafford's forehead furrowed. "What was the second?"

"You mean the first. Before this stomach thing."

"Okay, what was the first?"

"It was so stupid, Doctor." She grinned and grimaced at the same time. "I reached into the backseat of my car to grab a package that had fallen off the seat. I couldn't reach it. I was kind of annoyed. I came out the passenger side, opened the door to the back seat and stretched out to grab the package. When I came back up, I hit the back of my head on the top of the backseat doorway. I saw stars—I hit it pretty hard. But I didn't think anything of it until I got a headache, and even felt neck pain and a little low back pain. The next day, I was real sore. Now I get this awful virus to go with it."

Stafford scratched his head. "What're you taking for it?"

"For the virus?"

"No. For the neck and back, for the headache."

"Oh nothing. I never even saw the doctor for it."

Stafford looked down at her chart, searching for the medication section.

"I mean, nothing really. Just some over the counter stuff."

Stafford looked at her. "Ma'am, those count. When we ask about medications, those count."

"Oh." She seemed genuinely surprised. "Sorry."

"It's okay. Tell me everything you've taken."

"Well, I took two aspirin for the headache, every four hours, like it says. And I took a few Tylenol, until I remembered I really needed an anti-inflammatory. I took two Advil, about every fours hours, except when I slept."

Stafford frowned. He couldn't believe where his mind was taking him now. But, he would act on it, even if cautiously. "Roll over on your stomach."

She turned over. Her gown opened at the back, exposing her bare back. Stafford felt just below her head, at the top of her neck. Reed would know—Stafford couldn't be sure—were these vertebrae out of alignment? He felt one of the cervical vertebrae, two bones down from the base of the skull, that seemed clearly mismatched with its partner.

"You still have lower back pain?"

"I think. It's hard to tell, with the medications."

Stafford felt the lower area of her spine. He fought a grin as he found two definite mismatches.

"Okay," he said. "Roll back over."

"Is my back okay?"

"X-rays would tell you for sure, but I would bet you have some back strain."

Stafford stepped over to her i-v drip. He turned off all the medications. "I'm making an adjustment. I'll check back with you."

"Do you think it will help?"

"I wouldn't have done it otherwise. When I check back with you, I'll give you my recommendations. Let's see how the new, uh, medication regime works out." Stafford walked away, out of the emergency room, out into the parking lot. He surprised himself with how fast he had moved.

He pulled out his cell phone. He still had Galen Reed on speed-dial. "Eldon?"

"Galen. I'm in. I'm all the way in. We'll do this your way now. I'll listen first, ask questions later."

No answer came.

"Galen?"

"Sorry. You took me by surprise."

"I'm a little surprised myself. And I'm past the dreamer phase, the tiptoeing through fairy godmother-land phase. We'll have issues to work out. But I get it now. If I'm going to make Susan's death mean anything in the way of a lesson, or something positive, I need to go all the way with this. Tell me when we meet."

"Tomorrow night. The Grill."

"I'll see you there. By the way, one thing we absolutely need for sure. Be thinking of a chiropractor in the emergency room."

"For the emergency room?'

"Absolutely."

"Um, how's that going to go over with your hospital buddies?"

"I'm Chief Consulting Physician. I'll get it through. Be thinking of a colleague or colleagues."

"Sure."

"I've got a few things to finish up here," Stafford said. "I'll see you tomorrow."

"Good."

The call ended.

Stafford felt energized. He wished they could get started right away. Room 5-0-6 could be disempowered as a demon after all.

He turned on his heel. He knew how he could occupy his mind.

"Eldon?" Lawrence Middleton summoned Eldon Stafford gently.

Stafford looked up from the computer terminal at one of the workstations in the emergency room patient area.

"Um, is there anything you need?"

Stafford shook his head. "No. Thanks." Stafford had a yellow pad with pages of notes scrawled on it.

Middleton had seen Stafford trudge through the emergency room as if in a fog, as if his mind was operating somewhere else in a parallel dimension. He'd watched Stafford snap open his phone as he walked out. And he'd watched Stafford walk back in and head straight for the computer terminal without a word to anyone. He had wanted to ask the venerable Chief Consulting Physician what he was doing, but Stafford didn't appear approachable for conversation. So he'd left Stafford alone. Now it had been almost two hours. Maybe he could get some clue about Dr. Eldon Stafford's peculiar behavior. "I mean, if you need some data, I can ask the programmers to-"

"Thanks anyway," Stafford said with an abrupt politeness. "I'm just looking at something on my own. No computer program for it."

Middleton shrugged. "Okay."

"Doctor," summoned one of the emergency room nurses. She was looking at Stafford. "The lady with the abdominal pain? She's asking for you."

Middleton looked at Stafford, then at the nurse. "What's she want?"

"She wants to know what Dr. Stafford gave her."

Middleton frowned.

Stafford stood up. "I'll talk to her." He walked toward the woman. The last time Middleton had seen her, her eyes had been half open, her face tensed with discomfort. What had Eldon Stafford done?

Middleton followed Stafford.

The woman looked transformed. The color was back in her face. Her eyes were wide open, primed for more energy than could be expended in a hospital bed. "What did you give me, Doctor?"

"You feel better?"

"I feel fine. I still have the neck and back stiffness, a little. But I have no headache, and I think my stomach virus is gone. It all started to happen after you changed my medication."

Middleton looked at Stafford for the explanation.

"I turned your medication off." Stafford stepped to her i-v. He reached down and carefully removed it himself. "You've been off medication, getting nothing at all since I switched it off. Go home, and stop taking all that crap."

Middleton's eyes widened. Was Eldon Stafford referring to medication as "crap?"

"What should I do about my neck and back pain?"

Stafford looked at Middleton, as if his presence caused a momentary hesitation. But then Stafford reached into his pocket, took out one of his business cards, and turned it over. He took a pen from his front shirt pocket. "Call this man," he said as he wrote. "Call their office. Set an appointment for tomorrow. I'll call and let them know you're coming." He handed her the card.

"Galen Reed?" She looked at the card.

"He's a chiropractor. He'll help you handle these injuries without all of the stuff that's been tearing out the lining of your stomach and stressing your liver. He'll let me know if you need anything from us."

Stafford turned to walk away.

"Thanks, Doctor," she said.

"Thank you," he said as he walked away. A nurse drew a curtain around the bed so the woman could get dressed in privacy to leave.

Stafford walked out of the emergency room without looking back.

Middleton scratched his chin.

Chapter 19

"I don't care if your dad had another change of heart," Clyde Minden told Brianna Stafford. They sat together at a hot dog/hamburger stand. Clyde was dressed in sweatpants and a t shirt. Brianna had on a cotton blouse and a skirt. "I'm getting this done."

She shook her head. "He saw a guy. A guy who could be you in-"

"He told me. That poor guy probably had bad surgeons. I'm sure the techniques have improved. Believe me, this is going to help me, not hurt me."

"This isn't about surgeons or techniques. There's just no good way to cut pieces out of your discs."

"It's called surgery, Brianna. When they cut you, and take something bad out, you can phrase it in a way that makes it sound awful. But these are established doctors. They wouldn't do this to people if it wasn't going to help them."

"Really?" She nodded. "I'll bet the guy getting his fifth surgery thought he had the best surgeons and the most modern techniques."

Clyde sneered.

Brianna could see logic was not working against stubbornness and a closed mind. "Damn it, Clyde! Why can't you just try it without the, the cutting, the cutting into your back!" Her lips curled and tears formed in her eyes. "Why can't you just, just do it! Go in for a few times!" Tears rolled down her cheeks.

"Aw Jeez." He looked uncomfortable, maybe even irritated. But he also looked like he was softening.

Maybe the waterworks would counter macho stubbornness where logic had failed. "I don't want you to be that guy on the fifth surgery without at least trying?" She reached out and took his arm. "Please, Clyde. Try it without the cutting?"

"What am I going to tell my doctor?" he asked, annoyance seeping through the words. "That my girlfriend cried so I'm putting off the surgery to go to a chiropractor?"

She started to feel anger. Would he actually refuse to try Galen Reed's treatment because he was afraid he would look awkward to his doctor? But she stopped herself. Arguments hadn't softened him. Tears had. "You can't tell your doctor you've changed your

mind, but you can tell me you'll let them cut you?" She sniffled and sobbed.

He clenched his fists and his face tensed. But he wasn't rejecting her pleas.

"Please." She sobbed again.

He breathed in and out. "I'll tell him I need another two weeks to straighten out things at work."

"Two weeks?"

"Two weeks. I'll go in to see Reed a few times, to give it a chance."

"But two weeks might not be-"

"Brianna, I'm going to see Reed. Two weeks is it." He shook his head disgustedly. "Mainly because I can't stand to see my girlfriend cry."

She giggled through her tears, ostensibly addressing the remark. But as she giggled, she realized this was victory for now. As the end of the two weeks approached, she would assess where things stood and figure out how to keep him away from the knife a little longer.

"I need ideas, Natalie. You can help," Galen Reed called through the front door of Natalie Corey's middle class townhouse in La Habra. He had waited for the gate to the security complex to open because he didn't want to give her a chance to turn him away.

"Galen." Her voice sounded on the other side of the door. "This isn't a good time."

"I won't stay long. I'm just so, so hyped about this."

No response came immediately. He heard latches on the other side of the door. The door cracked open. "I've got the boys tonight."

"I just want to talk for a few minutes."

Natalie Corey slipped outside the door and shut it behind her. "This isn't a good time."

"Don't you see? I did what you said. I talked to him. And now, we're really going to make it happen."

She wore a grim look, not a look of excitement at all, but a look of sadness and resignation.

"What's wrong?"

"I've done a lot of thinking about all of this. I'm really in a—I'm in an awkward position with this. I just see... I see a train-wreck coming. I'm in the middle of—I can't be in it with you."

"What?"

"Have you ever watched a show on t-v, where you know one of the characters is about to do something really awkward, something weird is going to happen, and you can't watch?"

"I'm not sure what you're talking about."

"Galen, do you still have that file, that Susan Stafford file?"

Galen Reed took a deep breath. Natalie Corey's grim mood was apparently contagious, because he had caught it. "Yeah, I still have it. So?"

She shook her head. "This is going to end badly. I'm too intertwined in it. I know too much. I can't watch."

"Natalie-"

"I'm sorry. I just, I just can't go on seeing you." She turned away, possibly hiding tears. "I'll get another rep assigned to your office." She opened her door. "I'm sorry. For both of us." She went through and shut the door quietly behind her.

"Nattie." Galen Reed stood, staring at the door.

"Good-bye, Galen," her voice told him through the door.

"Wait a minute. Let's talk about this."

He heard no response.

He knocked on the door.

There was still no response.

He took a deep breath. This wasn't "A Streetcar Named Desire" where he would scream her name. He would have to try to salvage this relationship at some other time. It was time to launch into the Stafford-Reed/Reed-Stafford collaboration. If he could make it work, make it rise to its potential, Natalie would come back to him.

"Stu Javolly said I should call you," Lawrence Middleton said to Seymour McTavish. "I'm telling you, Stafford said 'stop taking that crap.' Then he referred her to that chiropractor who has been fooling around with his daughter's asthma."

"Well, I see why Stu had you call me, and the trip over was worth it, even at this hour." McTavish looked at his watch. The digital read-out showed "11:38 pm" He frowned and chewed on his lower lip. "I thought this thing was settled. My source said their little operation fell apart."

"If it did, I'm betting it's coming back together."

McTavish's nostrils flared. Was Middleton manufacturing issues to get attention? "Alright, well, I have a prime source right next to all this. I'll tap it. I appreciate the heads up."

"Sure." He paused. "Just trying to maintain the quality and integrity of the hospital."

"I'll make sure Mr. Greevey knows about your help, and your apparent leadership qualities."

"Sure."

McTavish left the hospital. He stepped into the dark hospital parking lot. He pulled out his cell phone, snapped it open, then stepped under a light. He'd still maintained the number he wanted in his speed-dial. He pressed the button.

The line went straight to voicemail—some song he didn't recognize answered the phone.

McTavish sneered. He wasn't sure he should leave a message. But he wanted to make contact as soon as possible. "Need a call back from you. Looks like I need you again. Fill me in on whatever you know. I know you have my number." He snapped his phone shut.

Should he call Wyatt Greevey tonight? Not with so many uncertainties. Eldon Stafford acting strangely would not be worth interrupting Wyatt Greevey's night. When he had more answers, he'd bring his boss up-to-date.

"This time, I listen. This time, you tell me how this should work," Eldon Stafford said as they took their seats in a booth at the Imperial Highway Grill.

Reed nodded. "Okay. I'll start with the basic idea, and we can work it from there. The idea is that we start health care without the drugs, the surgeries, any intrusive care. And the way we do that is to make chiropractic healers the first responders, the first examiners, the first healers. So you send me everything. We bring in the drugs and the surgeries when the less intrusive healing does not work. And we still make sure the body is at its best even for people with the more serious conditions. So you also send me cancer, Parkinson's, MS—everything."

Stafford nodded. "Okay."

"There's more to this."

"Keep going…"

"People need to think 'wellness.' They need to come see us when they feel great, so we can work with them to keep them feeling great."

A waitress came over.

"Not yet," Reed told her.

She nodded politely and left the table.

"We check spine alignment, and discuss with them, in practical day-habit terms, how to stay healthy."

"Yeah, well of course."

"Come on, Eldon. You say 'of course.' But this hasn't been a priority. It gets lip service, from some MDs more than others. But it needs to be a priority. Like dentists. Periodic spine hygiene, periodic body hygiene. We go every six months for our teeth. Insurance companies pay for it. But for our whole bodies? We wait until we're sick to see someone!"

"Makes sense. So how do we make that work?"

"Yeah. That's the trick. Because the system isn't set up for it."

"True."

"Also, you mentioned chiropractors in the emergency room. We should line up around fifteen to start, to take eight hour shifts once or twice a week, and then make the referrals. We will eventually want to expand to more than one on a shift, with a plan to coordinate with nurses to reduce wait times and make the whole place more pleasant, which will help patients with their conditions."

"How about twelve hours shifts, to make sure we can cover all the hours?" Stafford asked.

"No. One of the problems with emergency rooms is the long shifts for emergency room doctors. They get so tired that decision making gets fuzzy, bedside manner certainly gets compromised—we don't want to repeat that problem with the chiropractors."

Stafford took in a deep breath. "Okay."

"We also need the surroundings to be better. Aroma therapy. More comfortable furniture. Warmer colors. Earth tones that ease the patients' moods instead of that clinically severe white paint that adds an in-your-face edginess to the experience."

Stafford grimaced.

"That's an important part of 'taking this all the way.'"

"I'm in complete agreement with you," Eldon Stafford said. "It's just that-" He took a deep breath. "I'll have to figure out how to get this past the numbers people. It might take a little time. But I'm with you, absolutely."

"Okay. I'll do some of the first chiropractic shifts."

"Good."

"Patients see the chiropractors first. Not the mangled bodies from an auto accident or a gunshot, or bursting appendixes or heart attacks.

But people with routine, less traumatic problems, who may not want to wait three hours for medical attention—send them to local chiropractors if there aren't enough chiropractors on duty."

"Tricky. But if we present it the right way, doable."

"And to make it work, we also need to expand the chiropractic office to include diagnostic tools. We need to give DCs access to all those tests and test results. To handle patients with acute complaints, we'll need x-ray capabilities, ultrasound, MRI, PET and CT scans."

Eldon Stafford nodded.

"This will allow me, allow the chiropractors who are first-responders, to assess the patient's condition and determine immediately if more intrusive care is needed."

"As far as in the office, we may have to slide into this. Budget and personnel might be an issue. But those machines are at the hospital, and effective immediately all chiropractors will have access to the testing and the results, whether on an emergency room shift or not."

"And authority to request tests."

"Absolutely."

"Including standing x-rays."

Stafford smiled. "Okay. Yeah."

"Don't forget. At my office, I make sure we keep away that hospital smell everyone hates. That antiseptic atmosphere that oozes cleanliness, but a sense of sterility without warmth or comfort. At my office, I create a soothing atmosphere. We need to do the same thing at the hospital."

Stafford nodded again. "You mentioned that before. The old guard may have a fit. Fragrances at the hospital? But I know some nurses who will love the idea."

"Not fragrances, Eldon. Aroma therapy. We're not talking about some over-the-top phony smelling air freshener. We're talking about aromas that heal. Peppermint to settle upset stomachs. Eucalyptus to help breathing. Lavender—something to relax patients who are likely to be upset from long waits and whatever discomfort they've come in with."

"All right. The therapeutic benefits will help me slide it past the ad-min people."

"Good."

Stafford grinned. "It'll probably take the patients by surprise. But it should ease their moods and help their healing."

Stafford brought up his briefcase from the floor.

The waitress came over again.

Stafford gestured they were not ready to order yet with a palm up.

The waitress shrugged and nodded as she walked away.

Stafford laid his briefcase on the table, then popped open the latches. "I'm with you." He pulled out a pad and pen. "Let me make some notes. Let's set a specific timetable for various specific elements of this to happen."

"Good."

"Maybe we better order."

Reed smiled. He caught the attention of the waitress and waved her over.

"Oh, and I don't want to wait for us to put all this together for Clyde. I also sent a lady over with-"

"I saw her today. Clyde's coming in tomorrow."

"He still wants the surgery. He's talking about two weeks."

Reed raised his eyebrows as he shook his head. "I'll try to see him immediately. Two weeks is not a lot of time. I'll do what I can."

"Good."

"You're ready to order?" the waitress asked.

"Yes." Eldon Stafford looked at Galen Reed with a grin and a twinkle in his eye. "And I hope you don't need this table for awhile."

Reed nodded back. Stafford was on board. Reed's ideas about reforming and improving health care were going to get a real chance to work. He felt his stomach jump. Now the real drama would begin.

Chapter 20

"That's right. I'm part of the service at this hospital now," Galen Reed said to a woman in her late forties. The woman wore a blue hospital gown. She had visible abrasions on her face, and one of her fingers was in a splint. She sat on a gurney in the emergency room patient area of Orange County Memorial Hospital. "We are working toward having a chiropractor on duty all the time. Right now, we have enough staff committed to fill about twelve hours a day."

"I knew something was different when they did the standing x rays," she said with a smile. "The last time I had those was in my chiropractor's office in L-A."

"So you know something about chiropractic care."

"I figured I would go see my chiropractor in the next few days."

Reed nodded. "Well, you're getting the benefit of both types of care here. You took a big hit in that impact—airbag in your face and no doubt of a forceful back-and-forth on your body, broken finger trying to protect your face. My physical examination indicated some vertebrae out of alignment. We'll look at the x rays to confirm this. I'll do an adjustment right away if the x-rays confirm no fractures or other bone pathology. I should have those in just a few minutes. Now I know they gave you some prescriptions."

"Three. For pain. And a muscle relaxer. And an anti-inflammatory."

"Three." Reed's eyes darted away, then quickly back. "Well, that is another way to treat these injuries." He stifled his desire to say more, recalling that he was there to offer an alternative, not get in confrontations over it.

"He said to take the pills for a couple of weeks, then check with my doctor for possible physical therapy."

Reed's stomach churned. Drugs, which to him were intrusive forms of medical care, were not supposed to be the primary, first treatment offered. Here he was offering his treatment course as a competing plan instead of a primary plan. Didn't this mock the lessons of the Susan Stafford tragedy? He decided he needed to be frank. "Look," he said quietly, "the drugs will cover your symptoms. Physical therapy can be very helpful. But spinal manipulation to get the vertebrae in proper alignment is the most direct care for these injuries. Your spine has been thrown out of alignment by this event. We will put the bones of your spine back in alignment. We will address the actual cause of your symptoms directly."

The woman nodded.

Reed looked around and saw Lawrence Middleton behind him to the right. Middleton sneered a disgusted expression.

Reed turned to the woman again. "I recommend you see your chiropractor and begin a series of adjustments. Use the drugs only if they are absolutely necessary."

"*Mister* Reed, did you give our patient the disclaimer notice?"

Reed's nostrils flared. "Yes, *Larry*, I did."

Middleton stepped over to the patient. "The notice we are handing out, to all patients who are part of this, this experiment Dr. Stafford has foisted on us, clearly states that the opinions of alternative health-care givers here are to be acted upon at your own risk."

"Thank you, Larry, for that helpful information," Reed said. He looked back at the patient.

The woman looked concerned and confused.

"The idea here is to offer you a choice to start with the least invasive care first," Reed said. "You have the advantage of some familiarity with chiropractic care."

"Sure."

"You do have some nasty scrapes from airbag, and the broken finger. If you need help with the pain, you have it. Just"—Reed grinned as he looked back, saw Middleton, and continued anyway—"just read all the information about the side effects. Make an educated choice—taking the drugs should be considered a tradeoff."

Reed caught a glimpse of Middleton sneering. He looked back at the woman. "Feel better soon."

"Thanks, um, thanks, Doctor."

"You're welcome."

The woman looked back, apparently making sure Middleton was out of earshot. "I don't know why he's so hostile. I'm glad there is a chiropractor in the emergency room."

Reed smiled.

The woman started collecting her paperwork.

Reed walked away, toward a private, unoccupied area of the emergency room. He snapped open his cell phone and punched Eldon Stafford's name in the contact menu.

"Galen?"

"Hi Eldon. Middleton's still doing it. He waves that crap the hospital attorneys shoved down your throat, the cover-the-ass, we're-afraid-of-getting-sued memo—he waves that in patients' faces whenever he hears me talking to a patient. Only two other D-Cs will do a shift with him."

"I've talked to him. He's-" Eldon Stafford paused, as if choosing his words. "He's having a hard time adjusting to this idea."

"He's not adjusting to it. He's trying to sabotage it."

"Okay. Probably. Just do the best you can."

"Any real change at the hospital level is going to be tough with that disclaimer and fools like Middleton undermining the program."

"It'll take time. I'm working it from my end. Don't let him get you down, or get you off track. The situation is-"

A commotion sounded at the entrance to the patient area from the waiting room. Two nurses flanked a gurney. Lawrence Middleton jogged toward it.

"I gotta go," Reed told Stafford. "I'll call you." Reed jogged toward the gurney.

Middleton sneered at him as he approached.

"What do we have?" Reed asked, mainly making eye contact with the nurses, but glancing at Middleton.

"He's having another seizure," one of the nurses said.

A boy in his early teens was lying on his right side. His body shook with convulsions. His eyes appeared to roll toward the back of his head.

The nurse put a small cloth in his mouth. She looked at Reed. "He's been having seizures all afternoon."

"All afternoon?"

"He's prone to seizures," Middleton told Reed. "He had a terrible head trauma a couple of years ago. We've been able to control them with medication. This is a neurological problem, not a fender-bender, Mr. Reed. We don't need you."

Reed frowned and even growled softly under his breath. He spotted a woman who he figured was the boy's mother. "I'm Dr. Galen Reed, chiropractor on duty. I'd like to have a look."

"I have a waiver for you to review and sign if you decide to-"

"In a minute, Dr. Middleton. A few questions. Did he miss his medication?"

"No," she answered. She looked at Middleton, who seemed to scold her with accusing eyes. "We really did not miss a dose."

"Alright, alright," Middleton quipped. "I believe you. We'll have the CAT scan results in just a minute."

Reed stepped to the boy, who had stopped convulsing, but seemed to be tensing for another round of seizures. "Did they do an x-ray?"

"No," the nurse said.

"I need to see that scan. Upper neck area?"

"Yes."

"Please get it here." Reed felt the base of the boy's skull. Right at the top vertabra, C1, at the "atlas," he could feel a significant alignment problem.

The boy went into more convulsions.

"We need that waiver signed," Middleton insisted.

But no one seemed to react.

Reed saw the nurse on the phone. "You calling on the CAT scan?"

"Yes."

"Just ask them if there is any fracture or bone pathology in the neck area."

The nurse spoke into the phone. Reed felt further down the neck. More than one of the cervical vertebrae were far out of alignment, possibly from the original head trauma.

Reed saw the nurse hang up the phone. She thumbed through the chart, then moved over to Reed quickly. "No fractures on the scan. No problems. No reports of any fractures from any previous studies of the head and neck area," she reported as she showed Reed the portions of the chart that confirmed her statements.

Reed glanced at the chart. "Thanks." He turned to the mother. "Has he ever been adjusted?"

"What?"

"Has he ever been to a chiropractor?"

"No. We don't believe in them."

Reed looked down at the boy, now once again in between convulsions. "Ma'am, your son's neck is way out of alignment. Let me see if an adjustment would alleviate this. It won't hurt him. I promise."

"Excuse me." Middleton moved toward Reed. "The waiver."

Reed looked at the mother.

The boy started convulsing again.

"Okay," she said. "Try."

Reed positioned the boy's head, then moved it. A loud crack sounded from the boy's neck.

"My God," Middleton said with a squeamish look on his face.

The convulsions abated.

The boy spoke. "That felt-" He grunted and let out a burst of air. "Felt weird."

"Get him to x-ray," Middleton said, with annoyance, even a little panic. "I think this man just broke his neck."

"Felt good, though," the boy added, as if he hadn't heard Middleton. "Felt... good."

The mother looked at Reed. "That was an adjustment."

"Yes." Reed handed her his card. "That's a start. A grasping-in-the-dark start. I need to see him and get a complete medical history. But I think I can help."

"You don't mind if we do some real doctor work here, do you?" Middleton asked. "Like wait for the complete CAT scan results?"

"Sure." Reed looked at one of the nurses. "Please get him some standing cervical x rays also."

Middleton's lips tensed, but he nodded his approval of Reed's request to the nurse.

The mother looked at Reed. "We'll be in to see you the minute we can set an appointment."

"I'll tell my staff to give you priority."

Middleton walked away without saying anything.

"Okay. I'm all strapped in." Clyde Minden was secured to the inversion table, face up. There was a strap across his waist, straps around both legs, around both arms, and across his chest. Galen Reed stood over Minden, making sure all the straps were in place. "I'm yours, Doc. Where am I going?"

Reed grinned. "You're going upside down."

"Right."

"I'm going to rotate this table so your head lowers and your feet raise. This will use gravity to open the disc space. Your own body weight will open up the intervertebral foramina, allowing the bulge to slip back into place. Now, I need you to tell me how this feels."

Galen Reed tilted the table about five degrees.

"You okay?"

"Hmmm." Minden seemed to study the sensation. "Yeah."

"I'm adding some more." Reed added five more degrees.

"More," Minden said.

Reed nodded and added another five degrees. "Let's hold this a moment."

"Okay."

Reed watched Minden's face. There were no signs of stress. Minden's body remained relaxed. "You seem okay."

"I'm fine. You can go more."

"Good. Another five degrees." Reed tilted the table.

Minden squinted, but grinned. "This actually feels good. Let's go some more."

Reed nodded. "You got it." Reed tilted the table again.

"Yeah. Okay." Minden took in a deep breath. "But I'm starting to feel like everything's rushing south."

"Need me to pull it back?"

"No. I can stay with this for a few minutes. But this is good enough."

"Okay."

"It does feel good, on my back, I mean. It feels like things are stretching, loosening, kind of blotting out a tightness."

Reed nodded.

"Any way I could just walk around like this?" Minden asked with a smile.

Reed laughed. After enjoying the remark a moment, he said: "So give me a few tries at this. You're never going to need that surgery."

"It's set in two weeks."

Reed looked at Minden. "So are you going through with it?"

Minden seemed to puzzle over the question. "I honestly don't know," he finally said.

"Then you shouldn't do it, Clyde. You've got to give this a chance."

"I know what your opinion is, Doc. And I have to say, if a bill for 'inversion therapy' had come across my desk last week, I would've laughed before sending out the denial letter. They still might make me send the denial letter, but I would be wondering if we should pay it. I mean, I admit this seems to make me feel better."

"That should tell you something."

"But I'm not sure what."

"Clyde, I'll say it again. If you're not sure, you should hold off."

Minden shook his head. "I can't keep blowing off this surgeon. I could tell he was annoyed the first time I delayed. If I delay again, he'll probably drop me as a patient, or at least postpone me for a long time. This could turn out to be just some weird respite, and I really need it. Then I'll have to wait longer."

"Give this more time. Then let's run an MRI and see if we've made any measurable progress—we'll see if the test will back up what you felt today. I'm sure it will."

"Maybe I should do that right away."

"It's too soon. We need more time with the inverted traction."

Minden paused. "I don't know. I need to think about it."

"Call me before you decide."

"Sure."

"If you're really set on going through with it, let's go ahead and do the MRI before you do anything."

"Okay."

Reed stepped toward the door.

"If I decide not to do it, I'll have to tell my doctor about this."

"You mean your back surgeon."

"Right."

"Well, you probably should. Tell him you're trying anything possible before going to the drastic step of surgery."

"Yeah."

Reed turned to leave.

"Will you talk to him?" Minden asked.

Reed turned back to Minden. He smiled. "Yes. Of course."

"I always thought guys like him would be against this sort of thing."

Reed shrugged. "It's been that way. But it doesn't have to be." He nodded. "We could actually all work together. It would bring great benefits—to the patients."

Minden nodded.

"What the hell is going on over at that hospital?" McTavish asked rhetorically as he and Stu Javolly rode an elevator toward the underground parking area of Havitol Pharmacy.

Javolly shook his head. "I don't know. After I went to the hospital lawyers and got them all wound up about malpractice, and they forced that waiver on Stafford and Reed, I thought the whole thing would fall apart. But Middleton tells me the patients barely pay attention to it, or it isn't even offered to them at all."

"Not offered to them…"

"If no one insists on it, it doesn't get to them. And they've had some successes. Lots of referrals to the D-Cs. Away from drug-based solutions."

"The old man's been griping about the lower drug orders from the hospital."

"Believe me, I know."

The elevator reached the parking lot level. It opened and McTavish walked out into the underground parking area.

McTavish frowned. "So we're back to voodoo medicine and witch-doctors."

"Back-cracking."

"Yeah. Magic wands."

"The problem is," Javolly said, "People are buying it."

McTavish took in a deep breath.

"The old man has another angle on this thing, through the health insurance company he has a piece of, and his connections in that industry," Javolly said.

"He told me."

"But he's still riding us."

"Yeah. Me especially. 'Plan B,' he keeps saying. What're you doing about 'Plan B?'" McTavish sneered. "My source." He paused, wondering how much he should say to Javolly. But he saw little downside to sharing this information, considering that Javolly had shared similar information with him. Maybe Javolly would offer an effective idea he had not thought of. "My source has lost position. At least that's what I've been told. I wonder if it isn't a loss of enthusiasm. Plan B looks tougher."

"I'll bet he didn't want to hear that."

McTavish frowned. "Well, I'm trying to correct the situation before he needs to know."

"Ah," Javolly said as he nodded. They arrived at Javolly's car.

"I need to apply some pressure, push a few buttons. I'll get repositioned and crank it up again."

"Need anything from me?"

"Just keep letting me know what that twerp Middleton has to say."

"He's with us," Javolly assured McTavish. "Havitol has never had a better friend."

"And Havitol has never had a worse friend than Eldon Stafford, or, a worse enemy than Galen Reed."

"True."

"We will bring them down. The old man has decreed it. I will make it happen."

Javolly got into his car. "See you tomorrow."

McTavish nodded.

Chapter 21

"Doctor, I'm really stuck," Clyde Minden said to Doctor Randolph Collier over his cell phone. Minden laid back on his couch, dressed in a loose-fitting sweat-suit. He looked without seeing at a basketball game on television with the sound off. "I'm feeling so much better. I'm just not sure-"

"Clyde, believe me, you need the surgery. Your film is definitive."

"It's a big step."

"We've been over this. I've explained this to you—how the surgery will work, and what we'll accomplish." He paused. "I'll tell you what. The night before, when I check in with you, I'll bring in the charts and the plastic model I use to explain things. We'll get you completely comfortable with-"

"I'm telling you, I'm better."

"Now listen, Clyde." Collier's tone was gentle, but in a superior way, almost patronizing. "All of us have had that toothache that goes away just as you pull into the dentist's parking lot. The tooth doesn't miraculously heal. It's a psychological reaction. Your mind is now more focused on what you perceive will be the unpleasantness of the surgery, an unpleasantness you now fear more than the discomfort of your back condition. Think back to how painful your back has been. You'll know what to do."

"But that's just it. I know it's been getting better." Clyde paused, trying to figure out what to say to demonstrate this was more than just a psychological phase. He said the first thing that came to him, about an activity that was foremost in his mind. True, it was personal, but the man was a doctor, after all. "Doc, I'm gonna tell you something. My girlfriend. She likes to ride me on top, if you know what I mean."

"Uh-huh."

"I hadn't been able to, you know, do it that way. Until last week. It was no problem."

"Maybe she has lost some weight…"

"Trust me, she's in great shape. She's been exercising more, now that her asthma is under so much better control."

"Look kid, I understand your jitters. But we've got to fish or cut bait on this thing. I can't keep rescheduling. There's just no medical reason why you should suddenly be better."

Clyde Minden paused. "Actually, there is."

"These conditions don't just-"

"I've been getting treatment from a chiropractor. Some kind of upside down thing that-"

"You've been delaying this surgery to go to a chiropractor?"

"Well, my girlfriend-"

"This guy's probably done more damage."

"I don't think so. He's practically cured my girlfriend's asthma. I was hoping you could talk to him, kind of coordinate your efforts. I'm thinking I should get an MRI to see if-"

"You're a college-educated guy. Ever heard of the placebo effect?"

"I don't think this is just the power of suggestion."

"An MRI right now is silly, a waste. We have what we need with the recent one we just did. And I am not going to waste my time talking to some half-assed so-called back healer. They have been proven over and over again to be fakes and phonies. At best, you're getting a placebo effect. Forget another MRI. Let's get on with what needs to be done."

"He agrees with you on the MRI. But he also says I should give non-surgical methods a chance to-"

"We did that already, remember? The injections did not work.

What he means is that he wants to give his non-surgical methods some time to work. A long time. And a lot of money. Of course he doesn't want you to have the surgery. He doesn't get paid when I do the surgery. And if it is successful, as I know it will be, he doesn't get to soak you any more."

"But if I use his methods, you don't get paid. Right?"

There was a tense pause over the phone. Minden wondered if he had gone too far. "Look, I'm not going to waste any more time on this. I've got people waiting for a time slot, for a time slot you've taken and used—twice. You want to fool around with nonsense, and talk garbage to me? Then I'll help someone who is serious."

"I'm sorry, Doctor. I shouldn't have made that crack about you not getting paid. But this is serious. Eldon Stafford's been advising me all the way, helping me make-"

"Then I'll have a chat with him about tampering with my patients."

"He's not my doctor. He's not trying to take me away from-"

"I've been hearing about him—going a little crazy. He's liable to get yanked right out of his spot at the hospital, and even put his license in jeopardy if he doesn't snap himself out of it. I've got no time for this. Are you in or out for the surgery?"

"Let me get an MRI to see if-"

"I'm not waiting around for a meaningless MRI."

"Then let me get the treatment for another month or two, and then get the-"

"I take that as a no. Please call another doctor to treat your back after the chiroquacktor is done screwing it up."

"Wait. Maybe I should just do it."

"Kid, I need a decision."

"When?"

"Twenty-four hours. You're scheduled in four days."

"I'll call you."

"Call my office. Tell them yes or no. If I get no call, I assume we're done." The line clicked off.

Clyde Minden closed his cell phone. He sat up. His back seemed to stiffen. Was it in his mind? Was this a "placebo effect" situation? He was feeling better, wasn't he? Or did he really need the surgery, like so many of his fellow athletes?

"That's great," Galen Reed said to Shenelle Washington, the mother of Jerelle Washington, the boy who had been in the emergency room with seizures just a week before. She had walked up to Reed as Jerelle Washington left his examining room, concluding his treatment for that day. "He told me he's had no seizures for three days now, after all those seizures at once."

"It's true. It's such a relief."

"Your son has been sleeping properly?"

"On his back, with a pillow under his neck, knees bent—yes, absolutely." She smiled. "He does not want those seizures back."

"Good."

"And he really likes the swimming. Seems good at it."

"I'm glad. Exercise is important for someone his age. Important at any age."

"Yes."

"I noticed his posture is slipping back into bad habits today. I reminded him, the whole spine needs to be kept healthy."

"I'm glad you're telling him." She smiled again. "Sometimes a boy his age does not want to hear anything from his mama."

"And every child has heard his parents say 'sit up straight.' That is good advice for anyone. But for him? With that trauma to his cervical area? For him, it's essential."

"You've got no argument from me, Doctor."

"It's pretty certain that the misalignment of the atlas, the top vertebra of the cervical spine, which was probably knocked out by the original injury, and never really corrected, caused your son's problems. It's not always this simple, or the results this dramatic. And we need to keep monitoring him closely as he dries out from the medication he's been taking. But I like what I see. And the report of no seizures—it's just simply great news."

"This is by far the best result we've had, from any medical care." She shook her head. Tears started to form. "I thought he would never be the same after he fell down that staircase." She grimaced. "So stupid, grappling with his buddy. But kid stuff, not something he should he penalized for his whole life. Thank you, Doctor. You may have given him his life back. And thank Dr. Stafford for putting men like you in the emergency room."

"That means a lot to me. It will to him too. Thank you."

"See you Friday," Jerelle Washington said, smiling as they left.

"See you," Galen Reed said.

Reed walked to his office. His patient Kevin McDorn was waiting, and he wouldn't take too much time. But he had to celebrate this triumph of Jerelle Washington, if just for a moment. He picked up his appointment book. Under it was the file, the old yellowing file labeled Susan Stafford. Once the Stafford-Reed collaboration had started, it had been his habit to keep the file with his appointment book so he would see it before his day started. He opened the file and looked at the pages inside for just a moment, not really studying any of them, but thinking of how the failures of the past were being converted into life-changing successes in the present. What else could anyone expect in the way of vindication? He closed the file and put it back with his appointment book. There were patients waiting. Kevin McDorn was waiting now.

"How are you feeling?" Galen Reed asked as he entered the examining room where Kevin McDorn lay face down on an examining table.

McDorn turned his head slightly. "You know. Good days. Bad days."

"And today seems to be a bad day."

"Yeah. Every joint seems stiff today. My balance seems more off than usual, like a dizziness that just swirls around me all the time. My stomach is aching—I don't want to eat at all."

"Yes, your weight is down."

"Happens when I don't eat."

"You've got to eat."

"I know. It's just hard when this gets bad. I've got the constant headaches too."

Reed nodded. "Any changes that brought this on?"

"They're cutting back at work. I got a kid who's a junior at UCLA. Doing real well. But no scholarships. I lose my job, he has a hard time finishing."

"Stress."

"Yeah."

"Stress itself can be an enemy. It charges your body up in the short term, but then the body needs to recover. With your condition…"

"I know. And I may have compounded my stress."

"Compounded it?"

"Yeah. I went and saw my primary."

"Okay."

"He chewed me out for dumping the anti-inflammatories." He snorted and grinned. "He especially chewed me out for seeing you."

"Of course."

"But Dr. Reed, he says all the medical research shows that the anti-inflammatories, and the other medications he wants me to take, will help me. He says if I don't take the drugs, I'll die."

"And that's got you even more stressed."

"Yeah."

Reed grinned as he shook his head. "I can see why." He shrugged. "Those anti-inflammatories they push on you are exactly wrong for you." Reed knew he had explained this to him before, but the man obviously needed to hear it again. "In your condition, the Myelin Sheaths, around your nerves, have broken down. The electrical impulses don't travel through your nervous system the way they should. It affects everything—your joints, digestion—everything you mentioned today. The anti-inflammatories suppress your immune system, something you need operating at peak."

"I know. You've explained this before. I guess I just needed to hear it again."

"Okay. I thought so. Listen, let me remind you of one more thing. Your body is the greatest producer of healing medicines, better than any pharmaceutical factory. The body is a chemical factory and warehouse beyond anything created by humans. We need to unleash as much of that as possible to heal your body. That's why we've been working on your entire body's health. And you've been doing well, off the meds. Stay on that diet we gave you. 60% carbs, 20% fats, 20% proteins. Fish, chicken, fresh fruits, vegetables, soups, and lots and lots of water. Swim if you're strong enough. At the health club, with supervision."

McDorn nodded.

"I want you to come in for some Chironosis™. We'll try to get you out of these stressful thought patterns."

"Okay. Thanks."

"We'll do some gentle adjustments on some out-of-place vertebrae. That will place your spine at optimal alignment."

Reed completed the adjustments and got McDorn started on a gentle setting at the intersegmental traction table.

He noticed the next patient was ready. He entered the examining room to find Jimmy Puccinelli face down on the examination table.

"Hello," he said to Puccinelli. "Let's see how you're doing."

"Good," Puccinelli said.

Reed ran his fingers along Puccinelli's spine, from his neck toward his lower back. "You seem to be doing real well. The vertebrae seem to be in excellent alignment. Just a slight problem at L4-5. I'll do an adjustment there."

"So I still have problems," the man said.

"You have a basically healthy spine."

"'Basically healthy.' Not totally healthy."

"Everyone's spine needs attention, and periodic adjustment." He positioned his hands. "Breathe out." As Puccinelli breathed out, Reed pressed down.

"Alright, let's get down to it," Puccinelli said. "Am I healed up from the auto accident?"

Reed paused a moment. "I'd say that whatever ill effects you sustained from the accident are behind you."

Jimmy Puccinelli raised up on his elbows and turned to eye Reed. "So I'm okay now."

"Sure."

"So why is my attorney telling me you aren't going to issue a final report?"

Reed let out a burst of air. He hated this kind of conversation. "I have talked to your attorney about your case. You should talk to him."

"I'm talking to you. You're my doctor."

Reed pursed his lips. "Your attorney tried to tell me what I should write in my report. I told him I didn't do that. After some additional discussion, we decided it would be best if I simply sent over the records. My staff is working on that."

"So you didn't write a report..."

"Not one your attorney is interested in."

"Hmph."

"Step over here please." Reed motioned to the intersegmental traction table.

Puccinelli wordlessly went over and lay down.

Reed set the roller controls where he recalled that Puccinelli found them comfortable, then left the room. He remembered when he and Eldon Stafford had first encountered this patient. Stafford had suggested they send him away. Maybe they should have.

Reed walked into the next examining room. "How are you feeling?" he asked.

Sheila Watanabe looked back at Reed with tired eyes. She had a blue bandanna tied across the top of her head to obscure her lack of hair. She was thin, dressed in loose-fitting clothes. "I had chemo yesterday. Tuesday afternoon."

"How many more to go?"

"Another two weeks. Then they check."

"Have you been able to keep up with the nutrition plan?"

"It's tough right after treatments. But I'm pretty close. Same with the exercise."

"Good. Lie face down for me."

Sheila Watanabe laid face down on the examination table which Galen Reed elevated to nearly a vertical position. He felt along her spine.

"I never would have thought to come to a place like this for cancer," she said. "I couldn't believe Dr. Stafford would suggest this. But I have to say, I really believe these visits have helped. I'm not sure why. I just feel better—a little bit better than I would have without this."

Galen Reed nodded. "Your body is going through incredible adversity as you fight the cancer, and the effects of the treatment. My job is to give you every advantage in your fight to heal. We're making sure your spine, and therefore your entire central nervous system, is lined up for optimum performance for your struggle. And our focus on your entire body helps us maintain your health in the areas not affected by the cancer so your entire body is at its strongest."

"I think it's working."

"Good."

Reed found some misaligned vertebrae at T3-4 and L5-S1. "Relax and breathe out." Reed pushed down on her back. A slight click sounded. "On your side, please." She rolled on her left side. Reed applied a burst of pressure to her lower back. "Other side, please." She rolled to the other side. He repeated the maneuver. "I'll get some ice. Relax."

Reed left the room and went to a freezer in a central spot in the hall. He pulled out two ice packs. He scowled as he caught a glimpse of the room Jimmy Puccinelli was in. The door was wide open, not the way he had left it.

Reed entered the room Sheila Watanabe was in and placed ice on her mid and lower back. "I'll be right back," he said.

Reed stepped to the room Jimmy Puccinelli was in. He looked in. The room was empty. He moved into the hall and started toward the front to ask if anyone had seen Puccinelli leave. But as he did, he noticed his own office door was open.

Reed moved quickly to his office and saw Puccinelli going through papers on his desk. Reed felt his stomach jump and his teeth clench. "What are you doing?"

"Trying to find my file?"

"In my office? Snooping through my stuff?"

"My lawyer says my insurance company won't pay what my claim is worth. He says my file doesn't look good somehow. I wanted to see what's in my file."

"Thought of asking your attorney and talking to him about it?"

"I don't trust him. I asked your office manager and she said she couldn't find my file, that it was probably in your office. I didn't have time to wait for her to look for it."

Reed squinted. "Make time."

Puccinelli sneered, but walked out of the office.

Reed found the file under a stack of two others. He left his office and joined Puccinelli. "Come with me."

Reed and Puccinelli walked into the reception area at the front of the office. "Wait out here," he said to Puccinelli.

The sneer hadn't disappeared from Puccinelli's face, but he did what he was told.

Reed turned to one of his two support staff. "Please make a copy of this file for Mr. Puccinelli. He is discharged from care."

"Hey. Wait a minute. What if I need another follow-up?"

"Find a new doctor."

"Yeah? Well if my attorney can't get the insurance company to pay, then you can whistle for it."

Reed did not want a full-fledged debate with this man in the reception area of his office. "We can work all that out later, Mr. Puccinelli. For now, please leave once your file is ready, without further disturbing my patients." To discourage a response, Reed moved quickly away as he completed his last remark. He didn't hear one as he walked away.

He walked back into Sheila Watanabe's examination room. She seemed comfortable. He removed the ice packs. "You up to the rollers?"

"On a gentle setting, they would be great."

Reed smiled.

Sheila Watanabe got off the examining table and moved to the intersegmental traction table.

Reed got the table started.

He walked back into his office. His face tensed as he noticed his appointment book had been disturbed. What else had Puccinelli looked through? He noticed a few piles of papers had shifted position. Some bills for him to sign, and some insurance company claim rejection forms, were among the piles disturbed. He grunted as he noticed the Susan Stafford file had shifted position. It was no longer with his appointment book—it was exposed on his desk, on top of papers on the opposite side. He doubted Jimmy Puccinelli had any idea of the significance of the file, but Reed's nostrils flared with anger at the idea of this invasion of his privacy.

He sat down, leaned back, and shut his eyes. This brief incident would not mar the triumphs of his day.

"I want you to meet someone," Eldon Stafford said to Clyde Minden as they pulled in front of a large two-story home, fronted by a perfectly trimmed green lawn north of Brea in La Habra Heights. There was a "For Sale By Owner" sign in front of the house.

"I thought we were going to meet Brianna for lunch."

"We will."

Minden frowned.

"I just want you to meet one of Randolph Collier's patients." Stafford opened the driver's door of his car and stepped out.

"Wait a minute." Minden stayed in the passenger seat. "Is this the five-surgery guy Brianna keeps talking about?"

Stafford bent down and looked back into the car. "Yeah."

"I don't want to impose on the guy."

"He's okay with it," Stafford assured him. "He's expecting us."

"I don't know."

Stafford tipped his head up. "Come on. It'll be a quick visit."

Minden's lips tensed. He pushed a burst of air through his nose.

He took off the lap and shoulder belt and grimaced as he got out of the car.

"He won't be up to a long visit," Stafford added.

Clyde Minden took in a nervous breath and shook his head, but joined Eldon Stafford as they walked up a bush-lined walkway to the front door of the house.

Eldon Stafford rang the doorbell.

Clyde Minden took in another long deep breath. He fidgeted.

A pretty, thin, middle-aged woman, wearing a sweatsuit and no make-up, answered the door. "Doctor," she greeted. "A house call?"

"A visit," Stafford answered. "How are you?"

"I'm doing the best I can, under the circumstances."

"Good. Can you let him know we're here?"

"Yeah." She clipped her response with a tone of not wanting to say much, or let her emotions slip out through her words.

"This way. He's in... he's in our bedroom."

Chapter 22

"Hey doctor," said the patient from Room 507, who Dr. Stafford now knew as Victor Amistero, lying in a hospital bed. The man had a little more color in his face, and seemed to have gained some weight. But he still looked older than his age. Amistero looked at Minden. "You're the next victim?"

Minden grunted. "Sorry. This wasn't my idea to come here."

"Of course not." Amistero's jaw pushed forward. "It wouldn't have been my idea either, before my first surgery. I wouldn't have wanted to see the worst-case scenario."

Minden's face had a look of nausea and puzzlement combined. "What?"

"I know it wasn't your idea for you to come here. It was my idea. After Dr. Stafford mentioned your situation to me, it was my idea. Nothing like seeing, as a prelude to believing."

Stafford remained quiet. The awkwardness was serving his purpose.

"This probably isn't the best time to see you," Minden said. "I mean, Dr. Collier told me says rehab puts people out of commission for awhile, even for a first surgery. I imagine that after five-"

Amistero looked at Stafford. "You didn't tell him."

Stafford shook his head.

"Young man, I had what they call a 'bad result.'"

Minden filled the awkward silence with the question he seemed hesitant to ask. "What happened?"

"The pain's gone below the waist. Totally gone." He paused. "I'm paralyzed."

Minden's eyes widened.

"From the waist down."

Stafford turned and saw that Amistero's wife had quietly slipped into the room.

"Can you get him to at least try to use the wheelchair?" she asked Stafford.

"What the hell difference does it make?" Amistero grumbled. "The pain is still throbbing away above the waist. I'm useless. I'm through. God Damn Dr. Stafford here doesn't know any Kevorkian wannabes or I would have checked out for good by now."

"That's stupid," Amistero's wife said. "You may just need some therapy. You may be able to come back from it."

"What happened, I mean, what went wrong?" Minden asked.

"They don't know," Amistero said through clenched teeth. "They just kept carving on me, telling me with certainty that they knew they needed to keep carving on me. But now? They don't know."

"I agree with Galen Reed on this," Stafford said. "It could be scar tissue, or shock to the cord. And it could reverse. They can't find evidence of any permanent damage. But yeah, no one's sure."

Amistero nodded smugly. "So, you still don't like my description for you—'next victim?'"

"I'm sorry." Minden looked at Eldon Stafford with a desperate look on his face. "I'm sorry we bothered you. It wasn't my idea."

"We've established that," Amistero said.

"I'm sending Galen Reed over," Stafford said to Amistero. "Don't give up. We will find a way to help you."

Amitero shrugged. "Sure."

Stafford looked at Minden. "Okay. Let's go." He looked at Amistero. "I'll check back with you."

Amistero's eyes watered. "Thank you."

As he walked out, Stafford took Amistero's wife by the hands. Tears rolled down her cheeks. "Keep encouraging him. Galen Reed is the guy to help, if anyone can. And he will, under no circumstances, be talking about another surgery."

Amistero's wife nodded as tears rolled down her cheeks.

"It's been a success," Reed said to Stafford as they sat together in Reed's office after Reed's last appointment of the day. "I've been phenomenally busy, and we're helping a lot of people."

Stafford shrugged as he raised his eyebrows. "I have to agree with you, from a patient perspective. But there are some other problems."

"Not patient-related."

"Not directly. I'm facing some major trouble at the hospital."

"You mean Middleton? He's actually dialed it back since-"

"Not Dr. Middleton. The insurance companies. They're not paying on almost every one of the chiropractic charges."

"They're not used to chiropractors in the emergency room."

"They should be. It's been done before. There are hospitals that have chiropractic departments. It's as if this particular hospital has been singled out for denials for chiropractic care."

"So let's contact those other hospitals to see how they bill it."

"I've got Delores on it. She'll help us bill it better."

"Delores?"

"Delores Hart. She's been with my office forever. She started out with me years ago just to pick up some part-time money. Her husband, the record producer, did reasonably well with some artsy-type rock in the early 1970s. She'd bring some of it in—I can't say I understood it. But I did understand enough about what was going on in music to watch disco and punk squeeze the guy out. Delores went to being their full-time breadwinner. Then the marriage went south— she's been with me ever since. She's definitely behind what we're doing, and she's great with billing."

"You're going to have her work with the hospital?"

"I've got to. We've got to do something about this problem. The business office didn't care about bringing chiropractors into the emergency room. They got a little huffy about the aroma therapy and some of the new décor. But we got some nice press in the local papers, so they stayed quiet."

"I saw that." Reed grinned.

"Yeah. But now that we're not getting compensated for the chiropractic services, but still paying them for their shifts, the hospital is losing money. So they're down on that, and they're starting to breathe down my neck. About everything. About the stuff we brought in to tone down the atmosphere."

Reed frowned. "These are legitimate charges."

"Of course. They're more than 'legitimate.' The care you and your colleagues are giving is simply good medicine. It's better medicine than some of the stuff the insurance companies pay without a whisper."

Reed nodded. "Thank you for that."

"You don't have to thank me. I can see it. You know, I used to hear about this all the time from some of my more reflective colleagues. I admit, I kind of brushed it off with 'so-what.' But they would say 'we don't get paid for the best care. We get paid for procedures, for tests, for marked-up drugs.' I admit now, that's part of what has to change."

"Absolutely. Can the hospital get some lawyers working on this, to hammer the insurance companies? Does the hospital have someone good?"

"I talked to a guy who I think is their best. He says we could try it in court. The insurance industry is not exactly well-loved. But he pointed out that these policies have been written with pages of fine print devised by lawyers who are expert in this area of the law. They hire anal poindexters to implement the lines of fine print, under layers of supervision from more poindexters. They could have their bases covered with some line forty-seven of page three-oh-six, and we might spend all kinds of time and money and lose."

Reed let out a deep breath. "I'm having the same problem in my office. I'm helping cancer patients face chemo, and getting MS patients off of anti-inflammatories. What I am doing will lower the insurance company's drug costs, and could reduce the chemo period by strengthening the patient, but they won't pay me a dime. Not compensible chiropractic care, they say. Or we're getting cut to manipulations only, which they give a pittance for. I have to admit—I'd been trying not to—my cash flow may be headed for a crisis."

"I'll send over Delores Hart to help you too."

"I've got good billing people too. I should sit down with them."

Stafford nodded. "I'm sure your people are good, and I'll make sure Delores knows not to step on anyone's toes. But she's got two things going for her. She's been in this for many years, so she knows a lot of people, and a lot of angles. And, the insurance companies are still backward about chiropractic care. She'll flash my name around. I think it could help."

Now Reed nodded. "I've known for a long time that MDs and chiropractors are not on an even playing field when it comes to insurance company compensation. An x-ray for me comes back at less money than the exact same x-ray for a back surgeon." He shook his head. "It's never been about the money for me. I hate to make this about money. And I hate that doing good for these patients isn't enough. But we've got to make a living."

"Of course."

Reed shook his head as he picked up a file. "I may never collect on this one, and it's one we usually get paid on."

"Back injury?"

"Auto accident. You remember the guy—he hung out in our waiting room the first day?"

"Him?"

"I caught him snooping around my office. I threw him out and told him to find another doctor."

"What was he doing in your office?"

"Looking for his file. He knows that whatever I put in there is not getting him what he wants. I think his attorney is souring on his case. But his objective findings don't support his complaints, and I won't ignore the discrepancies and say he was hurt in the accident."

"He got care?"

"I improved the health of his spine."

Stafford tightened his lips in apparent contemplation. "Let's see what Delores can do with it. You said the guy has an attorney?"

"Yes. But the kind of case an attorney might decide is a waste of time."

"Well, there'll be a collectable lien. She's pretty good with that stuff."

"Okay, sure. Put your billing guru on this. But it's scrounging for nickels and dimes when we need an answer for dollars."

"I know." Stafford paused. "I didn't want to say too much. But I have an angle on a huge development in all of this, on the financial front. I'll let you know."

Reed's eyes narrowed. "You should bring me in on this. Remember when we first started, you laid it out before we had much of a chance to go over it. That led to problems. We should try-"

"You are absolutely right." Stafford's jaw thrust forward. "I almost did it again." He shook his head, then locked eyes with Reed. "You free tonight?"

"The Grill?"

"No. My office. Where my notes are."

"You're on."

Stafford paused a moment. "I know why I held this close. I want to keep this idea confidential. I definitely don't want it leaking out prematurely into the health care community. I think you'll see why. But, you should be part of it."

"Good."

Stafford stood up. "Let's get some takeout—there's a great, healthy Chinese place just up the block from my office."

"My treat."

Stafford grinned. "Let me treat. Until we get this billing situation resolved."

Reed returned the grin. "Okay."

"I heard a crazy story," Natalie Corey said as she stood in the doorway of Galen Reed's office.

Galen Reed looked up from the file he was working on. He was holding a pen, completing some notes on the patient he'd just finished with. "I see my staff just lets anyone walk around the place," he said grinning. "People who pass on crazy stories—anyone."

"I called ahead. They said you'd seen your last one before lunch. I figured I could catch you."

"I'm glad you did."

"I was telling you, I heard a crazy story about some chiropractor over at the emergency room who cured a boy with seizures."

Galen Reed dropped his pen. "I'm not sure about cured. But he's doing real well under the treatment regimen."

Natalie Corey's eyes filled with tears. "I swore I wouldn't fall apart."

Galen Reed stood and walked to her.

She turned.

He tried to hug her.

"I feel so bad," she said. She would not reciprocate his hug.

"It's okay." He kept his arms around her.

She turned back and put both of her arms around him. "I'm so sorry. I shouldn't have bailed out on you."

He squeezed her. "It's okay."

"It isn't. It really isn't."

He didn't say anything.

"I've been hearing about you, what you've been doing." She looked at him, tears on her face. "I've been so proud."

He gave her a quick kiss.

"I should have been here with you all the way."

"Don't worry. You're here now."

She broke their embrace and backed up a step. "Stop being so reasonable. I don't deserve it."

"You want me to be angry."

She frowned.

"You'll be angry with me if I'm not angry."

She turned. "You must be mad at me. I can't believe you're not."

He put his arms around her from behind. "To be honest, I haven't had time to be mad. Maybe if I'd had the time, I would be. But I've been so busy…"

"So you just didn't have time to think about me."

"Um, I did think about you-"

"It's okay." She turned and smiled. "I actually believe that explanation for why you're not mad at me."

He kissed her again, then embraced. He wasn't going to debate what seemed to him to be some tortured logic. She was back, supporting him. And as he held her tight, he realized he missed her.

"I actually heard from two emergency room nurses about you," she said. "They say Larry Middleton has even pulled back his hostility."

"Yeah." Reed's lips tightened.

"You're doing it, Galen. You and Dr. Stafford. You're making it happen."

He nodded his head. "Not without some difficulty. We may be having some success bringing chiropractic healing into the M-D world. But we're having trouble getting paid for it."

She had a look of realization on her face. "The insurance companies."

"Yeah. They're mostly not paying. When they do pay, they don't pay enough. The hospital's starting to put the heat on Eldon and my office is bleeding money."

"Eldon?" She smirked.

Galen Reed shrugged.

"First name basis." She nodded. "Well, you've been trying to get to this for almost ten years."

"On and off, you could say that."

They released their embrace.

"You know the old saying—'be careful what you wish for.'"

She looked at him. "Come over to my place tonight. Tell me about it."

His eyes narrowed.

"The boys are with their father over in Nevada at his parents' home."

Galen Reed nodded. He looked down at the files and forms on his desk. "I was going to work through lunch, but all of this can wait. Let me just get this a little organized for later today." He went over to his desk.

Natalie Corey stood in the doorway, wearing a relaxed smile, with an apparent willingness to wait as long as he needed her to.

"It's been exhausting," he commented as he tidied his desk. "We're doing so much good." He shook his head. "But we're grappling with a system that just doesn't want to reward us. A system that has little boxes for everything to fit into, and no room for any alternative way of looking at things. Little bureaucrats who sit at their desks in their cubicles and make their little decisions based on their little guidelines. Fighting for Eldon's attention was challenging. Fighting this mono-lithic system made up of tangled webs of little rules administered by little people—I'm wondering if it is possible to clear even a little of it away. I'd say we need an Alexander to cut this Gordian knot, but if he showed up, some little bureaucrat would probably tell him it's against the rules to use swords."

She looked at him with an expression of gentle affection. "You've done so much. You've come so close. You really do sound tired."

Galen Reed stopped straightening his desk. "You know, this is what I have missed about you. Without you in my life, I simply work all the time. I love the work. Well, not this bureaucratic crap. But the patients, the healing, watching people improve their conditions—I love it. And I'll do it non-stop. But, it is exhausting. And spending time with you forces me to come out of it for awhile—to rest."

She smiled. "It's not the most romantic thing I've ever heard, but I'll take it."

They walked out of his office.

"What does the great Eldon Stafford say about the money?" she asked.

"He actually came to me about the problem. And he's got a

big-time solution to it."

"Really..."

They moved toward the front of the office.

"We sat down at his home almost all day last Sunday. We put together a huge presentation for some money people he knows. He thinks he can address the problem in a big way."

"But you're not sure."

They reached the front door and walked through. Galen Reed drew in a deep breath. "He doesn't want me along because he's afraid of how these money people will react to a chiropractor. Just when I think we've come a long way, something happens and I feel like I'm back to square one."

They walked toward Galen Reed's car. "You've come a long way from square one," Natalie Corey told him. "With everyone else around you full of doubts, you kept after this until it became real. Square one? You're on the verge of something phenomenal."

Galen Reed's face eeked out a weary smile.

"You come home with me tonight, after the end of your afternoon patients. I'll allow you to talk just a little more about all this. Then, you relax. Rest. You'll come back renewed and ready to go. You'll look out with your rested eyes and see that 'square one' is a long way behind you."

He nodded. "Thanks."

They arrived at Galen Reed's car and got in.

"The money will sink them," Seymour McTavish told Wyatt Greevey. They sat in Greevey's office; McTavish relaxed in a padded chair, Greevey hovering over his computer terminal.

"The money." Greevey nodded, then smiled. "Good. Yes. Good. Because I heard they were doing well."

"A few parlor tricks, maybe some feel-good hocus-pocus to make a few people feel better. But denial notices are piling up because insurance companies don't pay for magic tricks, and it's got to be crunching their cash situation."

Greevey flashed a sly smile. "I'm on the board over at Health Solutions Insurance. And I've got connections with some of the others. A few phone calls, to express concerns"—he shrugged as he smirked—"it seems to have filtered down to the claims examiners."

"It seems that they're pumped up about the results, but worried about the money."

"So they'll fold, but maybe not yet."

"That's what it looks like."

"I mean, if they're not making money, they'll have to fold."

McTavish frowned, his eyes narrowing as he thought. "My source did say that Stafford may be working on some financial angle, some plan to get money into this operation."

"Some plan."

"Right."

"What is it?"

"I don't know the details. My source doesn't know. Maybe loans."

Greevey scowled. "Or investors."

McTavish didn't say anything.

"Find out."

McTavish nodded.

"I mean beat the bushes."

"Okay."

"How good is this source?"

McTavish paused. "Maybe less enthusiastic. Less proximity, at least when we last spoke."

"What can you do to address this problem with the source?"

"Sometimes if a person's already in, it's hard to back out."

"I see. Is Plan B still available?"

"Yes. Pretty much all laid in. All I have to do his give the word. But there may be another way to sabotage the relationship between Reed and Stafford. We're going to try that first."

"Why that first?"

"It's less drastic, less risky."

Greevey nodded.

"I'll keep you current on this, without any superfluous details."

"Yeah." Greevey squinted. "I"m not sure I like that."

"Believe me, sir, you do."

Greevey nodded, but his neutral expression conveyed acknowledgement, not agreement.

Chapter 23

"They told me you're about to leave town," Randolph Collier said as he entered Eldon Stafford's small office at Orange County Memorial Hospital. Collier was a tall, gaunt man, with a small head and small hands.

Eldon Stafford looked up from his desk. He was standing over it, gathering some computer generated papers he had been sorting. "I am. Brianna, um, my daughter—she's due here any minute to take me to the airport."

"Well then I'll get right to the point. We have some issues, you and I."

Talking vaguely about "some issues" did not impress Eldon Stafford as much "getting to the point," and he was pressed for time. But he maintained a steady tone. "What's on your mind?"

"A patient of mine. Clyde Minden."

Stafford nodded. "My daughter's boyfriend."

"My patient who has postponed his surgery twice on your rec-ommendation. This is very unprofessional. I don't tamper with your patients."

"It's not tampering. I spoke to him as a friend, not as a doctor competing for a patient."

"But you did compete for him as a patient. He ended up over with that Galen Reed character, whom I understand has some sort of part-nership with you."

"My daughter pushed it as well. She may have had more influence than-"

"What influenced him was the MRI you ordered. An MRI that-"

"I didn't 'order'-"

Collier raised his voice as he continued his statement. "An unncessary MRI, just months after his last one, showing some trivial minimizing of the herniation that got this patient worked up enough to drop his scheduled surgery—a surgery he finally committed to three days before the date-set, and then cancelled the night before! This is thousands of dollars for me—lost! Thousands of dollars I don't have for my malpractice premium, for my office overhead."

Stafford tensed his lips as he waited for just a moment of silence to creep in, hoping Collier had talked himself out, at least for the moment. "First of all, I didn't 'order' the MRI. I made it available to Clyde, the patient, and one of his health-care providers, Dr. Galen Reed. We now allow D-Cs access to these tests."

"Dr. Reed?" Collier chuckled a belittling tone. "Doctor? A chiropractor? You should know it's nothing but a flaky medical cult of sorts, with a tradition going back, what, just a hundred years? To some farmer in the Midwest?"

"Actually, I've been learning quite a lot about this. This type of healing goes back much-"

"I don't want some bullshit history lesson. You've obviously been taken in. But I'm telling you to leave my patients alone. Or I will raise hell."

"I've done nothing wrong."

Brianna Stafford walked through the doorway of his office.

"Nothing wrong? Are you kidding me?"

"One other thing, Dr. Collier. I hear a lot of talk from you about your malpractice premium, and your office overhead, and your lost cash. I didn't hear one sentence, not a phrase, not a word about the welfare of that patient you accuse me of 'tampering' with. Just what are your priorities, sir?"

Collier's face flushed. His eyes radiated a steely glare. "You got your lumps coming to you. There's been a lot of talk about you, about all the crap you've been involved with lately. You've got your lumps coming to you, that's for sure."

"Yeah? Maybe. But you're going to spin that MRI result and call it 'trivial?' That's how badly you want to cut into this guy's back?"

Collier's nostrils flared. He took a step toward Stafford. "Now you listen to me." He pointed his finger, stabbing it in the air for effect. "Stop messing with my patients. Stop screwing up the hospital. Or we will do what has to be done—we'll stuff your license down your throat—whether it makes you look bad or not, whether you ever practice medicine again or not." Collier stormed out of the office.

Brianna looked at her father. "Another happy colleague?"

"Yeah. Clyde's doctor. From the Lawrence Middleton school of tolerance for new ideas."

"Well I'm glad Clyde finally saw this the right way. I just hope Galen is able to keep helping him."

"I see no reason why not."

"Isn't there a money problem?" she asked. "Isn't that why you're going on this trip?"

"Sure is." Eldon Stafford gathered up some papers and started placing them neatly in his briefcase.

"Is it a bank loan?"

"Not exactly?"

"I mean, there are banks down here."

"True." Eldon shut his briefcase. He looked over to a corner of his office next to the door where a packed garment bag lay. He moved to the bag and snatched it up in his other hand.

"Can I help carry anything?" Brianna Stafford asked.

"Got it all," he said.

She smiled. "You seem so much stronger, so much more energetic."

"You're not the only one who has benefited from the care of Galen Reed." He walked through the doorway.

Brianna Stafford followed.

"There's no doubt he pointed me toward some lifestyle changes

I should have made on my own," he said as they walked together through the halls toward the hospital exit. "But I cannot dismiss my healthier back as a real part of this as well."

"He has been a good thing in our lives."

"Yes, he has."

"So, this money thing in the Bay Area. You have to go up there? They don't have a branch down here?"

"I told you, it's not a bank. It's-" Stafford looked around. He spoke in a hushed tone. "There are people around here with big ears who are not rooting for me on this." He looked forward as they kept walking. "But I think we're okay talking about this here in the hall." He thought of how to explain his planned activities to his daughter. "When you're a doctor, especially a prosperous one, like I have been, you get on lists, the lists potential investors enterpreneurs come to. These investors don't dabble in neighborhood restaurants, or condo conversion projects. They do the big stuff. Like the time they came to me for start-up money for some crazy search engine, named after a weird-sounding very large number. It sounded like a loser to me, another dot-com disaster. After all, from what little I knew about it, Yahoo had cornered the market on search engines, right?"

"Yahoo isn't even a search engine, Dad. It's a directory."

"Yeah, um, I understand that now."

"You're telling me you could have been at the start of Google?"

"Yup. Could have had some of those Google dot-com millions. I did end up getting in on a less glamorous start-up, for an on-line dating service for over-fifties folks. That paid for a lot of your college."

"Instead of just buying a college for me, if you'd been in on Google."

"Yeah, I guess. You would have wanted me to buy you a college?"

"No. I just... can't believe it. Google."

They reached the exit from the hospital and walked toward the parking lot.

"You took my spot, right?"

She laughed. "I did. You should see the looks I got."

"From someone who doesn't know you're my daughter."

"Probably."

They walked toward Eldon Stafford's reserved parking place.

"So Daddy, you're going to invest in some internet company, or something, to get enough money to pay for your clinic with Dr. Reed?"

"No-no-no," he said. "No, this time, I'm the guy with the idea. A new way to handle health care. A new kind of insurance."

Brianna Stafford's eyes widened. "Wow. With all the health insurance turmoil going on right now?"

"Yes. If not now, when? Galen and I worked out quite a presentation. I'll either dazzle them—or baffle them."

"Do you want to try it out on me?"

Eldon Stafford smiled. "On the way to the airport, I'll explain some of the ideas. It'll be good practice."

She smiled back. "Okay."

They arrived at his car.

"I'm looking for Delores Hart?" Jimmy Puccinelli said as he approached the front desk of the reception area in Galen Reed's office.

"That's me," Delores Hart greeted, smiling. She looked up from a stack of bills and reports she was reviewing at a card table temporarily placed to the right of the receptionist's station. Delores Hart sat in an office chair on rollers at the card table.

"Uh, Delores? Can I talk to you a minute?" Rosie Jacinto, the receptionist at Galen Reed's office, wore a concerned expression. She was a young thin girl, usually perky, dressed almost too high-fashion for a doctor's office.

"Sure." Delores Hart shrugged. "Just a minute," she called out politely to Jimmy Puccinelli.

Rosie Jacinto scrutinized Jimmy Puccinelli, as if to establish exactly where he was before she turned to speak quietly to Delores Hart. "What is he doing here?"

"I've got some paperwork here that'll help us clear his bill and get it paid."

"I don't think Dr. Reed wants him here. Did you know he snuck into Dr. Reed's office and went through his stuff?"

"He told me," Delores Hart said. "He was trying to look at his file. He shouldn't have done it—that's for sure—but he's not going back in that area. And he's anxious to get his claim moving, which will get us paid. He wanted to come by and pick up the bill, which I reformatted in a way that'll allow us to collect it. He and I spoke over the phone. We have an arrangement, um, an understanding. Don't worry. He'll be in and out of here."

"Oh. Okay." Rosie Jacinto turned back to her desk.

Jimmy Puccinelli focused intent eyes on the two women.

Delores Hart stood. "Mr. Puccinelli, I'm going to print the bills. I'll be right back." She walked to the back of the reception area. She refreshed a computer terminal, hit a few keystrokes and pushed the mouse to the print selection where she clicked it.

"Brianna," she heard Rosie Jacinto say.

Delores Hart looked up from the terminal. She walked to the front of the reception area. "Thanks for coming on such short notice. Hang on just a second."

"I came right over," Brianna Stafford said, with an urgency in her voice. "What's so important?"

"Just… wait a second." Delores Hart took the print, picked up a manila envelope, then handed it to Jimmy Puccinelli. "Take this to your attorney. This should get everything resolved."

"I need to see it," he said.

Delores Hart nodded. "Sure." She looked at Rosie Jacinto. "Is there a room Brianna and I could use?"

"A room…" Rosie Jacinto seemed puzzled.

"I need to talk to her, um, not in the middle of the waiting room."

"Oh." She frowned in thought. "There's a small spare office in the back."

"I know where it is." Brianna Stafford held a grim expression as she walked toward the extra office.

Delores Hart took the papers out of their manila envelope for Jimmy Puccinelli. "No reason why you shouldn't see your records."

Puccinelli nodded. "Yeah." He looked around. "See how agreeable I can be when people are reasonable."

Delores Hart shrugged and smiled.

"Brianna," Galen Reed greeted with a broad smile as he walked from his office toward an examining room. "I just saw you, didn't I? You're on maintenance now, once a month. Are you okay?"

"I'm fine," she said. "Delores wanted to see me."

"Delores." Galen Reed raised his eyebrows with puzzlement. "Your dad's key office lady. Hmmm. Husband was a rock music producer."

"That was a long time ago."

"I know. She's here helping us out with the billing."

"She called, said she wanted to see me right away."

Galen Reed shrugged. "Okay."

"My father's up there for the big meeting."

"Yup." Galen Reed flashed another broad smile. "I cannot tell you how excited I am." He shook his head. "Segueway Capital. The big leagues. Your dad and I have a chance to make a big difference, to work wonders for people all over the country, maybe all over the world."

"All from just stumbling into taking care of little old me and my asthma."

"Right." Reed forced a chuckle. "Amazing. Fate, the way it works out."

"It is amazing."

"Natalie and I were just talking about this last night, what the potential is."

"The vitamin lady."

"Right." He shook his head with a smile. "When Natural Healing Remedies wanted to expand, to take the company public, they tried to approach Segueway. They couldn't even get a meeting. Natalie helped me realize how big this is!"

"I've rarely seen my dad nervous. He is nervous about this."

"Understandable."

Delores Hart approached.

Galen Reed looked up toward the front as Jimmy Puccinelli walked out of the reception area, leaving the office. "What was he doing here?"

"Um, he was just here to pick up paperwork," Delores Hart answered. "I listened to him vent a little bit. That calmed him down. I didn't let him near your office."

"Obviously."

"He heard you in the hall and high-tailed it."

"Good." Galen Reed motioned toward his office. "I told Brianna you two could use my office for whatever it is you need to discuss."

"Oh." Delores Hart seemed startled by the offer. "Oh, sure. Um, thanks." She carried a blank file jacket that had another file jacket inside of it."

"No problem." Galen Reed went toward an examining room to see his next patient.

Delores Hart looked around apprehensively. "This could get weird."

"What?"

"Let's go in his office."

The two women stepped into Galen Reed's office.

Delores Hart pulled the door to the point where the door was almost shut except for a crack. "Jimmy Puccinelli tipped me off on this," she said in a hushed tone. "That's why I had him come in here. He's a slimy guy, but I felt I should follow-up. He said he saw something, a file, in Galen Reed's office. About your mother."

"My mother..." Brianna Reed frowned. "You mean me, or my father."

"No." Delores Hart pulled the Susan Stafford file out of the blank file jacket she had been carrying it in. She looked around warily. "I found it. There is an old file. About your mother."

Brianna Stafford took the file. She opened it. Right on top were newspaper articles about her mother's death. Further down in the file, she saw treatment notes, and forms detailing her medical history. One note that seemed to blare out at her was scrawled at the top of the initial patient form: "Referred by Natalie. Husband is Eldon Stafford. Daughter-asthma."

Delores Hart looked toward the door. "I feel almost like part of the family—I couldn't just keep this to myself."

"I know you were there for my father when my mother died so suddenly."

"Well, your father was there for all my problems." She took in a deep breath. "I'd like to think he related to the more adventurous side of my youth. I know he went to Berkeley, but stayed with the books. Me? I was a little farm girl from out north of Bakersfield. I was goody-goody enough to get into UCLA. But my parents had no idea what they were sending me into. L-A was so cool. The L-A scene was so much more interesting than studying! I did all of it. Drugs, music, parties." She smirked. "Guys. One of the guys became my husband—a record producer. He had groups with music all over FM radio. But he was also more into the scene than working. When music changed, and he couldn't, I had to work for a living. Your father—he was a gem of an employer." She seemed to choke on emotion. "I felt a close-ness-" Her face contorted to a grimace as she looked like she was trying to contain her emotions. "Sorry. I'm-" She flared her nostrils and seemed to deliberately force her face into a tough expression.

"It's okay," Brianna Stafford said. "I know how much you mean to us, and I appreciate how much my father means to you."

"Yes, well, I'm getting carried away." Delores Hart's emotions appeared to be contained. "A lot on my mind, I guess." She blasted some air out of her nose. "But I do feel like a family member, even though I am just a long-time employee." Her eyes hardened. "I thought you should see this."

Brianna thumbed through the file again. "This is creepy," Brianna said. "Really creepy."

"Your father wanted me to help out here. I know he believes in this man. But I thought you should see this. I would've contacted your father, but he's already gone."

"Yeah. To pitch an idea he has with a person who has some kind of creepy obsession with us."

"Try to call your dad before the meeting."

Brianna Stafford pulled out her cell phone. She put it on speaker. She pressed her father's contact selection.

The line rang, but before one ring even finished, voicemail answered: "This is Eldon Stafford's cell phone. I am unavailable-"

Brianna cut the connection. "I don't know what to do. I don't want to confront Dr. Reed right now, not in his office with all these people here. I don't know—I need to think about this." Brianna held the file as she walked out of Galen Reed's office and headed through the hall of the office toward the front.

Delores followed.

"I'll keep trying to call my dad," Brianna said, walking as if in a daze, in shock.

"Okay, dear. Sorry. I thought you should know."

"I needed to know. We need to know what it means." Brianna swallowed, but a few tears came into her eyes, then rolled down her cheeks. "I might have convinced my dad"—she took a couple of shallow breaths—"to get involved with something really strange. I thought I was so brilliant on this—the brilliant daughter who was going to show her father something about health care."

"I'm sure it'll be okay."

"He's almost ready to talk to those money guys."

"You can keep trying him."

"I will. After I get out of here." Brianna held the Susan Stafford file as she moved briskly through the front area of the office out the door.

Chapter 24

"I beat the bushes, boss," Seymour McTavish said to Wyatt Geevey. "Segueway Capital. Stafford has a big meeting with Segueway Capital. It may have already happened, or it's going to happen, real soon. Segueway. What a weird name for-"

"I know these guys." Wyatt Greevey tensed. His teeth clenched. He let out a nervous breath. "I know one of the main guys, Horace Wright—I know him real well. Another guy, Ben Richards. He used to be a big investor in Havitol."

"So it's not some flaky debating society."

"Hardly. That's why I'm telling you not to take the name lightly. Segueway. Transition. Like from one stage, one reality, to another. They deal with big stuff. High-concept. World-changing."

"So what is Stafford going to do with them?"

Wyatt Greevey squinted. "I don't know." He paused. "And I want to know."

McTavish nodded.

Greevey grunted. "Everybody likes to bad-mouth the health care system. Congress just threw a big monkey wrench at us, even though we had some influence, a little seat at the table." He exhaled. "But people live longer than ever. Now some guy is going to get a big bug up his butt and try to monkey with the system." Greevey shook his head. "A lot of people have worked very hard to get this thing the way it is, to bring care to people, and the drugs they all need. We don't need some new flaky scheme messing it all up, especially with this new government stuff we have to deal with."

"I'll find out what I can about this. But if it is a flaky scheme, won't it just fail?"

"Sure. But parts of it may catch on just long enough to dupe people into changing how they deal with their health. Then all the assumptions we made, the payoffs we've been expecting, that we've been counting on, will be screwed up. Investors will lose their money. Stocks will go down. And by the time the mistakes are discovered, it'll be a big mess, tough to clean-up, too late to clean-up for some of us, who will be ruined."

"But won't the marketplace just kick the scheme right out before it takes hold?"

"Not if it's a nihilistic scheme, designed to toss it all out—that will mess everything up."

"How do we know that's what Stafford's doing?"

"He's got chiropractors in the emergency room. He's calling drugs 'crap.' Believe me, this will be an assault on the system, on the status quo, on us."

"Well, you get the big bucks for knowing the big picture. Let me know what you need."

"I will. But I think the next move's up to me. Ben's the guy for me to call, not Horace. Ben'll understand the stakes, or at least be in a position to put the brakes on this thing."

Greevey picked up the phone and selected the intercom. "Get me Ben Richards. Look under Segueway Capital. Call his cell if he doesn't answer at the office."

"Good afternoon, Doctor Stafford," said Ben Richards as he motioned to a plush chair at a long wooden table. Stafford wore a blue three-piece suit with a light blue shirt and simple blue and red tie. The chair was across from a man and a woman at one end of the table. Ben Richards, a white-haired man, obviously long in years, with the gravelly voice of a man who had used that voice authoritatively for many of those years, wore a sports jacket, slacks, an open, white silk shirt and sat at the head of the table just to Eldon Stafford's right. "May I introduce Fiona Patton." Richards gestured toward the woman at the table. "Dr. Patton is a computer scientist by training. She wrote code for some of the earlier video games and was smart enough to take stock as compensation in the two companies she worked for. She then started her own company, and successfully took it public. She has a great mind for starting new businesses and for cutting edge ideas."

"A pleasure," Eldon Stafford said to her.

Fiona Patton nodded, showing a slight but welcoming smile. She wore her short brown hair straight, chopped off at her shoulders, with a brown tailored woman's business suit and an off-white shirt.

Ben Richards continued. "You know Seth Mercoyan, who brought you to our attention. He is in real estate, but had the foresight to get into both Google and eBay at the ground floor."

Eldon Stafford smiled. "Yes, he loves to remind me about Google." He looked at Mercoyan, a thin man, with black and gray hair, wearing an immaculate Italian gray suit, and orange shirt, and a silk orange and black tie with an intricate pattern.

"To be honest, I missed that one too," Ben Richards admitted.

"Yeah. Ben is not a lover of dot-com," Seth Mercoyan said. "Don't kid yourself. He's been investing in some of the best-known companies in the world for many years. Including health care."

"Health care?" Eldon Stafford asked. He felt a twinge of concern. Would this man want to hear about new ideas if he had a big stake, or big connections, in the established system?

"Well, I don't have any money in that area right now," Richards said. "I think the whole industry may be headed for big trouble. I got out of the drug companies, health insurance, and hospital-clinic interests because I'm pretty sure a calamity is coming—either the industries themselves are going to fail, and-or the government's new meddling is going to really screw it up, more than they already have. Drove me nuts to hear idiots say 'we need to get government involved.' Government was already involved with health care. Big-time. Heavily tangled up in it. Insured everyone over sixty-five, and all the poor with Medicaid. And there are regulations in every state. Jesus. You know, in Vermont, government jumped in with all these regs on how they were going to get quality healthcare to everyone by requiring this thing and that thing. They made it so expensive that the percentage of uninsured, one of the best in the country, doubled from seven to fourteen! Idiots. And they cry about the so-called uninsured. Some of those people choose to be uninsured! Young single people. Before we jumped off the cliff into more government meddling, we should have looked at the real number to know, the number of involuntarily uninsured."

Richards stopped speaking and looked around the table. No one seemed to be speaking.

Stafford didn't offer any comment. His proposal wasn't going to get into government involvement with healthcare. But he wasn't completely against the government taking over healthcare. He wondered if people wouldn't be better off with a government system than with a system run by big business for a profit.

A slight grin appeared on Richards' face. "I know. The old guy's back on the soapbox again. This is your meeting. I'll just say that I'm out of healthcare to avoid the mess. A lot of investors feel the same way. But a new idea? I love new ideas. I'd like to know what it is. I know how the system works now, and what a mess we might be headed for. But mess is an opportunity for good ideas. I'd like a good idea of what we might do to clean it up. Who knows—maybe I'll wade back in."

"Sounds good," Stafford said. "I'll try to give you a reason to 'wade back in.'"

Richards nodded as he shrugged. "Let me explain how this will work," Richards said to Stafford. "This is a screening committee. Segueway sets these up in threes. The initial idea—the industry, the product area—has to interest all three of us to get it to a meeting with a screening committee. Seth here found the two of us. He speaks highly of you. Getting to a Segueway screening trio is not easy for an outsider."

"I know," Stafford said. "I am grateful to all of you for the opportunity."

"Well, we do not grant these meetings easily." Richards seemed to be growling. "We are not looking for people to be grateful to us. We are looking for great ideas, high-concept innovations, that we can invest in, that will cause us to be grateful to you."

Stafford nodded. "Yes, of course."

"We will listen to your idea. We will ask whatever questions we believe we need answered to study your idea. We will ask blunt questions. We will make blunt statements."

"Good. I welcome the scrutiny."

"After we have completed our time with you, we will decide if we want to go forward to study this in depth and present it to the entire Segueway group. The decision to go forward must be unanimous for the three of us. To avoid impulsiveness, we have an inflexible rule that approval to go to the study stage is never granted until at least seventy-two hours after the meeting."

Stafford nodded.

"Now, when I say study the idea to present to the entire membership, I am not talking about just hiring a few college professors to troll around the library and the internet and then do some peer-reviewed abstract analysis. We will commit up to six figures, sometimes even a little more, to get top-notch experts to make confidential examinations of the marketplace and give us specific scenarios and plans of action that will be ready to go if the membership votes to move on it. They will look at financial costs, potential profits, regulatory problems... During that research phase, people may call you, or any partners you have, umpteen times a day, 24-7, to nail down details the three of us have overlooked, or just didn't know enough to ask about. Their job is never to reject an idea. If an expert can't work on the idea, then the expert recuses himself and we get someone who can work on it. When they complete their analysis, we will have timetables—week-to-week, month-to-month, year-to-year—with ideas of costs, when profitability is possible, over the short term and the long term. And, an idea of when or if we might be able to go public. At the full vote, we vote with dollars. Each member votes by committing a percentage of the costs needed to start the thing up. If members have committed less than one hundred per cent of the start costs needed, the idea is rejected. A hundred or more, the idea is accepted and the contributions are pro-rated."

"I understand."

"That said, we are your potential partners. It would give me great pleasure if you would now dazzle us, please."

Eldon Stafford nodded. He raised his briefcase on the table and popped the latches. "Gentlemen and lady," he said as he reached into his briefcase, "gentlepersons I guess is the politically correct, but maybe stupid-sounding form of address, I am here with a new approach to health care." He handed a small, bound notebook to each of the three Segueway representatives. "We will look at three key perspective changes—first, a new look at how care is approached; second, a new way to handle the insuring and administering the care; and third, most importantly, and maybe most revolutionary, a fundamental shift in who delivers the care.

"The packets I handed you are a written version of this presentation. You may want to refer to them later as you consider these ideas. And some of the drier data is offered there, data and references that would surely put you all to sleep if I was to try to communicate it to you orally. If you wish to make notes-" Stafford noticed they all had pads and pens. "I'm sure you'll know what to do." He decided he had offered enough preamble for this group... maybe too much.

"First, there must be a shift from curing illness, diagnosing problems and then attacking them with drugs and surgery, to maintaining health. The fact is that the great advances in medicine over the last century have been cures for many acute conditions, diseases and traumas. With that triumph, we now face many more chronic conditions. But our system fails to address this development, continuing to attack every health problem as if it is an acute condition. Sure, we will still have a need to confront disease. But if we are oriented toward maintaining health, people need never get the disease. People need never develop the chronic condition. Our first priority should be to keep people healthy, not wait until they get sick to care for them.

"Medical doctors, like me, have given lip service to this for years. We say to our patients: 'You need to lose weight. You need to exercise. You need to change your diet.' But we place way too little emphasis on this type of maintaining health. Then, when the results of poor health maintenance present to us in heart attacks, diabetes, chronic neck, back and joint pain, and even cancer, we confront these serious health problems with expensive drugs and surgeries, with the most drastic cures available for the ailments. A new approach is needed, an approach that really emphasizes health over sickness, beyond lip service."

"Totally agree with you," Ben Richards said. "But how do we translate this into a business that Segueway Capital can invest in?"

"I'm getting there," Stafford said with a smile, glad for the "total agreement." "The business is a health insurance company that emphasizes health over sickness."

Ben Richards flinched as he scowled. Fiona Patton had a puzzled look on her face. Seth Mercoyan tilted his head, eyebrows narrowed.

"Take a look at almost any dental plan," Stafford told them. "A check-up every six months is encouraged and paid for. Regular teeth cleanings and check-ups are considered a necessity. The plans are structured to encourage the regular check-ups. My dentist has done almost no major work on my mouth because he and my dental hygienist watch my health, pointing out possible problems and often addressing them before they become big problems. In this way, dental plans are actually more health-friendly than most health insurance plans. Do we care more about our teeth than the rest of our bodies? How did the dentists get acceptance for this type of approach, and not those of us who care for the rest of the body?

"For this new insurance plan, regular health maintenance visits would be encouraged. In fact, not only would they be paid at one hundred per cent, but we would discount the premium for insureds who make and keep their regular appointments."

Ben Richards' eyes widened. "You're going to charge people less money to use more services?" He shook his head. "I hear the theory, but it just doesn't make any business sense."

"Oh it sure could make business sense," Fiona Patton said with a knowing smile. "Down the line—right?"

"Yes. Absolutely. The regular health maintenance serves to prevent the huge expense for a bypass operation, or a liver transplant, or kidney dialysis—you can go on and on—not to mention all the expensive drugs you won't pay for because the serious conditions never occur."

"But what about the lip service problem?" Seth Mercoyan asked. "If people come in for these regular visits, but just nod their heads, without acting on the advice..."

"I think many people will take the advice to become healthy. But, you're absolutely right. Many won't. So we charge a basic premium that we then discount for a healthy weight, healthy blood pressure readings, healthy blood tests for cholesterol and triglycerides, and treadmill tests for endurance, that will tell us if people have been engaging in regular aerobic exercise. Frankly, cholesterol is an issue to be analyzed carefully. My partner on this project, Dr. Galen Reed, has different ideas than I do on exactly what these cholesterol readings mean. He would point out that the numbers for what is considered healthy cholesterol keep getting lowered. He wonders—is that because of real clinical evidence, or because the drug companies want to sell more statins? Correlation and cause need to be examined closely. So a consensus on what tests to look at to offer the discount would be decided after some careful study. Another idea—we could even discount for patients who take basic nutrition courses and demonstrate a yearly proficiency.

"The idea is to reward patients for focusing on their health with a financial benefit because that behavior will benefit us. Those regular check-ups, and healthy choices demonstrated with objective tests, will require a lot less of the huge expenditures for major medical procedures. Also, the policy would specify that the least intrusive care for an illness would be utilized first. Those less-intrusive healing methods are less expensive, and generate less side effects, side effects that lead to other illnesses we will be caring for down the line."

Richards nodded. "That's an interesting idea. To use your dental analogy, it would be like giving discounts to dental patients who come in every six months and show they've been flossing."

"Sure. You could look at it that way."

"So we'd need a lot more G-P type doctors," Ben Richards said. "To handle all of these extra maintenance appointments, maybe even handle the tests you're talking about."

"I think the tests should be handled by an independent entity," Stafford said. "But that's not a major detail. And you mention G-P doctors. But there's a growing shortage of G-P doctors. The money's in specialization. My own career is an example. I went from a good G-P practice to cancer specialist in the early 80s. My income exploded. Doctors know that. Who wants to stay a G-P and fight the lower insurance company reimbursements and less patient time available? So the precise type of MD care-giver needed for this proposed shift is a shrinking group. That's why nurse practitioners, physician assistants and even pharmacists have been suggested as possibilities to fill the gap. But that would put the least trained professionals in charge of the most important part of what should be the key to an improved system—maintaining health!"

Stafford waited a moment to let this idea sink in. All eyes were on him. He had created some drama by offering a dilemma. He had them wondering how he would offer to solve it. They were primed. It was time to pay it off.

"The third part of the proposal, the most revolutionary part, is that we don't use G-Ps as the primary doctors for health maintenance. We use chiropractors."

"Chiropractors!" Ben Richards almost looked angry.

Seth Mercoyan smiled nervously.

Fiona Patton flashed a wide, confident smile. "Bringing the best of two approaches to health together," she said.

"That's the idea," Stafford said. He could jump in with an intense patter of words to try to persuade the clearly skeptical Ben Richards. But he sensed this was a time to be a counter-puncher. If he jumped in with vehement advocacy, he could possibly dominate the meeting, but would not know for sure what Richards' most vehement objections and doubts were. He paused, waiting for Richards to take the lead. Richards was a blunt, outspoken man. He would let Stafford know the nature of his skepticism. Then Stafford would be able to hit the objections head on.

Richards didn't wait long through the pause. "Okay, look, I was with you for a minute there. But chiropractors? We'll be laughed out of the medical community."

"I don't think so," Fiona Patton said. "I've been seeing one, for regular health maintenance. My M-D doesn't like it, so I don't put the two together. It would be nice if I could."

"And healthier," Stafford added.

Richards frowned.

"I was in a market about twenty years ago," Fiona Patton continued. "I slipped on a piece of fruit on the floor and strained my left lower back. My doctor said to use a heating pad and take Advil. I did. I covered up the pain, but my back was constantly going out, in the same area, every six to eight months. It would go out with the least provocation. I had a friend who was in an auto accident who went to a chiropractor in our neighborhood. She told me he completely fixed her lower back. And that car looked like an accordion from behind. So I went. After about a month, maybe ten visits, my spine was lined up the way it should be. My back doesn't go out anymore. I go about once a month to get my spine lined up. I've been healthier, less prone to colds, almost no headaches, more energy—it does work. This is a good idea. But I understand Ben's concerns, and we will have to explain this to the public. The initial public reaction may be similar to Ben's."

"Well, we first let people know that this is already being done, in informal collaborations, with referrals on small scales. Chiropractors are on staffs at some hospitals and urgent-care facilities. But most importantly, we explain that chiropractors are trained to maintain health," Stafford said. "The health of the spine—the health of the whole body. They are perfect for putting this part of-"

"Dr. Stafford, I'm sorry." Ben Richards shook his head. "It's a flaky thing. I'm glad it worked for you, Fiona, but it's some flaky thing from the late 1800s, along with snake-oil medicine show garbage back then, with people even bottling and selling cocaine as medicine! Somewhere out in farm country, some guy starts laying his hands on necks and backs and says he's healed them. He took in some of the gullible and passed on the scam."

All eyes turned to Eldon Stafford.

Chapter 25

Stafford grinned. He and Reed had discussed this challenge, or one like it. He was ready. "Mr. Richards, what you said is exactly what I thought a few months ago. That's what I was conditioned to believe, rarely explicitly, mostly implicitly, with a snide dismissiveness by the medical community that said more by omission than anything else. Chiropractic—a harmless silliness, to be tolerated, but not to be taken seriously. Years ago, they tried to stamp it out. But now? They try to kill it with indifference and condescension. I was part of that until recently. I have been proven wrong. I have personally benefited from the efforts of a gifted healer. My daughter also has. I've watched this man, and some of his colleagues, help a number of people during this period. The effects of his efforts can be explained clinically. And they are too consistent for too many people to be explained by coincidence or by the placebo effect.

"Also, it is true that what we call 'chiropractic' has been around for just over a hundred years. But chiropractic is a modern form of spinal manipulation, and that has been around since at least the ancient Greeks. I was surprised to find out that Hippocrates, the man whose oath my colleagues and I take, an oath almost 2500 years old, was a serious practitioner of spinal manipulation to heal people." Stafford looked down at some notes. "He wrote 'Look well to the spine for the cause of disease.' He looked for and recognized different degrees of vertebral displacement as something that needed to be corrected.

And he referred to this as an 'ancient art.' Around the same time, a slightly older man than Hippocrates, the historian Herodotus, apparently was doing some kind of spinal healing, because there is a record of Artistotle criticizing this practice a few generations later because Herodotus's methods 'made old men young,' prolonging their lives too long.

"Spinal manipulation as a method of maintaining a healthy body has been around for thousands of years, in cultures all over the globe. Chiropractic—you're right—is a more recent, American discipline. But when you realize that chiropractic is simply the method of spinal manipulation combined with modern medical knowledge, with knowledge unknown to Hippocrates or Herodotus, or to spinal manipulation practitioners through the centuries, then you will realize as I do, that this is an exciting opportunity to combine chiropractic with the health approach of modern medicine and science to increase the health of everyone. Those snake-oil people you talk about are gone. Their scams were long ago exposed. Chiropractic is still here because it is effective, and because it has roots that go deep into antiquity, as far back as any modern medical technology goes back."

Richards smirked. "You were ready for that, weren't you..."

Stafford chuckled. "Yes."

"Comments," Richards requested.

Fiona Patton smiled again. "This is very intriguing. And out of the box. And, exactly the kind of idea Segueway was formed to look at. There are a lot of details to review. But if the vote was now, I would certainly vote we invest in looking this over, in detail."

Seth Mercoyan frowned. "This would be an insurance company."

"Yes," Stafford answered.

"We'd be starting an insurance company right at a time of the biggest uncertainty for health insurance companies in fifty years."

"That's right," Stafford said. "We have to guide this change from the point of payment. For most people, that starts with an insurance premium."

"The premium discounts fly in the face of some regulations," Seth

Mercoyan said. "The companies in business now are in trouble for dumping unhealthy insureds. We may run into trouble trying to reward healthy insureds.

"It's canceling insureds that has gotten those companies in trouble, canceling insureds to deny them coverage," Richards said. "We'd simply be charging higher premiums for people who behave in a less healthy way. You know, like bad drivers pay more for car insurance, and overweight people with high blood pressure and high cholesterol pay higher life insurance premiums. And the new law prevents denying coverage for pre-existing conditions. This would give a company the way to manage those conditions." He shrugged. "And maybe we don't call it an insurance company. It's a health cooperative. People pay in. The cooperative holds and grows the money, then pays out as the members need it."

"You're describing a mutual insurance company," Seth Mercoyan said.

Ben Richards shrugged. "Yeah, I see that." He paused. "We could put Stan on this. He's real good with this sort of thing. He read that health care bill monstrosity line by line—I think he has parts of it memorized. If there is a way to navigate around the dumb regulatory stuff, Stan'll know the angles. Maybe there is a way we set this up so it isn't an insurance company, so we don't have the regulations. But if we're going that route, we better put in a litigation budget, because I suspect the government will come after us with both barrels."

"And our competitors in the insurance industry," Fiona Patton said. "But we could get around the entire regulatory issue if we could get some favorable legislation for the entity that answers all the regulatory questions. Congress will change. So will the Presidency. We could be ready with the right product at the right time."

Ben Richards nodded. "Well, we'll need to study that, in all fifty states, and at the federal level, if we're going to move forward on this."

"Federal level would be best," Fiona Patton said.

Seth Mercoyan frowned. "But if this is some kind of cooperative, along the lines of a mutual insurance company, how do we make money? You're talking about a not-for-profit entity."

"We can loan the company the start-up money and set interest for the loan at a reasonable return." Richards shook his head. "I think profit can really mess up this sort of industry. It forces a conflict between the insurance company and their own insured as the company tries to squeeze dollars in a way that may affect a person's health. This was one of the main aspects of the health care business that motivated me to get out."

Seth Mercoyan broke into a twisted smile. "Um, look, I'm basically with this. But our membership favors big ideas with big payoffs. The money doesn't appear to be there in this one."

"There are payoffs other than money," Richards said. "Starting a company that leads to a meaningful reform of the health care industry in this country could be a legacy for Segueway that would dwarf all our other projects." He paused. "We've all heard it. They're talking about Europe, about Canada, as some sort of ideal. I can tell you, Canadians are coming here because their system has created severe shortages. Where will we go when our system does the same thing? I'd love to be part of an answer to this."

Seth Mercoyan grinned. "I had a friend from Toronto come stay with me for a month last year so he could get an MRI and some care for a bad back. He's got money. What about the people who don't?"

"They get to wait in line," Richards said. "In all those government-run healthcare countries. Stand in line, Mr. General Public."

Stafford again hesitated to offer any thoughts on this issue. He had often wondered if a compassionate government could create a universal health plan that could operate without creating shortages, the cause of the long lines. The old Berkeley days learning about corporate greed and profit still tapped him on the shoulder from time to time. Shouldn't this essential service be protected from the profit motive with a good government plan? He wasn't going to risk antagonizing Richards by expressing this idea.

Richards looked at Stafford. "Not much to say on this, huh?"

"Um, no, um, this issue is not part of my presentation."

Richards nodded. "Ivy League in the 60s? Columbia maybe?"

"No. Berkeley."

Richards chuckled. "Right. And you think maybe the government can get this mess untangled…"

Stafford wasn't sure what to say.

"It's okay, Doc. I'm not going to bite just because we have a different idea on this. But I'm going to give you some food for thought. In these countries—hey, even here with the government run stuff—here's what happens: Government pays—government runs short of money. Every time. Because bureaucrats cannot runs things as efficiently as the market. That was the death of so-called Communism, you know. The economies fell apart because bureaucrats cannot run an economy as well as the market. So when they run short of money on the health care expense budget, they cut compensation. Then providers—the doctors, the hospitals, all the providers—struggle more and more to make a living. And some of them bail out, leaving fewer providers and more shortages."

Stafford considered this idea.

"It's okay, Doc. You don't have to agree with me for us to do business. I'm just putting this out there for you."

Stafford nodded. "I will give it some thought."

"Good."

Stafford wasn't sure what else he should say. He almost spoke, a concluding remark he had in mind, but stopped as it appeared Richards might be formulating another thought.

"Now, on what you brought in today, here's my main concern," Richards finally said. "I'm afraid my initial reaction to the chiropractor idea will be the general reaction of the public. The new approach to health care would require a massive public education."

Eldon Stafford nodded. "I can't disagree with that. I have seen the polls. It's still under twenty percent who use chiropractors and have an awareness of what they do. An advertising budget would be needed—publicity experts should be hired. We will get push-back from stakeholders in the current system who will get particularly bruised by this idea. Those MD specialists will howl. If this works, they will have a lot of empty spots in their appointment books. We need to think of ways to get the full idea out to the public to counter what will surely be efforts to discredit the idea. Another idea would be to print and distribute simple textbooks on how chiropractic and modern medicine can work together. Get one to every high school health class in the country. Get the youth on board early. Hand them out to anyone interested in alternative health."

Ben Richards' eyes darted up. He seemed to be contemplating. Fiona Patton was still smiling. She seemed to like most of what she had heard. Seth Mercoyan also smiled and gave Eldon Stafford a quick nod as if to say I'm glad I got you this opportunity—you didn't embarrass yourself or me.

"It's simple," Stafford said, sensing the presentation was over, and wanting to end strong. "We have networks of chiropractors ready to treat patients, to work fully integrated into the health care system, collaborating, dying to heal people, and keep them healthy. We have patients sitting in hospitals, undergoing preventable surgeries, over-treated with prescription drugs, subjected to virulent staph infections created through the overuse of antibiotics, also, in a different way, dying to heal, like my late wife Susan. The system is dying to heal. And with your help, we can get that healing started."

"Dying to heal." Ben Richards smirked a cynical grin. "Cute."

Stafford wasn't sure if this was a compliment or not. He just smiled politely and nodded.

"Well," Richards finally said, "this is a biggie. I think we should take a week on it."

"A week?" Fiona Patton asked.

"Yeah, I think so," Richards said. "Don't get me wrong. I love the big out-of-the-box ideas. I'd vote yes if we were voting right now. But, I know it would be an impulse vote." He smiled. "I like Dr. Stafford. We know from Seth that he's a great man in his field. I just think we should all take the time to look over the stuff he gave us—think it over a little more." He chuckled. "It'll give me a little extra time—uh, Fiona, who's your chiropractor?"

She gave him a look of bewilderment.

"I'd like to book an appointment to check this out for myself, this ancient healing technology updated for modern times. I've got a lower back that's always going out on me. Stiffens up at the least provocation. Stops me from exercising as much as I should. Which, frankly, has me gaining a few uninvited and unwanted pounds. Maybe he can help."

"I'm sure he can," Fiona Patton said. "I'll be happy to give you his information. I'll also let him know he should see you as soon as possible."

"Thanks."

"I'd also vote yes if we were taking the vote now," she added.

"Makes three of us," Seth Mercoyan said.

Ben Richards stood.

Everyone else stood.

"Thank you for coming. We'll be in touch. Have your cell phone on. We may call you with some questions over the next week."

Stafford shook Richards' hand. "Thank you."

As Stafford shook the other hands, he heard Ben Richards say "Phone conference, nine o'clock a-m, a week from today. My secretary will call you. Let her know what number you'll be at."

Fiona Patton and Seth Mercoyan nodded.

Eldon Stafford picked up his briefcase and headed for the door. As he walked out, he saw a woman walk in with some urgency to her step. "Mr. Richards. A Wyatt Greevey has called twice. He wants to talk to you right away."

Richards chuckled. "That's kind of a strange coincidence." He frowned. "I wonder what that old buzzard wants." He shrugged. "I'll try him before I head out to the golf course. This went quickly. Maybe I'll get in a quick nine."

Eldon Stafford took in a deep breath. He couldn't have imagined the presentation going any better. He wondered if Wyatt Greevey's call to Ben Richards had anything at all to do with him.

"Galen! Dr. Reed!" Brianna Stafford got out of her car, parked about two rows from Galen Reed's car. The lot was almost empty. It was late afternoon, and though the automatic lights in the parking lot had come on, there was still enough daylight to light the area.

"Brianna?" Galen Reed frowned, clearly not expecting this summons from this person at this time.

Brianna reached back into her car, turned off the car radio, pulled the keys out and shut the car door, almost in one motion. She held the Susan Stafford file in her right arm. "I need to talk to you."

Galen Reed walked toward her.

Brianna Stafford stepped toward him, grim-faced and with resolve.

"Have you been waiting here for me?" he asked as they met each other.

"Can you please explain to me what this is?" she asked. She thrust the Susan Stafford file in front of him.

His eyes fixed on the file. "Where'd you get that?"

"Delores."

"I've been looking all over for it."

"For an old file about my mother?"

"I keep it-" Reed seemed hesitant. "For inspiration."

"Inspiration?" She squinted. "What is this about?"

He let out a deep breath. "I'll explain it to you." He gently took the file from her. "Let's go back into my office."

Brianna Stafford looked at him warily.

"That's why you've been out here?" Galen Reed frowned. "You've got a look on your face like I'm a stalker, or a serial killer…"

"I don't know what to think."

"Come on. You should know I'm neither." He paused. "But, I should have come out with everything a long time ago."

"Before my father bought into your whole deal and flew up to the Bay Area to make a pitch, to make a fool of himself!"

"Everything we've done together is real. The thing that's, that's understated, is my connection... to you, to your family."

"Yeah?"

"You really want to do this in the parking lot?"

Brianna Stafford thought a moment. Galen Reed was a gentle healer. She knew that first hand. He couldn't transform from the man who had changed her health and her life to a threat to her safety just because of his odd possession of an old file. "Okay. Let's go."

They walked together back to Galen Reed's office.

Chapter 26

"Where did that file come from?" Brianna Stafford asked, unable to wait until they got to the office, and unwilling to endure an awkward silence while they walked.

"Your mother was my patient."

"That file—it's from your office?"

"Yeah. From a long time ago. From when I just started out."

"I just… find that really hard to believe."

They arrived at the office. Galen Reed unlocked the front door. They sat down at the first two chairs next to the door. "Your mother went to the vitamin store to pick up some supplements. She and Natalie started talking. Your mother mentioned back problems."

"Back problems?" Brianna Stafford frowned. "I don't remember my mother having back problems."

Galen Reed smiled. "We got things under control." He paused. "Natalie told her about a new up-and-coming healer—me. She came to see me. I saw the last name and knew instantly who she was, who her husband was." He nodded with the smile of a pleasant memory. "She also recognized me. I didn't realize it, but she had been in the hospital administrative offices one day while I was on the phone working on a collection, back when I did that to support myself. It was a tough case—I don't remember the details—but I felt bad for the family I was dealing with, and it showed on my end of the call. She apparently overheard and remembered me as a compassionate, caring person. So when she walked in and saw me, she had Natalie's recommendation, and her own stored first impression. She trusted me. We hit it off immediately. And I helped her, with her neck, and with approaches to staying healthy."

"So she saw you in secret? I don't think my dad knew."

"No." His lips tightened as his eyebrows went up and down. "I've always wanted to bring chiropractic healing into an alliance, a working collaboration, with mainstream medicine. I thought success with your mother could open the door to a really heavy-potential connection with your father."

Brianna's face tightened, almost into a pout. "Like you ended up doing with me."

"It worked out that way. Yeah." He paused.

"This is just weird, Dr. Reed."

"Let me finish explaining. Then you can decide if you think there really is anything to get upset about."

"I'm listening…"

"Your mother did not want to tell your father about me. And, I had to accept that—legally because of confidentiality, and really, just out of decency."

"Okay, so you finally got to my dad through me."

"There's more to it. If this was just your mom coming in for a few adjustments, I wouldn't have held that file."

"What else?"

Galen Reed took a deep breath that seemed to quiver as he exhaled. He tightened his lips as his eyes watered. "I heard she'd gone into the hospital. I forget how. I think because she missed an appointment, and we called and found out."

"I remember telling people when they called the house."

"Maybe we talked to you. Anyway, when I realized she wasn't just in for an out-patient emergency room type visit, I went to see her."

"You saw my mother in the hospital."

"No." Galen Reed swallowed. "I went to the desk. They told me no visitors—she was in ICU. I asked what was going on. They said they couldn't tell me. Brianna, I would have known instantly she was suffering from a drug reaction. I had her complete medical history, including drug allergies. We are trained to look for this. I would have known it, and with that knowledge, her outcome might have been-" He stopped a moment. "I told this nurse, this huge tank-like nurse, like a female wall, that I was a health-care professional, a doctor, one of your mother's doctors. She asked for my card. I could tell she didn't like me, didn't want to deal with me, and suspected me of something—I don't know what. I handed her the card." He took in another breath. "I'll never forget the expression." He squinted. "An expression of, of disgust, of pure condescension, superiority. 'Young man,' she says to me, as if she's a second grade teacher talking to a kid she just caught throwing spitballs in class, 'we only allow real doctors to see patients here.' I told her I was a real doctor, and wanted to help with my patient's care. She said 'Missus Stafford would not see some phony doctor, someone like you.' 'Phony doctor,' she called me. She told me she'd call security if I didn't leave right away." He swallowed again, but tears rolled down his cheeks anyway. "I left. Brianna, God Damn me, I left." He shook his head as he looked away, wiped his face and sniffled. "I should have stayed and fought it out."

"Like you did for me, when I was in the hospital for my asthma."

Reed seemed genuinely taken by surprise. "I hadn't thought of that."

She smiled as her eyebrows raised. "You didn't have any problems dealing with nurses, tank-like or otherwise, when it was my turn."

He nodded. "And that was good for the present-day. But back then, I also should have stayed. I should have fought it out then too. I think I could have saved your mother. I think I could have made a difference. But, I was a young man. I thought I was confident, but I didn't have the guts to stand up for my health-care knowledge. I walked away." He paused. "And your mother died."

Brianna's eyes filled with tears. "I had no idea."

"I probably should have told you and your dad. I've wanted to. But it just never seemed like the right time."

Brianna nodded.

"I almost quit back then. It was a terrible time for me. I thought if I didn't have the ability, the courage to stand up for my training, my knowledge, my ability to heal, then I didn't belong in the business of healing people."

"But you do. You proved it. With me."

Galen Reed smiled. "It took some time to get there. And what kept me in was people like you, who believed I could help them. When I thought about quitting, I realized I would be abandoning people who had come to depend on me. I was like a shell. I stumbled around, alive as I helped patients, but dying inside from the guilt. I kept going. But it took a long time to come out of a"— he paused a moment—"a general funk, a malaise." He shook his head. "I had this idea of myself as someone people would hate if they really knew how weak and ineffectual I was. I did come out of it. Years of success brought me out of it. But I have never forgiven myself for Susan Stafford's death." He looked into Brianna's eyes. "I may be able to, if your father and I can make this collaboration launch into something truly wonderful, something that could change the world. In a way, your father and I are both trying to construct a meaning, a purpose, for your mother's death."

"Mm-hmm." Brianna Stafford took a deep breath as she paused. "There's only one problem. My father doesn't know he's part of a master plan for your self-vindication."

"I know." Galen Reed twitched his nose. "I know this is meant to be. I never really put your mother's death behind me. I put it back, but never left it. Then I saw your name on Sal's list for the nutrition consultation and it looked like Fate. Yes, I moved in. Was it deception? Was it 'creepy,' as you have called it? I don't think so. This time, I seized an opportunity, to do something good, to do something great. I could see how it all would fall into place, and I acted on it. I think— no I'm sure—it has all been for the good."

Brianna Stafford nodded slowly. "Well, I hope my father agrees with you." She pulled out her cell phone. "We need to call him."

"Isn't he coming back tonight?"

"I'm meeting his plane in about two hours."

"Let's meet it together."

Brianna Stafford handed the Susan Stafford file to Galen Reed. She smiled. She understood what Galen Reed was asking. If they met the plane together, she would seem to be satisfied with the disclosure he was going to make. Her presence would take some of the tension out of the moment. She nodded. "Okay. Dinner at The Grill. Then we'll meet him together. I'll help you. I think you are, as you said, doing what you do, 'all for the good.'"

"Thank you."

"You're buying."

"Of course."

They stood to leave. Galen Reed brought out his keys to relock the office door.

"I've been trying to call that old guy back," Ben Richards said to his assistant, a lady in her mid forties, plain-looking, with an efficient manner that radiated competence. She had just appeared in his office doorway. Richards was up from his desk, with a small carrying case for a few papers. "He's not picking up. Not even his cell phone."

"Um, he's here. He's waiting in the reception area."

"Here?"

"Sure is."

Richards looked at his watch. It read 4:36. "Aaah. No golf today." Richards shook his head. "These fat cats with their corporate jets."

"You like yours well enough."

"Yeah. Hope I'm not this obnoxious with it." Richards sat back down. "I guess I have to see him."

"Well... you don't have to..."

"You see, I'm not the jerk everyone thinks I am. If I was, I'd tell him to make an appointment. People think I'm a jerk, but you know I'm not."

"Yes, I know. Benjamin Richards has a soft spot for fellow aging near-billionaires who fly in for a chat."

"Okay. Enough embarrassing me about my tender side. Tell the fat cat to come on in."

Richards thumbed through some of Eldon Stafford's proposal. He slipped it into his desk as Wyatt Greevey walked in.

"Hi Ben. It's really good to see you."

Ben Richards stood and lifted his eyebrows as they shook hands and he motioned Greevey to a couch in his office. Richards sat in a chair at a diagonal angle from the couch. "How was your flight?"

"Smooth. Perfect."

"Good."

"How are the grandkids?"

"Wyatt, come on. Do we pull out our wallets and do show-and-tell with the baby pictures, or do you get to whatever it is that caused you to drop everything and fly up here?"

"Okay. It's late in the day. I'll get to the point."

"Good."

"You had a meeting with Eldon Stafford?"

Ben Richards maintained a smirky grin. But his lower lip twitched a little as he wondered how Segueway's confidential meeting had leaked to an outsider. "Well, Wyatt, my old friend. I'm not sure who Elmer Stafford is. But we have confidentiality here. Don't want speculators hovering around. It's a strict rule here. Sorry. No exceptions, not even for an old friend."

"I see. Well, if you'd met Eldon Stafford, you wouldn't have called him 'Elmer.'" Greevey smirked. "Unless you deliberately mangled the name to try to throw me off."

"I'm just an old guy," Richards said. He flashed a broad smile. "Eldon? Elmer? Pretty close to these old ears."

"I see. Well, I heard a rumor. So I thought I should help you guys out. You might want to write the name down if he approaches you— Eldon Stafford. We've been having a little trouble with him down our way."

Richards didn't change expressions, and didn't move to write down the name. If he had, he would be overacting. "Trouble? What, is he a rival drug guy or something?"

Greevey grinned as he squinted. "No. Old Elmer—he's a doctor."

"Elmer?"

Greevey let out a burst of air through his nose. "Hypothetically."

Richards smiled. Greevey had surrendered. He'd obviously given up trying to trap Greevey into admitting he'd spoken to Eldon Stafford. "Hypothetically" would allow them to focus on the issues without naming the parties. "Hypothetically," Richards repeated. "Good."

"Suppose a doctor, down my way, or wherever, started monkeying around with the health-care system? Started telling people not to take their prescription drugs. Started involving chiropractors who can't prescribe medications so exclude them from their methods. Suppose this doctor, highly respected, came wandering up here with big ideas about how to reform the system?"

"Send your hypothetical Elmer up. Segueway likes these kinds of ideas."

Greevey chuckled. "I always wondered what it would be like to be across the table from you."

"Are we across the table from each other on something?"

Greevey chuckled again. "I think so. You remember, we've been on the same side of the table for a lot of this stuff."

"That is true."

"Health care's touchy right now." Greevey's eyes bored in on Richards. "Precarious. The wrong people want to play around with it, worst of all, the government. And investors don't want to touch it."

"Yup."

"The problem is fairly easy to understand, tougher to solve. Medical science can keep us around much longer now. Great advances in procedures and drugs—well, we hear it all the time: '40 is the new 30,' '50 is the new 40,' hell, '80 is the new 50.'"

Richards laughed.

"We want all this stuff, to live longer, to eat our big diets and neutralize the effects of our, well, our lifestyles that would seem downright self-indulgent to even our grandparents. We want the drugs—we want the procedures. But no one wants to pay for all of it, for the research and investment that goes into developing these things that'll have many of us living to over a hundred. I mean, providers of all these technological advances deserve to be paid."

"Yes, of course. You didn't come up here to argue that companies deserve to get paid for innovation. That's what Segueway's all about."

"It's different from a dot-com, or a new gizmo to juice up a computer hard-drive. We've got a system with a lot of stakeholders who have committed to it. We need to keep it functioning smoothly."

"You think it's functioning smoothly now?"

"Of course it isn't, especially with this new garbage from the Congress. But we need to keep the damage contained. As the best of all possible alternatives, keeping in mind the problem, that everyone wants to live longer, but no one wants to pay—the system does not need any more challenges. You start attacking the whole structure and we'll have a real mess."

"I'm not sure we don't have a mess now."

Greevey eyed Richards. "You know how it works. You and I helped set it up. Over the last twenty years, I've been on the boards of three different insurance companies, two hospital conglomerates, in addition to my stake in Havitol. Computer power has made it possible to put a system in place, a system to control the mess."

Richards knew this information. But as he listened to Greevey, his mind wandered to the Stafford proposal. The more he listened to Greevey try to describe how orderly the current system really was, the more Richards liked the idea of shaking it up. So Richards would let Greevey talk. This would help inform Richards' thinking.

"With computer power, with juiced-up spreadsheets, we can control behaviors we had no chance of getting a handle on even ten to fifteen years ago." Greevey beamed a proud smile. "We reduce everything to numbers. Everybody's got a computer terminal. We can record every keystroke and analyze it all in any way we specify. So we can sit in our offices, as the people with the big picture, and command what the numbers will be. We set up the processes and procedures that'll make the numbers happen. We hand down our numerical commands through a few layers of middle management—less, now that we have computers to monitor behavior—just enough to insulate the real power from the front lines. Because scarce resources for care, for drugs, need to be doled out. We can't give everything to everyone because we can't afford to. So we set the procedures. We give the front lines no power at all. We tell them you hit these numbers to get your salary increases, to advance your careers, to get promotions and praise from the hierarchy. Even the first level of management has little authority—they're too close to the front lines. The people who have to say no can blame the procedures, or a process, or a system, or a nameless, faceless God of Insurance.

"We actually have this kind of thing on T-V, 'Deal or no Deal,' my favorite show—I want the whole country to watch it over and over. My favorite guy is the banker, the nameless, faceless curmudgeon who communicates through the affable host. The banker can be rude, even cruel. He never faces the contestant who has the big dreams he toys with and often thwarts. The affable host can present the rudeness, even the cruelty, face-to-face, eyeball-to-eyeball with the contestant, because he's just a messenger for the nameless, faceless banker. That's what insurance companies do—all day long. Nickels and dimes for the front lines to dole out. And we can even measure these. When employees dole out too many nickels and dimes, they don't get rewarded, and eventually they leave. We keep the ones who are best at being the affable game show host. That show conditions people to fall right into line with the system."

"Hmm."

Greevey smiled. "They're getting real good. One of the companies I worked with started using personality tests to evaluate potential employees. I like it so much, I've been using something similar at Havitol. Hundreds of questions. The applicant does the thing, along with a grueling detailed test of whether the person can read a procedure and apply it accurately, down to every last word. The test goes into a computer that spits out a result—it's a go or a no-go for the employee. Nobody knows what was really measured. Only at the top levels. Middle managers don't know. Personnel doesn't know. At this company? They measured for creativity and compassion over a strict adherence to rules. And, of course, they dump the ones who show a preference for creativity and compassion over the rules and a desire to please superiors! Brilliant."

"Yeah. I hear you. But in your numbers game, some things can't be measured. How do you measure the effectiveness of a specific treatment on a patient outcome? Did the patient, the health-care consumer, experience a quality outcome? No way to measure that."

"We're working on it. I have a company working on a quality control survey right now. They're pretty close to giving us a good set of questions that will give us the right result."

"Right result..."

"Yeah, that the system needs to be kept as it is. We've made our deal with the government. They call us a few names, but leave us in charge."

"You think this is good..."

"It is—you know it is. Otherwise, the system'll fall apart. You know what they say. It's the worst system except for all the others."

Richards shook his head. "Wyatt-Wyatt-Wyatt. Wyatt Greevey. You've become a conservative in the worst possible way. You think any change, any innovation, is a 'mess.' Let me tell you, last year I got tangled up with some of those rules-and-regulations people you love so much, in that little system you're so proud of. A niece of mine was having trouble getting approval for a procedure for her son who broke his leg and needed a complex, expensive surgery. The company said it wasn't covered—experimental care, they called it—they said in a six page form letter that it was not 'reasonable and necessary.' My sister got me involved in it for her daughter because of my past connections with some of these companies. I didn't have any pull in this particular one. I tried to make a few calls, even wrote a letter or two. After a few bouts with voicemail hell and incomprehensible, over-lengthy denial letters, I finally just paid for my niece's son's surgery. It was easier than all the hassle. But where does that leave the people who can't just write a check?"

"Settling for 'reasonable and necessary care,' and making sure the system does not fall apart."

"Is that right..."

"Look, some cases are bound to get caught in the cracks. But the system as a whole has to have the gatekeepers to keep it functioning."

"Or, maybe the system could use a little innovation."

Greevey snorted as his face tightened in apparent frustration. "Bring me a car that runs on weeds and gets a hundred miles to the bushel. Bring me a computer I can carry in my pocket."

"We have those."

"Exactly. That's a great innovation. This industry, Ben, it's different. You cannot threaten its stability or we're courting catastrophe."

Ben Richards scratched his chin. "Hypothetically."

"Yeah. Right."

"Hypothetically, I just can't agree with you."

Greevey nodded grimly. "Will you agree to think about it?"

Richards stood. "Always. I never stop thinking."

Greevey stood up as well. "Call me to talk about it."

"If it comes up here at Segueway, and I need your input, I will call you."

Greevey squinted. "Okay," he said with no expression.

They shook hands.

"Thanks for seeing me." But Greevey did not smile. He left the room.

Chapter 27

"McTavish," Greevey said into his cell phone. He pushed a button to roll up the window in his limousine, assuring a soundproof passenger area for him.

"Mr. Greevey?" McTavish answered.

"I need that Plan B of yours."

"It's in place."

"I need it to go forward."

"Um, it could take a week or two."

"I need it in action by Monday."

"I don't know."

"You have whatever resources you need. Make it happen. Come to me directly."

"Okay. It'll take pulling some heavy strings, dealing with people who aren't used to moving this fast."

"Do what you have to so it becomes a priority for them."

"With whatever resources I need."

"That's right. Let me know."

"I'll do my best."

"I don't care if you do your best. I only care if this succeeds. Monday."

"Yes sir."

Greevey ended the call and leaned back. He poured himself two fingers of Scotch.

"Both of you!" Eldon Stafford beamed with a triumphant smile. He stood at the sidewalk just outside the American Airlines terminal at John Wayne Airport in the Santa Ana community of Orange County. He held a garment bag and a briefcase. He had on the light blue suit he had worn during his meeting with Segueway Capital, without the tie. "Thanks for coming along with Brianna," he said to Galen Reed, who got out of the passenger seat to let Eldon Stafford step in.

Galen Reed smiled politely as he got into the back seat.

Eldon Stafford placed his garment bag in the back seat opposite Galen Reed and sat in the passenger seat next to Brianna.

"How was your flight Daddy?" Brianna Stafford asked. She watched for an opening, then pulled from the curb into a thru lane of traffic to leave the airport.

"The flight was fine," Eldon Stafford said. "The meeting was even better."

"That's great," Galen Reed said. "Are they going forward with it?"

"It's not official, because they hold off on approval for at least seventy-two hours. But they seemed very positive."

"That's good," Brianna Stafford said, but without much energy. She pulled up to an intersection that would take them out of the airport, stopping at a red light.

"I tell you, their old guy, Ben Richards—I thought he was going to torpedo the whole thing before I could even get started. But he came around."

No one said anything.

Eldon Stafford was confused by the lack of enthusiasm for his news. He wondered if they were just tired. It was late, and they didn't have the advantage of being energized by the success of the meeting.

"Well," Eldon Stafford said. "It was good of you to both come meet me."

Brianna Stafford fidgeted. The light turned green. She pulled away from the light.

"Um, I need to tell you something," Galen Reed said.

Eldon Stafford frowned. "Okay."

"I haven't been completely straight with you about"—he paused, as if searching for the right words—"about my relationship with you and your family."

Eldon Stafford's lips tightened. "Not straight with me. About what?"

Galen Reed looked at Brianna Stafford, then back out toward the front of the car. "About all the circumstances involved in my contacts with you."

"What circumstances?"

Galen Reed looked at Brianna Stafford again.

"He needs to level with you, about everything," Brianna Stafford said.

"I think I'm pretty clear on this," Eldon Stafford said. "You treated my daughter for asthma, which led to your contact with me."

"There's more to it," Galen Reed said.

Eldon Stafford shook his head. "What else could there possibly be?"

Galen Reed took a deep breath. "I treated your wife also."

"My wife." Eldon Stafford frowned. He wondered if Galen Reed was confused, or had misspoken. "Brianna and I lost her years ago." He shook his head. "You know about that. We got those hospital records together."

"I knew her back then." Galen Reed paused. "She was my patient. I know you will find this hard to believe or accept, but she came to me for a bad back, and I helped her with that, and then other health issues. I was successful with her treatment—we had a great rapport."

Eldon Stafford raised his eyebrows. "That was you?"

Brianna Stafford looked over at her father. She looked back to keep from driving off the road.

Galen Reed didn't respond. Eldon Stafford sensed he was surprised into speechlessness.

"Well I know she was seeing someone for her back problems. Some alternative healer. I didn't know who."

Brianna Stafford glanced at her father again before shifting her eyes back to the road. "I don't remember Mommy having a bad back."

"She had problems off and on. I had medications on hand for her. One evening, a few months before she died, I was going through the medicine chest and noticed the use-by date was going to expire. I asked her if I needed to bring home some more, and remarked she hadn't taken any for awhile. She told me—she seemed a little embarrassed, even a little concerned that I would be angry—that she was getting help from someone recommended by a lady at the store where she bought nutrition supplements and vitamins. God bless her, I think she thought I would demand to know who it was and that she stop seeing him." He smiled and shook his head. "Whatever she was doing was working. I looked her over—whatever she was doing wasn't causing her any harm. As far as I was concerned it was money well spent. I figured it was probably psychological, a placebo thing. But of course, I told her to keep going." Eldon Stafford's eyes widened as his smile broadened. "And that was you. What a bizarre coincidence."

Brianna Stafford exhaled a burst of air. "It wasn't a coincidence."

"Not completely," Galen Reed said.

"Not at all," Brianna Stafford added.

"When I saw Brianna's name on my nutritionist friend's list, I sought her out."

Eldon Stafford shrugged. "Because you knew my wife?"

"He had an agenda," Brianna Stafford said. "Even then."

"I've had the idea to bring chiropractors and MDs together for a long time. I knew who your wife was and hoped her successful treatment would put us together."

"Like it did with you and Brianna."

Galen Reed didn't respond immediately, but then offered a quiet "Yes."

"Well it was, and is, a great idea." Eldon Stafford smiled. "Just ask Segueway Capital."

"This doesn't bother you?" Brianna Stafford asked.

Eldon Stafford's eyes narrowed. "No. Why should it?"

"He has Mommy's old file," Brianna Stafford told her father.

"Well of course he has a file for her if he treated her as a patient."

"He carries it around with him, as some sort of inspiration."

Eldon Stafford turned around and looked at Galen Reed. He wanted to hear his explanation about how an old medical file could provide inspiration, but was curious, not disapproving.

"I don't carry it around with me. I do have it at my desk." He breathed in and out, a long breath. "I was at the hospital."

"At the hospital." Eldon Stafford frowned as he tried to make sense of this statement. "You mean when she-" He thought how to phrase it. "At the end of her life?"

"Yes."

"I don't remember seeing you."

"They wouldn't let me see her. I never got past the nurse's station."

Eldon Stafford turned back around.

"I wanted to see that hospital file as badly as you did."

Eldon Stafford scratched his chin. "Hmmm. Yes. You were down-right pushy about it."

"Her death has haunted me, Eldon. I could have helped—I know I could have. But I let myself get intimidated. This big, stocky nurse—brown-haired, built like a tank—I let her chase me out of-"

"Nora Sulkowsky," Eldon Stafford said. "She left nursing three years ago to become dean at a middle school. An inner city middle school." He smiled. "You were trying to get past Nora Sulkowsky to see my wife?"

"I showed her my card and she-"

"You identified yourself as a chiropractor and tried to get past Nora Sulkowsky?" Eldon Stafford almost laughed out loud. "Galen. You had no chance. Believe me."

"I could have helped your wife," Galen Reed said again.

The statement took the smile away from Eldon Stafford. "No doubt." He looked down. "But none of us knew that back then."

"Not true." Galen Reed seemed to choke up. "I did. I should have pushed until all of you did too."

Eldon Stafford turned around again. He looked into Galen Reed's eyes and saw visible signs of intense emotion. He shook his head. "You had no chance. Believe me. You were courageous even to make the effort. But you had no chance." Eldon Stafford smiled as his eyes glistened with forming tears. "And now, you and I are going to change that."

Galen Reed smiled.

Brianna Stafford looked at her father again as they pulled up to a signal light. "You don't find it weird, or creepy, that he's been sort of pursuing our family?"

Eldon Stafford lifted his head and looked up, then over at her. "Actually, this makes a lot more sense to me than the 'coincidence' explanation. Look what's coming out of it. 'Weird?' 'Creepy?' No." He shook his head. "Brilliant. Visionary. Ambitious and courageous."

"You keep saying 'courageous,'" Galen Reed said. "But I was a coward at the hospital."

"You think of yourself as a coward?" Eldon Stafford asked, wondering how Galen Reed, who had pursued this relationship with such singlemindedness in the face of doubt and hostility could possibly think of himself this way. "You're one of the bravest men I know. You couldn't have saved Susan. Not because you were incapable, but because, well, because the whole hospital staff would have backed the attitude of Nora Sulkowsky. If you had tried to push past her, you would have simply created an incident with hospital security. That would not have been a good way for you and me to meet."

"So this is okay with you," Brianna Stafford said. She pulled the car away from the signal light that had just turned green.

Eldon Stafford shrugged. "It's more than 'okay.' It brings us together more." He turned around again to look at Galen Reed. "Partners in finding some sense, some purpose, from Susan's death."

Galen Reed nodded. "Thank you."

Eldon Stafford turned back around. He swallowed a lump in his throat.

Brianna Stafford lifted her eyebrows. "Okay, then." She nodded. "It's all up front now. Everything's cool."

Eldon Stafford frowned. "I'm not sure about that. What brought all this up?"

"Delores showed me the file," Brianna said. "Jimmy Puccinelli told her he had seen Mommy's file in Dr. Reed's office. You know, she's almost like family. She thought we should know."

Eldon Stafford rubbed his nose. "So Puccinelli tried to sabotage this relationship?" He turned back around again. "Why?"

Galen Reed took in a nervous breath.

Eldon Stafford faced front again. "They knew about Segueway. That old Wyatt Greevey was calling Ben Richards even before the meeting." Eldon Stafford paused. "We need to find out how they knew."

"Did Puccinelli overhear something?" Brianna asked.

"Paperwork in your office," Stafford suggested.

"He was there recently to pick up some records." Reed frowned. "Did I talk about it while he was there?" He paused. "I did." He looked at Brianna. "I spoke to you, while he was waiting for his records."

Brianna nodded. "I think so."

No one said anything for a moment.

"Any other possibilities?" Eldon Stafford asked. "I mean, that would be pretty amazing timing for Puccinelli."

Reed frowned in thought. "I know I did mention it to-" Reed stopped. "She wouldn't."

"Who?" Eldon Stafford asked.

"No. She wouldn't." Galen Reed paused. "I mean, she was against all of this at first. It looked like we would break up over it."

"Vitamin lady?" Brianna asked.

"It can't be," Galen Reed asked.

"Well it's somebody with inside information," Stafford said.

"Puccinelli's upset with me. He could have mentioned the file to Delores Hart out of spite. He knows she's with Eldon's office. He was in the office for that first collaboration."

"Wait a minute," Brianna Stafford said. "Could Puccinelli have planted a bug in your office when he was snooping around? Maybe he saw Mom's file then…"

"I don't know," Galen Reed said.

"We'd better solve this," Eldon Stafford said. "We're on the verge of something incredible, something that may threaten those with less vision and openmindedness. This could get rougher."

"I'll talk to Natalie," Galen Reed said. "And I need to think and consider just how much access Jimmy Puccinelli has had to this information."

"Check the office for bugs," Eldon Stafford said.

"I know just the guy for the job," Galen Reed said.

"Have them check my office too," Stafford said. "Let's cover all the bases."

Galen Reed nodded.

Chapter 28

"Dr. Middleton." Wyatt Greevey walked to the entrance of his office with his hand extended. "Thank you for finding the time to stop by." Wyatt Greevey smiled, deliberately projecting warmth and respect.

"I appreciate you getting started so early to accommodate my schedule," Lawrence Middleton replied.

"I'll get right to the point," Greevey said. "You came to see me not long ago. Right here in this office you told me you were concerned about Eldon Stafford allowing hospital access to some flake wanna-be healer."

"I remember."

"Well sir, you were right. I was not impressed with the issue you brought to me. I was wrong. You showed vision and insight—I have been blessed with it often during my long life, and have profited from it. But not this time."

Middleton nodded.

"I can't always see every potential problem by myself. So I like to surround myself with people who can help me. You are one of those people."

"Thank you."

"Now the fact is, some changes are coming. Dr. Stafford's leadership at the hospital has been-" He paused, searching for the right words. "Hmm. Let's just say he has lacked judgment. This chiropractic experiment of his, well, it needs to come to an end."

Lawrence Middleton shrugged. "I agree with you. But the fact is, there have been some successes, and the overall buzz around the hospital is that a lot of people think it has been a good idea."

"A lot of parlor tricks." Greevey pushed a burst of air through his nostrils. "Some hocus-pocus for the easily impressed."

Lawrence Middleton looked as if he was about to say something, but didn't.

Wyatt Greevey raised his eyebrows and tilted his head, inviting Middleton to express his thought.

"I don't think a lot of people believe these are parlor tricks."

"You one of them?"

"Of course not."

Wyatt Greevey squinted. "It took some finagling, but I've got a good idea of what these people want to do."

"These people?"

"People Eldon Stafford is meeting with. A confidential meeting with people who start new businesses, and have a lot of money to put in play."

Middleton looked surprised.

"Yeah. He's taken it that far. Don't ask—I'll just say that I found out he met with a company called Segueway. Always make friends with the secretaries, especially when you need a copy of something." Greevey picked up a stack of papers.

Middleton's eyes diverted to the papers.

"They want chiropractors to take over a lot of the care. Do away with drugs. Do away with surgeries. Do away with the great medical advances of our age."

"Luddites."

Greevey smiled. "Exactly. And sure, eventually everyone will see the folly of it when people's health goes into the crapper. But while they're mesmerized with parlor tricks, you MDs'll take a big hit. Patients'll avoid you in droves. Drug company stocks will drop like a bowling ball rolling into a swimming pool. We've got a lot to lose. And we're not giving up a bit of it without a fight. We've got to stop this before it gets started."

"Good." Middleton's determined expression told Greevey the doctor was connecting with his message.

"I'm just making sure you're with me, and that you're ready to assert your leadership."

Middleton didn't speak right away. "I'll be ready," he finally said.

"Trust me. Eldon Stafford is about to find himself with a pack of troubles. The hospital board is ready to move you into his position."

"A pack of troubles."

"That's what I said."

"You're-" Middleton seemed squeamish, with a look of nausea on his face. "You're not, not going to hurt anybody…"

Greevey's eyes rolled as he frowned. "You mean send hired thugs to take him down?"

"Something like that…"

Greevey smiled. "You've been watching too many Oliver Stone movies, reading too many John Grisham novels. You think powerful companies, or organizations, or the government, behave like organized crime syndicates." He shook his head, still smiling. "I do not employ minions of conscienceless thugs, standing by to carry out extreme measures at my whim. There's nothing like that going on." He shrugged. "Don't need 'em. I am one of the owners of the system. I can wreak more havoc with that than with gangs of hired killers."

"You just scared me with your 'pack of troubles' line."

"Not physical troubles."

Middleton's inquisitive expression invited more explanation.

"Reed's crash-and-burn down here is all I need. It'll take Stafford down too. And it's already in place, in progress."

"I'll be ready."

"Good." Greevey stood and extended his hand again. "Thanks for stopping by."

Middleton smiled and shook hands vigorously.

"I haven't found anything," Steve Weiss told Galen Reed as he stood up from looking under Galen Reed's desk. He wore a tool-belt, tightened around dusty jeans, separating them from a worn, brown t shirt. His face was covered with stubby gray whiskers and a red Los Angeles-Anaheim Angels cap covered his thinning, grayish black hair. "But people can get pretty creative with this stuff. Let me spend a little more time on it."

"Thanks. And thanks for coming out on such short notice."

"Doctor, you have given my family and I so much help with our health issues." He smiled. "My wife was talking about you just the other day. If it wasn't for you, she would have had neck surgery and I'd probably still be on medication for depression and probably still drinking too much. You changed our lives. My business is up because my health is up. And my wife and I get along better. So when you told me someone was trying to do one on you, to stick bugs in your office, you better believe I got over here as fast as I could."

"That's nice of you."

"Give me a few more minutes to look in some nooks and crannies. And if I still can't find anything, I'm going to call a few p-i buddies to see if they have any ideas."

"Thanks. Take all the time you need."

The intercom buzzed. Reed pressed the receive button and picked up the telephone. "Yes?"

"Natalie's here."

"Natalie?"

"She's asking to see you."

Reed took a long deep breath. "Any more patients?"

"No. The last one before lunch just left."

"Okay. Tell Natalie I'll be right out." Reed put down the phone. "I'll be right outside the office. Let me know if you find anything."

"I will keep at this until I find something, or I tell you I am sure nothing is here." He walked to some shelves in the corner of the office with a device that looked like a metal detector hooked up to a black box.

"Thanks." Reed left his private office and walked out to the front.

Natalie Corey stood waiting at the counter.

"Natalie. This is a surprise," he said.

"Well I've been dying to find out what happened with Eldon Stafford and the Segueway meeting. I thought we'd be getting together this weekend to celebrate. Or, commiserate?"

"I've just been, well, I guess overwhelmed? Sorry. I should have called back to tell you."

"I did leave a few messages…"

"Yeah. Sorry."

"Okay, so what happened?"

Galen Reed looked at her. How much should he tell her? He still couldn't get himself to believe she could be the source of inside information that had been leaking to enemies of his project with Eldon Stafford. But she seemed aggressive in the way she was asking for updates. Or was she asking as a caring "girlfriend?" "Eldon, uh, Dr. Stafford, uh, made his presentation. They'll let us know next week."

Natalie Corey looked puzzled.

"He thinks it went well."

"Good." She paused. "You seem, well, not very talkative about it. Sort of blasé."

"Yeah, well, it's best not to get too worked up about things like this."

Her face broke into another puzzled look. "Is that right…"

"Yeah, of course." He tilted his head toward the door. "Let's step outside a minute."

"Outside."

"Yeah." He took her arm and ushered her out the door.

"What's going on?" she asked.

"I have a man in my office looking for bugs. We think someone may be listening in our conversations."

Natalie Corey smiled, then chuckled. "What?"

"Someone knew about this Segueway thing and told people unfriendly to the idea."

Natalie Corey's expression became serious. "Wow."

"Someone knew about the Susan Stafford file and tried to use it to disrupt my relationship with the Staffords."

"So they know about it now?"

Galen Reed paused a moment, then shrugged. "It's fine. They're fine. But someone didn't want it to work out that way. We know who tried to use the Susan Stafford file against us. But there has to be more to it. That person had to know what the file meant, and have access to the other information. We're still looking at this, trying to figure out if anyone else is working against us."

She looked at him, but seemed out of the moment.

Galen Reed looked at her, trying to assess her reaction.

Her eyes narrowed. "And you think it could be me." She turned away.

"I didn't say that."

She turned back, red-faced, seeming on the verge of tears. "You didn't have to. What you haven't said, my calls you haven't returned, the way you don't want to say much—you think it's me!"

"No. I don't-" Galen Reed cut himself short. "I'm in a real state right now. On one hand, the collaboration is taking off. On the other hand, someone may be betraying me, or bugging my office. It's just, a bit overwhelming."

Her lips tensed. Tears flowed. "I can't believe you think it's me!"

"I didn't say that. I said—I started to say I don't know."

"And that means you think it could be me!"

Galen Reed felt frozen. He couldn't think of anything to say that wouldn't cause more emotion for Natalie Corey. He wanted to deny he thought it could be her, but the truth was that he wasn't sure.

"Damn it!" Natalie Corey's face twisted with anger. "How could you believe something so horrible about me?"

"I don't. Not really."

"But you're not sure."

"I'm sorry. But you've just been so negative about all this. It was hard not to, to at least consider, to consider all the possibilities."

"I see." She raised her chin. "I came to try to catch you for lunch."

"I'm not really hungry."

"Yeah. Me neither." She walked away toward her car.

Galen Reed let out a nervous breath. That had gone badly. He'd hoped to find a listening device in his office, something that could explain all the inside knowledge someone was getting about him without having someone close to him as a turncoat. He had wanted to hold off contact with her until he had established the truth. This premature contact, that he was not prepared for, had gone badly.

"Galen."

He looked in the direction of Natalie Corey's voice.

She was walking back. "I need to talk to you."

He watched as she rejoined him.

"I'm admitting to you that I'm consumed with guilt."

He waited for her explanation.

"I was about to just... walk away."

Galen Reed was not sure what to say because he was not sure what she was going to tell him.

"I owe you an apology."

This took him by surprise. Was she about to admit her culpability?

"This is my fault."

He did not say anything, still waiting for the explanation.

"Not because I'm some sort of spy—I'm not. It's my fault because I abandoned you at a time when you needed me. And this allowed you to even imagine I could betray you."

He wasn't sure what to say.

"I'm not going to walk away this time. I shouldn't have before, and no matter how hurt I feel right now, I will not walk away again. It's a bad habit I seem to be developing. It feels awful every time I do it. So I won't do it, not this time."

"I appreciate that."

"You're not the type of person who will yell and scream and carry on when someone who is supposed to love you disappoints you. But your reaction comes out this way."

"I'm not-"

"I deserve it, Galen. Don't argue with me. I do feel hurt. I am maybe a little angry that you suspect me, even a little. But I brought this on by not standing by you when I should have. So I will stand by you now."

"Okay. No argument. Apology accepted."

"And I don't want you to give me any more inside information until you figure out how the other information leaked out."

"Natalie, the-"

"I'm still dying to know all about what is probably a very exciting time for you. But I don't want you to think I'm standing by you now just to get more information."

"Why don't you let me decide how much to tell you?"

"That's fine." She smiled. "Now let's go to lunch."

"I can't right now."

She frowned.

"I've got a guy in my office."

She tilted her head.

"Looking for listening devices."

She raised her eyebrows. "Ah."

"Tonight?"

"I've got the boys. But come over anyway."

Galen smiled. "I'll be there."

Galen Reed walked back into his office.

Steve Weiss was hunched over in the far corner, using his metal detector, and holding a magnifying glass.

"Find anything?"

Weiss sat up, still on the ground, but now up to face Reed. "I did." He stood. "Stuck to the bottom of your phone."

"So it's a bug. That's it. Mystery solved."

Weiss walked over to Reed's desk and picked up a small round metal object with a tiny metal mesh on one side. "This."

Reed nodded as he looked at it. "Okay. Good."

Weiss shook his head. "This thing doesn't seem to have any

function. It's a decoy. Taped to the bottom of the phone in haste. Not anything that would fool an expert, but it looks high-tech enough to fool someone just taking a quick look through the office. There may be another one in here they don't want us to find."

Reed took some initial comfort from the idea that this meant Natalie Corey couldn't be involved. But with a second thought, he realized the device could have been planted long ago, or that more than one person could be working against him and Eldon Stafford. "You're still looking…"

"Yeah. Every way I can think of. I'll let you know."

"Thanks."

Chapter 29

"We have a warrant to search these premises! Everybody freeze! Stay still!"

Galen Reed looked up from his examination of Sheila Watanabe. "Excuse me," he told her, maintaining a calm demeanor even as his stomach did flips.

He walked into the hall toward the front of his office. He saw three police officers holding up plastic shields, wearing helmets. They did not have their guns drawn, but they wore clearly displayed pistols in holsters on their waists, with their hands close to the guns.

"Stop right there! Raise your hands in the air, palms out!" The voice was the same voice Reed had heard while he was examining Sheila Watanabe. The man wore a gray pin-striped suit and stood behind the police officers. Another man dressed in an open-collared light blue shirt stood next to him. Behind them was a third man wearing a sport jacket and tie.

Reed slowly raised both hands and rotated them to show they were empty. "What is this about? This is a doctor's office. I'd prefer you not disturb my patients."

"Are you Galen Reed?" the man in the gray suit asked.

"Yes I am. Now kindly tell me what this is about. I'm assuming this is a mistake."

"There is no mistake. You are under arrest for violation of California Penal Section 550 A, Sections One, Two, Five and Six, 550

B, Sections One thru Four. Place your hands on your head."

Reed brought his hands slowly to the top of his head. "What? What is this about? What is Section 550A, One-Two whatever?"

One of the officers moved toward him with handcuffs.

"Excuse me, but why don't we just sit down and discuss this?" Reed remained compliant with these seriously armed men, and maintained an even temper though he churned with emotion—with anger, and yes, as he saw the handcuffs, fear.

"We are executing a search warrant." The man in the gray suit looked around the office, and still spoke as if he was addressing everyone, not just Galen Reed. "Part One. Any documentation pertaining to patient Jimmy Puccinelli. Part Two. Any documentation pertaining to billings for accidents. Part Three. Any documentation pertaining to billings for alleged services provided to Orange County Memorial Hospital."

"Alleged services?"

The officer took Reed's hands from the top of his head and clasped them together behind his back.

"Hey!" Reed called out "You! You in the gray suit who's doing all the shouting! Let's talk about this! You've made a mistake!"

"It's no mistake," the man said with hard eyes that barely seemed present.

"Sir," the officer said, politely but insistently.

Reed realized he had brought his hands away from behind his back. He put his hands back behind him.

The officer placed the handcuffs around his wrists and clicked them shut.

Reed pursed his lips as his nostrils flared. "I don't have anything to hide. I haven't done anything wrong." He felt a slow-building anger rising to a rage, but knew he had to fight allowing the adrenaline rush to overwhelm his reason. In fact, he used the building anger, and the knowledge it was there, and that he needed to keep it under wraps, as a means to focus his behavior. He felt acutely tuned to the moment. "I will cooperate fully. I can do it better without the handcuffs."

"We need to take you downtown," the officer told him.

"Fine," Reed said, becoming aware that these people had not arrived to reason with him. He turned to the man in the gray suit. "Rosie here will help you." He motioned to Rosie Jacinto. "Get Melanie to help also," Reed told her. He turned back to the man in the gray suit. "These are confidential patient files. I ask your discretion and your courtesy as you complete your review."

"We will behave within the parameters of the search warrant," the man said. "Now, may I have the Puccinelli file?"

Reed nodded to Rosie Jacinto.

She walked timidly to the man in the gray suit and handed him the file.

The man opened the file. "Yes. Here it is. Notes that say this man did not sustain the injuries in this car accident that you billed for."

"What? I'd like to see that."

"It's your file, sir. Don't you know what's in it?"

"I don't have all my files memorized. And I have staff working in them as well. I'd like to see the file."

"Downtown." The man in the gray suit nodded, and the officer with Reed took his right arm and nudged him toward the door.

"Rosie. Tell the patients here there's been a problem and we'll have to reschedule. And call Ted Butler. Tell him what's happened."

They reached the doorway. "You can call him from downtown," the man in the gray suit said.

"Tell him what's happened!" Reed shouted as they pushed him ahead through the doorway. "Tell him to come out as soon as he can!"

Reed was through the doorway now. The last few words had been uttered outside the office, but Reed was certain they'd been heard. He hoped help was on the way.

Seymour McTavish trailed behind Phil Hedges, from the Department of Insurance, and the man in the gray suit, Thomas Pendleton, Orange County Deputy District Attorney. He smirked as he watched Reed placed into a police squad car.

Two television news cameras rolled, and McTavish recognized a reporter from the Orange County Tribune he had worked with before.

"Nice job," he said to Phil Hedges as he smirked.

Hedges frowned.

McTavish flipped open his cell phone. "Greevey," he said into the phone.

"Is it done?" Greevey asked, answering the call from McTavish.

"Done and done. Went perfectly. Two television stations. And the Trib."

"Good work."

"Sure."

"Thank our friends on this."

"I will."

McTavish snapped his phone shut. He walked over to Phil Hedges. "Your boss knows how much we over at Havitol Pharmacy appreciate your department's fast attention to insurance fraud."

"He'll appreciate all your gestures. He's got a reelection campaign coming up, at some point."

"Good." McTavish watched the car door to the squad car shut. The car pulled away.

McTavish walked back into the office. He saw Deputy DA Thomas Pendleton sitting in one of the waiting room chairs, looking through a file. There was a stack of files on the floor. "Mr. Pendleton. Thanks for your quick action."

"We hate insurance fraud," Pendleton said.

"I know. So do we over at Havitol Pharmacy."

Pendleton looked up wearing a sly smile. "I can tell."

"We're showing our gratitude-"

"Not here, McTavish." Pendleton looked around. "I hashed this out with your boss last night. We have a clear understanding."

McTavish nodded.

Pendleton went back to looking at a file.

McTavish left.

"Okay, slow down," Eldon Stafford said into his cell phone. He walked through the hospital parking lot toward his car.

"He's under arrest. Handcuffs. They searched the office," Delores Hart said, seeming to gasp for air between phrases.

"Delores. Slow down. Take it from the beginning. Who is under arrest?"

"Galen Reed. They took him to jail."

Eldon Stafford's eyes bulged with disbelief. "Who arrested him?"

"They were here with plastic shields, and helmets, and guns. And they had a search warrant. They took files."

"What files?"

"Jimmy Puccinelli. They named that one."

Stafford tried to think. This turn of events was beyond anything he had anticipated.

"Dr. Stafford?"

"Yeah, I'm here." He arrived at his car. He stood next to it, absorbed in thought. "Does he have an attorney?"

"I think so."

"All right. Thanks for telling me."

"What should I do?"

"You're at Dr. Reed's office?"

"I just stopped in for a few hours to finish up a few things."

"Okay. Just head back to my office."

"What do you think happened?"

Eldon Stafford thought a moment. "I don't know," he finally said. "I'm not sure."

"It was just awful."

"Who's there?"

"Rosie. The lady who files sometimes. And some people who came in with the search warrant."

"Find out who Dr. Reed's attorney is."

"Find out…"

"Ask Rosie, or anyone there who might know."

He waited as he heard Delores Hart asking for the attorney

information. He heard "Ted Butler" from someone in the background.

"Ted Butler," she said.

"I heard. Thanks. I'll see you back at the office."

"Okay."

Stafford shut the phone. He got in his car, putting his briefcase in the back seat. He put his keys in the car, but didn't start the engine. He pulled out his phone and snapped it back open. "Brianna," he said.

The line connected. "Dad?"

"Are you on line?"

"Yes…"

"Can you get me a phone number for an attorney, Ted Butler?"

"Let me see." He heard the clicking of computer keys on the other end of the phone. "From Irvine?"

"Criminal Law?"

"Yeah."

"That's it. Give me the number."

"714-555-7410."

"Thanks," Eldon Stafford said as he jotted the number on the back of a business card.

"What is this about?" Briana asked.

"Galen got arrested. Sounds like some kind of problem with his files."

"That couldn't be."

"I know. Thanks for the number."

"Sure. Let me know what's going on."

"I will." He ended the call and quickly entered the phone number for the attorney.

"Law Offices," the efficient female voice said.

"Ted Butler, please."

"He's not here right now. Would you like to leave a message?"

"This is Eldon Stafford. I'm a partner with Galen Reed. Can you put me through to Mr. Butler?"

"Galen Reed?" The voice paused. "One moment, please."

Stafford waited. He knew she was contacting Butler on his cell phone to see if he wanted to take the call. That was fine with Eldon Stafford, and to be expected.

"Mr. Stafford?"

"Doctor. Yes."

"Dr. Stafford. I'll patch you through to his cell phone."

"Dr. Stafford?" Ted Butler's voice asked. The sound of auto travel permeated the background.

"Yes. What's going on?"

"I'm not sure. But for this type of case, this is massive overkill. It doesn't make a lot of sense."

"It might make more sense than you think. Galen and I have been involved in a huge project. There are indications that some people don't want us to succeed, some powerful people. Spare no expense. I'll help with the costs. Subpoena every document. Drag every witness in for a deposition. Dig into every motivation."

"I'm on my way to see him now. They're actually holding him like a criminal."

"Damn."

"I'll let him know you called, and keep in mind what you've said."

"Thanks. Please call me with a report on the situation as soon as you can."

"Okay, Doctor."

"Thanks." Eldon Stafford snapped his phone shut. His face tensed with a grim expression as he started his car.

"Page three," Wyatt Greevey said to Seymour McTavish. They sat in Wyatt Greevey's office just after dawn. Greevey tossed the paper down. "Page three in the LA Times. Page six in the Orange County Tribune."

"Well, these types of incidents don't get much play in the press."

"I need more play out of this than we've gotten."

"Doesn't this put your friend Reed out of business?"

"What difference does it make if Segueway decides to go through with it? If the thing gets going, Reed's problems won't matter. The concept'll be bigger than the man."

"I don't know."

Wyatt Greevey nodded as his lips tensed. "Of course you don't."

"Uh, is there something-"

"No. This isn't on you. It's on me. You did a good job. Playing this next angle is my move, and I may have underplayed it."

McTavish didn't say anything.

"I'll let you know if I need your help."

"My cell phone is on twenty-four/seven."

"I know. I appreciate it. Good work. Thanks for coming in so early"—Greevey held up the newspapers they had been reading—"with these."

"No problem."

"I should have known this would need some nudging, not just from the level you were playing. It was a mistake. My mistake." He raised his eyebrows. "But a mistake I can still fix." He smiled. "Still a good way to play this."

"Do you need me?"

"I'll let you know if I do."

Seymour McTavish took this as his cue to leave. He stood, nodded, and left.

Wyatt Greevey pulled open his lower desk drawer to find some old business cards. He fumbled through them until he found the one he wanted: Nate Wilson, Managing Editor, *San Jose Times*.

Chapter 30

Wyatt Greevey punched in the number handwritten on the card, Nate Wilson's direct line.

"Wilson." He had a thin voice, almost squeaky. His words came fast, rushed, as if he was in too much of a hurry to speak slower.

"Nate. Hey, my old friend. It's Wyatt Greevey."

"Wyatt. Long time."

"Yeah. I shouldn't wait so long between calls. But I think I have something for you."

"We love a good story."

"Chiropractor busted for insurance fraud."

"Where?"

"Brea."

"In Orange County? That sounds like a local story. For southern California."

"There's more to it. I have it on good authority that this chiropractor, along with another doctor down our way, was in the process of trying to scam money out of one of the big venture capital outfits up your way."

"Really. Now that could be something. Which venture capital company?"

"Segueway."

"Really. What do you have?"

"I can fax up a copy of their presentation to Segueway, and a copy of the article about the chiropractor's arrest."

"Yeah." Nate Wilson seemed to perk up. His voice sounded enthusiastic. "That could be good. Thanks."

"Glad to help out with a front page scoop."

"Well, I thank you for the lead, but I'm not sure this is a page one story."

"Sure it is. Segueway? Big money? Scams?"

"Look, I'll check it out. We've got a couple of good people who have some connections over there. We've built up some favors from our handling of some press releases on a few of their ventures. At least, I think they feel obligated to us. But I can't say it's page one."

"Well, sure, it's your call, of course."

"Yeah. Do you have any other information?"

But Wyatt Greevey was not letting go of the page-one idea. "Most newspapers, metropolitan newspapers, are having some problems."

"Problems..."

"Financial troubles."

"The internet. Twenty-four hour television news. Sure, we're a little tight on funds, like everyone."

"Well, Havitol needs to increase its visibility in the Bay Area. I'm thinking of a huge, ongoing advertising campaign. Frankly, a medical story on the front page, a sexy story that gets people thinking about medicine, would be a great way for us to kick off the campaign."

"Really."

"Absolutely."

"Well, maybe this is starting to sound more and more like a front-page story."

Wyatt Greevey smiled. "Good. Those faxes'll be out to you in five minutes. Have your reporters call me for more details. And have your advertising people call me, to get the ad campaign going."

"Sure."

"Nice to talk to you."

"Likewise. Thanks for the story."

"My pleasure."

"I'm sure it is, Mr. Wyatt Greevey. I'm sure it is. And I reserve the right not to run it if it doesn't check out."

"It will. But I reserve the same rights on my ad campaign."

"Of course you do. Call me again. Any time you want to talk about a story. Or, an ad campaign."

"Right."

Wyatt Greevey disconnected the call. He smiled. Maybe he had failed at first to handle the Galen Reed arrest perfectly. But this move would rescue the initial mishandling, perhaps even surpassing the event's original potential.

Wyatt Greevey reflected that not every decision he had made in his career had been perfect. But he had the ability to bounce back from mistakes, from adversities, a quality he had inherited from his father. He had been a boy in kindergarten when World War Two had begun. At that time, his father was a thirty-five year old grocery store assistant manager, the sole support of the Greevey family. So his father remained in the United States while so many went off to war. Eventually his father became the owner-operator of the store, through hard work, obsessive savings, and an eagle eye for opportunity.

But Wyatt Greevey had heard many times from his father about his father's life before the grocery store. Walter Greevey had been a rising young stockbroker in New York when an October day in 1929 destroyed so many fortunes, and in his case, took away a lucrative livelihood. He had watched two of his co-workers leap to suicide deaths, a cliché Greevey's father had personally witnessed at its origins. But young Wyatt Greevey heard from his father how he never gave up. "Guard your flanks and look for opportunities. I went to that store, and a bunch of other places, every day for six months until I got that clerk's job. Sweeping floors, stocking cans—I was glad to get it." When the teenaged Wyatt Greevey griped about hours helping out at the store—sweeping floors, stocking cans—his father would relay the story again, with a little embellishment each time.

Greevey's father had expected him to take over the store. But Greevey had better ideas. He turned around his father's advice.

"Watch for opportunities and guard your flanks." Greevey performed his responsibilities at the store, but went to school at night. He got a Bachelor of Arts in Finance, and was working on a Masters in Business Administration when his father had his first heart attack. Now was the time to take over the store, with his father standing by in an advisory capacity. But Greevey went a different direction. With some sharp moves, and meticulous research, Greevey positioned the store for a lucrative sale to a national chain. With the money, he bought three small drug stores in the area, in effect, setting up his own small chain, a move he made against his more cautious father's wishes. From the three stores, Greevey pursued a relentless strategy of expansion and profit. The expansion included moving into other parts of the health-care industry, and even some involvement with insurance companies. His father lived to see him reach a net worth of one million dollars, pleased to see how the family of the displaced stockbroker had evolved. His mother lived to see him accumulate nine figures of net worth.

He'd gotten where he was by looking for opportunities and guarding his flanks. Here was just another manifestation of the same concept. He had no doubt he would make this situation work for him, as he had manipulated situations to his advantage so many times in the past.

"We are asking bail of five hundred thousand," Deputy District Attorney Thomas Pendleton stated as he stood at the prosecution table in the Orange County Criminal Courthouse in Santa Ana. He wore a blue pinstripe suit (a slight variation on the gray suit from the day of the arrest) with a white shirt and blue tie. The court was about half full, mostly with attorneys and parties present for the morning calendar.

Galen Reed sat in an orange prison jumpsuit, with ORANGE COUNTY stenciled on the back. Eldon and Brianna Stafford sat behind the defendant's table. Reed took in a weary breath as he heard the district attorney ask for the huge bail.

"Your Honor, half a million is ridiculous," Ted Butler said. He wore a brown suit with an off-white shirt and gold tie. "Dr. Reed is a respected member of the community with strong roots here. And, Your Honor, we take deep exception to the way the prosecutor has manipulated the custody to keep my client confined over night when we could have had this handled yesterday! My client is an innocent man who the district attorney is trying to intimidate and harass with-"

Thomas Pendleton interrupted. "We are looking at this defendant for many more counts. He may be the head of an organized fraud ring, which will expose him to violations of the RICO Act, so with federal implications-"

"What?" Butler seemed genuinely incredulous. "Your Honor, this is one count. If they have evidence of more, let them bring those counts. Otherwise, five thousand is reasonable bail for this charge."

"Bail must guarantee the defendant's appearance at trial," the prosecutor said in a lecturing tone. "The defendant faces much more criminal liability than this one count, and is therefore a risk to flee."

The judge shook his head. "Ten thousand."

"You Honor, this is a serious-" But the prosecutor was not allowed to finish his objection.

"Counsel, I am not setting a six figure bail for this one count. You get more? Come back." The judge flipped the file toward the clerk. "Next."

Galen Reed let out another weary breath. He closed his eyes, then opened them. This ordeal was at least about to shift from the bowels of the county jail to a more benign locale.

"I'll post whatever you need," Eldon Stafford told him, leaning forward from the row behind, gritting his teeth.

Galen Reed turned to look at him. "Thanks."

"Something's going on, Galen. Someone's playing dirty."

"Dirty." Reed shook his head. "You ever stay over night in the county jail?"

"I'll get the paperwork going," Ted Butler said. "You won't be in here much longer."

Reed nodded as the sheriff's deputy took his arm.

"This is all so over-the-top," Ted Butler said. "Somebody is pushing this hard, someone with some serious juice." Galen Reed, Eldon Stafford, Brianna Stafford and Ted Butler sat at a worn cafeteria table on the second floor of the courthouse. The attorney drank a cup of coffee. The other three drank bottled water.

"I don't know," Galen Reed said. "I just want to go home, clean up, and get some rest."

"Of course," Eldon Stafford said. "We just need a brief conversation."

"Sure," Galen Reed said.

"Someone is working against us from the inside," Eldon Stafford said. "We've suspected it, but the ramifications are getting critical."

"You figure the person on the inside had something to do with my arrest?" Galen Reed asked.

"Absolutely."

"Well doesn't that rule out Natalie?" Galen Reed asked.

"Who can we 'rule in?'" Eldon Stafford asked.

"It was Puccinelli's file they say caused the trouble," Galen Reed said.

"Yes," Ted Butler said.

"So he sneaks in the office and plants a bug, then somehow manages to engineer this?" Galen Reed puzzled over this idea.

"Not without help," Eldon Stafford said.

Ted Butler shook his head. "Finding out who the insider is, the defector—you need to find out. The government is after you. I'm not sure why."

"Greevey," Stafford said. "He's got to be behind this."

"If we can find out who the insider is, we should be able to connect it to Greevey," Butler said.

"So how do we figure out who it is?" Stafford asked.

"You set a trap," Butler told them. "You feed some information to the people you suspect. False information. Different to each one.

Then you wait to see what ends up getting out."

"How do we trap Puccinelli?" Reed asked.

"With him, if I understand you, he might have planted a bug," Ted Butler said. "Go into your office and drop some tidbit there."

"Steve Weiss found a decoy. Nothing else. There were no functioning bugs."

"Try it anyway," Ted Butler said. "Your friend might have missed something."

Galen Reed nodded. "And I suppose I need to drop something for Natalie to leak."

"If you're going to check this," Eldon Stafford said.

"It can't be the vitamin lady," Brianna Stafford said.

"I don't think so either." Galen Reed's lips tightened as he paused in thought. "She told me she doesn't want any inside information."

"Clever ploy if she's the one," Ted Butler said. "So you need to leak something to her inadvertently."

"I hate it," Galen Reed said. His eyebrows moved together as another idea occurred to him. "Brianna," he said. "Remember when Puccinelli tried to drive a wedge between you, your father and me?"

Brianna Stafford nodded as her eyes narrowed in reflection. "He called Delores."

"Suppose there was no call?" Galen Reed asked.

The table was silent.

"Delores?" Eldon Stafford frowned with apparent doubt. "She's been with us for years. She's extremely loyal. How could any of these problems benefit her?"

Brianna shook her head. "She's almost like a family member. She helped get me summer jobs. Her kids babysat me when I was little."

"You should lay a trap for her also," Ted Butler said.

Eldon shook his head. "There's simply no chance that-" He appeared to stop himself. "Okay. Her too." He paused. "Anyone else?"

"I can't think of anyone right now," Galen Reed said.

"Let me know what you find out," Ted Butler said. "If the authorities were involved, it could be the basis for a legal defense. In the meantime, I will press for immediate discovery on their evidence. I do not believe they will be able to sustain the charges."

Galen Reed squinted as his face tensed with anger. "I couldn't agree more." He stood. "Let's get out of here."

The other three stood. They grabbed their empty drink containers to discard them, and headed out of the cafeteria.

"New development on the Reed-Stafford situation," McTavish said as he walked into Greevey's office. "I wanted to let you know right away."

Greevey looked up from his desk. He took his reading glasses off. "Of course." He motioned McTavish to a chair near his desk.

"From my source. There's a fax from Segueway to Stafford—came in this morning. We think it's probably stored in the fax machine memory. We're trying to get ahold of it. I'll stand by with you. As soon as I get a call we can-"

"Wait a minute," Greevey said. "What do you mean 'a fax from Segueway?'"

"Some sort of proposal or contract. That's what I'm hearing. We can check it out when we-"

Greevey shook his head. "Something's wrong. That's not the way they do things."

McTavish looked puzzled.

"They're in a decision-making mode. They call. They do a lot more work before they start shooting out proposals."

"So my source got it wrong..."

"Your source is probably walking into a trap." Greevey nodded grimly. "Our friends are starting to fight back."

"I better call right away." McTavish pulled out his cell phone.

Greevey shook his head. "I'm betting it's too late. You don't want your call coming in while the trap is being sprung."

McTavish nodded. He put his phone back in his pocket. "So it's damage control."

Greevey shrugged. "Not a problem."

"Sir, I'm one step away."

Greevey shook his head and smiled. "We're driving this thing. I'll just pick up the phone and call it off."

"So if they're not digging into this anymore-"

"You're one step away from... nothing."

McTavish smiled.

"I'm not making that phone call just yet though. I think we have this set up to work out just right."

"Okay..."

"Well, I would have preferred not to have our source burned this soon. Didn't expect them to push back. But I think we've already gotten it done."

"Good."

"We'll see."

Eldon Stafford walked into the small office and storage area where he kept his fax machine. "Find what you're looking for?" he asked.

Out of the fax printer came one page. It read, in bold black letters: "WE GOT YOU."

Delores Hart picked up the page as she turned. "Dr. Stafford?" She trembled.

"We sure found what we were looking for," he said. His eyes bored in on her. "How could you—so many years we worked together—how could you?"

She bit her lip. "I'm sorry." Tears rolled down both cheeks. "I'm sorry."

Stafford's teeth clenched.

"They came to me." She sniffled. "When this thing with Galen Reed started. They asked if I could get involved in this, this project you were starting, and then tell them things about it."

"Who came to you?"

"Some guy. He didn't say much about who he was."

"Did he tell you to try to make it look like Jimmy Puccinelli was behind this?"

She bit her lip.

"With a phone bug taped to Dr. Reed's phone?"

"I'm sorry…"

"Yeah, well, an apology—not quite enough here, Delores. You're going to have to tell us a lot more about the people you've been helping."

"I don't know if I can tell you."

Stafford's eyes narrowed so much they almost closed.

"They offered me a little money to tell them what was going on. He said he worked for an organization that protects people from flaky medical schemes. That's what chiropractors are." She seemed to harden. "I'm surprised, Doctor, that you seem to have forgotten that."

"Hmm-hmm."

"I didn't want to do it anymore. He kept pushing me, offering me more money and threatening to tell you what I'd already done." She sobbed. "I was in too deep."

"So you set up my friend, my partner—you set him up to be arrested…"

"They told me what to put on the bills. I just did it. I had no choice. I didn't know they would stick him in handcuffs."

"You had no choice." Eldon Stafford looked away from her, then back. "You had a choice not to sell me out."

"You know, Doctor, that's easy for you to say." Her tear-stained voice hardened again. "It was just a little extra money. To keep them informed." Her nostrils flared. "I've watched you bill half a million to a million a year. I've been with you year after year. I was there for you when your wife died. I felt for you. I tried to be there, as more than just a staff-member. If you'd been a little more-" She seemed to be fighting with how much she would verbalize. "I could have been-" She paused again. "We could have-" She stopped speaking. Eldon Stafford read her expression as the anger of someone who had apparently felt rejected, and had suppressed those feelings for years. "I contributed a lot more than you paid me for, Doctor. Why shouldn't I make some money from my position? After all, we have a business relationship, right? Nothing more than that."

Eldon Stafford found Delores Hart's newly uncovered bitterness infuriating. He had increased her salary to well above the market value for her position with him. Did she think she was a partner? Apparently she thought she should have become his wife, because she was the lady in his life with the most seniority? Because it was the next logical promotion? He chafed at the foolishness but did not want to engage her at all in any sort of discussion. "Well, I hope for your sake that they paid you a lot, because you're fired. Effective immediately. Don't expect any severance pay." He paused. "And I if I can figure out a way to rain down more consequences on you, I will. Do not give me as a reference."

She threw down the paper that read "WE GOT YOU" and walked out of the room.

Eldon Stafford followed her. These wouldn't be comfortable moments, but he would stay with her as she collected her belongings, assuring that she could do no more damage.

Chapter 31

"Everybody's on?" Ben Richards asked.

"Yes sir," his assistant answered.

"Thanks." Richards leaned back in his plush chair behind a dark brown wooden desk. He wore a bluish-green San Jose Sharks sweatsuit. His office overflowed with comfort, from the refrigerator off in the far corner from the entrance, to the big screen television and surround-sound stereo on the opposite wall from Richards' desk.

Richards put on his phone headset. "Fiona?"

"I'm here," she said.

"Seth?"

"I'm on to."

"We're doing this a day early, for obvious reasons."

No one spoke.

"You've all seen the paper?" he asked.

"Yes," Fiona Patton said, with a flat, emotionless tone of voice.

"I've got it in front of me," Seth Mercoyan said.

Richards glanced down at the front page of the San Jose Times, also sitting in front of him. The headline read: "Chiro Pitching Segueway Capital Arrested".

"I took calls and emails all day yesterday," Richards told them. "I've been reminded, as the senior member of the panel for this prospective investment, that Segueway does not like publicity, does not like headlines, especially headlines that make us look like scam victims."

"The chiropractor is not the one who pitched us," Fiona reminded them.

"Not directly," Richards answered. "But indirectly? Sure, he was part of the partnership pitching us. It's clear in the articles."

"So what do we do?" Seth Mercoyan asked.

"This little mess notwithstanding, it's still a good idea," Fiona Patton said.

"I wouldn't argue with that," Ben Richards said.

"I hate to say it," Seth Mercoyan said. Ben Richards could almost hear him shaking his head through the phone. "But we can't go through with this thing. With this big cloud over it, the membership will never vote to go forward."

"That is the problem," Ben Richards said. "Not only will they not vote for it, but I'm getting calls and emails insisting we distance ourselves from this thing immediately. If we don't, they're afraid every scam artist and flake-with-an-idea will deluge us."

"But it really is a great idea," Fiona Patton said. "That hasn't changed at all. The more I think about it, the more I like it. But"—she paused—"I'm getting the same calls Ben is. Embarrassment. 'Segueway can't be on the front page like this.'"

"And they're right," Seth Mercoyan said.

"I'm afraid so," Fiona Patton said. "So... I don't see any reason to go forward on this when the membership is already hostile."

Richards nodded. "We've all come to the same conclusion. A unanimous conclusion. A reluctant but unanimous conclusion. We pass on this."

"Yes," Seth Mercoyan said.

"As you said, reluctantly. Regretfully. Yes," Fiona Patton added.

"I'll call Dr. Stafford," Seth Mercoyan said.

Ben Richards frowned. He wanted to make the call, but did not want to seem too anxious. "Well, sure, you could. He is your friend."

"That's why I think I should be the one to tell him."

"I understand," Richards said. "But it is customary for the senior panel member to make the call. I mean, I have no problem doing it—comes with the territory."

"I appreciate this. But I brought him to us. What happened wasn't his fault—I want to make sure he knows that."

"I can get that across to him. And I think he deserves the respect of hearing from the senior panel member."

"You put it that way, as a way of offering respect." Seth Mercoyan paused. "All right. You call him."

"And as far as this being his fault." Ben Richard's jaw moved up. "I think these adverse circumstances were created, and I think I know who did it."

"There were an awful lot of ads for Havitol Pharmaceutical in the Times," Fiona Patton said.

"Yeah. I noticed that too. And that son-of-a-bitch Greevey was calling me about this. But we can't prove any of it, and we could sound paranoid even raising the issue."

"You don't think my friend Dr. Stafford was taken in by this chiropractor fellow?" Seth Mercoyan asked.

"No I don't," Richards answered.

"So the Times got it wrong," Seth Mercoyan said.

"Yeah." He blasted a jet of air out of his nostrils. "You believe everything you read in the papers?"

Richards heard a chuckle from Mercoyan. "No."

"You know how many times they've completely bollixed the facts on something of ours, even in the business section," Ben Richards reminded them.

"What if we can prove this was a manipulation?" Fiona Patton asked.

Richards shook his head. "We can't do it through Segueway. They won't want to take the time and energy to dig up all the crap we'd need to uncover. The pressure is for us to immediately put down some distance."

"I know," Fiona Patton agreed. "It just... doesn't seem right."

"No." Ben Richards took a deep breath. "It doesn't. But we all know that stuff happens in business all-day, all-the-time, that doesn't seem right."

No one spoke.

"I'll report to the membership," Richards said. "I'll call Dr. Stafford."

"Agreed," Seth Mercoyan said. "Tell him I'll call him later today."

"Okay," Ben Richards said.

"Give him my best," Fiona Patton said.

"Right."

"Bye," Seth Mercoyan said.

"Good-bye," Fiona Patton said.

The three-way call ended.

Ben Richards looked down at the file he had, labeled "Eldon Stafford Project." He smiled as he opened the file and looked for Eldon Stafford's cell phone number. He called it.

"Dr. Stafford."

"Dr. Stafford, it's Ben Richards, with Segueway."

"Yes. You've got your meeting set for tomorrow. We're looking forward to your decision."

Richards realized Stafford probably didn't know about the newspaper story up in San Jose. "Um, we just met."

"A day early."

"Yeah." Richards paused. "There was a newspaper article, front page, about Galen Reed's arrest—and Segueway Capital."

"Front page?" Eldon Stafford's disbelief oozed through the phone connection.

"Yup. Segueway was in the headline."

"Ridiculous."

"It may be. But it leaves Segueway with even a wisp of a p-r problem. And the membership doesn't like that kind of thing."

"I see."

"So we have to pass on this project."

Eldon Stafford did not immediately respond.

"It was not a happy decision for any of us. But it was unanimous."

"I understand."

"Seth will call you later. But this is the official call from Segueway."

"I see. Well, thanks for considering us."

"Sure. Now, um, for some unofficial communications."

"Unofficial."

"Right."

"What's on your mind?"

Richards smiled. "I'll tell you what's on my mind, what really has me preoccupied."

"Okay."

"It's my neck. And my back."

"Your neck and back…"

"They feel great. Haven't felt this good in years."

"And that's got you preoccupied."

"Yes it does. Because I went to Fiona's chiropractor."

Stafford did not respond.

"I'd never been to a chiropractor before. Thought I should check it out."

"Makes sense."

"I didn't expect anything much, really. But I feel fantastic. I've now had two visits and I'm going back a few more times before I go on some kind of regular maintenance program."

"It really does work. Take it from an MD."

"I'm a believer, Doctor."

"So if it wasn't for this Reed problem-"

"And the front page story up here-"

"There would have been a commitment of some serious funds to this idea."

"There still could be," Richards told him.

"I thought that Segueway-"

"Not from Segueway."

"Okay…"

"I want us to stay in contact. I want you to know you have friends up here, allies. Keep me posted on your successes. I just might shake the trees up here and see if I can put together a private group. It gets trickier, setting the legal arrangements, and the funds available could be lower, and it'll take longer to manage, without the structure of Segueway. But... well, my neck and back really do feel better." He straightened up in his chair as he grinned. "This idea is growing on me."

"Good."

"You see, in light of the government's latest attempts to get involved in health care, you may have come up with the best answer for millions."

There was a pause. "I have to be honest," Eldon Stafford said. "I haven't thought of this in terms of Congress's new law."

"Sure. That's not the first thing you think of. But I think big-picture economics. And the experts say this new law, if it comes in full-force, will create shortages. If there are shortages, people will look for alternatives. And we'll have it available, under one big tent."

"And if the people calling for repeal and revamp get their way?"

"We'll still be well-situated. They'll be talking about a consumer-driven healthcare system, with less regulations and more free market aspects, with patients choosing among a wide variety of healthcare options and reimbursement plans. There is only a miniscule fraction of possible options available to the public right now. Your idea could be a really good option for many people."

"That's encouraging."

"I want you to be encouraged, even though this is technically a negative call. But this is not over."

"Okay. That's good to hear. I'll tell Dr. Reed."

"I'd like to meet him sometime. I'm willing to bet his troubles will be history soon. Trust me, those troubles were only created there long enough to produce this result."

"What do you mean?"

"I mean there was a hell of a lot of Havitol Pharmaceutical advertising in the issue that had that front page article."

"Greevey. Of course. Well let's get the word out on that. He shouldn't be allowed to kill a good idea, should he?"

"Doctor, I don't know how much time you've spent in court. For your sake, I hope not too much. But one thing I have learned from my little skirmishes there—knowing and proving, two different things. Kind of like legal and moral, innocent and not guilty."

"Too bad."

"You might be able to get something more solid down your way, if they're stupid enough to keep coming after your Dr. Reed after they got what they wanted. Just keep me posted. I'll help you however I can."

"Thanks. I'll be in touch."

"Good. Bye."

Ben Richards ended the call. He flexed his shoulders and rolled his neck. He picked up some papers on his desk. Nothing else was on the calendar for the day. Tomorrow, he would listen to a pitch for a new program to share music files. Later in the week, a pitch for a new website for social networking with an occupational slant. He frowned. More high-tech, dot-com stuff. Lucrative, but sometimes tedious. Health care. What a huge tangle of intersecting messes. What a seemingly insurmountable set of unsolvable dilemmas. Ben Richards smiled. What a wonderful challenge! His mind raced. The cogs wouldn't stop turning. He tossed down the paper he had been holding, that couldn't hold his attention. He picked up the phone.

Chapter 32

"They seem to have totally lost enthusiasm for the case," Ted Butler said to Galen Reed, Eldon Stafford, Brianna Stafford, Clyde Minden and Natalie Corey. They sat together at a booth at the Imperial Highway Grill. They all had their orders, various snacks with drinks.

"Good lawyering," Galen Reed said, smiling, relaxed to be out of potential legal jeopardy.

"No." Ted Butler shrugged as he paused. "I mean, I'd love to take credit for it, but that's not it. It's really as if they just completely lost interest."

"But you called them on it," Galen Reed said. "You pointed out that the forms and reports on Puccinelli were not signed by me, not directly authorized by me to go out. Delores Hart sent those papers on to the insurance carrier."

"All true. But that prosecutor barely listened to me. It was like he knew he was going to drop the case before I even called, but didn't want to admit it."

Eldon Stafford shook his head. "Does this make sense?"

"Sure it does," Ted Butler said, "If someone is pulling the DA's strings."

Eldon Stafford nodded. "Ben Richards mentioned this possibility."

"Well, whatever it is, I'm glad my legal troubles are over," Galen Reed said.

"They sure are." Ted Butler said. "This shuts everything down, discovery, any legal capability we have to issue subpoenas and compel information."

"We could sue," Eldon Stafford said.

"Who?" Ted Butler asked. "Any of the possible defendants, the government, Havitol, even Jimmy Puccinelli—there's no cause of action against any of them that would survive a motion to dismiss, before we could even get the first interrogatories out."

No one spoke.

Ted Butler turned to Galen Reed. "But at least your legal troubles are over, including your bill from me, which I am writing off."

Reed's eyes widened. He nodded. "Thanks."

"Thank you. For all the great care you've given me. For the great things you and Dr. Stafford are trying to do." Ted Butler offered a warm, broad smile.

Reed nodded again, returning the smile.

"I have a question," Brianna Stafford told them. "I can understand how everyone feels good now, because the legal battles are over, and we caught Delores, and sent her on her way. But what are you going to do now? These are still good ideas."

No one answered.

"Clyde's a believer," Brianna Stafford said, elbowing him. "He walks around on his hands and says 'what do I need Dr. Reed's inversion therapy for—I can just do it myself.'"

Galen Reed smiled at Clyde Minden as he shook his head. "I know Clyde's on board. He's been bringing in Victor Amistero. The guy is starting to respond, at least a little, to our treatment plan."

"The guy saved me," Minden said. "I owe him a lot."

"What's this?" Ted Butler asked.

"The poor man had five back surgeries," Stafford explained. "The fifth one put him in a wheelchair, paralyzed from the waist down. He may never walk again, though we're trying to work with him. There are no objective findings of damage to the cord. He got Clyde to make his final decision on the back surgery."

"My never back surgery." Minden raised a glass of water. "Here's to Dr. Collier, and early retirement."

"Exactly," Natalie Corey said. "Retire those old ideas of surgery before all other alternatives have been tried. Brianna was saying it before. The ideas are still good. Dr. Stafford, you still have the power of your position over at Orange County Memorial. You can keep the-"

"Not anymore."

Natalie Corey froze.

"What happened?" Galen Reed asked.

"The hospital board voted me out, within hours after Galen was arrested."

"Fight it!" Brianna Stafford pounded the table with her fist. "There's your lawsuit!"

"I don't think I have any basis for it," Eldon Stafford said. "The hospital board has complete power to choose my position." He shook his head. "They actually gave me a chance to spin my way out of it. They implied, in kind of an indirect, sleazy way, that if I said Galen had manipulated me, sort of scammed me, and I got rid of all the changes, including the chiropractors in the emergency room, and stopped working with him, that I could keep my position." He looked at Galen Reed. "I wouldn't do it. I would not throw Galen under the bus for their trinkets."

"Trinkets?" Galen Reed smiled. "Prestigious position. Big salary. Trinkets?"

"Big trinkets, but trinkets never-the-less."

Brianna Stafford smiled proudly.

Natalie Corey nodded her appreciation as well.

Ted Butler spoke. "Well, send me a copy of your contract. I'm sure there is some sort of at-will clause in there that gives this prerogative to the hospital board. With all the publicity…"

"There is an 'at-will' clause," Eldon Stafford said.

"Publicity." Galen Reed's nose twitched, registering his disgust. "The article reporting that the charges were dropped was buried in a one-and-a-half inch box on page eight."

"They didn't even run one in the San Jose Times." Eldon Stafford pulled a copy of the paper from his briefcase and slapped it on the table. "But there are a lot of ads for Havitol Pharmaceutical. Wyatt Greevey. He's on the hospital board too. I'll bet he is behind a lot of our troubles."

"Go after him," Natalie Corey said. "We've been dealing with the sleazy tactics of those people for years. Maybe we can nail him with this."

"Nail him how?" Ted Butler asked.

"With his sleazy tactics, with Delores, with whatever we can uncover," Natalie Corey said. "We need to go on the offensive."

No one spoke immediately.

Galen Reed finally commented. "One thing I've learned—we do not have the power. This system we're working in is enormously complex, even convoluted, and we do not have the power within this messy bunch of power concentrations. If we take these people on, head-to-head; if we try to attack these rich, powerful people and their organizations with all their connections, like strangling tentacles into every center of power, we will lose. We will be crushed. Truth and fairness will mean nothing."

"So we just fold?" Natalie Corey asked, almost pleading.

"No." Eldon Stafford's face radiated a stern, determined expression. "We fight a guerilla war, with guerilla tactics. We chip away at all those tentacles, until the grip eases, and the tentacles lose their power and melt away."

Galen Reed looked at Eldon Stafford. He didn't have to say anything. His knew his expression asked "And how do we do that?"

Eldon Stafford's cell phone rang. He frowned as he looked at the number. "This is strange."

Everyone at the table looked at him for an explanation.

"It can't be." Stafford punched the green button to connect the call. "Eldon Stafford."

"Hello, Doctor," said the voice of Ben Richards. "Didn't expect to hear from me so soon, huh…"

"No. And, well, we were just talking about you."

"Hmmm. Good. Who's 'we?'"

"Um, well, Dr. Reed's here. His lady friend. His attorney. My daughter and her boyfriend."

"Where are you?"

"Where are we..." This sounded like a strange question. "You mean our location."

"Yeah. Not esoterically, or spiritually, or mood-wise, or politically. Just—where are you right now?"

"Um, the Imperial Highway Grill."

"One second." After a brief pause, Richards said "we're twenty minutes away. Everything's on me. So don't go anywhere."

"What?"

"Oh, we impulsive fat-cats and our corporate jets. Wyatt Greevey's not the only one, you know."

Stafford didn't know what to say.

"Sorry. Inside joke. I've got Seth and Fiona with me. We hashed a bunch of stuff out on the plane. We'd like to chat."

"I'll get them to put us at a bigger table."

"Good."

The conversation ended.

Chapter 33

"Forget Greevey," Ben Richards said to Ted Butler as he munched on a pickle. "He won this one. Let him have it. We can just move on ahead."

"Let him get away with all this?" Natalie Corey asked.

Ben Richards smirked. "He's not going to get away with anything. Not if we take him on the right way."

"People like Greevey want to fight as close to the gutter as possible," Fiona Patton said. "They're good at it. But in the battle of ideas, his are tired and worn. They belong to another time. That's where we beat him. And it will be a victory he will have no way to overturn."

"And the idea we beat him with is what Eldon presented to you," Galen Reed said. "What he and I came up with.".

"That's about it," Ben Richards said. "Now, a few things have to happen, but these are all within reach. First, it would be better for us if the government retreats from its push into the health care system. I explained that we could still prosper with the idea if the government stays in it. But we'd be trying to thrive in a system besieged by shortages. Government running health care is a European idea. It's not American. Keep it in God Damn Europe! When we get the word out about what is really going on in Canada, and other places where the government runs health care, we'll get the government to back out of the system. This could take a few years, but we will try to send that European import back across the ocean!"

"You might just convince this old liberal," Eldon Stafford commented.

"I'll make a capitalist out of you yet, Doctor," Richards said.

"I am a capitalist," Eldon insisted. "What do you think running my own practice is?"

Richards smiled and nodded, apparently conceding the point.

"I've got a friend who lives in Canada," Clyde Minden said. "He's got great health care."

"Has he been sick?" Ben Richards asked.

Minden frowned. "I don't know. Nothing serious; I know that."

"Yeah," Richards said. "It's the greatest system in the world until you get sick. You don't pay any insurance premiums, and can bask in the glow of the security of knowing you have coverage. Things get a little tougher actually getting that free care when you need it."

Minden shrugged and nodded.

"There are so many horror stories. We just need to get them out there."

"So where does that leave us?" Eldon Stafford asked.

Reed was smiling.

"He knows," Richards said grinning.

"I've got a good idea."

"I'll bet you're damn good at your back-cracking thing," Richards said. "I ought to give you a try."

Reed smiled again as he squinted. "I'd be happy to give you good, quality chiropractic care. I don't crack backs."

Richards also smiled again. "I like you." He looked at Stafford. "No more hiding this guy from us."

Stafford shrugged.

"Here is our thinking in a nutshell," Richards began.

"Probably a very large nutshell," Sy Mercoyan said.

Richards smirked. "Um, well, yeah—it's a complicated issue. But I'll give it a shot. My big-picture take. Americans want three things from their healthcare. They want to be able to get care when they need it. They want to be able to get quality care. And many are used to being almost completely insulated from the costs. The problem is, those three things are not mutually compatible. The government plan promises insulation from costs, which may or may not be true, but access and quality will likely be gone. When that becomes clear, the system'll change again. And really, the American way is to give up being insulated from the costs, but keep the other two—accessibility and quality. And gentlemen, that's where your collaboration comes in."

Eldon Stafford shook his head. "Good. Because I was starting to think I had entered the land of the policy wonks."

"It's all right," Richards said. "I'm just telling you what the three of us are thinking about." He exchanged knowing smiles with Seth Mercoyan and Fiona Patton.

"But how can the market come into play?" Brianna Stafford asked.

"I'm getting there," Richard said. "We need to push for a shift in the way health insurance is provided. And let me tell you, it's already happening with small businesses. You see, during World War II, wages were frozen. So big companies lured quality talent with benefit packages, and one of the most desirable perks was health care. So people got used to paying nothing for health care—employers kept taking care of it. But smaller businesses can't afford to do this. They're not big enough purchasers to get good deals on coverages. So they set up healthcare spending accounts. You see it more and more. And the big companies are starting to balk at the expense. When the little guys start outbidding the big guys for salaries for qualified people, you'll see the big guys dropping off to the HCSAs too."

"Okay," Brianna Stafford said. "More policy wonk stuff. I'm immersed in stuff like this in my classes. But you still haven't connected it up."

"What're you studying?" Fionna Patton asked.

"Foreign affairs."

Fiona Patton nodded. "So you want to work for government..."

"I'm no lover of government programs," Brianna Stafford said.

"Yeah. Miss Right Wing," Eldon Stafford said. "Reverse rebellion against her Berkeley-trained dad."

"No," Brianna Stafford said. "I just see it—the more governments I study around the world, the more I know the optimum society has as little government control as possible."

"Let the government facilitate," Ben Richards said. "Offer business incentives to set up tax-free spending accounts for healthcare. From their healthcare spending accounts, people can use before-tax money to pay for insurance coverage, or medical expense, including deductibles and co-pays, in whatever combination they want. We've studied this. The best policy for most people will be a policy for catastrophic coverage, but with people paying the smaller medical expenses up to a cap. When people are paying for the smaller medical expenses, either with the money in their HCSAs, or with their own money when the HCSA runs out for the year; when they're paying for the visits, and the tests, and the drugs, and the procedures, they will shop price. They will question necessity. They will look for the most efficient way to spend their money. And they will look for a way to minimize all their medical expenses.

"Market forces will return to health care. We don't have employers paying for essentials like food, and clothing, and housing. The government only helps with those items for the indigent, and we already have health care for the indigent. So we get the market back into this, and the efficiencies of the marketplace can act to reform the system."

Eldon Stafford beamed. "And Galen and I have a great option for efficiency, quality and cost."

Ben Richards nodded. "Exactly."

Ted Butler also nodded. "We have HCSAs at my law firm."

"Case in point," Richards said. "Small business."

"Right," Butler agreed.

"The other great thing about this approach is that people do not lose coverage with a company just because they switch employers," Fiona Patton added. "They pay a premium direct to their health insurer from their HCSAs. And they can choose from every company offering a plan."

"So," Ben Richards said, "here's what the three of us have come up with. We're going to set up the insurance plan you talked about, Dr. Stafford. We are also going to monitor government changes and the policy-legislative issues that need to be worked on to make this option viable. We will want the two of you to help us set up the precise mechanism, the network, the personnel, from the care end." Richards turned to Reed. "Keep doing your great back-crack-" He stopped himself. "Your great chiropractic care, my boy."

"Count on it."

"One thing," Seth Mercoyan said to Eldon Stafford. "We will also invest in some similar models involving nurse practitioners and physician assistants."

Reed frowned.

"Oh yeah." Richards nodded. "Some people will be slow to use the chiros. And we'll want to be in those other options as well. But don't make any mistake about it—the most efficient care system is going to be this one. I ran some quick numbers. Non-drug treatments first. Non-intrusive care emphasis. Emphasis on staying healthy and preventing illness. This care system will cost the least. So the public will pay the least to utilize it. And they'll vote for it—with their dollars."

Reed smiled. "Competition."

"Right," Richards said.

"And you like to play both sides when you can." Natalie Corey said as she smirked.

"Wyatt Greevey won't be on this side," Eldon Stafford commented.

"No," Ben Richards said. "But we'll be ready for him."

Eldon Stafford's stern expression became a smile of grim determination. "And we'll have a few rich, powerful allies of our own."

Ben Richards gave him a stern nod, reflecting determination and agreement.

"We'll keep on refining this integrated care system," Galen Reed said. "We'll reach out to more MDs and DCs to work together. We'll look for ways to publicize our successes. We'll use every word-of-mouth tool we have to spread these ideas among the grass roots."

"Natural Healing Remedies will be with you on this," Natalie

Corey said. "I'll make sure every store prominently features information about what you two have accomplished, and the potential for more. It'll be good for business."

Reed looked at Stafford. "So it's redemption. For both of us."

Eldon Stafford nodded. His eyes moistened as he thought of his wife. "Yes. Redemption and a lot of hard work to come, going against current conventions."

"I'm ready. I've been ready a long time." Reed looked up, away from the group.

"I know," Eldon Stafford said. He looked at Reed.

Galen Reed looked back at Eldon Stafford.

"We will accomplish some amazing things… together."

Galen Reed nodded.

Author's Note

We are indebted to *Crisis of Abundance* by Arnold Kling for Ben Richards' description of what he calls "a set of three principles that 'must' be satisfied by a perfect health care system." Kling discusses these ideas starting on page 46 of his book.

We are indebted to *The Cure* by David Gratzer for information about Canada's often lauded health care system. Dr. Gratzer practices medicine in both Canada and the United States. His book is a must-read for anyone who wants to import the Canadian healthcare system to the United States.

We are indebted to *Chicken Soup for the Chiropractic Soul* for wonderful success stories from the chiropractic profession, some of which inspired fictional events created for this book.

www.ingramcontent.com/pod-product-compliance
Lightning Source LLC
Chambersburg PA
CBHW021321250626
47155CB00002B/570